1

How We Confederates Won Our Independence, 1861 and 1862

Book 1 of The CSA Trilogy

An Alternate History/Historical Novel

By Southern Historian, Howard Ray White

You are holding in your hand the first book of a fictional alternate history/historical novel about our vast and beautiful Confederate States of America – a happy story in three parts of what might have been. You are reading Book 1. Below are the titles of the three books of our trilogy.

Book 1 – This is the book you are holding in your hand: *How We Confederates Won Our Independence – 1861 and 1862.*

Book 2 – You will want to get this book next: *How We Confederates Invited Cuba, Northern Mexico, Russian America and Hawaii to Join Our Federation of States – 1862 to 1877.*

Book 3 – You will want to get this book last: *How We Confederates Preserved Our Values while Developing the World's Greatest Economy – 1878 to 2011.*

Our trilogy was written by a proud Southern Historian Howard Ray White

Note to Reader: This trilogy of alternate history/historical novels are a happy, non-violent, non-racial, story of what might have been. So, please enter into the pages of this trilogy knowing that you will be experiencing far less of the violence, racial hatred and political hatred than exists in the truthful history of mankind. Just set aside notions of American politically correct thought, open your mind, and live through a refreshing historical novel about the Southern people as they expand in territory and progress across 150 years of alternate history while, along the way, creating the "Greatest Country on Earth."

Other Books by Howard Ray White

Truthful history books by Howard Ray White. See Amazon.com and book stores or contact the author at 704-242-0022 or howardraywhite@gmail.com:

Bloodstains, An Epic History of the Politics that Produced and Sustained the American Civil War and the Political Reconstruction that Followed. Four volumes: Volume 1: *The Nation Builders* (Ancient British Isles to March 1848), published in 2002; Volume 2: *The Demagogues* (March 1848 to April 1861), published in 2003; Volume 3: *The Bleeding* (April 1861 to May 1865), published in 2007; and Volume 4: *Political Reconstruction and the Struggle for Healing* (May 1865 to March 1885), published in 2012.

Understanding the War Between the States, and *American History for Home Schools,* both written by 16 Writers who belong to The Society of Independent Southern Historians, co-founded by Howard Ray White, the first book published in 2015.

Understanding Abe Lincoln's First Shot Strategy (Inciting Confederates to Fire First at Fort Sumter), published in 2011.

Understanding "Uncle Tom's Cabin" and "The Battle Hymn of the Republic" – How Novelist Harriet Beecher Stowe and Poet Julia Ward Howe Influenced the Northern Mind, published in 2003.

Understanding Creation and Evolution, which explains how the Biblical story and todays scientific story do not disagree, published in 2018.

R. E. Lee, Edmund Ruffin and Slavery, a novel set in wartime Virginia where a slave family struggles to keep safe and stay together, while seeking to identify their true friends, Whites of the North or Whites of the South. published in 2019.

How Southern Families Made America, a large, detailed history that illustrates, from the beginning of the colonial era to the success of the Republic of Texas, how it was primarily the people of the Southern Culture that settled and "Made America" published in 2020.

How to Study History when Seeking Truthfulness and Understanding, a quick read with color illustrations that teaches the reader "How to Study History", published in 2019.

Why and How the North Conquered the South, a quick read that helps the reader rapidly understand the "Why" and the "How" of America's most horrific conflict, published in 2020.

Rebirthing Lincoln, a Biography, here you find the most accurate and revealing biography ever published of Abraham Lincoln, covering from his birth in North Carolina to his first two months as President of the Remaining United States, published in 2021.

Reviews by Readers of the 3 Books of *The CSA Trilogy*

Eight people who are skilled in writing and reading history related to the South read *The CSA Trilogy* manuscripts prior to publication. Of these, the assessment by Dr. Fred Moss is thought to be the most helpful:

"It was my privilege to review this fascinating series prior to publication! . . . In this fun and informative read, Howard Ray White turns his considerable writing skill to a unique combination of fiction and historical non-fiction composition. His Trilogy is what I call a 'two by two' read! The fictional story of a group of twelve impressive young people of diverse backgrounds coming together for a special four-week-long seminar provides the framework that carries the storyline. . . . The included historical material will be new to many readers. . . They will love reading the revealed truth – truth all nicely documented with excellent clarifying footnotes, less fiction be confused with non-fiction. It also contains several accounts of the twelve engaged in outside weekend adventures with physical dangers, rescues, and at least one budding romance. Something for everyone! I highly recommend this most impressive, informative, and enjoyable series of three parts! *The CSA Trilogy* offers a new model for alternate histories of the American Civil War and what followed afterward. The South fought for what it believed to be a new classical Greek type of democracy. Thus, the war was for state's rights and democracy, not slavery."

Foreword

Thanks for your interest in beginning to read Part 1 of this trilogy. Grouped together as three parts, this alternate history covers 150 years of the Confederate States of America, from its formation in early 1861, to the celebration of the sesquicentennial of what has become the Greatest Country on Earth. The three parts of this trilogy match the three major stories of the Confederate States. Please read these books in sequence 1, then 2, then 3.

Book 1 – How We Confederates Won Our Independence, 1861 and 1862.

Our alternate history of the years 1861 and 1862 differ remarkably from truthful history. In our alternate history you learn how Confederates won recognition of their independence, guaranteed by a peace treaty between the United States and the Confederate States. Confederates did not fire on Fort Sumter, instead allowing Federal tax collection agents to operate in Charleston harbor. By choosing a campaign of passive resistance, Confederates will gain many months of time to build military strength and to organize a brilliant defense. You will learn how Confederates influence Northern political thought in their secret service campaign aimed at weakening support among the people, and among Republican governors and state militia, for an invasion of the seceded states. You will learn how Confederates used propaganda to encourage people of the North to fear that a Federal conquest of the Confederate States would result in free people of color migrating into their states and communities and becoming their neighbors. Of course, in 1861, in the Southern States, free people of color, with very few exceptions, had no desire to migrate into the Northern States and suffer the abuse prevalent there – but Confederates cleverly encouraged fear in the North that a war of conquest would produce that result. Furthermore, people of African ancestry, whether slave or free, were a valuable resource in the South – providing skilled labor in agriculture and animal husbandry – many with the obvious potential to farm land on their own.

When the North eventually invaded the Confederacy in May 1862, you will learn how Confederates overwhelmed the first wave of Federal invaders and forced the Lincoln Administration to agree to peaceful separation. Stated another way, you will read herein the alternate history of that remarkable Confederate success – made possible by employing tools of passive resistance, propaganda, political activism and military preparedness, thereby preventing the Lincoln Administration from gathering sufficient military strength to conquer the seceded Confederate States. The negotiated treaty settlement between the United States and the Confederate States will involve giving the portion of Virginia along the Potomac and the Ohio rivers to the United States in exchange for the arid land west of Texas – New Mexico Territory, Arizona Territory and Southern California. An important feature of the settlement agreement will be the Federal demand that Confederates accept all free people of color who are living at that time in the states and territory that remained within the United States. This resettlement south, into the Confederacy, was forced upon people of color by the northern states, for the White people of the Republican states were insisting that all people of color no longer be their neighbors. Federals also demand the emancipation and deportation of all slaves who lived in what remained of the United States – Delaware, Maryland, the transferred portion of Virginia, the remaining portion of Kentucky and the remaining portion of Missouri. Confederates agreed, and these emancipated free people of color were rounded up by Federals, handed over to Southern officials at the border, and resettled in various areas within the Confederate States as free people. This agreement satisfied several major objectives: it gave the remaining United States full control over the valleys of the Potomac and Ohio River; it allowed Northern white people to forevermore prohibit free people of color or slaves from living among them; it allowed the Confederacy to expand westward to the Pacific and to transfer into their country a small amount of southern Kentucky and southern Missouri. [1]

Book 2 – How We Confederates Invited Cuba, Northern Mexico, Russian America and Hawaii to Join Our Federation of States, 1862 to 1877

This is the next book, which you will want to read second.

With the Confederate States now established and unchallenged, we proceed to Book 2. Here our alternate history follows, to a remarkable extent, truthful history of the subsequent 1860's and 1870's. What makes our alternate history possible is the presence of the Confederate States as a new and prosperous country. It is really amazing to understand how the successful defense of the Confederate States quickly snow-balled into successful

---

[1] In truthful history, the political movement in the Republican Party to free slaves did not gain traction until after two years of war and over one hundred thousand Federal military deaths. Remember that the "underground railroad" did not help slaves find homes in the northern States; it kept moving them north into Canada. The New York City draft riots of July 1863 illustrated the hatred whites of the north held toward free people of color. And several states, including Illinois and Oregon, by constitutional law, prevented free people of color from moving into their state to live there. Excluding free people of color from Northern communities was the dominant passion in the Republican States. The Northern passion was not a crusade to force the emancipation of slaves who lived far away in the South.

independence movements in Cuba, in the northern region of Mexico, in Russian America (known at Alaska in truthful history) and in the Hawaiian Islands. With Confederate help and encouragement, these successful independence movements will result in the invitations and the additions of nine more states within the Confederacy – the State of Cuba, 6 states out of Northern Mexico, the State of Russian America and the State of Hawaii. These rapid events, to a great extent consistent with truthful history of those regions in those times, will tantalize the reader – elevate his or her imagination concerning what might have been. All of this takes place between 1863 and 1877.

Book 3 – How We Confederates Preserved Our Values while Developing the World's Greatest Economy, 1878 to 2011

This is the final book, which you will want to read last.

With the Confederate States now expanded in territory to span from mid-Virginia to Hawaii, and from Russian America to Cuba, we enter into Book 3. Here we witness the alternate history of how Confederates created a vibrant modern economy in the subsequent 134 years, to the sesquicentennial celebration of 2011. Most importantly, we learn the history of how Confederates encouraged immigration into their country of men and families of remarkable inventiveness and talent, thereby facilitating a rapid industrial expansion. We also learn how Confederates accomplished that remarkable achievement without losing the cherished principle of State Rights, while continuing to encourage respect for the country's very diverse population. Regulations over slavery remained the prerogative of each State, but that does not impede a rather rapid transition from slavery to independent living for families of African descent – a complete emancipation that included education, full citizenship and equal rights. Book 3 concludes with the heart-warming, televised celebration of the Confederate Sesquicentennial in the All Saints' Chapel at the University of the South in Sewanee, Tennessee.

The industrial expansion within the Confederate States will be remarkably complete and far more rapid than we recall in the truthful history of the South. Much credit goes to immigrants who brought terrific scientific and industrial skills – men like Thomas Edison (father was Canadian), Cyrus McCormick (of Chicago, but originally of Virginia), Henry Ford (from Michigan, father Irish), Antonio Luchic (Croatia), Orville and Wilbur Wright (Ohio), Paul Heroult (France), Nikola Tesla (Serbia) and Guglielmo Marconi (Italy).

The Confederate States became engaged in the Pacific and maintained good relations with China, so, when Hawaii, a Confederate State, was attacked by Japanese Imperialists in 1941, Confederates are drawn into a

Pacific War and the outcome is remarkably different than we recall in truthful history.

Why the Confederate States are the Greatest County on Earth.

Although this trilogy is primarily an alternate history of 150 years of the Confederate States, the writer has overlaid a novel upon this story, which presents twelve individuals of remarkable ancestry who are studying these 150 years and preparing essays to explain "Why the Confederate States are the Greatest Country on Earth." In the closing chapter, these twelve will be reading their essays in the All Saints' Chapel before you and a before a world-wide television audience on the evening of the Sesquicentennial Celebration. You will be following and getting to know these fictional characters – impressive and accomplished young people – through the three books of our trilogy. You, the reader, will enjoy following them, their interactions, and their experiences, over the four weeks that they are together, including some thrilling weekend adventures. You will also enjoy getting to know their professor, who is guiding their studies and essay preparations.

Let Us Compare the Happy Story Herein to the Real Horrific Story.

The three books of our trilogy are a happy story, so much happier that the truthful history of the conquest of the Seceded States – a four-year military nightmare that resulted in the death of approximately one million people, about half from the United States and about half from the Confederate States.

Let us ask ourselves, "Did this calamity have to happen?" This writer submits that the answer is "No!!" Alternate futures are always possible in the course of human events. Looking back from our vantage point today, we realize that a change in certain historic circumstances could have frequently and dramatically changed the course of human history, and, moving forward, even to redefining the world as we know it today.

Drawing upon his knowledge as an historian of the Civil War and mid-1800's American political events, the writer has reflected upon numerous plausible alternate circumstances that might have gained prominence during that era, storing away a "tool-kit" of possible historical alternatives. From this "tool-kit", he has picked a set of alternatives he believes would have been the most likely to result in successful independence for the Confederate States, agreement on a boundary between the two countries, and transfer southward of emancipated African Americans who lived north of that boundary. He believes the resulting alternate history is a tribute to what mankind is capable of achieving when goodness is allowed to prevail.

Bonds of Friendship

The three books of our trilogy are also a story about the bonds of friendship between whites and people of color, whether free or slave. My friend, of African descent, wrote the following to help you, as a reader, understand why black people would have been successful living in the Confederacy over the course of 150 years:

> "The truth is that most free people of African descent knew and understood that the South offered the greatest opportunities for success and did not look to the North as the Promised Land. There are accounts of free people of color who wrote to their friends and families in the North encouraging them to move south before the Civil War because free people of color enjoyed economic success in the Colonial and Antebellum South. Our readers need to know this history to understand why black people would have been able to be successful in the CSA. They need to know that this is real history and not based upon our having to imagine what could have been." [2]

And you are invited to join this writer, Howard Ray White, within the pages of this book -- invited to set aside existing prejudices and historical knowledge, toss a bit of magic dust before your eyes, and engage with him in a happy novel -- a story of the Confederate States surviving as an independent country; a story of African Americans transitioning from living as slaves to living as free, productive, prosperous and moral people; a country expanding many-fold in land area and population; a people encouraging talented immigrants and thereby experiencing unprecedented inventiveness and industrial expansion; a land belonging to a great and diverse people who are recognized world-wide as being fortunate to be living in the "Greatest Country on Earth."

Toss a bit of Magic Dust before Your Eyes, then begin Reading.

If your interest is primarily of a military nature, hoping to herein read about many battles over many years the three books of our trilogy may disappoint, because in this alternate history you read that success in defending State Secession was greatly enabled by declining to fire on Fort Sumter; engaging in passive resistance and deception; dispensing propaganda among people of the North, and using the months thereby gained to modernize and expand weaponry to be better prepared to successfully defend against the anticipated military invasion. Only through such political efforts, the writer

---

[2] This account of relations between Southern whites and free people of color is the result of studies by Barbara G. Marthal of Tennessee, the author of the book, *Fighting for Freedom, A Documented Story*.

believes, could success have been achieved by the Secessionists. Again, why not toss a bit of magic dust before your eyes and engage with him in a happy historical, alternate history novel?

Today many writers tell stories called fantasies. This is not one of those, but as a reader, you might choose to think so. This is a good-feelings story of a fictional country, viewed as of 2011, celebrating its sesquicentennial and its great and successful population diversity – a might-have-been country celebrating how it had remained successful without giving up "Individual Liberties" and the people's right to govern themselves at the state level. Yes, those two guiding principles have remained and continued to work for 150 years – for the benefit of all Confederates. How was this accomplished in today's complex modern world? You have to read further to find out. If you are more comfortable thinking of this story as a fantasy, you need not apologize.

The Novel's Thirteen Characters and the "Sewanee Project."

Our trilogy's three books are, to a significant degree, a novel. Although most of this *Trilogy* reads like an alternate history, parts read like a novel. Enjoy the experiences and interpersonal relationships developed during these four weeks at the University of the South, Sewanee, Tennessee. And enjoy the story of three weekend trips away from Sewanee: the adventure of six engaged in an overnight sailing adventure off the coast of Cuba; the adventure of two exploring an historic cave west of Sewanee, and the adventure of five enjoying a weekend overnight backpacking trip on the remote Fiery Gizzard trail east of Sewanee.

A list of the thirteen characters follows below:

- Joseph Evan Davis IV, 64, professor of history, University of the South, Sewanee, Tennessee.
- Isaiah Benjamin Montgomery, 27, corporate farmer, of Mississippi.
- Marie Saint Martin, 23, beginning her career in business, of Louisiana.
- Emma Cathrine Lunalilo, 22, working toward her Ph. D., of Hawaii.
- Carlos Jose Cespedes, 24, cane sugar farmer, of Cuba.
- Chris Withers Memminger, 22, veterinary medicine student, of South Carolina.
- Benedict Christian Juárez, 27, Ph. D. in Philosophy, teaching professor, Costa Este (of former Mexico).

- Allen Bruce Ross, 26, bison rancher, Sequoyah (in truthful history the US State of Oklahoma).

- Conchita Marie Rezanov, 23, working on her Ph. D. in political science, Russian America (in truthful history, Alaska).

- Robert Edward Lee, IV, 23, BA degree in political science, of Alabama.

- Andrew Houston, 23, BS petroleum engineering, of South Texas.

- Tina Kathleen Sharp, 26, nuclear engineer, of North Texas.

- Amanda Lynn Washington, 25, working on her Ph. D. in Education, Virginia.

You will read about the ancestry of these 13 people and discover that they are descended from men who played major roles in the success of the Confederate States, including Cuba, northern Mexico, Russian America and Hawaii. You will enjoy the past family connections of these thirteen and appreciate how those relationships enabled them to tell the story of our Confederate States from the perspective of especially meaningful family experiences.

You are encouraged to read all three books in this trilogy. In the final chapter of the Book 3, you will arrive at a dramatic conclusion, the celebration of the sesquicentennial, July 4, 2011. Here you will read the twelve essays presented before a world-wide television audience by the twelve young Sewanee Project team members, each, from a different perspective answering the question, "Why are the Confederate States the Greatest Country on Earth?"

We conclude the Foreword here. To learn more, one must continue reading.

The narrative presented within the three books comprising this CSA Trilogy are in the voices of Joseph Davis, 64, professor of history at the University of the South – a truthful and lovely college setting from which our story is told. We now go to Sewanee, Tennessee to hear our fictional character, Professor Davis, begin what is called the "Sewanee Project." He will explain. Hope you enjoy this alternative history presented with a novel overlay.

Table of Contents

A Quick Orientation for the Readers of this Book

Professor Davis: "This year, 2011, all across the Confederacy, citizens are celebrating the 150th aniversary of the founding of our country, The Confederate States of America. But first, perhaps I should introduce myself. My name is Joseph Evan Davis, IV, age 64, professor of history and political studies at the University of the South at Sewanee, Tennessee, CSA. You may have not heard of me, but I am confident that you have heard of my great-great-grandfather, Jefferson Davis, the first President of our country, so I need not say much about him as we begin. Instead, a few words about our University are now appropriate.

"We are renouned at the University of the South for our excellence in educating past and future leaders of our country, and in providing academic advice to governments both here and abroad, because the CSA is the recognized world leader:

- In political anaylsis and synthesis,
- In building successful governmental structures that are broadly beneficial to a diverse citizenship, and,
- In advising governments around the world concerning improvements that will help them sustain themselves and beneficially govern their diverse populations.

"Sewanee is located on the top of the southern Cumberland Plateau, and although remote by some measures of geography, we are only 150 miles east-north-east of our country's capital at Davis and 20 miles north of the Alabama State line. I presume you know that the capital of our country, Davis, is located on land donated by Tennessee, Mississippi and Alabama, at the junction of the boundaries of those three States, at the point where the Tenn-Tom waterway joins the Tennessee River, thereby providing water transport from the Gulf of Mexico into Alabama, Mississippi and Middle Tennessee. Davis, named for Jefferson Davis, is surprisingly small for the capital of such a huge country as ours, but here, unlike countries elsewhere, government reponsibilities are decentralized to such an extent that obligations at Davis, at the Confederate (federal) level, are far smaller than obligations at the State and local levels. And here, at the University of the South, we have historically advocated for government that is heavily decentralized and have witnessed rewarding results over the past 150 years. I suppose it was toward ensuring such a governmental structure that the Southern States seceded in late 1860 and early 1861, and as late as early 1862.

"Furthermore, it is here today, on June 6, 2011, that we begin the "Sewanee Project" in support of our sesquicentennial celebration and toward a better understanding of the question put to us, which I repeat here:

By analysis of our history and our culture, answer the question:
"Why are the Confederate States of America the greatest country on Earth?"

"We anticipate that this inquiry will result in 12 essays, each authored by a visiting guest, who is noteworthy because of his or her descent from particularly influencial leaders in our history, and because he or she has been recognized for his or her exceptional power of analysis and keen judgment – in spite of the fact that all twelve are yet young and unmarried."

Book 1, Chapter 1, Day 1 – The Sewanee Project Introduction
– at the University of the South, Sewanee, Tennessee, CSA,
Monday Morning, June 6, 2011

Our Story Now Begins

So, dear readers, having finished the brief orientation via
Professor Davis's voice, we begin telling the story of the CSA. Just
pretend you are there in the Confederate States of America in the
year 2011 witnessing it all yourself. Here we go. . .

Professor Davis is addressing the twelve young men and women who
have been selected to spend four weeks at studying assigned aspects of our
history in preparation for delivering their relevant essay. We now listen in on
that first meeting, an oreintation.

Professor Davis:

"It is so good to see all twelve of you assembled here this morning. Yes,
it is today, Monday June 6, 2011, that we are beginning our work together,
which, for no better name, I am calling "The Sewanee Project." Consider this
Orientation Day. But, before we break up this morning for lunch, we will also
engage in our first study, that being the history of the Nation-State of
Sequoyah, located west of Arkansas and north of Texas. The program we
begin this morning will last four weeks and one day. The last day, Monday,
July 4, will be the main objective that all of us will be shooting for, that being
presenting your essays, the twelve essays you will be writing and presenting
as part of the televised Confederate Day Celebration event, which will be held
here on the campus, be televised throughout the Confederate States and be
seen by many around the world. Since you and your essays will be featured
on the event schedule, take your work seriously and good luck to all.

"I will present nineteen lectures, one each morning, starting tomorrow
and continuing on Mondays through Fridays until concluding on Wednesday,
June 29. The schedule for these lectures follows:

1. Tuesday, June 7: Secession of Seven States.
2. Wednesday, June 8: The Confederacy's First 10 months.
3. Thursday, June 9: Confederates Decline to Fire on Fort Sumter,
   Choose Passive Resistancce.
4. Friday, June 10: U. S. Congress Chooses War – Four More States
   Secede.
5. Monday, June 13: Federal Invasion and Victorious Confederate
   Defense.
6. Tuesday, June 14: Montreal Treaty Negotiations.

7. Wednesday, June 15: Boundary Settlement.

> This concludes the first of three climaxes in our trilogy. We continue to the lectures that will be presented in Book 2.

8. Thursday, June 16: French Intervention and Mexican State Secession.
9. Friday, June 17: The Heroic Story of Russian America.
10. Monday, June 20: Hawaii – From Kingdom to Republic to Confederate State.
11. Tuesday, June 21: Cuba Wins Independence from Spain, becomes Confederate State.
12. Wednesday, June 22: The Great Confederate Expansion.

> This concludes the second of three climaxes in our trilogy. We again continue to the lectures that will be presented in Book 3.

13. Thursday, June 23: Early Confederate Industrialization Studies.
14. Friday, June 24: Confederate Population Studies.
15. Monday, June 27: Overview of Confederate History 1870 to 1890.
16. Tuesday, June 28: Overview of Confederate History 1891 to 1920.
17. Wednesday, June 29: Overview of Confederate History 1921 to 1938.
18. Thursday, June 30: Fascist Japan, Emerging China. Pearl Harbor, and the War Against Japan.
19. Friday, July 1: Overview of Underlying Confederate Principles.
20. Saturday and Sunday, July 2 and 3: Events leading up to the Sesquicentennial Day Celebration.
21. Monday, July 4: Televised Sesquicentennial Celebration Event and Presentation of Twelve Essays.

> This concludes the third of three climaxes in our trilogy.

"Before proceeding any further, let us get to know a bit about each person in the room. I will begin with a brief story about myself."

Professor Joseph Evan Davis, IV

At this point, with all twelve essayists before him in the lecture room, professor Joseph Evan Davis, IV, age 64, begins the round of introductions. As a reader of the three books of this trilogy, you will be involved with Professor Davis and the twelve young men and women throughout the three books of this amazing alternate history.historical fiction novel, all the way to the final pages, where you get to read the twelve essays as presented to the worldwide television audience at the close of the celebration of the Confederacy's 150 years. So use this opportunity, dear reader, to begin to get to know theses characters, which represent the novel that overlays this alternate history of 150 years of the Confederate States. Joseph Davis is the senior professor of history and political studies at the University of the South at Sewnaee, Tennessee, CSA. He now begins to address the twelve:

"My great-great-grandfather, Jefferson Finis Davis, was born in Kentucky in 1808, attended West Point, and served in the United States army both in the upper Mississippi Valley and in the War Against Mexico. He and his brother Joseph raised cotton on large adjacent farms alongside the Mississippi River in the State of Mississippi in a region called 'Davis Bend.' He was elected United States Senator from Mississippi and lived in Washington several months of each year from 1847 to 1851 and from 1857 to 1861. Soon after returning home, he was asked to accept the position of Provisional President of the Confederate States of America, later confimed by the votes of the people. The rest of the story is too well known to repeat here.

"My great-great-grandmother, wife of Jefferson, was Varina Anne Howell Davis, born in 1828. She was of Natchez, Mississippi, a river town of notable Native American heritage, stretching back many centuries.

"My great-grandfather was Joseph "Joe" Evan Davis, born in 1859, son of Jefferson and Varina, named for Jefferson's brother, Joseph and his grandfather, Evan.[3] My grandfather was Joseph Evan Davis, Jr., who spent most of his life in the Confederate State of Virginia. My father was Joseph Evan Davis, III, who spent most of his life in South Texas, where I was born and raised.

"I received my bachelor's degree in history at Houston University and my doctorate in 1976, here at Sewanee, at the age of 29 years. I have been married to my lovely wife Judith for 40 years. She is a professional musician, playing first chair, French horn section, in the Nashville Symphony, and often backing up country music stars at recording sessions. That keeps her away from Sewanee some days and nights, but she does love her music and I am glad that she has a career she enjoys. We have four children, Varina, Billy, Evan and Mary

---

[3] In truthful history little Joe Davis died in an accident on April 30, 1864, apparently falling from a balcony at the Confederate White House in Richmond, Virginia. The little boy fell thirty feet to a brick-paved walk below, dying within moments. The conquest of the Confederacy would occur only 12 months into the future, and prospects for defending the new country's independence were already dismal. It may not have been an accident. It may have been murder by a Federal spy. The truth was never firmly established. But the father continued with all his might to preserve the country he was charged with defending. Little Joe's death was a terrible blow. In her *Memoir*, Varina Davis would write, "On Joe [Jefferson Davis] set his hope. This child was the greatest joy of his life." In our alternate history, the Confederacy is not struggling for survival in April 1864 and little Joe Davis does not suffer this fall.

Katheryn and are expecting our first grandchild soon. Oh yes, we stopped the Joseph naming convention at me, the fourth. There are no plans for the fifth.

"What are my interests? Although I am not accomplished I do play a banjo and sing. Several of us in my church get together regularly. I still play tennis, was rather good in my former years, but age has trimmed my game. Our family likes to hike the ridges and mountains, back packing and camping out occasionally. Sewanee, here atop the Cumberland Plateau, is a great jumping off point for hiking and backpacking. I have researched and written a few non-fiction books about history and political struggles.

"So that's a little story about me and my Davis ancestors."

The Twelve Visiting Guests

"So, at this time, let me welcome each of you, our essayists. Perhaps each would like to take turns telling about yourself and your relevant ancestry, and the area of our history which each of you has been charged with analyzing and reporting upon.

"Isaiah perhaps you will lead off for the twelve visiting guests. Your essay will concern **Understanding Human Diversity**. Mr. Montgomery, please come forward and tell us about yourself."

Isaiah Benjamin Montgomery

At this point Isaiah Montgomery came forward. Six foot one inch tall, 170 pounds, muscular, athletic, and of three-fourths African ancestry, Isaiah is both handsome and intelligent – a young man who people quickly learn to admire – a man who others look to for leadership. Isaiah began to introduce himself:

"I am 27 years old and presently reside in Mound Bayou, Mississippi, where I am a field supervisor for Section 8 of the Mound Bayou Corporate Plantation. Overall, MBCP farms 110,000 acres. Section 8 contains 3,400 acres. I received my BS degree in Agricultural Science at the Montgomery Agricultural Institute, named for my ancestors, located in Oxford, Mississippi. In Section 8 we grow cotton, field peas, various legumes, soybeans, alfalfa and sweet potatoes. Cotton covers about 35 percent of the land most years. My ancestry is three-forths African and one-forth European. Played quarterback on football teams in high school and college. Had a lot of fun, but I am rather small for the pros and, to be honest, I love the land and the farm life. I am not just an employee at MBCP. Like many with a long family tradition of working there, I am a significant stockholder. Continued success for our corporation will be more meaningful to me than the salary I make working there. I expect you all understand.

"My great-great-great-grandfather was Isaiah Thornton Montgomery, son of Benjamin (Ben) Thornton Montgomery, both slaves owned by Joseph Davis, the brother of President Jefferson Davis. Both Davis brothers owned large cotton plantations along the Mississippi River between Vicksburg and Natchez. The Montgomery family was remarkable, including the father, my ancestor Isaiah, and his brother Thornton. Although a little white blood does flow through my veins, my ancestor Isaiah's parents were born in America as were his parents and grandparents. Yet, by blood, they were of pure African ancestry. Ben, the patriarch of this family, was self-educated and exceptionally enterprising, even though a slave -- the result of his remarkable ability and steady encouragement from the Davis brothers. He set up a mercantile store, soon gaining enough money to buy emancipation for the family. The store grew into a major business, Montgomery and Sons. In 1887 Isaiah founded the community of Mound Bayou, which grew to 800 African American inhabitants and 30,000 acres of farmland, which, after years of hard work, was well protected from Mississippi River flooding by an amazing span of high dikes. [4] There, in upstate Mississippi, over the generations, Colored people built a huge farming cooperative that benefitted from the most advanced agriculture science. This is now a corporate farm that owns and manages 110,000 acres of upstate Mississippi farmland. The stockholders in the Mound Bayou corporation, this closely held enterprise, are all farmers, are all working the land, and are all former slaves."

Professor Davis:

"Thank you, Mr. Montgomery. Now, Miss Saint Martin, your essay will concern **ensuring State Rights and Individual Liberty.** Please come forward and introduce yourself."

Marie Saint Martin

Several young women are among the twelve. Marie Saint Martin will be the first lady introduced to you as a reader of Book 1 of our trilogy. She may have a slight degree of African ancestry, but it is not very noticable.

---

[4] In truthful history, Mound Bayou, Mississippi was founded as an independent black community in 1887 by former slaves led by Isaiah Montgomery and other slaves from Davis Bend. Its founders envisioned an all-black, self-sufficient farming community.

Attractive and tall at five foot eleven inches, tanned from days at the beach, her long black hair is easily spotted in the crowd. Her athletic build might be deceiving in that she is also both smart and an accomplished musician. In fact, as our story unfolds, it will be Marie that organizes and leads the musical endeavors that several of the twelve discover they enjoy as the course of the four weeks of togetherness moves forward. Marie:

"I am 23 years old and mostly of South Louisiana French Creole ancestry, very close to 100 percent European blood. I tan really well and spend time at the beaches east of my home in New Orleans. Love to swim. Played volley ball and ran cross country in high school and do love tennis. But do not consider myself exceptionally athletic. Love to sing country music, New Orleans style. Five of us have a band in my home town: two guitars, a string base and drummer, and I sing lead. We do have a CD, which can be my gift to you all. Love the band, but doubt we will ever become popular enough to make it our career. Like they say in the music business, we will need to "find a day job to earn a living." Anyway, the passions mentioned above are secondary to my major career ambition. I want to be an entrepeneur, to start up and run my own business. I want to work for myself. That goal dovetails into my essay topic rather well. State Rights and Individual Liberty are the foundation that makes successful entrepreneurship achieveable. In the way of preparation, I have earned a degree in accounting and business administration at the Benjamin School of Business at New Orleans and am working various entry-level jobs to gain hands-on experience while I save every penny I can and consider business ideas as they materialize. My mom and dad send me ideas on occasion and I network with others of my persuasion. Glad to be here. Have an idea for a venture? I'm all ears.

"Jules Saint Martin, my great-great-great-grandfather, was Judah Benjamin's nephew who worked alongside him during his term as Attorney General in the Davis Administration and as the leader of the Confederate Secret Service during the successful Defense of Independence. My Study and subsequent essay will concern the **importance of ensuring State Rights and Individual Liberty**. You see, the Confederate Constitution ensures State Rights and Individual Liberty, because those limits on Confederate federal power are unassailable. Of course, there is much more to our story."

Professor Davis:

"Thank you Miss Saint Martin. Emma Cathrine Lunalilo will be presenting the third essay. It will concern **how State and local**

governments compete for citizen loyalty. Miss Lunalilo, please come forward and introduce yourself."

Emma Cathrine Lunalilo

Emma Cathrine Lunalilo is the Hawaiian member of the team of twelve essayists. At barely under six feet tall, her powerful 129-pound suntanned swimmer's physique reminds you of a confident life guard on a beach where the scarry big waves come crashing in. As a reader of our trilogy, you are getting to know a little about each of the twelve characters who will be along with you from the beginning to the end. Enjoy getting to know them. Although, exceptionally intelligent and capable in many ways, these twelve represent the diversity for which the Confederate States are known. Emma:

"I am 22 years old and call home the Big Island, Hawaii. Attended Hawaiian Cultural, a private school, through 12th grade. Received a BA in Political Science and Diversified Government at Qween Emma University in Honolulu and am presently at Guadalajara University in the State of Costa del Sur. I am there working toward my Ph. D. in Politics and Government Affairs. Friends sometime call me "Surfer Girl," because so much of my free time growing up in Hawaii was spent on the beach and out in the big surf. Of course I greatly miss having access to the surf in Guadalajara. Can get to the ocean only about once a month. My ancestry is about half and half, mixture of European and Hawaiian. I really do feel passionate about the importance of maintaining individual liberty in the modern world. So I purposely chose to diversify my living experiences by going to a former Mexican State to study for my doctorate. Friends sometimes complain that I talk too much and have trouble settling down to serious study. Let me know if you see me bouncing around too much. But if you want to really get my attention and my focus, just holler "Surf's up!

"My great-great-great-grandfather was William Charles Lunalilo, former King of Hawaii and grandnephew of Kamehameha I, the king who united the Islands in the early 1800s. As you know, with help from Russian Americans and Confederates, the the Hawaiian Islands – the group of mid-Pacific islands so important to the early days of marine shipping and whaling – we Hawaiians overcame take-over schemes by New England missionary families, traders and businessmen, to peacefully emerge as an independent democratic republic. Soon thereafter, the Republic of Hawaii accepted statehood in the Confederate States of America. We know it now as simply Hawaii. My Study and subsequent essay will concern the **importance of ensuring that each individual State compete for the loyalty of her citizens**, for citizenship is first to the State, second to the country. That is the Confederate way. We insist that local governments retain important control over all local matters that require government oversight."

Professor Davis:

"Thank you Miss Lunalilo. Carlos Jose Cespedes will be presenting the fourth essay, which concerns the principle that a citizen's **right to vote is defined by the State where he or she lives**. Mr. Cespedes, please come forward and introduce yourself."

Carlos Jose Cespedes

Carlos Cespedes is the Cuban member of the team of twelve essayists. He is no athelete, but, at six feet one inch and 165 pounds, he will tell you he is "rugged enough." He is a good sailor of the Gulf of Mexico waters off the northern side of the island. Handles his family's ocean-capable sailboat well and has a bit of a windswept, suntanned complextion, even at this young age. Let us hear what he has to say:

"At 24 years old, I fall in the middle of the pack here today. My ancestry is European, mostly of Spanish origin. I don't play sports, but it seems everybody loves to hear me play Spanish and Classical music on my guitar. Sing along, too. I have CD's for sale, but each of you will receive one as a gift. I have been an ocean sailor since becoming a teenager. Hey! Good news! Dad has promised that he will send up our company airplane and take six of us down to Matanzas, Cuba for a twenty-four hour, overnight sailing trip. More on what should be a great week-end adventure later. My family home is there, in Central Cuba, on the north coast in the seaport city of Matanzas. We have been sugar producers for 167 years. How sweet it has been. No, not really; like all agricultural enterprises, owners and workers encounter ups and downs. World sugar prices historically fluctuate -- occasionally so wildly that large losses must be sustained and then overcome. But Confederate trade policy has been a leveling force over the years. Neither the Confederate Government nor the State of Cuba hands out price supports in needy years, but the Confederate Sugar Association does step in with occasional voluntary quotas to balance supply to demand, and the Confederate Government will retaliate against countries that suppress world sugar prices by subsidizing their inefficient growers. But I love farming and, although the sugar business is not always sweet, I love every year, both the good and the bad. Confederates love their cane sugar as well. Soft drinks and store-bought deserts that are sweetened with processed corn syrup, so common in the United States, are shunned in the Confederacy. I think we are healthier as a result. I sought a double major at Zulueta and

Poey University in Havana, Cuba. One was Governmental Philosophy and Political Science. The other was Comparative North American History.

"Carlos Manuel Cespedes, my great-great-great-grandfather, was the leader of the successful Cuban Revolution of 1868 which led to independence from Spain, admission into the Confederacy as the State of Cuba and the first, step-by-step emancipation program for people of African descent who were held as slaves. My study and subsequent essay, concerns the **importance of ensuring that the right to vote, as defined in each State, results in governments that are sufficiently reflective of the voices of their citizens, who facilitate their existences.**"

Professor Davis:

"Thank your Mr. Cespedes. Now, our next essay will be by Chris Withers Memminger. It will concern **the importance of low tariffs and vigerous international trade**. Mr. Memminger, please come forward and introduce yourself and your subject."

Chris Withers Memminger

Chris Memminger is a South Carolinian as were his Memminger ancestors. Growing up on a farm with fine thoroughbred race horses, he knows that life well. At five feet eleven inches and 143 pounds and looking every bit the part of a White South Carolinian, he is as confident and capable on a horse as his background would suggest. He now tells his brief story:

"Good morning, you all. I am 22 years old and call Aiken, South Carolina home. Going back four generations we Memminger's have been engaged in corporate farming and raising and racing prime thoroughbred horses. We are proud of our five championships at the Confederacy's premier annual race: the Old Hickory Stakes, run the second Saturday in May at the Hermitage Race Track near Nashville, Tennessee. I do love horses and the seasonal swings and struggles that farmers contend with year after year. I earned my B.S. in Agricultural Science at The Citadel in Charleston, South Carolina, and am presently working toward a degree in Veternary Medicine at Davidson University in Nashville, Tennessee. Love being close to those Middle Tennessee thoroughbreds. Amazing horses.

"About my essay. Confederate farmers understand the importance of vibrant and balanced international trade. Much of the passion in the late 1850s and early 1860s for State Secession came from a determination to enjoy low-tariff, balanced export-import trade. I look forward to addressing the importance of vigorous international trade.

"Christopher Gustavus Memminger of South Carolina, my great-great-great-grandfather, was Secretary of the Treasury during the Davis Administration. My study and subsequent essay will concern the **importance of ensuring that international trade and our tariff structure contribute to a vibrant economy**. We believe that the United States, just to our north, suffers from heavy reliance on high tarrifs on imports. Here in the Confederate States, tariffs are low to zero, and international trade is fair to both importers and to exporters, and also vibrant and profitable."

Professor Davis:

"Thank you Mr. Memminger. The sixth essay in our Project is the responsibility of Benedict Christian Juárez who has accepted the essay assignment converning **what makes a wise immigration policy**. Mr. Juárez, please come forward and tell us about yourself, your illustrious ancestor and the subject of your forthcoming essay."

Benedict Christian Juárez

From Costa Este, one of the Seceded Mexican States, Benedict Juárez complements the team of twelve by virtue of his mostly Native American ancestry. He is the shortest of the men, at five feet eight inches, but his broad, muscular body proves he is no pushover. On the other hand, his mild mannered, easygoing temperment suggests everything will be just fine. Benedict:

"I am 27 years old, and my ancestry is seven-eights Native American and one-eighth European. My home is at Monterrey, a large manufacturing city in the State of Costa Este. Our motto is, "If it can be made, we can make it best." Jobs are abundant for folks of all walks of life, but I am particularly proud of the great job opportunities for people of largely Native ancestry. Opportunities are there for Native Americans from entry level positions to upper levels of management. I completed my B.A. degree in World History and then my Ph. D. degree in Philosophy at Juárez University in Ciudad Juárez, in the State of Central Norte. My thesis, completed two years ago, was titled, "Quantifying the Distribution of Human Talents, Strengths and Weaknesses within Races and Ethnic Groups." I have just begun teaching in the Philosophy Department at Freedom University in Queretaro in the State of Central del Sur. My family has been active in government service and education ever since Mexican State Secession. So, I have just followed in their footsteps, I suppose. What are my other activities? I like to make things, and should have been an engineer, but my family ghosts must have pulled me toward the career I have undertaken. On the side, I do construction work for myself and other family members. Have just about completed a small house that is becoming my bachelor pad, I suppose. I am always looking for ways to be more effiient at whatever I undertake. Seems like that is the Monterrey way. What did I say? "If it can be made, we can make it best."

"Benito Juárez of Mexico, my great-great-great-grandfather, was the recognized leader of the northern Mexican States in their 1865 War of Mexican State Secession. During the fight against dictatorial rule from Mexico City, many northern Mexican states, then reduced to mere departments within the autocratic Mexican government, rose up and proclaimed State Secession. With Confederate help and the resolve and determination of northern Mexico secessionists, independence from dominantion by Mexico City was secured. This resulted in the admission of six Mexican States into the Confederate States of America. My study and subsequent essay will concern **Confederate immigration policy**."

Professorn Davis:

"Thank you Mr. Juárez. Our next essay will be by Allen Bruce Ross. His will be explaining **what makes the Confederate electorate exceptional**. Mr. Ross, please come forward and tell us about yourself and your subject."

Allen Bruce Ross

Allen Bruce Ross adds knowledge of, and ancestry from, the Cherokee Nation to the twelve essayists. He is not a cowboy, for his herds are bison, not cattle. The Confederate State of Sequoyah, the location of his family ranch, is just north of the four Texas states. Allen introduces himself:

"I am 26 years old, and a little over one-fourth Cherokee in ancestry. My Ross family have been ranchers in Sequoyah for three generations. Ross Brothers Buffalo Ranch consists of 4,500 acres of Native-leased prairie grassland in upper Sequoyah upon which 1,900 head of bison are raised for market. Our animals are 100 percent grass-fed and the meat is among the top choice and healthiest anywhere in the world. As a teenager I worked the fences and looked over the herds in summer and winter, including that heavy snow we suffered in 1999. I love ranching, but I have three brothers and two sisters and it does not need all of us. So I have struck out on a career in Native American Law. I completed by B.A. in government studies, history and creative writing at The Cherokee Nation University in Cherokee City, Sequoyah. I then received my law degree using interdisciplinary exchange, attending Cherokee National for two years and here at Sewanee for the other two years. The interdisciplinary exchange program is popular with Native Americans seeking to become lawyers because our challenge is to be competent in law in typical Confederate states, such as Georgia or Texas, as well as competent in the Native American law issues within the State of Sequoyah. Interdisciplinary exchange is also popular for aspiring lawyers in Russian America and Hawaii. I passed the Sequoyah bar last year and am just starting to practice law. I am 6 feet tall and as rugged as one would expect for a man of my background. Folks don't call us "cowboys." We are known as "bisonboys." Bisonboys are tougher than cowboys because it takes a tougher man to manage a herd of bison and keep the fences in repair. I participated in rodeo contests in earlier years, but, after sustaining a bad fall, I have reasoned, "been there; done that." So I just play a guitar and sing country music ballads. I am looking forward to my essay, **"Because the Two Political Parties Compete by Appealing to an Informed Electorate**." I come from a strong, self-reliant and freedom-loving family. I am grounded in a firm faith and rock-solid code of morality. I have benefited from great teachers and mentors. I abhor biased education of our youth and efforts to mislead voters through political demagoguery. So do not be surprised if my essay is focused on those themes. By the way, Ross Brothers buffalo will be featured for dinner this coming Sunday. You will love it!

"My ancestors and I have lived in the Nation-State of Sequoyah going back over 160 years, and before that, for many generations, near or not far from the Great Smoky Mountains. My great-great-great-great-grandfather was Principle Chief of the Cherokee Nation, Koo-wi-s-gu-wi, known often by his English name, John Ross. He was the leader of the Cherokee Nation from 1828 until his death in 1868. His wife, Quatie, was my great-great-great-grandmother. John's father was Scottish and his mother was three-fourths Scottish, so John Ross was only one-eighth Cherokee, but he was a great leader of the Cherokee people during very difficult times. I am a bit more than one-quarter Cherokee myself, being descended down through the male Ross line (William Allen Ross to Robert Bruce Ross, and so forth). My study and subsequent essay will concern the political parties over the 150-year history of the Confederacy and the extent to which citizens have demanded and secured for themselves **an electorate that is excceptional**."

Professor Davis:

"Thank you Mr. Ross. Our next essay is being undertaken by Conchita Marie Rezanov. Her subject answers the question: **Is Davis no bigger than it ought to be?** Please come forward Miss Rezanov and tell us about yourself and the question your essay will answer."

Conchita Marie Rezanov

You now know a bit about seven of the twelve essayists. All are young men and women. So far, none are married or in serious romatic relationships. This will be the situation for the remaining five, suggesting that a budding romance may just flower during the upcoming four weeks in beautiful Sewanee. Of the five remaining, one of the most interesting is Conchita Marie Rezanov of the Confederate State of Russian America. [5] Tall at six feet two inches, athletic, a blue-eyed blond and lovely to look at, Conchita is both smart and extremely difficult to beat on the tennis court. Conchita is beginning to speak:

"I am 23 years old and presently residing in San Diego, South California. B.A., History, Baranov University, Sitka, Russian America. Presently in second year of a Ph. D. program at Argüello University in San Diego. Captain of the Argüello tennis team. Some of you may know that I am among the top 50 Confederate amateur female tennis players. Born in Sitka. At age 13 moved with family to San Diego, South California where Dad became a professor with the designation of Professor of Political Philosophy, the Baranov Chair. My Ph.D. thesis will concern a comparative study of human consequences of limited federal government power, as enjoyed by Confederate citizens, versus the centralized government power experienced by other nations of similar human, financial, and natural resources. What am I passionate about? Resisting the world-wide movement toward very powerful centalized governments. Hey, it seems like we Confederates are the world's last great hope. Tennis, anyone?

"My great-great-great-grandfather was Nikolai Rezanov, an important leader in the settlement of Russian America as was his wife Concepción, their son Jose Rezanov, and their grandson, also named Nikolai. The Aleksandr Baranov and the Rezanov families were the most important leaders in Russian America over the generations, and key in arranging for Mother Russia to expand settlement of the region and then to grant independence in exchange for payment in gold, a payment that the Confederate States advanced on our behalf. You see,

---

[5] In truthful history the Confederate State of Russian America is known as Alaska.

these Russian American leaders knew where the gold was and the Emperor of Russia did not. We know this vast region as the State of Russian America, the largest of all Confederate states in land area. My study and subsequent essay will concern the limited growth of the Confederate Government at our capital city of Davis, and the question: **'Is Davis no bigger than it ought to be'?"**

Professor Davis:

"Thank you Miss Rezanov. Our ninth essay is the task of Robert Edward Lee, IV. Mr. Lee's essay will concern **how Councils of Confederate Governors ensure cooperation among neighboring States**. Mr. Lee, please come forward and tell us about yourself, your famous ancestor, and about your important subject."

Robert Edward Lee, IV

Robert Edward Lee, IV is of the Virginia Lee family that is well known to Confederates for his leadership in defeating the Federal invasion of his State. Of the five commanders that led the defense against the Federal's simultaneous invasion launched on May 1, 1862, General Lee is considered by military historians to have been the most capable. The fourth Robert calls himself a regular sized fellow: six feet tall, 150 pounds. Let us listen in:

"I am 23 years old and recently began working at the Department of Interstate Affairs in the Confederate Government at Davis, in the Confederate District. Going back four or five generations, my Lee family hails from Virginia, North Carolina, Tennessee and Alabama. My home is in Montgomery, Alabama, where my family has been in the insurance business for over 100 years. But insurance is not for me. I love studying people, especially leaders in government, commerce and industry. I constantly am asking myself:

- In government, what makes a statesman?
- In commerce, what is the source of long-term success?
- And in industry, how do winnners emerge from the competitive struggle?

"I want to become a writer, but not a college professor. Just want to focus on the study of an issue that moves me and then write effectively to move my readers. Just want to be a positive force for the good of our country. As you know, it is not easy to navigate a hierachy of government from the bottom up -- from local to state, to Confederate -- in a manner where interstate conficts can be resolved and progress can be sustained. In other nations, government is far more centralized and politicians at the top level decree what lower level governments will be doing, and how individuals are expected to comply. It is far different here, and, in reality, far more difficult to manage for the good of the people. So I have prepared myself for this career by gaining a B.A. degree in Political Science at Jefferson Davis University in Jackson, Mississippi, and a Masters at the Calhoun School of Government Studies in Athens, Georgia. I chose both schools because of their historical depth. But, I consider my education just beginning. I love to read and observe and analyse events and people, their actions and reactions. What makes them tick.

"But I do love the outdoors. I love taking my horse on mountain pack trips and camping out wherever it suits me. Do love the Great Smoky Mountains and the rugged landscapes in West Texas and Costa Sudoeste. Back at my family's home, my collection of mounted hunting trophies is modest, but growing. I am a caver, too. I enjoy exploring caves in northern Alabama and the Cumberland Plateau here in Tennessee. By the way, there are some big caves near here that some of us might like to explore. It's a thought.

"Robert Edward Lee of Virginia, my great-great-great-grandfather commanded the Confederate army that defeated the Federal invasion force attempting to conquer Richmond, Virginia. I am descended from his son, Robert, Jr., and so on down the line.

"My study and subsequent essay will concern the **importance of State Cooperative Commissions as effective governmental organizations,** created to ensure that each State retains its constitutional rights, while, as technology and populations expand, to ensure that effective coordination is maintained among the necessary State and Local government regulations and programs, thereby keeping such coordination out of the hands of the Confederate Government at Davis and within the authority of the various States, jointly acting through coordinating bodies."

Professor Davis:

"Thank you Mr. Lee. Mr. Andrew Houston has agreed to address the next essay, which concerns **the excellence in our Confederate Transportation Network.**"

Andrew Houston

We now move west to Austin, South Texas, and learn about Andrew Houston, a descendant of the most important leader in the struggle by Texans to win independence from Mexico and in the subsequent ten-year era of the Republic of Texas, an independent nation. Like the sterotypical Texan, Andrew is tall at six feet, six inches, and muscular. With his height and red hair Andrew is easy to spot in a crowd, and resembles a rugged outdoorsman, which he enjoys being when time permits. He now describes himself to the other eleven:

"Hello folks, here I am in a nutshell. Twenty-three years old and presently residing in Austin, South Texas. [6] Have a B.S. in Petroleum Engineering from Hughes-Sharp School of Science and Engineering, Houston, South Texas. Graduated two years ago. Presently on leave of absence from Texas Oil Company while working on my Masters of Business Administration at The University of Austin, South Texas. I love to hunt, hike, kayak, crew on ocean sailboat adventures. Played on the Hughes-Sharp tennis team. An avid student of Confederate history, have published a study guide for high school students titled, *Making Confederate History Easy to Comprehend – A Concise Study Guide*. Rather unusual for a 23 year old engineer to put time into publishing a history study guide. But I began work on it at age 17 and over the course of 5 years polished it off. With the internet, e-books and print-on-demand publishing, I found getting the final booklet out to students was not all that difficult. I sure learned a lot in the process. That old saying is true: 'you never really know a subject until you teach it to others.'

"Sam Houston, my great-great-great-great-grandfather, is best known for his leadership in Texas. He was commander over the Texas military force that captured Santa Anna and forced the Mexican Government to grant independence to the Mexican state of Tejas. Subsequently, he was twice President of the Republic of Texas. After merger into the United States he was, for ten years, a Senator in Washington City, after that the Governor of the State of Texas. Before arriving in Texas, Houston had spent three years as a teenager with Eastern Cherokees and had as a young man become a military and political leader in Tennessee, for a time being the state's governor. Late in life, following his service in Texas, he lived again with the Cherokee people where he helped facilitate the union of the Five Civilized Tribes and their acceptance as the Nation-State of Sequoyah. His wife, my great-great-great-great-grandmother, was Tiana Rogers Houston, of the Cherokee Nation. I am descended from their son Andrew. [7] My Study

---

[6] You are coming to realize that the Texas of truthful history is divided into four States in our alternate history.

[7] In truthful history Tiana Rogers was Sam Houston's wife for a few years while he lived with Cherokees in what is now Oklahoma, but there is no record of a child named Andrew. Andrew is a fictional character in our alternate history.

and subsequent essay will concern the **importance of excellence in our country's transportation network**."

Professor Davis:

"Thank your Mr. Houston. Miss Tina Kathleen Sharp will be researching, writing and presenting our eleventh essay. It concerns the **importance of excellence in our country's energy production and distribution**. Miss Sharp, please come forward and introduce yourself and your subject."

Tina Kathleen Sharp

Two young women complete the group of twelve essayists. Next to last is Tina Kathleen Sharp, also from one of the Texas states and also pursuing an energy-related field. To that extent, she and Andrew Houston have complementary careers. He is in pertoleum; she is in nuclear power. A real smart lady, for sure, and her ancestor was very important to launching the original Texas oil boom. Let us listen in:

"I am 26 years old and working as a nuclear power engineer at the Comanche Peak Nuclear Station, north of Fort Worth in the State of North Texas. Because Comanche Peak was built over 35 years ago, I am helping with design and planning to upgrade the plant for reliable performance over the next 25 years. Five years from now I will probably be working on the design of a new nuclear station in the State of Russian America. I am proud that we Confederates have never suffered a nuclear power plant failure such as Three Mile Island in the United States, the Soviet's Chernobyl reactors, and Japan's Fukushima Daiichi Nuclear Station. No other country in the world generates more electricity with nuclear power than ours. I grew up in West Texas, and earned my B.S. degree in nuclear engineering at the Confederate Science and Engineering Institute in Atlanta, Georgia. I went on to earn a Master's degree there. So, now I am working in my field and happy to be here in Sewanee this summer. Other interests? It has to be history. I am a nut about Confederate history. Would have majored in that, but felt I could contribute more to our country in the field I chose. Music. I play the French horn rather well. West Texas State Youth Orchestra, Atlanta Civic Orchestra and the Comanche Peak Brass Quintet. Love to cook great meals from scratch. Learned a lot from Mom and Dad as well as my high school Home Economics teacher.

"Walter Benona Sharp, my great-great-grandfather, of Tennessee and Texas, was a leading Texas oil man and inventor of the Sharps-Hughes hardrock drill bit. His pioneering work made possible the Texas oil boom, which began with the Spindletop gusher in 1901 and helped make the Hughes Tool Company a leader in oil field drilling equipment. [8] His son, my Great Grandfather Dudley, was Sectretary of the Confederate Air Force from 1956 to 1960. My study and subsequent essay will concern the **importance of excellence in our country's energy production and distribution**. In the Confederacy our electricity generation is 60 percent nuclear. No nation produces and distributes electricity as cheaply as we do. Furthermore, our oil and gas reserves mean our petroleum and petrochemical industries are by far the most efficient on earth. The price of our gasoline? People who are not Confederates appear to be, how should I say, jealous?"

Professor Davis:

"Thank your Miss Sharp. Our final essay is the task of Amanda Lynn Washington. Her subject will concern the **importance of excellence in our country's schools, colleges and universities**. Miss Washington, please come forward and tell us your story."

Amanda Lynn Washington

Amanda Washington completes the team of twelve essayists, and is probably destined to become the team's most important contributor. Her appearance clearly shows her ancestory is about 50-50, from Africa and from Europe. Athletic, five feet eleven inches and 135 pounds, she looks the part of a former high school basketball guard. She wraps up the intoductions:

"I am 25 and presently residing in Lynchburg, Virginia and expect to complete my Ph.D. in Public Education late next year. I earned a joint B.A./B.S. degree in Education at Jefferson Davis University in Jackson, Mississippi three years ago. After one year of classroom teaching experience I came to Lynchburg to Washington University to earn my Ph. D. My thesis is titled, 'Achieving Excellence in Educating a Diverse Population.' My ancestry is close to 50 percent African, 40 percent European and 10 percent Native American. I have participated in athletics in several ways in public school and college. I love to run. Played a rather good game of basketball, mostly as point guard. I love to sing and have a great deal of experience in chorus and piano. Gospel music is a favorite. Love jazz. Want to race me in the 100 yard dash?

"Booker T. Washington of Virginia and Alabama, my great-great-grandfather was a leading educator of students of full or partial African ancestry, notably at the Tuskegee Institute, which he founded.

---

[8] The history of the Sharps-Hughes hardrock drill bit and its importance is truthful history. The story of Walter Benona Sharp is truthful.

My father, Dr. Larry Washington, a physician, is the son of Booker T. Washington, III. My great-great-grandfather's pragmatic approach to teaching studens of color and his advocacy for similar educational programs all across the Confederacy had much to do with the successful training of our people to succeed in technical work in many fields, ranging from agriculture, to manufacturing, to transportation, to construction, to medicine, and so forth. And, as we all know, the pragmatic training of which he pioneered has been a major contribution to the excellence our Confederacy has enjoyed in intelligent and capable craftmanship across diverse fields of endeavor.

"My study and subsequent essay will concern the **importance of excellence in our country's schools, colleges and universities**, to ensure that a non-political educational culture is sustained and that the brightest students are encouraged to study and succeed in the important fields of business, technology, medicine, science and engineering -- fields key to the economic progress of everyone in our country. Our high schools are very good and we realize that a college education is not worthwhile for well over three-quarters of Confederate young men and women.

"Entrepreneurship is very strong in our country, and college does not help much with that. Unlike to our north in the United States, we see very few college graduates flipping hamburgers. There is a good reason for that."

Professor Davis:

"Thank you, Miss Washington. This completes the introductions."

Our Plans for the Next Two Weeks

With the introductions complete, Professor Davis begins to tell the twelve essayists about the schedule for the next four weeks at the University of the South, all leading to their presentations of essays before the worldwide television audience on July 4, 2011. Professor Davis:

"Personally speaking, I could not be more pleased with the way the Sewanee Project is lifting off the ground this morning. You are here as individuals and also as part of a team that is designed to be greater than its indiviuals. By that I mean by personal interactions and discussion among yourselves, I anticipate much greater outcomes will resullt from interpersonal associations and comaradary within this team. You inspire me and I hope each other as well. Thanks go to each of you, our twelve Sewanee Project Essayists. Each of you is charged with the task of studying relevant facts and relevant history, analyzing what you find, and writing your essay, each answering from the chosen perspective the burning question that seems to so puzzle the world: 'What has made the CSA the greatest country on Earth.'

"Now about some ground rules for the next four weeks that we will be together.

"Saturday and Sunday are days for free time, but Monday through Friday you will be fully engaged in the project from the time you wake in the morning until you go to sleep. The following are the rules for those five days.

"Breakfast will be eaten together at 7:00 am each morning. We will be together at the big round 12-seat breakfast table in Davis Hall and you will note that rotating seat assignments will be in place to facilitate getting to know one another and to talk together about experiences and progress on writing individual essays. Eat a full breakfast because lunch will not be served until 1:15.

"Class will begin at 8:00 am and conclude at 1:00 pm."

"Lunch will began at the big round table at 1:15 pm and conclude at 2:00 pm. Seating will be reassigned each day. Get to know each other a bit more and use this time to hit upon some discussion inspired by the morning's class.

"From 2:00 pm to 4:00 pm you are expected to be in the library engaged in independent study to improve your understanding of the Confederacy and the essay subject which you have been assigned. Four library assistants have come in from summer break to be here for you over the next four weeks, so please use their talents to help with your individual research. The library at Sewanee is among the world's best and our staff there is eager and qualified to help.

"You will have two hours in late afternoon for free time and exercise, from 4:30 pm to 6:30 pm. I know you will enjoy that. I hear talk of tennis and other endeavors.

"You are to be at supper from 6:30 pm to 8:00 pm. Here the seating is different, for you will not be eating together at the big round table. You will find a nice spread of traditional Southern Cooking on that table. But you will not be seated there to eat. You will serve your plate, choosing from among the nice spread of offerings. Then you will move to your assigned private dining table to eat and to better get to know another person among the eleven, one-on-one. Every evening the pairings will be changed. No one looking over your shoulder, no one else talking, just the two of you alone to share whatever interests you. Of course, part of your conversation ought to be discussing the day's events. Using portable sound-deadening high-profile partitions, our campus maintenance men have set up 6 private dining tables near the big round table, so everything will be convenient and easy to maneuver. Every evening you will be assigned a two person table for supper, table one, two, three, four, five or six. Over the course of 11 days, you will have held a supper-time discussion with every other essayist. Then the table assignment scheme goes into repeat mode.

"After supper, there will be time for relaxing, and music, and further conversation. There are several musicians among us. Something might emerge from that interest.

"Before retiring for the night one more task remains. That is completing your private diary. On the table at the back of the room are 13 bound, 7-inch-by-10-inch diary books containing 150 pages of blank ruled paper. Every day I want you to make a diary entry before retiring. I will be starting my diary book, the thirteenth one, as well. I will begin each day's entry on a fresh page listing the day and the date, followed by "Joe to diary." From there the diary notes will flow. Now, I want you to make your diary entries at the close of the day, not the next morning or some later time. Why? Folks, your next four weeks will be greatly exciting and stimulating. But you need a good night's sleep more than ever before. Believe me when I tell you that recording notes about the day just closing and about possible plans and ideas for the day to come will help you relax and go to sleep. Those who do not do that will often toss and turn and mull over experiences and ideas for an hour or so, failing to slow down the brain and put it to sleep. I have this on high authority, so trust me on this.

"We shall make an exception in our schedule this afternoon. Instead of library time, please return here after lunch for a presentation on The Sequoyah Story. Allen Ross and Andrew Houston have agreed to help me with it, so I know it will be special for all of us."

The just-before-bedtime-diary-note assignment surely made sense to Professor Davis. He believed that putting notes on paper just before bed would prevent such issues from interferring with sleep. But there will be an additional benefit. As readers of our amazing story, you will have an opportunity to see a few selected diary notes at the close of each chapter (each day will be a chapter). Through this sampling of diary notes, you, as a reader, will get to better know the twelve essayists – their thoughts about the day's lecture – their thoughts about each other – plans for weekend adventures – musical interests -- occasional romatic notions – and so forth. For that reason you should enjoy reading a page of diary notes at the end of each chapter.

You may wonder why the twelve essayists selected for the Sewanee Project were descended from notable leaders in the early days of the

Confederates States. "Why not include some young people whose ancestry is not notable?", you may ask. Well, as it turns out, Professor Davis and the administration of the University of the South had decided that it was not necessary to showcase young people whose ancestry was not noteworthy. All Confederates in the year 2011 knew that opportunity for success in their country was open to all. That fact did not need to be illustrated through the selection of the twelve. So, what was special about the twelve? They were specially positioned to tell about important leaders and accomplishments in Confederate history from the viewpoint of **family history** as well as public history – a very special addition – an addition that enhances the popularity of the project.

Professor Davis continues: "Now, your are in for a special treat. Among you are descendants of perhaps the two most important men in the history of the Cherokee Nation and in the founding of the Nation-State of Sequoyah. I personally know of no more heroic and charitable event in the history of the Confederate States of America than the story of Sequoyah. Three of us will be presenting this history over the next two hours. I will present the core history, Allen Bruce Ross will present that part that relates directly to his ancestor Principle Chief John Ross, and Andrew Houston will present that part that relates directly to his ancestors Sam Houston and Tiana Rodgers Houston. I will now begin."

How the Nation-State of Sequoyah Came to Be

As we all know, the Nation-State of Sequoyah is today's homeland for Confederates of Native American ancestry. How did that come about? How did Native Americans persevere through broken treaty, after broken treaty, after broken treaty to retain a part of North America as their national homeland? First we need to understand that those broken treaties had been made between Natives and earlier governments – during colonial days with certain European nations (England, Great Britain, France, Spain and the Netherlands) – and afterward, with the United States government. Most of these had been broken prior to State Secession. [9]

But in our own history, following the creation of the Confederate States of America, treaties between Natives and Confederates have always been honored. The Five Civilized Tribes, between 1817 and 1840, had been forced by treaty and/or the U. S. Army to relocate to the land west of Arkansas and North and east of Mexican Tejas. Those resettled had been promised that a large stretch of land west of Arkansas would be their national land forever, and there they would be free to operate a government of their own creation. [10] This land, promised to the Five Civilized Tribes, was a region of 64,273 square miles – a vast area for the relatively small Native population to occupy. An example for comparison is helpful. The land granted to these five tribes was twenty-six times the size of little Delaware, which would be supporting a population of 112,216 people in 1860. Soon after Secession, the Confederate

---

[9] In truthful history, such treaties with Native Americans would be broken by the United States in subsequent years.

[10] This large stretch of land resembled what in truthful history is today called Oklahoma, but without the western "panhandle" appendage that was carved out of the Republic of Texas.

Government promised to honor the former commitment by the United States to support a Native American nation across those 64,273 square miles. Confederates promised to support a Native nation-state if the Five Civilized Tribes living there would support the cause of secession for the adjacent Southern States and fight, if necessary, to defend it against attack from Kansas, northern Missouri and elsewhere.

The Five Civilized Tribes of Southeastern North America consisted of the Cherokees, the Choctaws, the Chickasaws, the Creeks and the Seminoles. Living east of the Mississippi River and south of Virginia and Kentucky, they had been farmers who raised beans, squash and corn in field crops and acquired meat by fishing and hunting. Most advanced were the Cherokees. For a long time Whites had occasionally married native women and the children of those mothers were called mixed blood and were perceived as citizens of the relevant native Nation, be it Choctaw, Chickasaw, Cherokee, Creek or Seminole. Mixed blood citizens were most prevalent in the Cherokee Nation, and by 1861 a significant number of Cherokees were far more White than Native. The people of the Civilized Tribes were remarkably different from the Woodland Indians to the north and the Plains Indians to the north-west.

Before arrival of Europeans and the diseases they brought to the Americas, people in the Civilized Tribes had numbered in the millions and many lived in towns, some of them being very large towns on raised mounds. But by 1861, the Native population had been drastically reduced. So the land exchanged with them, lying west of Arkansas, was large enough to support their remnant population for many generations into the future.

Meanwhile, to the North, during the 1850s, across the Northern States, the Republican Party was new, was becoming powerful, and was promoting an attitude that the land being settled in the Plains, the Rocky Mountains and the Pacific Northwest was exclusively for White people of European ancestry. This extreme racial attitude, encouraged by Republican leaders, portended dangerous times for Native Americans living in those regions – a future without bison, being restricted onto so-called reservations, onto the worst, driest land available. Sadly, Confederates would refuse to accept Natives seeking to flee the North's wide-spread passion for ethnic cleansing with regard to Natives – its negotiators would insist on prohibiting southward immigration of Native Americans from United States land, unless invited by leaders of the Five Civilized Tribes. Northern Natives would remain on assigned reservations.

In mid-1861, President Davis had appointed Albert Pike to negotiate alliances with the Five Civilized Tribes and with any other smaller native groups then living in Indian Territory. Assisting Pike was General Ben

McCulloch, commander of Confederate troops in the region. Pike and McCulloch first won an alliance with the Creek Nation, the Chickasaw Nation and the Choctaw Nation at a gathering of chiefs and headmen at North Fork Village. Subsequently, the Seminole Nation agreed at its council house gathering. Pike even won support from small bands of Wichitas, Kiowas and Comanches who were then living in the western part of the territory. Finally, on October 1, 1861, at a great mass meeting of the Cherokee Nation, the decision was reached to also make an alliance:

> "All of the treaties which Pike signed with the Indians were very much alike. The Indians agreed to join the South, and the Confederacy agreed to take the position toward the Indians that the United States had held. It agreed to pay them their annuities, to guarantee to them their lands, to furnish them with arms, and to protect them against attack by the North. The Indians were to have delegates in the Confederate Congress, and they were encouraged to believe that eventually they might become a State within the Confederacy."

Essentially, Confederates promised the Five Civilized Tribes: if you support the Confederacy against anticipated aggression by the United States and the Lincoln Administration, we will support you. If we are successful, after the immediate danger passes, we will recognize a Native American nation that will encompass the land west of Arkansas, south of Kansas and north and east of Texas. Furthermore, we will negotiate an arrangement whereby this Native American nation can become a special nation-state with voting power in the political structure of the Confederate States of America. And we will support your right to control immigration into your nation-state.

Warriors of the Five Civilized Tribes fought bravely and heroically in Defense of the Confederacy, earning a place of deep gratitude in the hearts of fellow Confederates. And the Confederate Government did keep its promise: Indian Territory would become a Nation-State reserved for Native Americans and controlled, with regard to all internal matters, by Native Americans living under their rules of government.

The boundaries of what would become the State of Sequoyah are easy to define. The eastern boundary was the westward boundary of the State of Arkansas. The northern boundary was the southern boundary of Kansas, a State in the United States. The southern boundary was the Red River westward to where the headwaters fork and from there further westward along the northern branch. The southern and western boundaries were shared with Texas. Within what would become the State of Sequoyah, the initial Tribal boundaries were as follows (these were not rigidly observed, and would be less so as the years advanced):

The Choctaws settled in the southeastern part; the Chickasaws settled west of the Choctaws; the Cherokee settled the northeastern part; the Creeks settled southwest of the Cherokee, and the Seminoles, a small population, settled in a modest region just beyond their Creek kinsmen. Land west of these allocations was not clearly allocated, but the inference was clear that all land to the west was for the use of the Five Civilized Tribes, and they would be empowered to control immigration into it and the governance of it "as long as the waters run." [11]

Sam Houston played a major role in bringing together leaders among Choctaw, Chickasaw, Cherokee, Creek and Seminole and winning their agreement to give up each Tribe's authority in exchange for collective sovereignty for the whole. By this agreement, the Choctaw-Chickasaw-Cherokee-Creek-Seminole Unification Treaty of July, 1864, Houston's supporters elevated the authority of the Union of the Five Civilized Tribes into a bulwark of unquestioned United Authority. This led to the Sequoyah Constitutional Convention of 1865, where the Sequoyah Nation-State Constitution was drafted and signed. It provided for a bicameral legislature, a House and a Senate, an Executive headed by a Governor (Joint Principle Chief) and a system of tribal courts, district courts and a supreme court. The Secretary of Native Immigration was a powerful position, for, by agreeing to allow Sequoyah to become a homeland for Natives further west in the Confederacy, the Five Civilized Tribes gained the good will essential to winning approval of its bid for admittance as a Nation-State under the Confederate States Government. Leaders of the Five Civilized Tribes started from a disadvantaged position, for Sequoyah was large in land mass but small in population. This is where Sam Houston was most influential.

Before the Confederate Congress, on April 5, 1866, Sam Houston, speaking as ambassador for the Choctaw-Chickasaw-Cherokee-Creek-Seminole Alliance, explained the great benefit to both Confederate Native

---

[11] In truthful history, most of the natives in the Five Civilized Tribes supported the Confederacy and suffered greatly during repeated Federal invasions of their lands during and after the War Between the States. In our alternate history, because peace was achieved in 1862, after only one great battle west of the Mississippi, the Five Civilized Tribes avoided the massive destruction and death among the population that was suffered in truthful history. This enabled the Five Civilized Tribes to move forward toward unifying under a nation-state government – first under the protection of the Confederate States and eventually as a nation-state government with all the rights of statehood – plus an additional right to control immigration and preserve Sequoyah for settlement by Native Americans from within the boundaries of the Confederacy, such as from the Upper Rio Grande and the Lower Colorado rivers.

Americans and Confederates of European ancestry who were settling near-vacant lands from west Texas to the Pacific.

"Andrew Houston, please step forward and read the portion of you ancestor's address to Congress which gives us a flavor of what he said.

"I have read this many times before and am always thrilled each time I do so."

The words of Sam Houston as read by Andrew:

"My fellow Confederates, it is my belief – and I encourage you to share it with me – that no matter from what lands a people's ancestry originated, our Lord understands that they have a right, even an obligation, to occupy underutilized land, to make it fruitful and to multiply upon it. This God-given right exists even though the existing occupiers have resided upon that land for many, many generations. That is a God-given right to mankind, the right to occupy underutilized land and build a flourishing God-fearing society upon it. Some have called this our 'Manifest Destiny.'

"But that right carries with it a serious obligation to deal fairly with those who had long been living on that underutilized land. Our Lord wants us to be gracious and helpful to those less fortunate than ourselves, and that, too, is our obligation. The Natives living in this hemisphere were living as stone-age people (did not possess metals technology except for gold and silver) when Europeans first arrived. We brought diseases and chaos that severely decimated the tribes of Native peoples; in some regions hardly a remnant remains living today. My friends, we cannot change the past, but we can change the future. We can give Native Americans a home in a nation-state of Sequoyah. Choctaw, Chickasaw, Cherokee, Creek and Seminole are already there. These we call the "Five Civilized Tribes." These we have come to know well, for they were farmers, hunters and fishermen living in what became North Carolina, South Carolina, Georgia, Florida, Tennessee, Alabama, Mississippi and eastern Louisiana, where so many of our ancestors settled. No Native peoples in North America are more advanced than the Choctaw, Chickasaw and Cherokee. Believe me. I know them well. These and the two others have united under the Choctaw-Chickasaw-Cherokee-Creek-Seminole Unification Treaty of July, 1864. They have named their region Sequoyah, to honor the Cherokee who invented the easily learned Cherokee system of writing. They have approved a Sequoyah Nation-State Constitution, establishing a government well suited to their needs, which promises to enable Native advancements not dreamed of just a few years ago.

"My friends, Natives deserve their Nation-State under the Confederate States Government. Our Lord beseeches us to grant it to them. Not just for their sake – also for everyone living in the Confederacy today and tomorrow. Under the tutelage of Sequoyah's leaders, other Native Americans will migrate to this new Nation-State and benefit from opportunities found there. From east of the Mississippi, most remaining Choctaw, Chickasaw, Cherokee, Creek and Seminole will come, as well as Lumbee from North Carolina. From western Louisiana, Houma will come. But most importantly, from west Texas to the Pacific will come Apache, Navaho, Pueblo and smaller groupings from the southwest, including Cheyenne, Comanche, Paiute, Pima, Shoshone, Tohono O'odham and Yaqui. But Natives presently living to the north, in the United States, shall remain there and this will be enforced. The government of Sequoyah will grant migration rights and oversee the process. We believe Natives are best at such oversight and guidance. I stand today embarrassed, so greatly embarrassed, over the suffering and lives lost in the Cherokee Nation during its forced westward migration known as the "Trail of Tears." That alone tells me that Choctaw, Chickasaw and Cherokee are bound to do a better job than can we. We only have to let them do it!"

The Nation-State of Sequoyah

After thanking Andrew Houston, Professor Davis launched into the history of the Nation State of Sequoyah: [12]

"The Confederate Congress admitted the Nation-State of Sequoyah into the Confederate States of America on July 4, 1870. This decision was one of the most beneficial decisions Confederates have ever made. The 2010 Census has shown that 1,352,941 people of full or partial Native ancestry live in Sequoyah. During 2010, a little over 100,000 people of no Native ancestry also lived in Sequoyah at some point, being permitted to be there because of work or visitation permits. Today, Sequoyah remains a Nation-State where only its government can grant the right of residence. And the Sequoyah constitution stipulates that only persons with at least 1/16 native ancestry are permitted to live there (children who fall below 1/16 must move out upon reaching adulthood).

---

[12] We are departing from truthful history with regard to Sam Houston – in our alternate history, Sam Houston and his family would play a major role in uniting the Five Civilized Tribes around a decision to denounce the United States and team up with the Confederacy, and later to help unify the tribal leaders to cooperate in creating a Nation-State government for Sequoyah.

"The story of the Sequoyah prairie grassland deserves inclusion. In the early years, the 1840's and 1850's, the population of the Five Civilized Tribes was too small and the business/ranching skills too marginal to successfully develop the economic potential of the vast prairie grassland in the western half of Indian Territory. This region promised to be sustainable prairie grassland when properly managed and not overgrazed. Leasing grazing land in the western region of the Indian Territory began with many leases from the Cherokee Nation to Texas Ranchers, who moved large herds of their longhorn cattle north into what was called the prairie grassland of the Cherokee Outlet, allowing them to gain weight, then moving them further north through western Kansas to railroad heads from which they were shipped to Chicago and points east. Lease revenue served to strengthen the Cherokee economy, and taught Cherokees valuable lessons about the longhorn cattle ranching business and the importance of moving cattle to top-dollar markets. By the 1850s, ambitious mixed-blood Cherokees were operating a few cattle ranches and hiring Texans to move Cherokee longhorns through Kansas to railheads. After the Montreal Treaty, Cherokees could no longer market longhorns to the north. So, they were soon moving cattle to river ports on the Mississippi and Red rivers. From there Cherokee cattle went by riverboat to New Orleans and Mobile, and by rail across Tennessee and on to North Carolina and Virginia, and by rail across Alabama, Georgia and South Carolina. [13]

Choctaws and Chickasaws were quick learners. Cattle ranching soon developed into a major industry for the Natives and part-bloods living in what would become the Nation-State of Sequoyah and beyond. And cattle ranching diversified into Bison ranching in the Native Game Lands. Native cattlemen became bison ranchers, managing the growing herds as those amazing animals thrived on the Native Game Lands. The key was herd population management and grassland conservation. When the historic drought would strike the Native Game Lands in the 1930s, laying waste to the plowed lands elsewhere in that part of North America, Native management of

---

[13] In truthful history, Native Americans have no nation-state and many live on reservations. Apache, Navaho, Pueblo and others in the southwestern United States live on reservations. After Federal forces defeated the Confederacy, many northern tribes were relocated to Indian Territory, which became Oklahoma Territory. Then Oklahoma Territory was opened to "Land Rush" settlement by people of European ancestry. The Federal Government made sure that, when Oklahoma was granted statehood, Native American residents would be forever a minority unable to protect themselves against the demands of the White majority. Whites plowed up the prairie to grow cotton, etc. The drought years arrived in the 1930's, the top soil blew away, and Oklahoma became a "Dust Bowl," a land of great sorrow. It recovered but slowly. The population in 2010 was 3,762,000 persons, of which 321,687 were of full or partial Native ancestry. In our alternate history, Native Americans are gathered together on the land as citizens of the Nation-State of Sequoyah, most of the prairie remained intact as grazing land, the population grew more slowly, and the Native residents controlled their destiny and prospered.

the virgin prairie grassland paid off. During those "dust bowl days," many bison were moved east to pasture in Arkansas and Louisiana and the population was thinned moderately. Recovery was excellent after the rains returned, and today Cherokee grass-fed bison is considered the finest red meat available anywhere in the world.

"Moving rapidly forward to present days, the story of the Nation-State of Sequoyah is a picture worth painting. Let us look at population, industry, education, nature of the people, political organization, tourism, racial mix and race relations, immigration rules, and influence in Confederate politics.

"At this point I am going to ask Allen Bruce Ross to step forward and tell us about four Cherokee families: Sequoyah, the Major Ridge family, the John Ross family, and the John Rogers family."

Major Cherokee Leaders: Sequoyah and the Ridge, Ross and Rogers Families

At this point, Allen Bruce Ross continued the history:

"The story of the State's namesake, Sequoyah, although familiar to most, needs telling again. A Cherokee, Sequoyah was born about 1770 to Wut-teh — a full-blood Cherokee of the Red Paint Clan and related to Chief Old Tassel and Chief Doublehead. The baby's father was Nathaniel Gist, a half-blood Cherokee fathered by an Englishman or Scot by the name of Gist or Guess. So Sequoyah was three-fourths Cherokee. He spent his youth in the Cherokee village named Tuskegee. As an adult, he fathered four children with wife Sally Waters and three with wife Utiyu. Like many Cherokees who allied with Andrew Jackson's militia, he fought the "Red Sticks" in the Battle of Horseshoe Bend (the 'Red Sticks" were a faction of Creek warriors who were aligned with the British during the War of 1812). Later he became a silversmith and found that Whites were often his customers. Frequent contact with Whites and his business experience inspired him to tackle the task of teaching members of the Cherokee Nation to read and write. Finding the Cherokee language difficult to express through the 26-symbol alphabet of English-speaking neighbors, he resolved to create an alphabet of 86 characters, each of which represented a syllable in the Cherokee language. Stringing together these syllables created words and then sentences. Use of this alphabet enabled many Cherokee to communicate by written messages. In 1825 the Cherokee Nation officially adopted Sequoyah's writing system. The *Cherokee Phoenix*, the first regular newspaper for the Cherokee Nation, subsequently began publication using a special type face of 86 characters. Afterward Sequoyah travelled west to join the Western Cherokees in Arkansas;

later further west into Indian Territory. There, he established a business as a blacksmith and periodically represented Cherokees in negotiation between his people and American authorities. Later in life, he visited other Native tribes west of Texas, learning their language and striving to adapt his alphabet to their tongue. He crossed into Mexico to engage with Cherokees who were experimenting with relocating there. Sometime in 1843, 1844 or 1845, he died when engaged in this last mission. Although a powerful concept of writing, the only language to successfully adapt his method was the Cherokee's. The story of Sequoyah and the Cherokee system of writing is important to our understanding of why and how the Cherokee rose to become the most capable leaders of all the Native Nations of North America.

"There are three prominent names in Cherokee history, each of which deserves mention. These names are "Ridge," "Ross," and "Rogers." We can call them the three "R's." We now turn to the first of the "R's," Major Ridge.

"Major Ridge (also known as Nunnehidihi) was born about 1771, near the Great Smokies in a Cherokee town along the Hiwassee River in what would become Tennessee. He was three-fourths Cherokee, his maternal grandfather being of Scottish ancestry. Ridge helped lead Cherokees in joining with General Andrew Jackson at the Battle of Horseshoe Bend. He grew rather prosperous, developing a sizable plantation of nearly 300 cleared acres, planted in tobacco and cotton and worked by 30 African-American slaves. Furthermore he operated a profitable ferry service and trading post.

"Along with several other Cherokee leaders, Major Ridge, without proper authorization, signed (made his mark) on the Treaty of New Echota, which allegedly bound all Cherokee to accept removal to new lands west of Arkansas. Principle Cherokee Chief John Ross declared Ridge's treaty illegal and resisted Cherokee removal with all the force he could muster.

"We now turn to the second "R," John Ross. John Ross was the longest serving Principle Chief of the Cherokee Nation. Born in 1790 near the head of the Coosa River in northern Alabama, John Ross was the son of a one-fourth Cherokee mother, Mollie McDonald, and father Daniel Ross, of Scottish descent. Since all babies born to Cherokee mothers were deemed full members of the tribe, the baby's Cherokee ancestry was derived from his mother's mother, Anna, who had been born to Ghigooie, a full-blood Cherokee, and her husband, John McDonald, also of Scottish ancestry. Such marriages of Cherokee women to men of European ancestry were common in the Cherokee

Nation and history would show that children born to these unions would become a great strength in the Cherokee people. This tradition would enable them to become the most advanced and most politically capable of all Native populations. John Ross grew up in the vicinity of what would become Chattanooga, Tennessee. As a young man, he was with Cherokees allied with Andrew Jackson at the Battle of Horseshoe Bend. He became a farmer, raising tobacco on 170 acres in Tennessee with the help of 20 African slaves. And he ran a ferry across the Tennessee River at Ross's Landing, which would become the city of Chattanooga.[14]

"Elected to the Cherokee National Council, Ross, being the most fluent in English, became a major leader in negotiations on behalf of the Cherokee Nation at discussions in Washington City that took place between 1818 and 1824. He was elected Principle Chief of the Cherokee Nation in 1828, which had organized under a constitutional National Government, complete with judicial, legislative and executive branches. At Washington City, Principle Chief Ross encouraged recognition of the Cherokee people as belonging to a distinct Nation, appealing to major United States government leaders and filing a claim in the U. S. Supreme Court (*Cherokee Nation v. Georgia*). Chief Justice John Marshall agreed that the Cherokee were of a sovereign nation, and that the State of Georgia could not impose laws upon Cherokee people, but President Andrew Jackson held the trump card. He persuaded Congress to pass the Indian Removal Act of May 1830, which ordered Cherokee, Chickasaw, Choctaw and Creek to relocate to Indian Territory west of Arkansas. Of the four, only the Cherokee refused to comply. Ross led the resisters, but as mentioned earlier, others, led by Major Ridge, chose to negotiate the best possible removal deal outside of Cherokee authority. Ignoring that the Ridge group had no authority to speak for the Cherokee Nation, the U. S. Government closed a deal with them at New Echota (a trick), creating a great feud within the Nation. Principle Chief John Ross had been circumvented. Sadly, signers of the so-called Treaty of New Echota would be charged with treason, condemned by a Cherokee court and sentenced to death. Ridge, his son and a nephew would be executed two years later.

"Ross did persuade U. S. General Winfield Scott to let him take charge of the final 1838 Cherokee removal to Indian Territory, but the extremely cold weather that winter and scarcity of provisions resulted in many deaths, including Ross's wife Quatle, who died of pneumonia near Little Rock. John Ross continued as Principle Chief for many

---

[14] The Ross house can still be seen, as of 2011.

years, and, on August 21, 1861 he advocated an alliance with the Confederate States of America.

"We now turn to the story of the third "R," John Rogers, Jr., who, for the years 1839 and 1840, was Principal Chief of the Cherokee Nation West, the name given to Cherokees who had migrated west long before the final "Removal" mentioned above. He was born in 1876 near the Great Smokies to John Rogers, Sr., of European ancestry, and Alice Vann, of partial Cherokee ancestry. His full brother was James Rogers. His half-sister was Tiana Rogers, the daughter of John Rogers, Sr. and Jennie Due. The Rogers clan is important to Cherokee history. By the way, the great American entertainer, Will Rogers, is descended from this family. But it is now time to tell about Tiana Rodgers, John Roger's half-sister.

"Tiana Rogers would become the wife of (General, Governor, President, Senator) Sam Houston of Texas fame. The story of Houston's Cherokee wife, Tiana, is both epic and heroic, so let us spend a few pages on that. We start with Tiana, daughter of Captain John James Rogers and Jennie Due, born about 1800 within view of the majestic Smoky Mountains. The baby's father was one of the most prominent White men in the Cherokee Nation and her mother was the part Cherokee sister of two prominent Cherokee Chiefs: Chief Tah-lhon-tusky and Chief Oo-loo-te-ka, the latter taking the name John Jolly when dealing with Whites. Also the baby was related to Sequoyah, who would create the Cherokee alphabet. The baby had been named "Diana Rogers" but Cherokee's had trouble making the "D" sound, so they called her "Tiana." Captain Rogers and his family lived among Chief Oo-loo-te-ka's clan of about 300 Cherokees on Hiwassee Island, a large island in the Tennessee River where the Hiwassee River rushes in from the Great Smokies. Rogers had two wives and many children. Sons John Rogers, William Rogers, and Charles Rogers were destined to become prominent among Cherokees. Sons John Rogers and James Rogers were to become teenage friends of Sam Houston, now to be introduced."

Professor Davis:

"Allen, we thank you for those splendid family stories.

Sam Houston and the Cherokee Nation

"Now, Andrew Houston, please come forward to tell us the rest. Tell us the relevant Houston family story." Andrew began:

"About 50 miles to the east of Hiwassee Island, where Cherokees and the Rogers family lived, was the pioneer town of Maryville,

Tennessee. Near Maryville, with a splendid view of the Cherokee Nation's Great Smokies, was the new farm of Elizabeth Houston, a vigorous pioneer widow and mother of an energetic family of 6 sons and 3 daughters, all born in Virginia. The Houston's had recently relocated to Tennessee, arriving in 1807. The fifth son, born in 1793, was named Sam for his late father, Captain Samuel Houston, who had died just before the family's pioneering immigration of 1807. Having purchased a 400 acre tract of raw Tennessee land, and, with 6 males, age 11, 14 and older, and some money left from selling the family farm in Virginia, the Houston family seemed destined to become successful Tennesseans. But one of the males, 14-year-old Sam, was not inspired toward farm work. He loved to read and explore the woods. At age 16 he did rather rebel against his stern, hard-driving older brothers, and he ran away, with books in tow, to the Cherokee Nation, to live the playful life of Cherokee natives based at Hiwassee Island. He stayed a long time – three years except for a few short visits back home. He loved spending time on the island with the Roger's family, especially brothers John and James Rogers. He also noticed their little half-sister, Tiana Rogers, seven years younger than he. Chief Oo-le-te-ka's clan welcomed Sam Houston, for the growing teenager was a popular companion and a source of useful learning. Handsome, ruggedly built, tall at six-foot two and intelligent, Sam Houston impressed as a potential important future leader of the Cherokee people. Chief Oo-le-te-ka decided to adopt Sam Houston as his son and gave him the Cherokee name, "The Raven," obviously a name suggesting greatness to come. Of his three teenage years with the Cherokee, Sam would much later write:

" 'It was the molding period of life when the heart, just charmed into the feverish hopes and dreams of youth, looks wistfully around on all things for light and beauty – 'when every idea of gratification fires the blood and flashes on the fancy – when the heart is vacant to every fresh form of delight, and has not rival engagements to draw it from the importunities of a new desire.' The poets of Europe, fancying such scenes, have borrowed their sweetest images from the wild idolatry of the Indian maiden. . . . There's nothing half so sweet to remember as this sojourn [I] made among the untutored children of the forest'.

"But would 19-year-old Sam Houston take charge of the family mercantile store in Maryville? Would he work the family farm alongside his brothers? Neither. He would join the army.

"We now fast-forward to January 22, 1829. Oo-le-te-ka's Cherokees are now living west of Arkansas on land given by treaty exchange to the Western branch of the Cherokee Nation, and Tiana

Rogers, now 29 and widowed, is living there with her people. Meanwhile, Sam Houston is now Governor of Tennessee and getting ready to marry. His career had been illustrious. He had risen to the rank of colonel in the 39th regiment of the United States Army; then become a prominent Nashville lawyer and close associate of Tennessean Andrew Jackson, now President of the United States. He was also Major-General of the Tennessee militia and had served two terms in Congress. Yes, Sam Houston, now 35 and the Governor of Tennessee, is to be betrothed to Eliza Allen, 18, the daughter of Colonel John Allen, head of a prominent, wealthy and ambitious Middle Tennessee family. They were married, but in three short months, the marriage crumbled. Eliza returned to her parents. The problem is not well understood. Governor Houston loved young Eliza to be sure. But had the father pushed his young daughter into a marriage that she did not want in order to gain prestige and advantage for his family? Governor Sam Houston, a sensitive man who held honor at the loftiest heights, was emotionally crushed and felt unable to faithfully carry on his duties as Tennessee's Governor. He resigned. He headed west to the land of the Western Cherokee Nation, to Oo-loo-te-ka's people who had been his happy refuge during his latter teenage years. The Raven flew toward the sunset, flew to his other home, where he had known happiness.

"With an adventurous male companion, Sam Houston rode a steamboat up the Cumberland River and down the Ohio to Cairo, Illinois, where the pair employed a flatboatman to take them on a drifting course down the Mississippi River to the mouth of the Arkansas River. From there the party poled upstream to Little Rock. There Houston bought a horse and rode 140 miles further up the Arkansas River Valley to Fort Smith, then further to the westernmost Federal outpost, Cantonment Gibson. From there he boarded a small steam packet to Webber Falls, where navigation terminated. Word of the Raven's journey had already reached Chief Oo-loo-te-ka and a large Cherokee welcoming group was on hand to greet the emotionally devastated traveler:

" 'My son', said Oo-loo-te-ka, 'I have heard you were a great chief among your people . . . I have heard that a dark cloud has fallen on the White path you were walking . . . I am glad of it – it was done by the Great Spirit . . . We are in trouble and the Great Spirit has sent you to us to give us counsel. My wigwam is yours – my home is yours – my people are yours – rest with us.'

"Of his June 1829 arrival, using the third person story-telling style, the Raven would many years later write: 'when he laid himself down to sleep that night, he felt like a weary wanderer returned at last to his father's house.'

"For three and one half years Sam Houston would live among the Western Cherokees, among Oo-loo-te-ka's people. He quickly found himself 'in a position of leadership over 7,000 Native Americans who controlled the country from Missouri to Texas and westward to the Great Plains.' During the first ten months, Houston kept busy helping Cherokee leaders make peace with the Osage, a plains-culture tribe which lived in the western region of what would be called Indian Territory; improving cooperation with the other four Civilized Tribes; dealing with Federal agents and military officers on behalf of the Cherokees and the Creeks; surviving a terrible case of malaria that almost killed him; traveling to Washington to personally appeal to President Andrew Jackson to honor the commitments Federals were attempting to make with the Five Civilized Tribes in exchange for their removal from east of the Mississippi to west of Arkansas; and, somewhat in secret, giving support to Chief Oo-loo-te-ka's dream of a Native American Nation within North America.

"In April 1830, 12 months following his resignation as Governor, Houston was back in Middle Tennessee seeking Eliza's final decision on reconciliation of their marriage. Bad news. Eliza and, or her family refused to consider reconciliation. What was Sam Houston to do? He had fulfilled his commitment to "honor." He had gone down onto his knees, professed his love and apologized profusely. He could do no more. The beautiful Tiana Rogers was waiting for him in the Cherokee Nation. He now felt free to do what he had wanted to do for the past ten months, since renewing his life with those Cherokees he had known and loved in his late teenage years. He would return to Oo-loo-te-ka's people and take Tiana as his wife. He had no divorce paper, but he and Tiana would be living together as man and wife anyway. That summer of 1830, The Raven, 37, took as his wife Tiana Rogers, 30. The bride was tall, slender, intelligent, beautiful, and no family contained more important Cherokee leaders than did the Rogers. Sam selected land near the Neosho River, 30 miles from Oo-loo-te-ka's lodge and a little above Cantonment Gibson. He built or bought a large log house, set out an apple orchard, lived in style and entertained his friends.

"But, after two and a half years with Tiana; after two and a half years dealing with Federal agents, persuading Federals and President Andrew Jackson to honor the commitments made in past treaties, Sam Houston was drawn to a new field of opportunity – Mexican Texas! He felt he must cross the southern boundary of Indian Territory, enter Mexican Texas and search out the opportunities it afforded. He needed to understand the relations between recent Anglo immigrants recently arrived in Mexican Texas and officials at Mexico City, opportunities for Texas Independence, and how future events might affect relations with the adjacent Five Civilized Tribes in Indian Territory. He could not take Tiana with him on this adventure; she would be safer at their Cherokee home where she would be protected and provided for. But he could send for her when it made sense for her to join him. Sam Houston was heading for Texas. But he knew not that he was to become the most important political and military leader that huge land would ever know. [15]

"The story of the fight for Texas independence from Mexico, the Alamo, the capture of Mexican President Santa Anna, the creation of the Republic of Texas, and the election of Sam Houston as the Nation's president, is well known to most. However, there is insufficient time today to retell it. So I proceed to describe Sam Houston's return visit to Tiana and the Cherokee people."

"Sam Houston, no longer President, and with divorce papers from Tennessee finally in hand, is in Cherokee Territory by January 1839. While he is re-uniting with Tiana, she explains that he is the father of a son, Sam Houston III, who is 6 years old. Upon hearing this surprising news, Houston exclaimed, 'Why had you not sent word to me in Texas that you had given birth to our son? I never knew you were pregnant!' Tiana explained, 'I had not shown when you left. And I know you are a man of rigid honor, a man who, if he had known, would have returned, abandoning his calling to help the people of Texas. So I did not want you to know until after you were free to return to me.' Happily, Sam married Tiana Rogers, 39, in the Cherokee Nation on March 1, 1839.

"The Houston family returned to Texas in August, but not in time to prevent his successor, Texas President Mirabeau Buonaparte Lamar, from ordering Texas militia to drive Cherokee settlers out of Texas, in the process killing a great Cherokee chief, The Bowl, in the Battle of Neches. Houston was furious. And his open support for the right of Native Americans to live in Texas would cost him political support from this point forward. But, you see, few men in history have been

---

[15] In truthful history Talahina (Tiana) would die of pneumonia in 1838. As she had waited for her husband's return, Sam, still needing official divorce papers from Tennessee, would be busy leading the Texas Independence fight and then serving his first term as President of the Republic of Texas. In truthful history, after finishing his first term as President, having learned of Talahina's untimely death, and after, about the same time, receiving divorce papers, Sam would marry Margaret Lea, 21, of Alabama on May 9, 1840 and bring his bride to Texas where the couple would eventually have seven children. In truthful history, Tiana would not give birth to a son fathered by Sam Houston.

more stubborn than was Sam Houston. He had told Texans that Tiana, a part-blood Cherokee, was his wife and Sam, Jr. was their son: 'You people of Texas, my friends, had better get used to it, for I will never abandon my family.'

"And in time Texans respected Sam Houston as a man of his word, a man who stood by honorable principles. They elected him to a second term as President of the Republic of Texas. Tiana stood by his side as Sam was inaugurated; Texans had grown to admire his beautiful and intelligent Cherokee wife. After Texas merged with the United States, Texans elected Houston to the Federal Senate to represent the new State of Texas from February 1846 to March 1859. From time to time, Tiana was in Washington City with her husband, but people of the Northern culture seemed far less congenial. Political sectionalism and racial exclusionism were passions too strong in the North. Also, from time to time, while Sam was in Washington, Tiana and their sons, Sam III and Andrew, spent time with their Cherokee relatives, thereby preparing them for positions of future leadership among the Cherokee people." [16]

"By the summer of 1859, as news of political sectionalism in the Northern States became ever more worrisome, Texans asked Sam Houston to leave the Senate and become their Governor. Sam had been Governor for 11 months when Abe Lincoln was elected President, 12 months before South Carolina seceded.

"We now proceed to March 16, 1861. Twelve days earlier, on March 4, the same day that President Abraham Lincoln was inaugurated, a Texas Constitutional Convention had declared the State of Texas an independent nation, seceded from the Federal Government of the United States. Union under the Confederate States of America followed and all Texas government officials were now compelled to swear allegiance to it. But, when the Secretary of the Convention called for Governor Sam Houston to swear his allegiance, he did not come forth. He was at home writing his letter of resignation. Like a replay of the scene in Nashville, Tennessee, Governor Houston was again stepping down from the office of Governor, handing the office to Lieutenant-Governor Edward Clark. How could this be? Sam Houston was Texas! He had been, by far, the most important leader in the Texas struggle to secure independence from Mexico – as Commander-in-

---

[16] In truthful history Sam Houston did serve a second term as President of the Republic of Texas and did serve as a Senator for the State of Texas as reported above. But Tiana was not with him, of course.

Chief of the Armies of the Republic of Texas, he had brilliantly led his troops to a resounding victory over Mexican General and President Santa Anna in April 1836 at San Jacinto and there received the defeated Mexican leader's admission that Texas was an independent nation – he had twice served as President of the Republic of Texas – he had encouraged the union of the Republic of Texas and the United States, thus transforming vast Texas into a State with the promise that it could divide itself into as many as five States in the future – for thirteen years he had represented the State of Texas in the United States Senate. On the other hand, having been elected Governor in August 1859, during the tumultuous sectional political turmoil of 1860, Houston had tried to calm enthusiasm for Texas Secession. [17]

"Sam knew what he planned to do, and Tiana understood it for sure. The family, Sam, 68, Tiana, 61, Samuel, III, 29, and Andrew, 20, would leave Texas for the Cherokee Nation in Indian Territory. Sam felt unable to help seceded Texas. But Sam knew without a doubt, that he, Tiana and their two sons would be useful in the land of the Five Civilized Tribes."

Professor Davis then stepped forward and said:

"Thank you Andrew.

"That about wraps up our story about the Nation-State of Sequoyah. There is so much to tell, but so little time allocated to it. There are many good books and biograhies and studies that you ought to read when time permits in the years ahead.

"Now, we are wrapping up Orientation Day for all of you. Enjoy supper together. Spend valuable time at the library at any time over the next four weeks and get to know the staff there. They have agreed to remain at their work through July 1 to be at your service. Regarding time there, I am handing each of you a suggested personalized reading list which is directed at studies for the essay to which each of you has been assigned. In addition to the essay-targeted list, at the library you will pick up your package of readings that all will find useful. They include the Confederate Constitution, double-spaced to allow ample edit notes; the first inaugural addresses of Presidents Davis and Lincoln; the Montreal Treaty; Secretary Benjamin's famous essay on the "Great Confederate Expansion"; The last annual report to Czar Alexsandr II by the Russian American Company and the Russian America Independence Acceptance Treaty; the Declaration of Independence for

---

[17] All of the above is truthful history except for Tiana. Our story now proceeds to our alternate history.

Seceded Mexican States and the Treaty of Saltillo; The Declaration of Independence of the Cuban People and the Spanish Accord signed at Havanah; the essay by Samuel Kipi, "How Hawaiian people became Confederates"; the Confederate Declaration of War against Japan, the Japanese Surrender Accord, and the Plan for Reconstructing Japan, its Government and its People," and, finally, *A Comprehensive History of the Confederacy*, by David Herbert Donald of Mississippi, which was published last year.

"All are now dismissed, but I will remain here to answer any questions you may have. Oh, yes! Please do not forget to make your diary entry every evening before going to sleep.

"See you here in the morning."

Dear reader: I will be posting selected diary notes as recorded in the evening of each day by Professor Davis and our 12 Sewanee Project essayists. The selections below were from Monday, June 6:

Monday Evening Selected Diary Postings

Diary note by Professor Davis said, "Near me at breakfast were four impressive fellows – Allen Ross, a bison rancher of Sequoyah; Andrew Houston, a petroleum engineer of South Texas; Carlos Cespedes, a sugar farmer of Cuba; and Isiah Montgomery, an African American corporate farmer of Mississippi. I expect excellent contributions will come from these fine young men."

Diary note by Allen Ross said, "Had supper with Conchita Rezanov, of Spanish-Russian ancestry, born in Russian America and now living in South California working on a Ph. D. in history. A beautiful blond, a highly ranked tennis player, and a gifted conversationalist, the fellows will be competing for her attention. Being a simple bison rancher myself, I doubt I will have much of a chance with her. . . . . I was honored this afternoon to be able to tell much of the story of my Ross Cherokee ancestors in conjunction with Andrew Houston. What a wonderful afternoon, followed by a lovely evening."

Diary note by Emma Lunalilo said, "Supper with Carlos Cespedes. I can't believe it. He invited me to go sailing this coming weekend, off Matanzas, Cuba. Says there will be six of us. Will fly Saturday morning from Tennessee to Cuba on the Cespedes' private jet, then take an overnight sailing trip on the family 50-foot sailboat. He said, 'Emma, no one here is more skillful on the water than you. I will be so, so disappointed if you decline to join the group.' Obviously, I said 'yes.' We were matched for supper and had a great conversation: two islanders I suppose, Cuba and Hawaii."

Diary note by Andrew Houston said, "Amazing afternoon! Such a wonderful chance to tell the story of my ancestor Sam Houston's relationship with the Cherokee Nation."

Diary note by Marie Saint Martin said, "Hard to believe that, among the thirteen of us, there are five musicians: Professor Davis plays banjo and sings. Carlos Cespedes plays guitar in both Classical and Country style. Allen Ross plays guitar in Country and Western styles. Tina Sharp plays French horn and is talented at singing. Amanda Washington plays piano and sings, too. I intend to get all of us together for some jam sessions and to see what we can do well when playing together."

Book 1, Chapter 3, Day 2 – The Secession of Seven States and The Confederate States Prior to Lincoln's Inauguration – Class Lecture, Tuesday, June 7, 2011

Professor Davis continued with his lectures as soon as the twelve were seated and ready to listen.

The Story of Judah Benjamin and Jean Lafitte

Here's a helpful hint: as a reader, just pretend you are in the class room with Professor Davis and the twelve essayists, listening to the day's lecture. Professor Davis begins now. (I am omitting quotation marks on Professor Davis' remarks).

Confederate actions prior to Abraham Lincoln's inauguration were in many ways key to eventual Confederate success in defending its independence. To be sure, Lincoln was determined to conquer the Seceded States [18] and his ploy to incite cannon fire at Charleston's Fort Sumter was designed to force Confederates to "fire the first shot." And he and fellow conspirators had every reason to believe the tactic would work. [19] But he had not figured on the influence of Jean Lafitte, his son Jean Pierre Lafitte and the son's relative by marriage, the exceptionally capable and savvy Judah

---

[18] The writer will be capitalizing more often than is considered proper style in the United States today. He is adopting style choices rather common during the mid-1800s, in situations where he believes the Confederate culture would have approved. For example, to stress that a State is sovereign over most matters in the CSA, he uses the capital "S". State Secession, like World War II, is an historic event deserving capital treatment. Much is said about race in *The CSA Trilogy*, and the White race and the Negro or Black race is capitalized. Also, the mixed race of White and Black is termed Colored people (today almost all Confederates of African ancestry are mixed race, so Black or Negro does not often apply). There are more examples. The writer thought you might like to know about the reasons for his style selections.

[19] In truthful history, President Lincoln was intent on implementing some scheme that would incite Confederates to fire first to initiate the war he planned to launch. That was a political tactic designed to support a propaganda campaign alleging that the United States was under attack and state militia must come forward to defend it. Any first shot might serve Lincoln's purpose, but Charleston was surely his preference. Fort Sumter was a partially completed large fortress in the middle of Charleston harbor. South Carolina had declared Secession on December 20 and, during the night of December 26, a small Federal garrison, under the command of Robert Anderson, had, under the cover of night, relocated from a shore fort, Moultrie, to the mid-harbor fort, Sumter, in violation of an understanding between U. S. President James Buchanan and the Nation of South Carolina -- an agreement stipulating that Anderson's garrison would make no aggressive move. Wishing to avoid any appearance of distrust, South Carolina troops had not been placed in Fort Sumter, allowing Anderson to sneak in at night and bring in cannon. A strict interpretation of international law infers that Anderson's action was an act of war.

Benjamin. [20] I am about to tell you the fascinating Benjamin-Lafitte story using lots of quoted conversation, which may not be entirely authentic, but let us not be fussy about such details as, together, we live this bit of important history as if we were there, listening in.

The scene is Montgomery, Alabama, February 18, 1861. Jefferson Davis has just completed delivering his remarks to the gathered crowd, accepting the office of President of the Confederate States of America. Immediately afterward, Jean Lafitte approached Judah Benjamin, both of Louisiana. They were related by marriage, for Jean's son Jean Pierre and Judah were married to sisters of New Orleans' rather prominent Saint Martin family. Jean Lafitte clasped Judah's hand and said, "That was a fine start to what ought to become a great nation, but we will need every trick we can muster to sustain it, Judah. What part will you play in the effort?"

Judah answered, "President Davis has spoken briefly to me about a position in the Cabinet, but only in generalities. I agreed to take any position where I could be useful. Attorney General was mentioned, among other possibilities. You look well. I did not know you were here. I know you miss your wife Catherine. It's been two years since she passed away. She was a fine lady. Your son Jean Pierre and his wife Marie are well I hope. Except for quickly passing through during my travels, I've not been in New Orleans for over a year; so busy in Washington and Mississippi."

Jean Lafitte then told Judah what he knew: "I arrived early this morning. My son Pierre had encouraged me to come and, well, I wouldn't

---

[20] We deviate from truthful history when Jean Lafitte, 79, enters the story on Monday, February 18, 1861 at Montgomery, Alabama. Jean Lafitte and brother Pierre Lafitte were famous in history as the Barataria, Louisiana pirates during the early 1800's and for the pirates' important support of Andrew Jackson during the Battle of New Orleans in 1814. In true history, Jean Lafitte was killed in a naval attack off the coast of Honduras in 1823, two years after his brother Pierre had died in 1821, while on the run from authorities -- struck down by illness near Cancun, Mexico. The wives and children of both brothers had been safely secured in New Orleans in 1820, the year that Jean's son Jean Pierre was only 5 years old. In the alternate history presented in *The CSA Trilogy*, Pierre Lafitte does die as history recorded it in 1821, but Jean does not die. Jean spends a few years in South America and eventually returns to New Orleans in 1830. Charges of piracy are dropped at the request of President Andrew Jackson, and Jean Lafitte joins wife Catherine in New Orleans in raising son Jean Pierre from age 15 to adult years. Son Jean Pierre does not die of the epidemic that struck New Orleans in 1832, as truthful history tells us, but lives on to play an important role in this historical novel. In 1840, at age 25, Jean Pierre Lafitte marries a sister of Natalie St. Martin Benjamin, named Marie St. Martin (age 21), the fictional wife having been born in 1819, two years after the birth of Natalie St. Martin. Catherine Lafitte dies in 1858 in accordance with truthful history. Natalie Saint Martin, in conformance with truthful history, marries Judah Benjamin in 1833. Both Saint Martin sisters are of a rather prominent New Orleans Creole family. So, our story creates a brother-in-law relationship between Judah Benjamin and Jean Pierre Lafitte.

miss this historic event for anything. Pierre had talked at some length with Mr. Davis when he was traveling from his farm, Brierfield, on Captain Leather's Mississippi paddle steamer, coming down from Davis Landing to New Orleans. Pierre is 46 years old now and, as you know, often captains Mississippi riverboats himself, mostly the long haul up to Wheeling and back to New Orleans, but on this trip Pierre was just an assistant to Leathers. Pierre advised me that Davis was a great choice for President but seemed too bent on doing the honorable thing. He said, 'Papa, you are a master at trickery and deceit when it is called for. Honorable men, such as Mr. Davis, seldom deal effectively with deceitful politicians. We have to be cunning and careful. Please go to Montgomery and see how you can help. You are better at circumventing deceit than any man I have ever met. If you mastered anything during your days of piracy, it was dealing with deceit. And talk to Judah. He can get you connected'."

Judah injected, "I don't see Pierre much these days. Since my wife Natalie spends all of her time in France, and I do so miss her, she does not get a chance to visit with her sister Marie and Marie's family. Tell me, do Pierre and Marie speak very often of Natalie and me?"

Understanding, Jean answered, "On occasion, but, although you and Pierre are brother-in-laws, the Atlantic Ocean keeps the wives apart and it seems like you and Pierre find little time to get together.

Then Jean continued with his report: "I am 79 years old, Judah -- blessed to have lived such a long life. Why, I was almost Pierre's age when my men and I, with our artillery, fought alongside Andrew Jackson in the Battle of New Orleans. That was 1815, 46 years ago. It was a massacre. The Redcoats were taken by surprise and slaughtered. And my men from Baratavia, with their cannon, were in the thick of it. If you had the right authorization papers for piracy on the high seas, there was some slight honor in being a pirate back then; at least I like to think so.

"But that was then, and this is now. Today, the rules governing right and wrong are altogether different. Which gets me to my worry over our new Confederacy: those damned Republicans – way up north from Massachusetts and westward along the Great Lakes out to Chicago – do not intend to obey the rules. Davis and our other leaders must not be deceived in hoping that the rules so clearly written in the Federal Constitution will protect each state's right to peaceably secede. We must not be overly focused on doing the 'right thing.' Honor among thieves is foolish thought, and Abe Lincoln and his cadre of thieves feel no need to be constrained by law or by 'honor.' And, I know that you know that – when it comes to understanding the behavior of 'thieves' – well, look me in the eye, now – what do you see? – Yes, Judah, you see me – an expert at understanding the behavior of thieves. Perhaps you can introduce me to President Davis so we can talk and figure out how this old man and his nefarious connections can be of help."

About mid-day on the following day, Tuesday, January 18, 1861, Judah Benjamin gained a brief audience with President Davis for the purpose of introducing Jean Lafitte. "Mr. President, thank you for these few moments of your time and allow me to introduce you to a wise old man from Louisiana, long a friend of mine, and a relative by marriage, Jean Lafitte."

President Davis replied, "Jean Lafitte, I am so glad to meet you face to face for the first time. I well know the story of how your men and their artillery helped Andrew Jackson defeat the British at New Orleans. So I am eager to learn from a man with your wide range of experience. We face a most difficult situation, as you surely realize, and must use all available resources at hand. Talked with your son Pierre coming down the Mississippi on Captain Leather's riverboat and was most impressed with him. He updated me on family activities and alerted me that he was going to urge you to come to Montgomery and offer your help. That is wonderful. Have a seat."

Jean then began explaining how his family might help: "Mr. President, your warm reception of a man, far less honorable than you in his career of early years, speaks volumes of your eagerness to use all available resources. My family's network of connections ought to be helpful -- at least you have our full and eager support."

Davis replied: "Jean, my friend, anyone as helpful as you and your men were to General Jackson at the Battle of New Orleans is eagerly welcomed here. Tell me what you know."

"First, Mr. President," Jean reported, "our Confederacy is up against men who have no respect for established law or personal honor. They have risen to power by agitating a majority of voting men in each Northern State to believe that the Democratic Party in each of those states is 'evil by association,' – evil because of association with the Democratic Parties of each Southern State – evil because the governments in each of those states permits slavery – permits the bonding of people of full or partial African ancestry. Accordingly, as justified by their "holier than thou" manner of reasoning, they have deluded themselves into believing there is a 'higher law' which permits them to seize every power they deem useful in advancing their agenda.

"And, Mr. President, their agenda is firmly against letting any seceded state go its own way in peace. Is there honor in violating the limits on Federal power clearly and unquestionably imposed in the United States Constitution? Is there honor in violating those limits to merely advance their party's political agenda? In their minds, they say, 'yes', – even in violating the highest law of the land, there is 'honor.' 'Yes,' because anything they do to conquer seceded states and force them back under the Federal Government imparts 'honor', – is authorized by their view of a 'higher law'."

Carefully listening, President replied, "Jean, I understand clearly your point, and witnessed it repeatedly in the United States Senate over the past four years. Senator Seward of New York, repeatedly referred to a 'higher law,' as if it superseded the Constitution. And President-elect Lincoln seems to be taking the same view. He left Springfield, Illinois on February 11, 8 days ago, on an extended travel and speaking tour, which my associates call the 'Republican Railroad Rally,' – all leading up to persuading voters in the Northern States to support some sort of military confrontation with our Seceded States. We get daily newspaper reports of his railroad stops and speeches, but have no person following the train to give us first hand reports."

Immediately seeing a way his family could help, Jean offered: "With your concurrence, Mr. President I believe I can have our man shadowing that train within two days. That is the nature of the help I wish to contribute to our cause of peaceful separation. My family, because of our operation of riverboats from New Orleans to Wheeling, have unusual ability to gather intelligence in the northern States, especially the important States of Missouri, Illinois, Indiana, Ohio and Pennsylvania, as well as Maryland and Washington."

Gratified that the conversation was becoming helpful, Judah injected: "Mr. President, Jean Lafitte and I talked at some length last night about his family's capabilities and his assertion that the Confederacy needs a secret service which is empowered to gather intelligence and distribute propaganda in support of our peaceful separation. For the most part, we Southerners have always sought to behave honorably and lawfully in our social and political lives. But Jean and I believe the time has come for dealing with our adversaries as we would deal with criminals. If I may suggest it, Mr. President, is there a time tomorrow evening when we can discuss this further? By then I am hopeful that Jean and I can lay out our thoughts in the form of a 2 to 4 page written policy proposal."

Davis concurred: "Mr. Lafitte, Mr. Benjamin, I would like to do just that. Say 5 o'clock at my hotel room. We will dine as we review your thoughts."

So, a very important strategy concept was being born during these first two days of the Confederate States Government – a strategy concept that would grow into a successful program for the Defense of the Confederacy. Jean Lafitte and Judah Benjamin worked late into the night developing their recommendations. They were at it after breakfast and, for a few hours during the early afternoon, discussed their thoughts and sought advice from Robert Toombs and Stephen Mallory. Toombs, of Georgia, had excellent advice on how to persuade Confederate citizens (a proud bunch to say the least) that it was in their best interest to appear weak and avoid any aggressive action, even to let Federals take control of Fort Sumter if it meant avoiding firing the "first shot" that Lincoln coveted. Mallory had great knowledge of the strength of the U. S. navy and saw some wisdom in a strong priority on defense against invasion down the Mississippi and Tennessee rivers, viewing that as more important that defense along the seacoast and at the Confederate seaports.

The Lafitte-Benjamin Position Paper and Preliminary Cabinet Debate

By 4 o'clock that afternoon, the first Lafitte-Benjamin position paper was written up. It consisted of four pages:

We see merit in basing the defense of the Confederacy on the following principles:

1. The strength of the Republican Party is in the Northern State governments that it controls and the governor of each of those states, each of whom controls his respective state militia. Collectively, those state Republican Parties and those Republican governors hold more power than President Abe Lincoln and the Republican political leaders in Washington City. Therefore, every effort must be made to persuade the people of each Northern state to support a policy of peaceful co-existence and to oppose calling up their militias to launch a War Between the States. Toward that goal, we must:

    a.   Send our spies and propaganda agents into each northern state to gather intelligence and to spread our message.

    b.   Send friendly delegations from each Confederate state to designated Republican northern states in search of friendly relations and settling differences (match up state assignments; Mississippi to Illinois and Michigan, Alabama to Indiana and Ohio, etc.).

2. While our Southern states are sending delegations and spies northward to designated "sister" Northern states, the Confederate Government must be doing likewise with respect to activities in Washington City and the workings of the upcoming Lincoln Administration. In that effort we must be especially attentive to activities related to communications between the Lincoln Administration and the Republican governors, and related to future Federal military action against Fort Sumter and Fort Pickens, which we foresee as being for the purpose of instigating a conflict as an excuse for calling up Republican state militia.

3. We must appear peaceful and conciliatory toward the northern states. A few specifics are worthy of discussion:

    a.   Promise to keep the Mississippi River open for the northern states, down to the Gulf of Mexico and back;

    b.   Promise to help collect Federal tariffs imposed on goods moving across the boundary between the Confederacy and the United States;

    c.   Promise to pay for any Federal property that resides in the Confederacy;

    d.   Promise to operate an independent postal system;

    e.   Place our defensive military fortifications 5 to 20 miles south of our northern border so they do not seem threatening to states to our north;

    f.   Begin planning in each state for introducing a tentative program for gradual emancipation of slaves. We are speaking of a plan that does not commit anyone to action, but is to be widely broadcast northward to counter the holier-than-thou crowd of radical Abolitionists, for this is to be primarily a propaganda activity, and

    g.   Encourage those among us of partial African ancestry to help in disseminating propaganda and collecting needed intelligence.

4. Also we should include in our propaganda messages the fact that the United States Constitution prohibits a state from using military force against a sister state and prohibits the Federal military from using military force against any of its states. We are dealing with criminals who will not obey the law and will use deceit to persuade the gullible that launching a military invasion force toward the South is not a violation of law.

5. Through state-to-state diplomatic efforts, we must encourage the Democrat-controlled states to our north (especially North Carolina, Tennessee, Arkansas, Virginia, Kentucky and Missouri) to support us in our independence and to join us in secession if forced to choose between 1), fighting against us, or, 2), joining in our mutual defense. Toward that end we should encourage them to:

    a.   Establish secession conventions and keep them active so each can quickly choose between joining in a military attack upon Seceded States versus seceding their state and joining in the defensive effort.

b.   Prepare their State militia for any eventuality.

c.   Make no aggressive moves that would alarm Republican-controlled states to the north.

6. We must use every means at our disposal to avoid appearing to be aggressive toward the North. If they bring naval warships into our harbors, we must not shoot. If they bring soldiers onto our shores, we must not shoot. We must not shoot until we have drawn their forces far inland to such a place that we can cut them off, envelope them, and force their surrender. Capturing prisoners is more important than defending every foot or our waterfront and soil. Toward that goal our strategy must be "Retreat, Envelope, Capture." The Lincoln Administration will probable try to coerce us into firing the "first shot." We must avoid doing that!

7. We must delay the foreseen invasion from the north as long as possible — hopefully until December of this year, 1861, when the Federal House and Senate are scheduled to convene. During these 10 months it is imperative that we strengthen all aspects of our defense.

8. We must take advantage of every month we put off facing a military invasion by using all possible means to enhance our preparations:

a.   Using Confederate bonds, purchase the vast majority of the cotton crop in our country and expedite shipment to safe havens in Cuba and elsewhere in anticipation of a blockade by the U. S. Navy. Use this cotton revenue to pay for arms, steam engines, tooling for firearms and ammunition manufacture, iron for armoring ships and laying railroads, telegraph wires, etc. Seek the most modern rifles and pistols in large numbers, especially arms that rapidly fire repeated rounds. Maximize the size and effectiveness of Confederate cavalry and make every effort to maximize the mobility of all ground troops.

b.   Our greatest vulnerability is invasion through armed river gunboats coming down the Mississippi and Tennessee rivers. Recognizing that the U. S. military will attempt to split our eastern States from our western States, priority should be toward defending against that line of attack as compared to defending against invasion from the seacoast.

9. An effective and dispersed Confederate Secret Service organization needs to be quickly established. It is suggested that the Service not be under the administration of the Confederate War Department, because their plate is too full to take on administration of

such a large additional responsibility. We suggest, instead, that the Confederate Secret Service be under the Confederate Attorney General's office because legal issues are significant and because that department can give rapt attention to rapidly building and dispersing an effective Service.

One hour later, at 5 o'clock, Lafitte and Benjamin met with President Davis. Every word of the 4-page position paper was discussed and analyzed in depth. Davis saw a great advantage in avoiding firing the "first shot." He saw a great advantage in delaying the day the Confederates would have to defend against a major invasion force. A cotton farmer himself, he even saw merit in a program for purchasing cotton and expediting shipment out of the country. Much he liked, but much worried him as well. Every fiber of his being was naturally committed to honesty and straightforward interpersonal dealings. He detested deceit and demagoguery, and knew that Republicans, such as Senator Seward of New York, had no qualms about such behavior. "How," Davis mused, "can we persuade our people to appear weak and non-aggressive? Will they tolerate a retreating response to U. S. Navy occupation of Charleston harbor and Fort Sumter? Will England and France judge us as unworthy to join the nations of the world if we appear weak and let the Lincoln Administration push us around?" The meeting concluded at midnight.

Davis suggested the following plan: "In the morning, first thing, I will call a preliminary Cabinet meeting for 10 am on Friday, February 22. That gives us tomorrow to further develop our thoughts. By then I expect to appoint to the Cabinet Robert Toombs of Georgia, as Secretary of State; Christopher Memminger of South Carolina, as Secretary of the Treasury, and LeRoy Pope Walker, as Secretary of War, and all three should be able to join us by then. Furthermore, Judah, I have known you for several years based on our time together in the United States Senate and have admired your legal mind and your ability to grasp a situation and present a lucid analysis of what it means and what ought to be the best response to it. My Cabinet needs representation from Louisiana. Please give consideration to my invitation to you, now offered, to become our Attorney General. If the ideas you and Jean are advancing win approval, I can think of no better place from which to administer a large and active Confederate Secret Service than from the desk which you will command."

Prior to the Friday morning Cabinet meeting Benjamin handed a letter to Davis formally accepting the position of Attorney General. Davis eagerly accepted and asked Benjamin to attend the meeting, and suggested that Jean Lafitte be available in the hotel lobby if called upon to answer questions. Therefore, the Friday morning meeting involved President Davis of Mississippi; Vice President Alexander Stephens of Georgia; Secretary of

State Robert Toombs also of Georgia; Secretary of the Treasury, Christopher Memminger of South Carolina, Secretary of War Leroy Walker of Alabama, and Judah Benjamin of Louisiana, Attorney General. Several topics were covered, but by far the greatest amount of time was spent discussing the position paper prepared by Benjamin and Jean Lafitte.

There was universal agreement that the Confederacy would greatly benefit by delaying the foreseen attack by the United States army and by state militia from the Republican states. Treasury Secretary Memminger said that delaying an attack "would give valuable time to raise money to support a military purchase program." Secretary of State Toombs said such a delay would "contribute to winning recognition from Great Britain and France," but warned that "an appearance of weakness might hurt our chances of winning recognition." So, he explained, the issue "could work for us or against us." War Secretary Walker agreed "more time would aid in building and equipping a Confederate army, especially with regard to obtaining rifles and artillery," but, he warned, the "same delay would help the North, but on balance the greater advantage would be ours." On the other hand, among the group, Walker was probably the most confident that the North would not attack. Vice President Stephens seemed not to offer any strong opinions, but did not object to a focus on building a "strong" Confederate Secret Service and placing the administration of the organization outside of the War Department. Davis explained that he "worried most of all about the Executive Department's ability to hold off the more militant" among those in the Confederate House and Senate -- and, within the Confederate States, the more militant among newspapermen and citizens. Davis supposed that, if and when a fleet of U. S. Navy warships and transports enters Charleston harbor and lands at Fort Sumter, "how can we hold back the eager young South Carolinians who will be determined to force them back out to sea, thereby giving the Lincoln Administration that 'first shot,' which we believe to be their strategy for rallying the people of the North? Turning such 'honorable men into timid tricksters' will be difficult, especially since most of our people live in rural areas, own a rifle, and 'half of those can shoot a squirrel perched in a tree 50 yards away'."

It would be only a few days before the full Cabinet would be appointed and the first full meeting would be held. That would be the time to strive for decisions pertaining to the suggestions in the Benjamin-Lafitte paper. The thoughts of the new Secretary of the Navy and the new Postmaster General could then be assayed.

Of the nature, character and agenda of one Abraham Lincoln, it was mostly a mystery. The Republican Railroad Rally Train had pulled out of Springfield, Illinois, 11 days previously, on February 11, taking the President-elect on a speaking tour across the Northern States. Realizing that the last known position of Mr. Lincoln and his train was New York City, where it had arrived two days ago, February 20, President Davis explained, "We know not what Mr. Lincoln is telling Republican leaders across the Northern States, but based on his public statements in speeches that we have seen reported, his agenda appears to be quite uncompromising and militant. It can be presumed he is rallying the people for military action and making arrangements with Republican governors to strengthen State militia and to be prepared for a call-up of troops." As he moved to close the meeting, Davis said, "As you leave, please, without raising suspicions, candidly introduce yourself to Jean Lafitte. You should spot him in the lobby of this hotel. Make whatever arrangements you choose so as to gain further knowledge of the man, his experiences, and how he proposes to help us. You can trust him to keep all secret, but make sure no one overhears you or becomes suspicious. Judah will be helpful in this regard. Keep your copies of the Benjamin-Lafitte paper for future contemplation but make sure to keep each sheet away from anyone outside of this Cabinet. Discuss strategy ideas among yourselves, but privately. This is Friday, February 22. Our next meeting will be on Monday, February 25. I expect we will have a full Cabinet present for that one. Let us target Wednesday, February 27 for decisions regarding the proposals in this paper. Oh, I am about to forget to make a special request of you, Secretary Memminger. You are of Charleston. At our next meeting I want a report from you on how you and other leaders of that important city can help us keep peace when, or if, the Federal navy moves in on Fort Sumter and attempts to incite our side to fire the coveted 'first shot'." With that the meeting adjourned.

President Abraham Lincoln and his Railroad Rally

This day, February 22 was also the day of Mr. Lincoln's last Republican Railroad Rally speech, a speech he delivered to the Pennsylvania Legislature in Harrisburg. [21] Afterward, as evening arrived, Lincoln's "handlers" decided upon secretly sneaking him into Washington City on a night train, leaving the Railroad Rally Train at the Harrisburg station, which would, the following day, resume the published route with all other members of the entourage, a tactic designed to fool newspapermen and everyone else, and, we must suspect, to create the false impression that Southerners in Maryland were out to kill the President-elect. So Lincoln donned a disguise and boarded a special train from Harrisburg to Philadelphia, where he transferred to a

---

[21] Abraham Lincoln's travel to Washington City and his first weeks in office is truthful history, as will be his eagerness to force the Confederates to fire the first shot. It will be several more months into our narrative before the history of the Lincoln Administration deviates from truthful history, and that transformation will be footnoted for you at the point it takes place.

scheduled night train down to Baltimore, where he switched to a scheduled night train from Baltimore to Washington City. Throughout this ruse during the night of February 22 and early morning of February 23, the future President was disguised in a long overcoat thrown over his shoulders, his long arms hidden within, the sleeves just dangling, and an uncharacteristic soft felt hat upon his head to minimize his height. He arrived with his bodyguard and, unknown to the public, entered into his room in Willard's Hotel. The Railroad Rally Train arrived without incident a few hours later. [22] By evening the ruse became known and news of it was telegraphed to Montgomery, Alabama. Jeff Davis read the report that evening and thought to himself: "What kind of a coward am I to be dealing with." In fact he went on to include that thought in a letter he wrote to wife Varina the following day. She was expected to arrive in Montgomery in a few days. A portion of the letter said:

Montgomery, Alabama, February 24, 1861,

My Dear Wife,

I am taking a few moments this Sunday to add a bit to the letter I wrote on February 20. Have met with Judah Benjamin and Jean Laffite, both of New Orleans. You know Judah from our time together in the U. S. Senate. I think you know of Jean Laffite, although perhaps have never met him. He is 79 years old now. His son Pierre is married to Marie Saint Martin the sister of Judah's wife Natalie. As you recall, Natalie spends all of her time in France to her husband's great disappointment. By the way, I talked with Pierre on the way down the Mississippi on Leathers' boat and found his insight useful. Pierre is a river man who often captains a boat for Leathers, but he was just an assistant when we talked. I am trying to remember that many years ago you knew Natalie and perhaps her sister, too. Anyway, when you get to Montgomery we will have dinner with Judah and Jean and talk over things.

Last night I received a telegram from our people in Washington City reporting that on February 23, Mr. Lincoln snuck into town in disguise pretending to be escaping some phantom threat from Democrats in Maryland. Of course, there was no threat. What kind of coward, what kind of demagogue am I going to be dealing with? That is

---

[22] In truthful history, President-elect Lincoln's bodyguards, of the Alan Pinkerton agency, alleged that some person or people in and around Baltimore planned to kill him while passing through Maryland. As a student of history and the writer of the three books of the *CSA Trilogy*, I believe the allegation was just propaganda to make the South look evil. President Davis' interpretation of the elaborate disguise is a reasonable reaction giving the circumstances.

certainly a strike against his character. It makes me worry all the more. Looking forward to hearing your interpretation, for your instincts are sharp and useful to me. The Lafitte's (who ought to know what they are talking about) believe we should deal with the Lincoln Administration as if they are criminal personalities without regard to law -- and that we need to keep such behavior in mind as we arrive at our policy toward them.

Again, devoted love to you and the children,

Your Husband

Davis, Benjamin and the Full Confederate Cabinet Meeting

The next day at noon, on February 25, President Davis held his first meeting with his full Cabinet. Postmaster General John Henninger Reagan of Texas had arrived and accepted his role, as had Secretary of the Navy Stephen Russell Mallory of Florida. So, all were present. Many topics were introduced and many opinions offered, but the topic that most concerns readers of *The CSA Trilogy* are the group's discussions centered on the four-page Benjamin-Lafitte position paper. President Davis, Vice President Stephens, Toombs of Georgia (State), Walker of Alabama (War) and Memminger of South Carolina (Treasury) had previously reviewed the paper and had engaged in discussions over the weekend, but the concerns and ideas presented were new to Reagan and Mallory.

As alternatives and opinions sparked across the makeshift conference table some basic positions were becoming clear: Toombs, Walker and Memminger felt more strongly that a response which delayed the anticipated calling up of militia in the Republican states would work to their advantage, even if achieved through a "timid trickster" strategy reeking of embarrassing weakness. Mallory of the Navy, new to the idea of purposeful timidity, reasoned that, because it was hopeless to challenge the United States Navy head-on, time gained for building a naval defense and inland river defense would be useful. Benjamin submitted:

"Jean Laffite tells me that he and his son have hopes that we can engage the talents of James Eads of Missouri, the most capable man in America at building Mississippi steamboats, including iron-clad gunboats. A project under his leadership would be most helpful in organizing a defense against attackers coming down the Mississippi and the Tennessee – another benefit from winning delay." [23]

Several saw merit in expediting the shipment overseas of the remainder of the 1860 cotton crop through immediate government purchase and hastened shipping even though only about 20 percent of the crop remained to be shipped. A strategy to raise and export the 1861 crop was needed with a target of 90 percent picked, ginned, baled and exported by the first of December.

Without question, all agreed that efforts to appear non-aggressive should be stressed and reported widely in the northern states, such as free navigation of the Mississippi and Tennessee rivers and assistance in collecting U. S. tariff duties at the northern Confederate border.

Midway through the discussions, Memminger delivered the report that President Davis had requested in the previous meeting – concerning how he and other leaders of Charleston can help keep peace when, or if, the Federal navy moves in on Fort Sumter, attempting to incite our side to fire the coveted "first shot". To that question Memminger offered the following suggestions:

> "We should establish a Department of Confederate Communication tasked to frequently disseminate news throughout the Confederacy to inform our people about the reasons for future measured responses to potential attacks by northern states militia and by the U. S. Navy. I believe if we are candid and open, we can win our people over to a timid trickster tactic, and we can do that in a way that will deceive the Lincoln Administration to our advantage. If we engage Southern newspapermen and give them honest news, I believe they will report it out in persuasive language. We must send people from the Executive Department to the Confederate House and Senate and to the governors and State legislatures for the purpose of delivering the same message. Every aggressive move Mr. Lincoln presents must be analyzed and delivered to the communication network we ought to establish. The people will support us if we steadily teach them to know the character and methods of the enemy we face."

Other issues were discussed, as well, but there is insufficient space here to report them.

The Cabinet meeting lasted all afternoon. At the conclusion, President Davis asked each man to study the issues and be prepared to state final opinions on the questions on the table at the next meeting, which would be

---

[23] In truthful history, river gunboats built by James Eads of St. Louis, Missouri were greatly responsible for the Federal victories on the Cumberland River, the Tennessee River and the Mississippi River.

held in two days, on Wednesday, February 27. At that time, he said, "we will be casting votes that are intended to afford me your best advice."

The Cabinet meeting on February 27 was held as planned. Votes were cast and much in the Benjamin-Laffite paper was supported by the majority. President Davis directed Secretary of State Robert Toombs to add the Confederate Communications Department (CCD) to his oversight and to do what was needed to be sure the Executive Department's decisions and strategies were made known to the people for the purpose for encouraging their support, especially their support of a potential "timid trickster" response to a potential U. S. military reinforcement of Fort Sumter. He also directed Judah Benjamin to proceed with establishing a strong and extensive Confederate Secret Service (CSS) within the Department of Justice. He advised that money and resources intended for the War Department would be transferred to the Secret Service as needed and that he, Davis, would mediate between the financial needs of the War Department and the CSS. But, he said, communications by the CSS will always be in code.

The Confederate Secret Service

So the CCD and CSS were launched on February 27, 1861 in Montgomery, Alabama, two events that would play major roles in the successful defense of State Secession:

> Toombs issued a press release to all newspapers in the Confederacy announcing the Confederate Communications Department (CCD) and how communications would flow back and forth. No coded messages here. To facilitate outgoing communications he recruited a team of 7 communications deputies, each a native of the state he was to serve; three surveillance deputies who were charged with gathering and cataloging readily obtainable intelligence; three secretaries, and two telegraph operators. Within two days new telegraph wires were run into the newly established CCD telegraph office and ample battery power was installed to ensure reliable electrical strength.

> Benjamin began building his Confederate Secret Service personnel one person at a time, giving priority to people who had vision and resources to build and organize teams of their own. As the size of the department grew, he reasoned, he would add layers of supervision and chains of command. But for a start, he felt an urgency to recruit agents and get them out into the field as fast as possible. Mr. Lincoln was already in Washington City plotting strategy and would be taking office in less than a week. Benjamin's immediate staff, stationed in Montgomery, would be Jean Laffite and Jules Saint Martin. Saint Martin, also of New Orleans, was his wife's young brother, available

and capable. Jules sent a message to Pierre Laffite to come to Montgomery immediately for discussions. With his steamboat traveling routinely back and forth between New Orleans and Wheeling, Virginia, Pierre would be valuable in transporting Secret Service agents and documents into the upper Mississippi states as well as Illinois, Indiana, Ohio and Pennsylvania. Over the next few weeks many other agents would be recruited.

Female Secret Service agents would number among the most effective, for Republican operatives generally considered the plantation Southern lady, with her charm and manner of speaking, too ignorant to be carrying secret Confederate messages. This misconception about the Southern lady was especially prevalent in the northeastern Yankee culture. They were wrong -- female agents would prove very effective in dispensing propaganda. Most helpful would be propaganda aimed at accusing President Lincoln of lying about his parentage, for there was substantial evidence in western North Carolina and eastern Kentucky that his father was North Carolinian Abraham Eloe, that he was two years old when his mother, Nancy Hanks married his step-father, Thomas Lincoln. In 1861, a man of illegitimate birth, who had lied about it, was not to be respected.

Men and women of color were also effective Secret Service agents. Although they sometimes had trouble with racial abuse in the Republican States because of their Negro ancestry, Republican operatives never suspected that they would be supporting State Secession. This freedom from suspicion allowed them to carry messages and report on observations in the North without interference. Most Secret Service agents of color were able to read and write, also not suspected by Republican operatives.

Confederate Secret Service agents would be lobbing politicians and newspapermen in Washington City and in Northern States capitals -- providing evidence that encouraged peaceful separation of the two countries.

Early Preparations for a Military Defense of the Confederacy

From the first few days, efforts were underway to procure improved weaponry for the new Confederate army. Heavy guns were already in position at the seacoast forts along with powder and cannon balls. But there were little field artillery and it was mostly in the hands of arsenals that served State militia. Regarding small arms, the weapons and ammunition in the State arsenals, although in modest quantities, were at hand, as were the weapons and ammunition at Federal arsenals, which had been renamed as Confederate arsenals. [24]

Of the former Federal arsenals within the Confederacy, the small arms inventory totaled 117,010 pieces.[25]

A few weeks earlier, Secretary of War Leroy Walker had recruited United States Colonel Josiah Gorgas to become the Confederate Chief of Ordinance. Accepting, Gorgas had resigned his command over the U. S. Frankford Arsenal, an ammunition plant near Philadelphia, and come south. Born in Pennsylvania and graduated from West Point in 1841, Gorgas had married the daughter of former Alabama Governor John Gayle and thought of himself as a Southerner. In the meantime Confederate purchasing officers were already in the northern states seeking opportunities to procure arms and ammunition, among them Raphael Semmes of Alabama, who was in New York and finding good opportunities to buy ordinance stores in considerable quantity and ship them to the Confederate states. Another purchasing officer of note was Caleb Huse, also buying in the northern states. Born and raised in Massachusetts, Huse married a woman from Alabama and eventually called that state his home. He would soon be sent to Great Britain as general purchasing agent for the Confederacy. His want list was long: a variety of machinery to produce military stores in new Confederate factories; artillery for fortifications and field batteries; rifles of the newest design; brass shells for bullets of the new cartridge design, which was superior to paper; lead for bullets; percussion caps and copper and fulminate of mercury to produce them locally; gunpowder, and steam engines. Furthermore, there was early discussion of the need to seek out and recruit men in the northern states and in Europe who were skilled in the manufacture of military stores. Recruiters would be instructed to pay travel expenses for top recruits. This was the beginning of a long-standing Confederate tradition concerning emigration: always seek emigrants who would bring to the country skills and character

---

[24] The Baton Rouge Arsenal in Louisiana contained 47,372 arms of great variety, consisting of U. S. rifle muskets; caliber .69 rifle muskets; new and altered percussion muskets; flint muskets; Harper's Ferry rifles; Colt rifles; Hall rifles; various types of carbines, and Colt and percussion pistols. At the Mount Vernon Arsenal in Alabama, the inventory of all types of arms totaled 19,455. At Charleston, South Carolina, the small arms inventory totaled 22,469. The small arms total at Augusta, Georgia, was 27,714. Altogether there were about 2,000,000 cartridges for small arms and about 100,000 pounds of gun powder suitable for making about 900,000 more cartridges.

[25] Fortunately, there was an ample supply of percussion caps, about 2,000,000, in Montgomery, Alabama. All arms were single shot. There were no revolvers, either as pistols or rifles, in the inventories of Southern arsenals. However, the Le Mat revolver pistol, first produced in 1856, was, in truthful history, ordered by the Confederate military immediately after Lincoln proclaimed war and became an important weapon for cavalry.

capable of advancing Confederate goals. In other words, Confederate immigration resembled recruitment.

Tuesday Evening Selected Diary Postings

Diary note by Professor Davis said, "At breakfast enjoyed conversation with Robert Lee of Alabama, an inspiring writer with a remarkable and inquiring mind; Marie Saint Martin of New Orleans, lovely to look at, athletic of build, and a musician of ability who aspires to become an entrepreneur; Andrew Houston, a petroleum engineer of South Texas, who impressed me the previous morning; and Chris Memminger of South Carolina, of a long-standing corporate farming family who loves to talk about his thorough-bred race horses and his work toward a degree in veterinary science. Chris and Marie seemed to be attracted to one another. Who knows? Romance may grow out of these four weeks of togetherness. All twelve of them are single and, as far as I have determined so far, none are seriously attached as of yet."

Diary note by Marie Saint Martin said, "Supper with the Cuban sailor and grower of sugar cane -- none other than Carlos Cespedes himself. Surfing Emma Lunalilo of Hawaii, who ate supper with him Monday, told me today that 'Carlos might brag too much about his family's wealth and political influence in Cuba,' but she was thrilled that he had 'invited her on the sailing trip he is planning for this weekend.' Well, I did not mind the bragging, and perhaps to call his pride in his family 'bragging' is really not fair. That sailing trip this weekend – he invited me, too. Fantastic. Oh, he claims to play Spanish guitar and classical music as well. Have to include him in some jam sessions. Allan Ross plays country, cowboy music on his guitar and Amanda Washington sings and plays jazz piano. I am for forming a musical group!"

Diary note by Robert Lee said, "Really enjoyed this morning's lecture on the secession of the first seven states. Of course, my famous ancestor's State, Virginia, was not among these seven, but that "Mother of States" was holding open its secession convention in order to be ready if Virginians found it necessary to quickly secede. By the way, the Lincoln Administration, soon after Abe took office, asked my ancestor, Robert E. Lee, to take command of the Federal Army. Was an attempt to make the Federal Army look like it was not opposed to slavery or opposed to Southern slave owners, make it easier to retain Southerners in the Federal Army. Lee refused, resigned, and returned to Virginia to be of service to his State if called upon." [26]

Diary note by Benedict Juárez said, "Being descended from President Juárez, I so much admire the decision of those first seven American States to

---

[26] Lincoln's invitation to Robert E. Lee to take command of the Federal Army and Lee's refusal and resignation is truthful history.

repudiate the oppressive agenda of that upstart Republican Party and simply exercise their individual constitutional right to secede from the United States Government. They were quick to join together to create the Confederate States of America, too."

Book 1, Chapter 4, Day 3 – President Lincoln's Scheme to Draw the "First Shot" from Confederates at Charleston – Class Lecture, Wednesday, June 8, 2011

President Lincoln's Schemes, Fort Sumter and the Confederate's Response

Editor's note: As a reader you are about to witness the actions of President Abraham Lincoln and his Administration from the day he took office until the day that a Federal fleet of warships and transports arrived off the coast of Charleston, South Carolina. All that you will read below concerning the Lincoln Administration is true history up until the moment of the arrival of the fleet positioned in the Atlantic just beyond Charleston Harbor. The corresponding Confederate response, as portrayed by the actions of President Jefferson Davis, Judah Benjamin and others, is an alternate history, not a true history. So, although you may be surprised to learn the history of how President Lincoln maneuvered a Federal fleet to Charleston for the purpose of inciting the coveted "first shot," rest assured the history reported here is the truth of what really happened concerning events in the North – spies, deception and all. Only the response by Confederates is an alternate history.

We listen in as Professor Davis continues with his lectures as soon as the twelve are seated and ready to go.

Five days after the February 27 Confederate Cabinet meeting, on March 4, 1861, Republican Abraham Lincoln of Illinois was inaugurated as President of the remaining United States. Except for recently admitted Kansas (of Bleeding Kansas notoriety), Lincoln was becoming President over seven fewer States than had existed prior to State Secession. He replaced Democrat James Buchanan of Pennsylvania, who rode off into the sunset, so to speak, with no intention to resume public life. Lincoln's address to the gathered crowd emphasized a twisted interpretation of the right to State secession and his intent to pursue Federal subjugation, by force if necessary, of the Seceded States, but minced his words just enough to not sound as militant as were obviously his intentions. Regarding the right to State secession he argued:

> State secession "heretofore only menaced, is now formidably attempted. I hold that, in the contemplation of universal law and of the [Federal] Constitution, the union of these States is perpetual. Perpetuity is implied, if not expressed, in the fundamental law of all national

governments. [27] . . . The [association of American States] is much older than the [Federal] Constitution. It was formed, in fact, by the Articles of Association in 1774. It was matured and continued by the Declaration of Independence in 1776. It was further matured . . . by the Articles of Confederation in 1778. And finally, in 1787, one of the declared objects for ordaining and establishing the [Federal] Constitution, was 'to form a more perfect union.' . . . It follows from these views that no State, upon its own mere motion, can lawfully get out [from under the Federal Government] -- that resolves and ordinances to that effect are legally void, and that acts of violence, within any [seceded] State or States, against the authority of the [Federal Government], are insurrectionary or revolutionary, according to circumstances. . . . Therefore, . . . to the extent of my ability . . . I shall take care . . . that the laws of the [Federal Government] be faithfully executed in all the States. . . .

"In doing this there needs to be no bloodshed or violence; and there shall be none, unless it be forced upon the [Federal] authority. The power confided in me will be used to hold, occupy, and possess the property and places belonging to the [Federal] Government, and to collect the [Federal] taxes; but beyond what may be necessary for these objects, there will be no invasion – no using of force against or among the people anywhere. . . . The mails, unless repelled, will continue to be furnished in all parts of the [former and present country]. . . . The course here indicated will be followed, unless current events and experience shall show a modification or change to be proper. . . .

"In your hands, my dissatisfied fellow-countrymen, and not in mine, is the momentous issue of civil war. The [Federal] Government will not assail you. You can have no conflict without being yourselves the aggressors. You have no oath registered in heaven to destroy the [Federal] Government, while I shall have the most solemn one to "preserve, protect, and defend it."

The inaugural address clarified Lincoln's strategy: he intended to maneuver a few Confederates into firing the coveted "first shot." His method would involve occupying forts and buildings that were formerly considered Federal property and in forcing importers to pay Federal tariffs on taxed goods brought into the Seceded States from foreign countries. Republicans believed those tariff collections would amount to a lot of money, because the duties on imported goods, expressed as a percentage, had been raised by a very large amount the previous month – the majority votes in the Federal

---

[27] Lincoln's legal deception – at this time those United States were a federation of States, not a singular nation. The notion of a "fundamental law of all national governments" is not relevant.

House and Senate for the tariff tax hike having been enabled by the resignation of Representatives and Senators from the seven Seceded States (logically speaking a form of taxation without representation). And the vast majority of import taxes collected by the Federal Government had historically been collected in Southern seaports, giving the North a bit of a free ride. Details of Lincoln's address were quickly sped to Montgomery and elsewhere in the South.

President Davis convened the Confederate Cabinet at noon the following day, March 5, to study Lincoln's address and discuss the best corresponding strategy. Everyone read the text of the message once more and discussions began – one paragraph at a time. After an hour two major elements of the address became their focus:

> 1. Lincoln's convoluted argument that legal State secession was legally void, and
> 2. "There needs to be no bloodshed or violence; and there shall be none, unless it be forced upon the [Federal] authority."

Secretary of State Robert Toombs submitted: "That means Lincoln will attempt to send a Federal military force against us soon and without advanced approval from the Federal House and Senate, which is not scheduled to convene until December 1, almost eight months into the future. Furthermore, Lincoln's address tells us that the Federal military objective will be to trick us into firing the coveted 'first shot.' The Federal army is far too small to subjugate us; he must call up many regiments of State militia from the Republican States to present a military threat to our vast country; and potential militiamen may not rally to his side and face possible death on the battlefield unless he can allege that their country has been attacked and must be "defended." His strategy requires that we fire the 'first shot.' I am now sure of it."

None could state the conclusion in more concise words. And none could present a logical alternative. In a way the discussions during the previous week concerning the Benjamin-Lafitte paper had conditioned the mind-set of Cabinet members to almost anticipate Lincoln's message. President Davis and all others agreed with Toombs's assessment. So, the discussion moved forward to the obvious issue: "How should the Confederate Government prepare to face this challenge?"

By the next day, March 6, the agreed strategy could be condensed into the following two directives:

> First, if Lincoln succeeds in rallying vast hordes of State militia out of the Republican States, all under the control of compliant Republican governors, it is probable that we will be subjugated, that we will be defeated. Therefore, it is imperative that we launch a

propaganda campaign to teach the people – both North and South – that we only seek peaceful separation, that the Federal Constitution forbids Federal military and, or, State military making war on a state that is behaving peacefully. The first message in that campaign is to be a letter to the people from President Davis. Carriers of this message and supporting documents should include newspapermen, diplomats, and Secret Service agents. We must ask our friends in the Democratic Parties of every Northern State and their respective newspapers to help us spread this message. It is imperative that Republicans not succeed in conjuring up the idea among their people that going to war against us is morally right or justified in any way. President Davis agreed and accepted the assignment of having a draft of a letter to the people ready for the Cabinet meeting the following day.

Second, it is to our advantage to delay as long as possible making any response that gives Lincoln an excuse for calling up State militia, such as refusing to pay Federal tariffs at seaports or firing against Federal military within view of witnesses. So how do we organize our seaports and our military to comply when we must, and retreat when we must, yet retain our strength and build rapidly upon it toward the day when the anticipated war does erupt? Toward those goals the following was outlined:

1.   Confederate artillery must be retained in any retreat and we anticipate that Charleston harbor is a likely target from which we will decide to retreat rather than give Lincoln his coveted "first shot." Therefore, the fixed artillery around Charleston harbor that cannot be modified into mobile artillery must be withdrawn to safe, hidden locations inland but done so secretly to keep Federals unaware. Where practical, fixed artillery should be converted to mobile artillery. Full retreat with all other weapons and supplies should be planned so all can be brought out quickly, in one movement, when the order is given. Similar plans should be made for the vicinity of Fort Pickens and other likely targets of the Federal Navy. Our artillerymen must be nimble and quick, capable of escaping capture and capable of rapidly supporting cavalrymen and foot soldiers when the enemy, in large or small groups, ventures inland and becomes vulnerable to being cut off, surrounded and forced to surrender, hopefully out of view of witnesses.

2.   Our ground forces must be capable of rapid retreat. We should consider building light personnel wagons that would enable one mule or one cavalryman upon his horse to evacuate several men with personal weapons rapidly down designated roads. Look into a light personnel wagon for rapid retreat, made

of wood, which our people can easily produce. Maximize the percentage of our fighting men who are cavalry. Procure horses and mules wherever possible, including to the north as far as Kentucky and Virginia.

    3.   If we are successful in avoiding giving Lincoln his coveted "first shot," when he does move to make war against us with massive State militia reinforcements, we hope the support he enjoys from militiamen in the Republican states will be less in number and less enthusiastic than otherwise. If we can delay the start of full-scale war until this winter, or even March, 1862, we must make the most of it so as to be best prepared.

    4.   The suggestion in the Benjamin-Lafitte paper regarding purchasing the remainder of the last cotton crop and expediting export is worthy and should be pursued. We need steam engines and skilled men to maintain and operate them on the railroads and on ships and riverboats.

    5.   We need rifles and pistols capable of six shots or more per loading. We need to seek brass cartridge technology and employ it as best we can. We need to scour the world for that technology and bring it in as finished weapons and ammunition, and also bring in machining tools and raw materials needed to make such weapons and ammunition in our States.

    6.   We need machinists and machine shop tools, so launch a recruiting effort to bring in immigrants with those skills and the tooling they will need, looking especially to the British Isles and Europe.

But all we do must enable greater mobility, for that will be most important when we face Federal incursions. And the list went on. More definitions of policy were noted that day, but space does not permit their inclusion here.

Just before the meeting broke up Secretary Memminger said, "I will contact authorities in Charleston immediately, and make sure that the good ladies of our city resume sending food out to Fort Sumter every day, and that newspapers report on that often. The last thing we need is for Lincoln to succeed at convincing the people of the Republican States that Federals at Fort Sumter are starving to death, for God's sake." And President Davis added, "Good, please see that is done. Furthermore, Robert Anderson of Kentucky, who commands the Federal garrison in the fort, was a friend of mine at West Point and afterward during my military career. I will consider going to Charleston myself and, perhaps, have a chat with him. Let us show good Southern hospitality where we can." [28]

Although the Confederate Executive had existed not quite one month, a plan for defending secession was taking place. This first month of the Jefferson Davis Administration would go down in history as one of the most effective government launches in recorded history.

Meanwhile, in Washington City, President Abraham Lincoln was selecting his Cabinet and moving forward toward his goal of inciting the "first shot." His Cabinet members were:

- Secretary of State: William Seward, Republican, of New York.
- Secretary of War: Simon Cameron, Republican, of Pennsylvania.
- Secretary of the Navy: Gideon Welles, Republican of Connecticut.
- Secretary of the Treasury: Salmon Chase, Republican of Ohio.
- Attorney General: Edward Bates, of what little Republican Party existed in Missouri.
- Postmaster General: Montgomery Blair, of what little Republican Party existed in Maryland.
- Secretary of the Interior: Caleb Smith, Republican of Indiana.

Prior to Abe Lincoln's inauguration, South Carolina Governor Francis Pickens had sent two Delegations to Washington City, both seeking to negotiate with leaders in the Buchanan Administration on the Fort Sumter crisis. But these Delegations had made no progress with those "lame ducks." And Republicans who were supposedly influential with Lincoln had given the South Carolinians no reason for hope. So, those Delegations had returned home with nothing but a stronger fear that Lincoln would stop at nothing in his quest to conquer the Seceded States.

In February, President Jefferson Davis had taken over control of the South Carolina militia at Charleston, and had sent a Delegation of three men to Washington City to again seek an audience with President Lincoln to find a way to defuse the Fort Sumter crisis. These men had departed on February 27 and had arrived 3 days prior to Lincoln's inauguration. They had notified the new President that they were emissaries from President Davis and that they earnestly sought an audience with him to discuss the crisis at Fort Sumter and all other matters of interest to both parties. Lincoln had refused to see them, probably more than once, in that they were most likely quite insistent. They

---

[28] In truthful history, Charleston ladies did attempt to send food to soldiers in Fort Sumter, but Captain Anderson refused to accept it, and President Lincoln falsely alleged that Federal soldiers in the island fort were facing starvation, requiring that he send the U. S. Navy with relief supplies to Charleston Harbor, complete with armed warships and troop transports.

were seeking opportunities to talk with new Secretaries in Lincoln's Cabinet and Federal Representatives and Senators, but it was Lincoln whom they most wanted to see. These men would keep at their mission in Washington City through March and into April. They would be keeping in touch with President Davis by telegraph and letter. [29]

The morning of his first day on the job, March 5, President Lincoln started considering various plans for maintaining Federal troops at Fort Sumter in South Carolina and Fort Pickens in Florida. He read a report alleging that the Federals at Fort Sumter would run out of food supplies in six weeks. But that was an old report and the ladies of Charleston were persistently attempting to deliver lovely food daily. Federals only had to accept those wonderful and nourishing gifts. That same day, Lincoln issued a verbal Executive Order to the Federal Navy directing it to immediately land at Fort Pickens the 200 troops presently on the offshore warship, the *Brooklyn*. These men had been sent by former President James Buchanan to reinforce Fort Pickens, but had agreed in consultation with Florida officials to remain a short distance offshore. Confederate forces had taken over the substantial nearby navy yard at Pensacola, but had determined that it was not possible to take control of nearby Fort Pickens without a substantial fight. The Confederates already had the good stuff. They had the shipyard. Seeking to avoid bloodshed and recognizing their practical limitations, Confederates had promised not to attack the Federals under siege in Fort Pickens if the men on the warship Brooklyn made no move to reinforce the Fort. Lincoln thought that, by violating that agreement unilaterally, he was underway toward achieving his goal of inciting the "first shot." [30]

Three days earlier, on March 2, 1861, Congress had passed an Amendment to the Federal Constitution. It was known as the Corwin Amendment and would have to be ratified by three fourths of the states to become part of the Federal Constitution. But seven states had seceded. Big problem. The Corwin Amendment would prohibit the Federal Government from passing any laws or enforcing any executive orders that would interfere with each State's right to regulated slavery. It was sponsored in the House by Thomas Corwin of Ohio and in the Senate by William Seward of New York, who became Lincoln's Secretary of State.

Clearly, incoming President Lincoln would have great difficulty mounting a moral outrage, an Abolitionist crusade against slavery in Delaware, Maryland, Kentucky, Missouri, Virginia, North Carolina, Tennessee or Arkansas, much less against the Seceded States. Freeing the

---

[29] The history of this Confederate Delegation is truthful.

[30] The history of Lincoln's first day in office is truthful.

slaves was totally off the table. But some figured that an Amendment to the Federal Constitution might encourage some Seceded States to return. [31]

Before long, Secretary of State William Seward agreed to talk, indirectly and unofficially, with the Confederate Commissioners through two Justices of the Federal Supreme Court, Samuel Nelson of New York and John Campbell of Alabama, the latter having chosen not to resign his lifetime appointment. Both Nelson and Campbell were totally against war. Claiming to be also speaking for Chief Justice Roger Taney of Virginia, Nelson was warning Seward, Salmon Chase and Edward Bates, all Secretaries in Lincoln's Cabinet, that Federal invasion of the seceded States would totally violate the Federal Constitution and be illegal use of armed force unless it was constructed as the invasion of a foreign nation, meaning the Confederate States had to first be recognized as a legitimate foreign government. Although negotiating with Seward through Nelson and Campbell was a far cry from the audience with Lincoln that the Commissioners were seeking, they shucked their pride and decided to work with whatever lines of communication they could pry open. They agreed to talk with Seward.

On the other hand, leading Democrats were anticipating a peaceful resolution to the secession crisis. Democrat Senator Stephen Douglas of Illinois, considered the leader of his party in the Northern States, was publicly praising what he alleged to be Lincoln's professed restraint -- alleging that Lincoln's inaugural message was a "peace offering rather than a war message," and claiming Lincoln gave "a distinct pledge that the policy of the Administration shall be conducted with exclusive reference to a peaceful solution of our national crisis."

But there is reason to suspect that Republican leaders were quietly letting Douglas have the spotlight, hoping that would retard the building secession movement in other Democrat-controlled States: Virginia, North Carolina, Tennessee, Maryland, Kentucky, Missouri, Arkansas and little Delaware. Keeping Douglas in the spotlight would buy time for Lincoln and his Cabinet to organize their Administration and complete their arrangements to wage war.

On March 11 Lincoln discovered that the Navy had not obeyed his order to direct the 200 men on the warship Brooklyn to land and reinforce Fort Pickens at Pensacola. Infuriated, he restated the order in writing, and, the next day, General Winfield Scott dispatched a vessel to steam to Florida and deliver the order directing the men to land at Fort Pickens. However, Captain Henry Adams, commander of the Federal naval forces in and offshore from

---

[31] The Corwin Amendment was never ratified by three-fourths of the States, so it never became law.

Fort Pickens would not act on General Scott's order. The order would either be pocket vetoed somewhere down the chain of command or Adams would personally veto the thing. It would appear that Adams did not want to unilaterally violate the armistice in effect at Fort Pickens and was intentionally procrastinating. Adams' sense of personal responsibility was heightened by the fact he was personally in possession of the initial papers that documented the agreement between the Federals and Florida State officials.

On March 15, a mere 11 days into his new job, President Lincoln opened a Cabinet meeting discussion about plans to re-supply and re-enforce Fort Sumter by sea. The discussions carried over to March 16. Postmaster General Montgomery Blair of Maryland was a West Point graduate and his wife's brother-in-law, a former Navy man, had developed a proposal to do just that. Montgomery Blair thought the plan had merit and persuaded Lincoln to give it serious consideration. Two options were contained in the Postmaster General's wife's brother-in-law's plan to send Federal warships into Charleston harbor. The mission would be only to re-supply or it would be to re-supply and reinforce. Secretary of State William Seward of New York took the lead in opposing the plan to invade Charleston Harbor. At that time he was definitely against creating a military incident at Charleston. Seward argued that a Navy expedition to put more Federals into Fort Sumter would "provoke combat, and probably initiate a civil war." In his position statement Seward added: "Suppose the expedition successful, we have then a garrison in Fort Sumter that can defy assault for six months. What is it to do then? Is it to make war by opening its batteries and attempting to demolish the defenses of [Charleston]? . . . I would not initiate war to regain a useless and unnecessary position on the soil of the seceding States." Secretary of the Navy, Gideon Welles of Connecticut acknowledged that under different circumstances he might advocate initiating war, but the Fort Sumter plan was not one of those circumstances. Wells included in his written position paper: "By sending, or attempting to send provisions into Sumter, will not war be precipitated? It may be impossible to escape it under any course of polity that may be pursued, but I am not prepared to advise a course that would provoke hostilities." Secretary of War Simon Cameron of Pennsylvania and Secretary of the Interior Caleb Smith of Indiana agreed with Seward as well. Secretary of the Treasury Salmon Chase of Ohio disliked the plan for he feared it would ignite a war of invasion that the Treasury was ill-prepared to fund, but he reluctantly agreed to offer his support if Abe Lincoln was sure it would not be the prelude to war. Chase wrote: "If the attempt will so inflame civil war as to involve an immediate necessity for the enlistment of armies and the expenditure of millions, I cannot advise it in the existing circumstances of the

[Federation] and in the present condition of the [Federal] finances." [32] Only Secretary Montgomery Blair of Missouri -- who, ironically, did not represent the political views of the vast majority of the people of his state, and was in charge of only the unrelated U. S. Postal Service -- strongly endorsed an invasion of Charleston harbor by the Federal Navy. Blair explained such action was needed to repudiate what he alleged to be southern States expectations that "Northern [States] men are deficient in the courage necessary to [force Seceded States back under] the [Federal] Government." Blair urged prompt action to "vindicate the hardy courage of [Northern States men] and the determination of the people and their President to [reinstall] the authority of the [Federal] Government."

So at this time Lincoln did not have agreement on a course of military action within his Cabinet. Seward, Cameron, Welles and Smith were eager to avoid war, and Chase was quite cautious. Only Postmaster Blair was eager to launch a militant incident to elicit the coveted "first shot." In Lincoln's view, negotiating with the Confederacy or the Confederate State of South Carolina was definitely out and opening a dialogue with President Davis or his Commissioners was impossible. Lincoln would never recognize that the Confederate States of America even existed. Lincoln refused to accept his Cabinet's vote. He decided to postpone any decision on the matter.

Meanwhile in Montgomery, on the next day, March 16, Confederate Secretary of State Robert Toombs instructed three Confederate Commissioners who had been chosen to present Confederate policy to Great Britain, France and other European powers:

"They were to make clear the absolute right, as stipulated in the Federal Constitution, of the southern States to secede from the Federation. They were to stress the importance of tax-free trade with the Confederacy. They were to warn that, if the Lincoln Administration were to make war upon the Confederate States, the essential raw material, cotton, would be cut off from British mills. Since African American bonding might be a stumbling block to recognition, they were to touch the subject lightly, but emphasize two facts. The Confederate Constitution prohibited the importation of bonded Africans. Some were already emancipated free people of color, and a trend toward eventual emancipation of all was being discussed among state leaders. Commissioners should emphasize that, even now, more than half of the free people of color in North America were living in the Southern States and many of them were successful landowners, farmers, skilled laborers, and business men and women."

---

[32] The editor of this book is substituting "federation" for "nation" to more accurately describe the country in 1861.

The March 18 issue of the Boston *Transcript* presented the underlying Republican argument for a Federal conquest of the Confederacy: specifically to keep prices of manufactured goods high by ensuring collection of Federal import taxes, not only in Seceded States, but in Federal States as well. African American bonding was not an issue. The newspaper argued, "It is apparent that the people of the principal seceding States are now for commercial independence." Believing it would be impossible to stop the smuggling of heavily taxed goods across the very long land boundary between the Confederate States and the United States, the newspaper alleged that Northern States west of the Appalachian Mountains would "find it to their advantage to purchase their imported goods at New Orleans [using smugglers] rather than at New York [City, where the Federal Tax could be efficiently collected]." Officials believed the high Federal import tax on foreign goods was only collectable in an efficient manner at established seaports. Yet, the Lincoln Administration could have obtained help from the Confederate Government in collecting import taxes had it been willing to talk to the Confederate Commissioners, who were patiently seeking an audience with Abe Lincoln.

Meanwhile, Commander-in-Chief General Winfield Scott presented the position of the Federal Army concerning Fort Sumter. He proposed the following message to the commander at Fort Sumter: "You will, after communicating your purpose to His Excellency, the Governor of South Carolina, engage suitable water transportation and peacefully evacuate Fort Sumter . . . [and] with your entire command embark for New York [City]."

But Lincoln had other plans.

Ignoring Scott's recommendation, Lincoln proceeded to gather independent military information by personally sending spies to Charleston:

1. Firstly, Lincoln personally sent Lieutenant Gustavus Fox to Charleston to check out the situation, alleging that Fox was going to Charleston to talk with the troops at Fort Sumter about evacuation plans. But in reality Fox was on a secret mission for the President to spy on Charleston's coastal defenses. Fox, a Massachusetts textile agent who had formerly been a naval officer, was Postmaster Montgomery Blair's wife's brother-in-law. Fox was the Navy man who had originally proposed the Navy reinforcement plan to Blair.

2. Secondly, Lincoln personally sent Stephen Hurlbut to Charleston. Hurlbut was an old friend from Illinois who had been born in Charleston. Lincoln instructed Hurlbut to make connections with people who had been opposed to State secession – which Lincoln in his naivety expected to be numerous – and to assess their political strength. As a native-born South Carolinian, Hurlbut would be able to circulate among the State's influential people.

3. Thirdly, Lincoln sent Ward Lamon to South Carolina to spy. Lamon was known in the southern States for his opposition to Abolitionism, so he would not be suspected of aiding the Republicans. Comfortable in bars and saloons, Lamon would be able to limber up loose tongues.

President Lincoln's deliberations about Fort Sumter were no secret. But most well informed people probably expected the Cabinet to have a dominating influence over the new President, simply because Lincoln was so inexperienced in Federal Government work, and in leading a large organization. [33] So, appeals for peace were directed at the Executive as a whole, not just at Lincoln himself. Just about every well-informed person in the Northern States, the remaining Southern States, and the Confederacy recognized that the Lincoln Administration was deliberating on reinforcement or withdrawal at Fort Sumter and Fort Pickens; and there was agreement that one path led to war while the other led to peaceful coexistence. Many well-informed Northern States people were concerned about Washington City becoming isolated between Maryland and Virginia, should secession spread to all Democrat-controlled States. But hardly anyone believed there was any real danger of the Confederacy launching an invasion of the Northern States. Many wise and powerful voices pleaded with the Lincoln Administration to let the Secessionists go in peace. These people did not want war, and they were hopeful that letting those seven States remain apart would deflate mounting State secession movements in the other Southern States. [34]

Horace Greeley, in his New York *Tribune*, a Republican newspaper which, among all newspapers, had been most influential in building the Republican Party throughout the Northern States, alleged that he opposed instigating war. In fact it was about this time that a newspaperman on the *Tribune* staff arrived in Charleston, encouraged by a joint invitation from Robert Toombs (State), Judah Benjamin (Attorney General), and Christopher Memminger (Treasury and a Charleston native). A second newspaperman had accepted a similar invitation. He was of the Cincinnati *Enquirer*, a very influential newspaper for southern Ohio and northern Kentucky, which was owned by Washington McLean, a Democrat. The third newspaper to accept an invitation to send a reporter to Charleston was a man from the New York *Herald*, a widely read staunchly Democrat newspaper edited by Frederic Hudson. The Davis Administration hoped the presence of these three newspapermen from three influential newspapers would be helpful in assuring the peaceful intent and friendly nature of the Confederate people. As

---

[33] In truthful history the biggest organization that Lincoln had ever led was his two-man law office.

[34] The foregoing is truthful history.

each arrived in town, he was witness to the festive and friendly ladies of the city who, every day, prepared fine southern food and arranged for and attempted to deliver it to the Federal garrison holed up in Fort Sumter. [35]

Furthermore, the Confederate Commissioners in Washington City, although officially ignored by the Lincoln Administration, observed political opinion within their view, and reported back to Montgomery that it appeared that Northern States public opinion strongly favored peaceful coexistence.

The March 21 issue of the New York *Times* editorialized, "There is a growing sentiment throughout the [Northern States] in favor of letting the Gulf States go." But the Lincoln Administration had different ideas. On that same day, Abe Lincoln's first spy, Gustavus Fox, mentioned previously as the Postmaster General's wife's brother-in-law, was arranging to row out to Fort Sumter to sharpen his plans for an assault on Charleston Harbor by the Federal Navy. He explained to Governor Pickens that he had merely wished to pcaccfully visit the Fort Sumter garrison. Obviously suspicious of Fox's intent, Pickens asked that he join him for lunch to discuss further the nature of his business. Deftly, Pickens managed to get the New York *Tribune* reporter to join in the discussion. So Fox found himself uncomfortably contriving excuses on the spot regarding the purpose of his visit. Fox claimed "he had come on pacific purposes." Although Pickens probably suspected that Fox was lying, he granted the man permission to row out to the Fort and then dutifully reported Fox's visit to Montgomery to keep President Davis informed. Fox probably had little confidence in Major Anderson's loyalty to the new Republican Administration, because he also deceived the Federal garrison of his intent. Then Fox set about to thoroughly survey the Fort and its surroundings and mentally firm his plans for landing Federals from a flotilla of Navy ships, which would force their way into Charleston Harbor from the Atlantic. After completing his survey, and without explaining Lincoln's intent to Major Anderson, Fox rowed back across the harbor to Charleston and hurried back to Washington to report to President Lincoln. A report of the visit also reached the press room at the New York *Tribune*, and Horace Greeley made brief mention of it in the next issue, closing with the question: "What was the real mission of officer Fox, brother-in-law to the wife of Postmaster General Montgomery Blair?" [36]

Lincoln's second spy, Stephen Hurlbut, did not visit Governor Pickens. Instead, he frequented a few bars about town and gathered a sense of the

[35] This Confederate effort to influence three influential Northern newspapers is our alternate history.

[36] Lincoln's spying trip by Gustavus Fox is truthful history except for the witnessing by the *Tribune* reporter.

attitudes of South Carolinians for or against secession, and found that an opponent of secession was a rare bird indeed.

A few days later Abe Lincoln's third spy, Ward Lamon, a personal friend from Springfield Illinois, spoke with Governor Pickens about the intent of his trip. Lamon alleged to Pickens he "had come to try to arrange for a removal of the garrison." Pickens listened a bit and likewise extended an invitation to lunch. This time the reporter from the Cincinnati *Enquirer* was found and brought to the table. Lamon struggled to invent excuses, but Pickens permitted Lamon to row out to the fort. Then he wired Montgomery a report of the encounter. Meanwhile, Lamon rowed out to the fort and talked with Major Anderson about the politics surrounding Fort Sumter. Anderson, well aware that he and his men sat upon a powder keg that could launch a dreaded brother-against-brother war, told Lamon that he strongly favored a policy to evacuate his men and turn over Fort Sumter to the Confederacy. When Lamon rowed back from the fort, he again called on Governor Pickens, and asked if an armed Federal warship might be given clearance to enter the harbor and take away Major Anderson and the Federal garrison. Recognizing that there was no logical reason to assign such a sensitive task to an armed Federal warship, Pickens replied that no armed ship of the Federal Navy would be allowed in Charleston harbor. With that, Lamon replied that he believed Major Anderson would prefer a passenger steamship anyway. Lamon concluded his meeting with Governor Pickens with the upbeat allegation that he hoped to return to Charleston in a few days to help remove the Federal garrison. Then, Lincoln's spy likewise hastily traveled to Washington City to report back to his Commander-in-Chief. News of this visit soon reached the press room at the Cincinnati *Enquirer*. Editor Frederic Hudson, sensing a significant story, headlined the item: "Why Was Lincoln Confidant Ward Lamon Snooping Around Fort Sumter?" People knew of Ward Lamon and his work for the Lincoln campaign, including printing hundreds of counterfeit tickets so Lincoln supporters could pack the galleries that day in Chicago when Abe had won the Republican nomination for President, and the many days he had spent on the Republican Railroad Rally train acting as a bodyguard for Lincoln. The *Enquirer* story raised significant questions about what the new and inexperienced President was up to. Was he operating a personal spy network? [37]

On March 25 Stephen Douglas stood before the Senate, recognized the Confederate States of America and its capital in Montgomery, and advocated a Federal policy of peaceful coexistence. Douglas advocated "withdrawal of the [Federal] garrisons from all forts within the limit of the States which had

---

[37] The spying trip by Ward Lamon is truthful history except for the witnessing by the Cincinnati *Enquirer* reporter.

seceded, except those of remote Key West and Dry Tortugas, needful to the United States for coaling stations." Declaring, "Anderson and his gallant band should be instantly withdrawn," Douglas argued that, unless the Federal Government intended to subjugate the seceded States, Fort Sumter rightfully belonged to Charleston and Fort Pickens rightfully belonged to Pensacola. So at this time Douglas claimed to stand opposed to a Federal invasion, declaring, "We cannot deny that there is a Southern Confederacy de facto, in existence, with its capital at Montgomery. We may regret it. I regret it most profoundly, but I cannot deny the truth of the fact, painful and mortifying as it is." Then Douglas concluded with, "I proclaim boldly the policy of those with whom I act. We are for peace." [38]

But not all people were advocating peace. Many Republican leaders were openly advocating an invasion. The Republican Party had come from nowhere to dominance throughout the Northern States in just six short years. Militant Republicans were peppered throughout the Northern States. Their recent political triumphs were rather intoxicating. Michigan Senator Zachariah Chandler argued, "Without a little blood-letting this [Federation] will not, in my estimation, be worth a rush." Pointing directly at Fort Sumter, Lyman Trumbull of Illinois introduced a resolution in the Senate stipulating, "It is the duty of the President to use all the means in his power to hold and protect the public property of the United States." Stooping to the exaggerated rhetoric typical of crisis-time politicians, a caucus of Republican Representatives warned the Lincoln Administration that failure to reinforce Fort Sumter would bring disaster to the Republican Party. But the March 4 through March 28 Special Session of the U. S. Congress would conclude soon.

About this time Secretary of State William Seward again met with the Confederate Commissioners who were hoping to win recognition and a pledge of peaceful co-existence. Apologizing for the delay, Seward, again with apparent confidence, alleged to the Commissioners that the Federal garrison would soon be withdrawn from Fort Sumter. But Seward was not in control!

Within a few days Lincoln's three spies were back in Washington City to report on their respective trips to Charleston. Lieutenant Fox advised Lincoln that, having seen the situation first hand, he was even more confident that his proposal to sneak Federals into the harbor by sea at night would work. Stephen Hurlbut, returning on March 27, exploded Lincoln's dream that opposition to State secession resided in the hearts of a significant remnant of South Carolinians. Hurlbut reported, "Separate nationality is a fixed fact; there is no attachment to the [past Federation of States] . . . positively nothing

---

[38] The Douglas speech is truthful history.

to appeal to." He reported that South Carolinians viewed themselves as citizens of a new nation. He believed they would protect their harbor from any ships that appeared intent on sustaining foreign occupation of their fort. Even "a ship known to contain only provisions for Sumter would be stopped and refused admittance," Hurlbut predicted. But all three reported that there would be no starvation at Fort Sumter, if the commander would accept the food that the ladies of Charleston were attempting to send out to the men every day. Although the "starvation" gambit was dead, the reports by Lincoln's spies bolstered his confidence that a military mission to re-supply Fort Sumter would be perceived as technically doable, and that such a mission would produce the desired result. South Carolinians would feel compelled to fire that useful "first shot," which Lincoln believed he needed to persuade the people of the Republican-controlled States and their respective State militia to support him when he began his war. Lincoln figured, with the "first shot" coming from Confederate cannon, Republican newspapers and politicians all over the northern States would, the next day, in orchestrated unison, cry out for patriotic men to take up arms against the alleged "aggressor." And Lincoln hoped that at least one soldier in Fort Sumter would be killed in the melee to properly get the blood flowing.

On March 28 Army Commander-in-Chief Winfield Scott recommended to Lincoln that both Fort Sumter and Fort Pickens be evacuated and turned over to the Confederacy. Scott told Lincoln that evacuating Fort Sumter, while continuing to occupy Fort Pickens, would be viewed as an aggressive move likely to influence other States, notably Virginia, to secede. Therefore, both forts should be evacuated and turned over to the Confederacy. Scott had been born on a large farm near Petersburg, Virginia, attended the College of William and Mary, studied law a bit and served as a Virginia militia cavalry corporal before embarking on a life-long military career with the United States Army. So he was of the Southern culture as were many of the Army's leading officers. The Army Chief's eagerness to avoid war troubled the President greatly.

Apparently, that very afternoon, Lincoln resolved within himself to move toward decisive military action as quickly as possible to arrest the growing peace sentiment. Coincidentally, that very night the President and First Lady held their first official state dinner at the White House. Most members of the Cabinet attended. At the conclusion of the affair, Lincoln asked the Cabinet to stay so he could speak with them about the forts. Lincoln told them that the Army Chief recommended abandonment of both forts, but, he warned, a decision on the matter was his and his alone. He directed the Cabinet to meet with him the next day to assist him in reaching a decision.

At noon, March 29, President Lincoln convened his Cabinet to press for their blessings to his plans to send warships, troops and transports to Fort

Sumter and to unilaterally break the agreement not to reinforce Fort Pickens. The earlier cover story, the imminent crisis story, the idea that those few Federals at Fort Sumter were running out of food, had been reduced to nonsense by the ladies of Charleston's attempted food delivery campaign, and newspaper coverage of their daily efforts. The Confederate Secrete Service had made sure that story received wide coverage in Northern newspapers. So a mercy mission to resupply was no longer considered. The proposed mission would be to re-enforce and the stated object would be to collect taxes on imports. [39]

Gustavus Fox had completed his initial preparation and planning work at the New York Naval Yard, and he had returned back to Washington City to present directly to Lincoln a practical and executable list of ships, men and war material needed to reinforce both forts. Fox told Lincoln that the flotilla could be assembled and made ready to steam south in about one week. So, by circumventing the command structure in the Federal Army and Navy, and by working through Gustavus Fox, a navy man and the brother-in-law of the wife of his Postmaster General, Lincoln now had the specific details he needed to directly order that two armed fleets be quickly assembled, and that they invade the Confederate harbors at Charleston and Pensacola. It is doubtful that, on March 29, Cabinet members fully comprehended the extent to which Gustavus Fox had already arranged for Lincoln's naval flotilla to be assembled at the New York Naval Yard. They were about to be asked to express their opinions as if Lincoln was still undecided.

Lincoln submitted to the Cabinet his proposal to reinforce either fort, or both forts. These were very serious proposals with great potential to propel the United States toward a military invasion of the Confederate States. So Lincoln asked each man to submit his recommendations in writing, and that they did.

Secretary of State William Seward remained firmly opposed to reinforcing Fort Sumter because he firmly believed that such action would lead to the war of invasion he was striving to avoid. However, Seward greatly feared Lincoln's militant attitude, and attempted to limit the President's aggression to the less politically sensitive Fort Pickens in hopes of maintaining peace at Fort Sumter. Applying that psychology, Seward wrote that he favored reinforcing only Fort Pickens. Caleb Smith agreed with Seward. Edward Bates supported Seward on reinforcing Fort Pickens, but would not commit one way or the other on Fort Sumter. Continuing to express hope such a move would not propel the United States toward war, Salmon Chase reservedly gave his blessing to reinforce both Fort Sumter and

---

[39] In truthful history Lincoln would stress that the Navy mission was to bring food to the Federal troops that occupied Fort Sumter.

Fort Pickens. Apparently changing his position on the issue, Navy Secretary Gideon Welles revealed he would support reinforcing both Fort Sumter and Fort Pickens. As before, Montgomery Blair was insistent that both forts be reinforced. In fact, Montgomery's father, Francis Blair, had come to the White House that morning and lectured Lincoln that turning over those forts to the Confederate States would be treason and would dangerously slow the Republican Party's momentum. Secretary of War Simon Cameron was absent, but he had supported Seward's peace-making stance two weeks earlier. So Lincoln's chief advisers, the Cabinet plus the Army Chief, were divided five-to-three on Fort Sumter: five opposed a mission (Army Chief Scott, Secretary of State Seward, Interior Secretary Smith, Attorney General Bates, and Secretary of War Cameron) and three, to differing degrees, supported a Navy mission to Fort Sumter (Treasury Secretary Chase, Navy Secretary Welles and Postmaster General Blair). Lincoln read over the written opinions and heard the discussion. We must surmise that he was disappointed that so few blessed the invasion of Charleston Harbor.

But Lincoln held the trump card. So, as he had seen courtroom judges do so many times in Illinois, Lincoln announced his decision: A Federal Navy fleet, to be under the direction of Navy Secretary Welles, would be ordered to Charleston Harbor with reinforcements, arms and supplies with the announced intention of placing them in Fort Sumter. Another Navy fleet, to be under the direction of War Secretary Cameron, would be ordered to Pensacola with reinforcements, arms and supplies also with the announced intention of placing them at Fort Pickens.

Abe Lincoln handed Navy Secretary Welles the following directive:

> "I desire that an expedition, to move by sea, be got ready to sail as early as the 6th of April next, the whole according to memorandum attached, and that you cooperate with the Secretary of War for that object."

The directive further specified that the flotilla to Charleston Harbor include the warships *Pocahontas* and *Pawnee*, that it include a revenue collection cutter, and that 300 Federal seamen and 200 other Federal soldiers be sent to New York City with combat supplies to go aboard and provide troop support for the mission. He directed that the two fleets depart for Charleston and Pensacola, respectively, by April 6 at the latest. Secretary Welles handed the order to Gustavus Fox with instructions to speed it to New York. Then Lincoln told the Cabinet that as soon as Secretary of War Cameron could be reached, he would be assigned responsibility for the mission to reinforce Fort Pickens, and that ships leave New York no later than April 6. Lieutenant Fox, whose loyalty was to Lincoln, left immediately for New York to ensure that the orders for the Navy mission to Fort Sumter were speedily carried out. Welles obtained Lincoln's agreement that the Federal Navy's most powerful warship, the *Powhatan*, would be commanded by Samuel Mercer and would lead the Navy's mission to Fort Sumter.

Secretary of State Seward was horrified. His Fort Pickens diversionary psychology had failed to defuse the Navy mission against Fort Sumter. [40]

Meanwhile, Confederate Treasury Secretary C. G. Memminger was having great success in selling the Confederate's first offering of $5,000,000 in new government bonds. When all sales would be totaled, the issue would be oversubscribed to $8,000,000 in Confederate money. The Confederate Government was on a sound financial footing and her treasury notes were so well regarded that they could be exchanged for gold. [41]

On April 4, Lincoln wired Lieutenant Fox with final go-ahead orders to set out for Fort Sumter to reinforce it. If the fleet met resistance from shore batteries, the relief force was to retreat and leave those in the fort to defend for themselves. At the same time Lincoln arranged to get a secret message to the garrison in Fort Sumter to expect the fleet to arrive about April 12.

The next day, April 5, a Washington City dispatch to the Montgomery, Alabama *Daily Mail* announced: "The frigate *Powhatan* goes to sea tomorrow morning, fully equipped and provisioned, and will probably take three companies of troops. The impression at the [New York] Navy Yard is that Forts Sumter and Pickens are both to be re-enforced." So people in both countries knew that the Federal Navy armada was about to steam out of the New York Naval Yard for Charleston harbor and Fort Pickens. The fleet of warships and transports ordered to enter Charleston harbor was very large, indeed, consisting of war-ships *Powhatan, Pawnee, Pocahontas*, and the revenue cutter *Harriet Lane*; steam-tugs *Uncle Ben, Yankee* and *Freeborn*, plus the merchant ship *Baltic* with 200 men and the necessary supplies. It was altogether a formidable little armada that was to enter Charleston Harbor consisting of 8 vessels carrying at least 26 guns, maybe more, and about 1,400 men.

At this time Seward warned Lincoln that he had earlier promised the three Confederate Commissioners – who were still seeking an audience in Washington City – that Fort Sumter "would not be reinforced without prior notice." So, apparently to accommodate Seward's sensitivities, and to further increase deception, Lincoln, on April 6, dispatched Robert Chew, a clerk in the Federal State Department, to Charleston with a letter to Governor Francis Pickens. Lincoln's order to Chew, dated April 6, said:

---

[40] Lincoln's Cabinet votes and orders to Navy commanders are truthful history.

[41] The success of Confederate bond sales is truthful history.

"Sir – You will proceed directly to Charleston, South Carolina; and if, on your arrival there, the flag of the United States shall be flying over Fort Sumter, and the fort shall not have been attacked, you will procure an interview with Governor Pickens and read him as follows: 'I am directed by the President of the United States to notify you to expect an attempt will be made to supply Fort Sumter with provisions only; and that if such an attempt be not resisted, no effort to throw in men, arms, or ammunition will be made, without further notice, or in case of an attack upon the fort.'

"After you shall have read this to Governor Pickens, deliver him the copy of it herein enclosed, and retain this letter yourself.

"But if, on your arrival at Charleston, you shall ascertain that Fort Sumter shall have been already evacuated, or surrendered, by the United States force; or shall have been attacked by an opposing force, you will seek no interview with Governor Pickens, but return here forthwith."

On April 7, Robert Anderson received his first written order since the Republicans had taken over the Federal Government. Up until this day the few verbal communications that had come to him had been intended to deceive him. The new message, from Secretary of War Simon Cameron, commanded that he remain in Fort Sumter awaiting resupply by the Navy. He added: "You will therefore hold out, if possible, until the arrival of the expedition." But Lincoln Administration had no real intention of holding Fort Sumter for the long term. Once the "first shot," was drawn, they intended to get Anderson and his men out of Charleston. A few killed Federals would be fine, but a fight to the last man might draw unnecessary criticism. So Cameron advised: "Whenever, if at all, in your judgment, to save yourself and command, a capitulation becomes a necessity, you are authorized to make it."

The same day, April 7, the Secretary of State William Seward answered a "strong letter" from Supreme Court Justice John Campbell demanding to know if past assurances of evacuation at Fort Sumter had been truthful or deceptive. Seward, rarely inclined to be truthful when a lie better served his purposes, replied in writing to Campbell: "Faith as to Sumter fully kept. Wait and see." Judge Campbell forwarded the "promise" to Montgomery, but Jefferson Davis was not deceived, for he personally knew about Seward's propensity to lie for best effect.

The next day, April 8, Robert Anderson, the commander in Fort Sumter, wrote a "distressed letter" to the Adjutant General, Colonel Lorenzo Thomas, in which he appealed for recall of the Federal Navy fleet. Clearly, Anderson did not want war. Yet he was the man who Lincoln had chosen to draw the "first shot." Anderson wrote a postscript asking Thomas to destroy the letter after reading it, for Anderson, a career officer who abhorred insubordination, knew his letter damned the Lincoln Administration. However, Thomas would never receive Anderson's letter, for Confederates in Charleston intercepted the dispatch and sent it to President Davis. Anderson had written:

> "Colonel: . . . I had the honor to receive, by yesterday's mail, the letter of the honorable Secretary of War, dated April 4, and confess that what he there states surprises me very greatly. . . . I trust that this matter will be at once put in a correct light, as a movement made now, when the [Confederacy] has been erroneously informed that none such would be attempted, would produce most disastrous results throughout our [country]. . . . We shall strive to do our duty, though I frankly say that my heart is not in the war, which I see is to be thus commenced. That God will still avert it, and cause us to resort to pacific means to maintain our rights, is my ardent prayer."

When Anderson's letter reached Jefferson Davis, he read it with considerable feeling, because they had been close friends during Jeff's military career. They had been together at West Point. Although Jeff had chosen to retire after 7 years of military service and settle down on a farm, Robert had chosen to make the military his life's career. [42]

On the evening of April 8, Lincoln's agent, Robert Chew, arrived in Charleston and called on Governor Pickens. Chew was the Federal State Department employee Lincoln had picked to attempt to deceive Pickens into believing that the fleet steaming for Charleston harbor was merely going to re-supply the Federal garrison with food, water and lamp oil. Chew read aloud to Pickens the following statement from Lincoln:

> "I am directed by the President of the United States to notify you to expect an attempt will be made to supply Fort Sumter with provisions only; and that if such an attempt be not resisted, no effort to throw in men, arms, or ammunition will be made, without further notice, or in case of an attack upon the fort."

Of course this letter was merely an attempt at further deception. The Federal Navy fleet was far more than would be necessary to deliver supplies to the few well-fed men within Fort Sumter.

By April 9, it was obvious to the Confederate Commissioners that the Lincoln Administration was intent on invasion. Lincoln had repulsed every effort they had made to open up dialogue. He continued to be fervent about ignoring them as if the slightest recognition of their existence might knock the underpinnings from the flimsy legal argument he would make to justify his

---

[42] The story of Robert Anderson is truthful history.

invasion. The dejected Commissioners – Roman, Crawford and Forsyth – wrote President Lincoln their final letter. They also prepared a copy and sent it to President Davis. Excerpts from their letter to Lincoln follow:

> "Your refusal to entertain these overtures for a peaceful solution, the active naval and military preparations, and the formal notice . . . that the President intends to provision Fort Sumter by forcible means, if necessary . . . can only be received by the world as a declaration of war . . . . The undersigned are not aware of any Constitutional power in the President of the United States to levy war, without the consent of [the Federal House and Senate], upon a foreign People, much less upon any portion of the People of the United States. . . . Whatever may be the result, impartial history will record the innocence of the Government of the Confederate States, and place the responsibility of the blood and mourning that may ensue upon those who have denied the great fundamental doctrine of American liberty, that 'Governments derive their just powers from the consent of the governed,' and who have set naval and land armaments in motion to subject the people of one portion of this land to the will of another portion."

Confederate Response to Lincoln's Aggressive Plans

The three Confederate Commissioners had been kept in the dark about the Davis Administration's plans to refuse to give Lincoln his coveted "first shot." It had seemed best to keep that a secret. So, they were left to assume that Southern pride would compel Confederates to repulse an attempt by Federals to enter Charleston harbor with a fleet of warships. Before departing, the Commissioners forwarded to Montgomery news from that day's issue of the New York *Tribune*: "The *Tribune* of today declares the main object of the expedition to be the relief of Sumter, and that a force will be landed which will overcome all opposition." That same day the New York *Herald* – in defiance of Republican pressures – courageously charged, "Our only hope now against civil war of an indefinite duration seems to lie in the overthrow of the demoralizing, disorganizing and destructive sectional Party, of which 'honest Abe Lincoln' is the pliant instrument." Lincoln Administration censors, backed by the Federal military, would eventually silence the *Herald* and other newspapers that editorialized against the Republican Party. But for the moment, the men in charge of the *Herald*, dared to defy the Republicans. [43]

---

[43] The *Herald* editorial is truthful history.

From Charleston, General Beauregard telegraphed Montgomery that he was assured by informants that the Federal fleet would soon be at Charleston Harbor, attempting to land men and war materials into Fort Sumter. [44]

Night fell in Montgomery while President Davis conferred with his Cabinet on organizing the Confederate States response to the Federal fleet's imminent arrival in Charleston harbor. A decision to avoid firing the "first shot" had been made two weeks previously, pending unexpected developments – and nothing unexpected had taken place. But Robert Anderson and his command, holed up in Fort Sumter, did not know that. Intentionally restrained from entering the city and receiving visitors without the approval of the Governor, the soldiers only knew that they were not starving, even though their commander was refusing the daily meal deliveries persistently attempted by the good ladies of the city. They did not know that heavy artillery had been removed and only easily withdrawn field artillery remained at various points around the harbor (some excuses had been published that a few heavy guns were being temporarily moved out of the city for repairs or were being relocated elsewhere along the harbor, giving the impression around town that, although movements were noted, defenses were still in place). The essence of the Confederate response, agreed to that night, was as follows:

> To prevent a trigger-happy artilleryman from firing an artillery piece, all cannon loads of gun powder was to be removed from the city a few hours before the fleet arrived.

> When the fleet was spotted, the following was to rapidly take place:

> > 1.   To ensure accurate reporting of the event, all newspapermen in the city (especially those from the Republican States, were to be encouraged to advance to the Battery to witness the proceedings (the Battery was the waterfront edge of the city, giving a fine view of Fort Sumter). The Confederate photographer would set up on the Battery to record the event.
> > 2.   The field artillery surrounding the harbor was to be withdrawn.
> > 3.   Confederate army troops and South Carolina State militiamen were to be gathered around their commander and read the message from President Davis, which would explain the importance of the strategy to avoid firing the coveted "first shot."

---

[44] The above history of Lincoln Administration activity is truthful. The Confederate non-militant response is our alternate history.

All would be ordered to stack their arms and take positions to watch the proceedings until further orders.

4. The mayor of the city was to speak to the citizens to explain the strategy of avoiding firing the coveted "first shot" and to seek their cooperation, ensuring them that the wisest councils had been consulted in arriving at this political decision, and that this decision is a sign of strength and wise council, not a sign of foolishness and weakness. They would be told that import and export activity would largely be diverted to other Confederate seaports and coastal places where landing and shipping out goods was workable, because the Federals would be intent on collecting Federal tariffs on goods within their grasp. He would ensure them that Confederate financial aid would compensate importers and exporters for taxes paid, but the major effort would be to relocate import and export activity elsewhere.

There had been a switch of assignments while the Federal fleet was steaming to Charleston: The most powerful Federal warship, the *Powhatan*, was directed to bypass Charleston and proceed to Florida. Command of the Charleston mission was to transfer to the Federal warship *Pawnee*.[45]

According to plan, on the morning high tide of April 12, the Federal warship *Pawnee* led the Federal fleet into Charleston harbor, guns at the ready, expecting shore batteries to open fire at any second. *Pawnee* was followed by *Pocahontas*, then the revenue cutter *Harriet Lane*, this being three warships in total. After them came the merchant ship *Baltic* with "brother-in-law" Gustavus Fox on board. The last three to enter Charleston harbor and anchor near Fort Sumter were the steam-tugs, *Uncle Ben*, *Yankee* and *Freeborn*. From shore, people just watched. General Beauregard stood at the ready to engage with any Federal official who came ashore. Newspaper men – both those representing newspapers to the north and those representing newspapers within the Confederate States – wrote their stories and headed off to the telegraph office. The Confederate photographer took photographs every hour to ensure he got the best lighting available that day. Some of the rougher sort about town complained loudly that Southerners were just cowards for letting the "damn Yankees" into our harbor. But, overall, the crowds were under control.

Meanwhile, the situation at Florida's Fort Pickens was becoming more grave. When Washington Gwathmey had been ordered to carry Lincoln's message to Fort Pickens, that Navy officer had refused and tendered his

---

[45] We now depart for truthful history with regard to the Federal fleet. In true history the fleet bobbed about off-shore watching the artillery duel it had incited. In this alternate history, the fleet enters the harbor and no artillery is fired.

resignation. Navy Secretary Welles had then selected John Worden to act as messenger, who had arrived at Pensacola on the afternoon of April 11. Without delay he had sought out the Confederate Commander, Braxton Bragg, and falsely alleged that his mission was to deliver a "verbal message of a pacific nature" to Henry Adams. Eager to maintain a posture of peaceful coexistence, Bragg had agreed to let Worden take a boat out to Fort Pickens.

So, on the morning of April 12, Worden took a boat out to Fort Pickens, wrote out Lincoln's order based on his memorization of the thing, and handed the order to Henry Adams, Commander of Federal forces at Pickens and of the Navy ships anchored further offshore. This order personally commanded Henry Adams to violate the standing truce and off-load soldiers, artillery and military supplies from the warship Brooklyn into Fort Pickens. This order undoubtedly demanded that the movement be undertaken secretly at first nightfall and without notifying the Confederates in any way. But word had reached Montgomery that Worden was delivering an order to unilaterally break the truce at Fort Pickens, and Confederate Secretary or War Leroy Walker rushed a telegram to Bragg advising him to intercept Worden. But Bragg was tipped off too late. He telegraphed Montgomery, "Mr. Worden had communicated with fleet before your dispatch received."

During the darkness of the Florida night, Federal artillerymen, artillery guns and military equipment were transferred from the Navy warships into Fort Pickens, in violation of the agreement between the Federal Government and what had been at that time the Nation of Florida, for, then, she had just seceded and not yet entered into the Confederacy. [46] The *Powhatan*, which had steamed on beyond Fort Sumter toward Florida was still 5 days away, but Henry Adams had finally decided he had no choice but to obey Abe Lincoln's order to unilaterally violate the armistice. The next day Secretary of War Leroy Walker would show Jeff Davis the telegram from Pensacola reporting the Federals "have violated their agreement. Reinforcements thrown into Fort Pickens last night by small boats from the outside. The movement could not even be seen from our side, but was discovered by a small boat reconnoitering." Worden would be detained when the train he was riding north passed through Montgomery, but he carried no incriminating papers and was released for lack of evidence. [47]

Editor's note: From this point forward, the history you will be reading is not truthful, but involves historically correct individuals placed in

---

[46] In international law it is understood that breaking an armistice by one party is an act of war and the party breaking it is properly accused of starting the conflict.

[47] The Navy action at Fort Pickens is truthful history.

historically correct offices of authority and reacting to events forced upon them in ways consistent with their prior thought processes and biases.

Wednesday Evening Selected Diary Postings

Diary note by Benedict Juárez said, "I really enjoyed supper with Tina Sharp. She grew up in West Texas and is presently a nuclear engineer working at the Comanche Peak Nuclear Station north of Fort Worth. I appreciated the sincere interest she showed in stories about my Juárez ancestor, but I was more interested in learning about her heritage, which is in Texas oil. Got a short course in ancestor Walter Benona Sharp and how the Sharps-Hughes hardrock drill bit launched the famous Texas Oil Boom at Spindletop in 1901. Her career also involves producing energy. Not with petroleum, but electricity generated with nuclear power."

Diary note by Chris Memminger said, "I am proud of my ancestor Christopher Gustavius Memminger of South Carolina, who was Secretary of the Treasury in the Davis Administration. He and those around him did such a good job at keeping the Confederate dollar strong and taking every advantage of the benefits of strong cotton exports in exchange for military equipment, steam engines and so forth. So much was accomplished in only those first ten months, as Professor Davis will be explaining further tomorrow. International trade will be the focus of my essay. Today was a good day. Goodnight."

Diary note by Marie Saint Martin said, "Tomorrow we will learn further how Secretary Judah Benjamin and my ancestor, Jules Saint Martin, were so, so important in the successful defense of Confederate Independence, perhaps mostly because of their superb management of the Confederate Secret Service. Operating throughout the Northern States during 1861 and 1862, Confederate Secret Service agents helped undercut the Republican arguments urging war against the Confederacy, and helped bolster opposition Democrat Party candidates in State and local elections and in elections for the Federal House and Senate. And they really confused the North about what was going on in the South, to make the North believe that the South could not or would not defend itself militarily. Passive Resistance was exploited to its fullest. . . . . Oh, yes, I talked with the musicians in our team and we agreed to get together tomorrow afternoon. Looking forward to that!"

Book 1, Chapter 5, Day 4 – Confederates Decline to Fire on Fort Sumter and Intensify Propaganda and Military Preparations – Class Lecture, Thursday, June 9, 2011

Professor Davis continued with his lectures as soon as the twelve were seated and ready to listen. We readers listen in. (Professor Davis' lecture is not on quotes.)

News that the complete fleet of Federal warships had peacefully entered Charleston Harbor arrived in Washington City on April 13. To those seeking war, this result seemed devastating. Lincoln was in shock! The coveted "first shot" allegation was not his to exploit. Instead he faced a political contest between Davis Administration operatives (former Democrats) and Lincoln Administration operatives (now Republicans) – and he already sensed that the Davis Administration was far more coy and manipulative than he and fellow Republicans had ever imagined. Republicans had been the masters of political demagoguery and deception. William Seward's maximum seemed to have always been: "Never tell the truth when a well-crafted lie will better serve our purpose." Confederates had always based their political arguments on the Constitution, on law, on individual liberty, on honor and honesty. Something had changed. But Lincoln had never met the Lafitte's.

The Spring of 1861: A Time of Political Maneuvering, North and South

Lincoln sensed that, with no fireworks at Charleston, and already suffering from effective "peace" propaganda dispensed by the Confederate Secret Service, he had insufficient justification to call up militia from the Republican states – too few would participate with any eagerness or commit to facing death on the battlefield – and messages from several Republican governors, especially governor Edwin Morgan of New York, confirmed the public's timidity, particularly concerning the people in New York City and the surrounding metropolitan area. And the Republican governors of Ohio (Dennison), Indiana (Morton) and Illinois (Yates) expressed concerns that many people of the southern half of each of their States were of the Southern culture and would strongly oppose an aggressive military invasion unless, the United States was previously attacked by Confederate military. The United States Army had only 1,080 officers and not quite 15,000 troops – a force that small could not even prevent secession in Maryland and Kentucky. If tied down in Maryland and Kentucky, no troops would be available to prevent secession in Virginia or Missouri, or invade states further south. What would Lincoln do with the troops in Fort Sumter and Fort Pickens? Those forces were too small to safely venture much beyond the city limits without being captured and rendered ineffective. He knew that he had to call up state militia to build an army of sufficient size to do more than prevent secession in Maryland and collect tariffs in a few seaports. Was he now moving toward a cat and mouse game – jailing Maryland political leaders and chasing down incoming merchant vessels to force payment of import taxes? There was 1,900 thousand miles of shoreline along the Confederate coast. Lincoln had not the navy to patrol it all.

President Lincoln held a Cabinet meeting of April 15, 1861, to discuss how best to respond to the peaceful reinforcement of Fort Sumter and the "peace" propaganda campaign coming out of the Confederacy. It was becoming more readily known across the Republican states of the north that the people of the seven seceded states only wanted to be left alone. The rather "fantastic" false demagoguery of the 1860 campaign, in which Republicans portrayed the "slaveocracy" of the south as ruffians and villains intent on bringing slavery into the northern States, always a farfetched and illogical argument, but scary none the less, was losing its edge. Lincoln's allegation that lawless elements within the Seceded States had somehow executed an internal revolution was becoming a hard sell, more so in the face of the Confederate's "peace" propaganda campaign. The excitement was dying down. Editorials were appearing again, recommending that the seven wayward sisters be allowed to leave in peace. The Cabinet seemed to be in disarray. Secretary of State William Seward, of New York, reminded everyone that he had consistently argued that the Navy campaign against Fort Sumter and Fort Pickens had been a horrible idea from the start. Postmaster General Montgomery Blair, of Maryland, who had advocated the Navy mission and facilitated it through is wife's brother-in-law, seemed to be at a loss for words when asked, "What should we do now?" Treasury Secretary Salmon Chase, of Ohio, seemed focused on collecting taxes on imports when ships arrived at Charleston, but Navy Secretary Gideon Welles, of Connecticut, reminded the group that he would be unable to prevent incoming vessels from seeking another Confederate seaport elsewhere. Secretary of War Simon Cameron argued that many of the men and officers in the United States Army were reluctant to venture as small bands into the South Carolina and Florida countryside, realizing they would be outnumbered and liable to be captured and thrown in stockades far from the view of comrades. The other two, Bates of Missouri and Smith of Indiana, seemed to want to skirt militant talk. And it would be a long time before Lincoln's Cabinet would be able to agree upon a pro-active plan for dealing with the Seceded States. The three Confederate Commissioners had returned to Washington City again and were always eager to talk. Would any member of Lincoln's Cabinet dare to interact with any of the three?

With his Cabinet undecided, President Lincoln consulted again with Orville Browning of Illinois over his frustration concerning his failure to incite the "first shot." A long-time political friend from Illinois, Browning had written before the inauguration:

> "In any conflict . . . between the [Federal] Government and the seceding States, it is very important that the [Secessionists] shall be [perceived as] the aggressors, and that they be kept constantly and palpable [allegedly] in the wrong. The first attempt . . . to furnish supplies or reinforcements to Sumter will induce [a military response] by South Carolina, and then the [Federal] Government will stand justified, before the entire [Federation], in repelling that aggression, and retaking the forts."

But the Confederates were not behaving as Browning had imagined they would.

Meanwhile, on May 3, in London, Lord John Russell, British Foreign Minister, received the Confederate commissioners to Great Britain, William L. Yancey of Alabama, A. Dudley Mann, a Virginian and former United States career diplomat, and Pierre A. Rost, of Louisiana. (After receiving instructions on March 16, Yancey, Mann and Rost had traveled to Charleston and boarded a ship to England, departing on March 24). Although the meeting at this point was "informal," Russell seemed to understand that, by allowing Federals to reinforce Fort Sumter, Confederates were demonstrating a great reluctance to give President Lincoln his coveted "first shot," while gaining for themselves valuable time to build a military. He deemed the strategy a good political move in that it gave Republican Party politicians – new to political power and with corresponding impetuous instincts – time to consult cooler heads. He intended to consult with others in his government and, when appropriate, arrange a second meeting. In short, the diplomatic contact had been cemented. Soon thereafter, Rost, who had been born and educated in France and had helpful contacts there, left London for Paris, for that had been his final diplomatic destination from the start.

The Seven States Negro Emancipation Conference

On Monday, May 13, 1861 the Seven States Negro Emancipation Conference convened in Montgomery. The Conference, essentially a committee made up of 21 men, three appointed by the governor of each Confederate State, were gathering to develop recommendations for a schedule, procedure and regulation for emancipating the enslaved negro population of each seceded State – a slow-paced program lasting many years, it was presumed, recognizing that, although coordination would be advantageous, the actual decisions would be made independently by each State, for the Confederate Constitution prevented the central government from ruling on anything concerning emancipation. As Confederate Attorney

General, Judah Benjamin was sitting in as a consultant, but he had no official authority. The 21 men appointed by the governors were all White men. But each governor also appointed one free person of color from his state, thereby making up a seven-man Advisory Panel of successful men who were of significant African ancestry. [48]

The immediate purpose of the Emancipation Conference was to dispense propaganda designed to encourage the Republican States of the North to let the South go its own way. But, this propaganda objective was hidden from the newspapermen who attended the opening part of the Conference.

The opening of the Conference, complete with introductions and statements of purpose, was attended by 14 newspapermen, 7 from seceded States, 3 from Democrat-controlled adjacent states and 4 from Republican-controlled states. And newspaper coverage was highly desired, for a program for eventual Negro Emancipation within the Confederate States was seen as a valuable propaganda tool, quite useful in impeding the Lincoln Administration's ability to gain the "high moral ground" as it sought to rally the people of the Republican states to support a call for state militia to reinforce Federal troops in a massive invasion of seceded sister states.

Although Judah Benjamin had no official capacity at the Conference, he did address the Delegates during the first hour, and those remarks were widely printed in newspapers across North America. A bit of his talk is presented below:

> "Delegates, allow me to first address the seven free persons of color in attendance here today, each appointed by the governor of his state and asked to participate as an advisory panel. Gentlemen of the Advisory Panel, your contribution to the success of our efforts should be very important. So please pay close attention, discuss ideas among yourselves and with the three delegates from your respective States. President Davis and I want to encourage each State to think about a schedule and procedure for emancipation within its borders. And regarding our urgent need to defend this Confederacy's right to independence, we seek your help, the help of other free persons of

---

[48] In truthful history there was never a seven States Negro Emancipation Conference. In our alternate history, a conference is held as a propaganda event, aimed at confusing the North and reducing anger in Great Britain toward slave holders in the Confederacy. A bit latter you will see how the press is invited to the opening part of the conference, then asked to leave. After they leave, taking their stories to Democrat newspapers in the North and to Europe, delegates to the Conference talk about ensuring that the process is for propaganda purposes and emancipation is to be gradual and carefully managed. This Conference is a significant propaganda tool and served to slow the efforts of the Lincoln Administration to win support for a war.

color, and the help of persons of color still under ownership. Again, President Davis and I thank you for your help and advice.

"Now addressing the twenty-one Delegates, I congratulate you on taking the initiative in beginning a long and thoughtful process of coordinating the eventual emancipation of the bonded Negroes in your respective states. To be sure, you will be motivated to embrace a program that is most beneficial to each category of your Negro population. You will consider the husband and his wife. You will consider the young children and their nurturing. You will consider the faithful older persons and not leave them wanting. You will consider the young men and women – many in the prime of young adulthood and eager and able to strike out on their own. You will remember that a relationship of bondage, between the owner and the slave, places well-understood obligations upon the shoulders of both – the owner is responsible for the welfare of the slave and, in the case of the woman, for the welfare of her children – the slave is responsible for being productive and cooperative to the best of his or her ability. And a responsible owner is sensitive to the desire of most bonded women to remain with her chosen husband. But, when children reach the productive age of, say 16 years, opportunities naturally arise for these young men and women to leave their parents and move on to a new life elsewhere when and if the owner sees wisdom in such a move, for the owner may, simply stated, have no remaining useful work for the maturing child and needs to ensure that, wherever that useful work can be found, a transfer to another owner might well be best for all concerned. Yet these decisions can be difficult, for so often, especially on rural farms, owner families and slave families have played together as children, and worked side-by-side as youths and young men and women. In short, many are close friends.

"As of our 1860 census, the Negro population in the seven Confederate states totaled 2,349,063 persons of which 36,811 were not slaves, but free and independent people of color. The corresponding population in the states to the north of our boundary totaled 2,090,450, of which 213,976 lived as free individuals in states that permitted slavery and 238,315 lived as free individuals in states further north, which are now controlled by the Republican Party. From the start of the importation of Negroes from Africa and the Caribbean, to its conclusion 53 years ago, only about 300,000 enslaved Africans were shipped into seaports along the shores of what is now the Confederate States of America. Yet, in our seven states we enjoy a Colored population that has expanded on the order of 800 percent, which constitutes evidence of, for the most part, good treatment with regard to bearable workloads, plus adequate food, shelter and medical care.

"Yet, many Negroes today naturally wish to join the ranks of their free and independent brothers and sisters. Furthermore, many owners of Negroes, especially those on very large and mature farms and plantations, are facing greater and greater problems in finding useful work to justify retention of the entire laboring group, especially in the future when advancing science, engineering and industrialization enables farm productivity improvements through new and exciting machinery and labor saving equipment, such as Cyrus McCormick's reaper. So, future economic concerns point to reductions in the work force on many farms, but some owners are reluctant to see some of their Negroes depart and face an unknown future under the ownership of another individual, perhaps hundreds of miles distant. Furthermore, the Republican states, for the most part, permit immigrants from Europe to freely come into their midst and settle there, but not the Negro. Enforced by its state constitution, Illinois, the home state of President Lincoln, prohibits immigration by a free person of color. [49] And movement by free and independent negroes within the states that do permit slavery can be a trying affair, for a counterfeit-proof method of issuing documents giving evidence of free status is badly wanting of improvement. So, I earnestly ask that you give some attention to the issue of improving our documentation of a person of color's free and independent status, including adoption of the photographic methods that are just now becoming available, for it is imperative that our free and independent people of color not be enslaved by criminals who circumvent our slavery laws.

"You will be looking toward drafting an emancipation schedule that will, perhaps, over a period of several decades, complete the emancipation of your entire population of slaves in your respective state. But you must show more urgency to advance emancipation than has Abraham Lincoln. For example, in a speech delivered at Charleston, Illinois, in debate with Senator Stephen Douglas, not quite three years ago, on September 18, 1858, before a crowd of 12,000, Lincoln said he envisioned a schedule for eliminating slavery that would exceed one hundred years. My, God, gentlemen, 100 years exceeds four generations. As Christian people, surely, we can do better than that.

"I quote briefly from Lincoln's 1858 speech:

---

[49] Prohibition of Free People of Color moving into Illinois is truthful history.

" 'I do not mean that when [opposition to slavery] takes a turn toward ultimate extension it will be in a day, nor in a year, nor in two years. I do not suppose that in the most peaceful way ultimate extinction would occur in less than one hundred years at least; but that it will occur in the best way for both races, in God's own good time, I have no doubt.' [50]

"So Mr. Lincoln envisioned that 100 years would be needed to complete a peaceful transition to a society where all Negroes would be free and independent. For God's sake, fellow Confederates, we can do better than that!

"Within the framework of an overall program for each of your states, you will undoubtedly be envisioning plans that foresee making free and independent even the last remaining slaves in far less time than one hundred years. And I leave those discussions to you, where they rightly belong. But let me make two recommendations for your consideration. First, if you find a way to begin a token emancipation process, on a very small scale to be sure, but in sufficient numbers to demonstrate the South's feelings of good will toward our loyal Negro population, then consider pursuing such a modest goal very soon, even this summer. Perhaps 2,000 of the most capable could be enrolled in a provisional program within weeks. Second, where the Confederate Government can be helpful over the next few weeks in providing security and transportation in support of a modest beginning of a token emancipation program, please ask us to consider participating. And give proper thought to where these newly-emancipated recruits would be relocated: consider four possibilities where they might settle:

1. Perhaps they would settle within the state where they presently live; or,
2. Perhaps settle in a sister state in the Confederacy; or,
3. Perhaps migrate to a state to the north of our boundary which also permits slavery; or,
4. Perhaps migrate even further north to a state, now controlled by the Republican Party, where a few free people of color presently live and where problems of reliable emancipation documentation would be a minimal concern."

At this point Judah Benjamin had concluded his presentation. This first phase of the Seven States Negro Emancipation Conference, which had been open to newspapermen and observers, was over. It had consumed just over one hour. The 21 Delegates, the Advisory Panel of free People of Color, and

---

[50] The quote and date of Lincoln's speech is truthful history.

Judah Benjamin thanked the observers and newspapermen and announced they would, at that time, begin their closed door meeting, and would announce at some later time when a press release was forthcoming. Several days were envisioned for the discussions, as Delegates anticipated needs to periodically communicate with governors and other leaders in their respective States.

When the closed door meeting began, Judah Benjamin presented further guidance, which, for our purposes is best condensed into the following concepts:

• All recognized that slaves in the Confederate States were of widely different ability and that, in many hearts, considerable White blood flowed, meaning they were not a pure race, but a racial mix of varying proportions. Almost all living slaves had been born in a Southern state, for the African immigrant was now seldom seen. All attending the Conference recognized that many slaves were skilled at agriculture and animal husbandry; many were raising fine, moral families; many were leaders on the farms where they lived, including acting as foremen over others; many were exceptionally skilled at a trade, such as blacksmithing or bookkeeping.

• The care of children of slaves had to be carefully considered. Many slaves were old and deserved the light work assignments and care given by those who had owned them for many decades. But most importantly, all recognized that each individual was a unique person whose future path from slavery to independent living needed to be designed to best suit everyone with whom he or she was involved.

• The Conference realized that limiting emancipation to only slaves who would volunteer to migrate into a Northern state would sharply shrink the field of candidates. The South was their home, and migrating into a Northern state might result in harsh treatment, hardship and even death. There were real risks. But the immediate need was for heroes to step forward and help the Confederate Secret Service induce fear in the North that a Federal conquest of the Confederacy would likely result in hundreds of thousands of free people of color migrating into their state to become their neighbors.

• Although there was sincere interest in developing thinking regarding future emancipation, the propaganda usefulness of a token start was of paramount immediate interest, because impeding the Lincoln Administration's effort to win state militia support for a large military invasion of the Confederacy was imperative. That was the reason Confederates did not force Federals out of Fort Sumter and that was the reason they believed, through propaganda emerging from this Conference and other targeted messaging, they could secure further high moral ground.

- Therefore, Benjamin advised, "this Conference needs to advocate an emancipation plan that our States can embrace, which is very gradual and not absolute, which can be modified as the years pass by, which makes good common sense and which will be useful in winning support abroad, especially among the honest and good people in Great Britain, and in the Republican-controlled States to the north."

- "The Davis Administration does not envision compensated emancipation by which tax payers pay owners to make their slaves free and independent. So the plan emerging from this Conference must be considerate of the investment of the owner as well as the welfare and aspirations of the slave, thereby striking a balance whereby both interests are somewhat balanced."

- "The Davis Administration believes an immediate and public message should emerge from this Conference. Should not this Conference suggest a specific program for the immediate emancipation of, say 400 carefully selected and willing Negro families, totaling 2,000 individuals who will accept emancipation within a few weeks and embark on journeys to the Republican-controlled states to the North? That needs honest discussion."

- "Please understand me – we all know that the newly emancipated free people of color of which we speak will prefer to remain in the Confederate States and thereby avoid migration into the Republican States. But we need for the North to learn to worry, seriously worry, that forcing seceded states back under Federal control will result in Negro migration into their communities."

- "Consider a partnership whereby owners voluntarily emancipate the individuals and the Confederate Government handles transportation, financing and brief training to make the relocation program a success. Should not that be the bargain to be struck in the next few weeks, for time is of the essence?"

- "Another path to emancipation is being discussed among military men: emancipation in exchange for military service. You should consider a second emancipation program where men of color are accepted in State militia as trained fighting men. They would be spread out among the militia units and represent a small percentage of troop strength. If slaves, they would gain freedom after honorable service under battlefield conditions, for we greatly worry that all we are attempting to do peacefully will fail, and we will eventually face a military invasion."

- At this point Benjamin became quite specific about emancipation in exchange for migration north into Republican states: "You may have a better idea, but President Davis suggests 400 individuals from South Carolina be asked to accept emancipation in exchange for relocation to Massachusetts; 400 from Georgia be asked in exchange for relocation to New York State; 400 from Alabama be asked in exchange for relocation to Pennsylvania; 400 from Mississippi be asked in exchange for relocation to Ohio, and 400 individuals from Louisiana be asked in exchange for relocation to Illinois. This would total 2,000 individuals. By the way, the best estimate of the number of runaway slaves that have passed through the so-called 'underground railroad' on their way to Canada is approximately 2,000 individuals. So, we are asking the Republican states to the north to, this time, allow our emancipated people of color to live among their people and forego pushing them north to Canada. If the people of those states accept Negro emigrants, we believe they will enjoy the benefits of a multi-racial society – and we encourage that. We believe you will have no problem getting enough owners to contribute the 400 agreeable families we suggest. President Davis will offer, from his Mississippi cotton farm, two very qualified families totaling 10 individuals, and he expresses confidence those will accept the proposal. We expect many more owners will strike such bargains with very qualified slaves."

- "Our emphasis on the propaganda purposes of our emancipation program must remain secret, and from time to time you will have to deny it."

The Seven States Negro Emancipation Conference concluded on Thursday, May 23, ten days after it had begun. The recommendations of the Davis Administration, as relayed by Attorney General Judah Benjamin were found worthy and became the backbone of the policy recommended to the respective States. A press release that Thursday afternoon was received by numerous newspapermen and forwarded to newspapers all across North America and to important cities in Europe. Because it was a sensational story, it received prominent publicity. It seemed to be a worthwhile propaganda tool, affording the new Confederate Government significant elevation toward higher moral ground.

Mr. Lincoln, less than three years earlier, had suggested that complete peaceful emancipation of all Negroes would require more than one hundred years – you heard me right – 100 years. The Seven States Negro Emancipation Conference recommended, as a general but not concrete guide, 50 percent emancipated by 19 years (1880), 90 percent by 29 years (1890) and 100 percent by 39 years (1900). And the Conference stressed marriage, keeping families together and keeping children with their mothers through age 16. The Conference recommended a work-for-emancipation apprenticeship program whereby young men and women who worked for owners from age 16 to age 23, a period of 7 years, if married, would have earned the right to request to become free and independent themselves and also any young children belonging to the couple. If not yet married, the age advanced to 25 years, resulting in a 9 year program (the status of young children belonging to an unmarried female at the 9-year stage was not clearly defined). The objective was to strike a balance between allowing the owner to receive the monetary value of at least seven years of work while also ensuring that the newly freed person of color was well trained and capable of successful independent living.

The delegates from five of the seven States also recommended that a limited number of adult Colored men be inducted into their respective State Militia. These men could be either free or slave. If slave, the owner was, of course, involved in the process. A slave who successfully supported his fellow militia men in peace and in war was promised emancipation by the thirty-sixth month of his service as would his wife and children. A free Colored man could also designate his wife and children to be emancipated by the thirty-sixth month should any be slaves. Colored men in the militia were to be armed and trained fighters, integrated into militia units in such a way that they were evenly distributed among the ranks. No Colored man could become an officer. Colored men were to be a small minority, representing not more than seven percent of troops (it was suggested that Louisiana allow up to ten percent). The Conference realized that White people would object to militia units made up entirely of Colored Men – to ensure proper behavior Colored men should be a small minority in the unit to which each man was assigned.

The Confederate Secret Service Infiltrates the Northern Mind

While the various Confederate States considered how to deal with the recommendations of the Seven States Negro Emancipation Conference, rapid progress was made in recruiting the 400 families (2,000 individuals) needed for the first emancipation phase – a propaganda action – and their relocation into the Republican states to the north. Within two weeks, secretly and without press coverage, by June 6, over one hundred newly-emancipated families from Louisiana, Mississippi, and Alabama were aboard steamboats moving north up the Mississippi and Tennessee rivers to Illinois and into the Ohio River and on to Ohio and Pennsylvania, and scores more were aboard steamships moving north up the Atlantic coast from Charleston and Savannah toward Massachusetts and New York. Agents in the Confederate Secret Service helped the groups move safely into new locations where they could settle down. Of European ancestry, each agent helped groups stay away from unnecessary public view and had handy papers showing the people in the groups were slaves being escorted into Canada or some other deception. The object was to get the groups settled within the targeted State before the commotion began. The typical family was a husband and wife and three children. The typical group was two families. The typical racial composition of recruits was nearly pure African ancestry, for it was considered helpful if the Negroes moving north were clearly African in appearance. However, a group leader was, on occasion, a man of mixed race with a noticeable European component in his ancestry. The agent brought money to allow each group to purchase a horse and wagon and some tools, and to buy food for two months. They brought clothing and blankets with them. But the summer weather was most helpful. These volunteers were brave people. They were moving into hostile regions in defiance of laws that excluded free people of African ancestry from taking up residence. They were pretending to be just passing through as persons bonded to an owner as long as that deception worked. Of course, they had been emancipated in exchange for volunteering for this Secret Service assignment, but that was their secret. As the weeks and months went by, some would suffer harsh treatment. Some would be robbed of everything they owned. Some women would be raped and some men would be killed, but the losses would not be nearly as bad as some had feared. In confronting these obstacles, the recruits showed immense courage, of which numerous monuments existing today throughout the participating States now testify. The Secret Service agents and the brief training the newly emancipated received before boarding the steamboats and steamships, and additionally while aboard, had been very helpful. Their presence in the North sparked controversies in many places and, after two or three months, news of such events became worrisome to many citizens of the Northern States. They were debating the question: "If we force the Confederates back under the Federal Government, will that not open the way for a million Blacks to come north and settle in our communities? If we just let the Confederates go, can we not easily exclude Blacks from our States?" [51]

The Confederate Secret Service, under the able leadership of Attorney General Judah Benjamin with the full support of President Davis and members of his Cabinet, grew over the summer of 1861 into a large and influential organization with agents working assignments all across the Democrat-controlled States to the north and, most importantly, the Republican-controlled States beyond. By the end of the summer the roster of agents out in the field and on the move who were working full time at their craft exceeded 1,000, and those who had lived and worked in their

---

[51] In truthful history free Blacks were excluded from settling in most northern States. They were excluded by State laws, and State constitutions. As a result, the presence of the volunteers in our alternate history was designed to challenge those laws for propaganda purposes, and to make citizens in the North eager to let Confederates go in peace in exchange for the racial purity they sought within their State.

communities in the North for many years and were supporting the cause on a part-time basis, gathering information and disseminating propaganda, could never be counted, but surely exceeded 5,000. Many of these agents were women. And many of these agents and their supporting contacts were of full or partial African ancestry, which was most helpful since Republicans, by their nature, never suspected Negroes of being capable of working as secret agents, and many of these agents were from Louisiana with easy access to steamboat travel as far north as Wisconsin and as far east at Pennsylvania. Many spoke French or broken French which afforded important cover in communications, especially in written communication further confused by being put down in code. Substantial rewards were promised to Colored agents. If slave, they would be emancipated, along with family members. If free, they would be given money to enable the purchase of land or to improve their living standards.

The work of Secret Service agents and their contacts was particularly influential with Democrat political activists, with people living in the North who had relatives in the South, and with newspapermen looking for a good story. Through these channels, the State Republican parties stretching from Pennsylvania westward lost considerable influence and the peace movement grew strength. From time to time during the summer of 1861, the Lincoln Administration and cooperative Republican governors thought they were close to justifying a large call-up of State militia, only to shy away and wait for a better excuse, for the threat of another massive wave of State secessions loomed large.

Virginia, North Carolina, Tennessee and Arkansas at the Ready to Secede

Since February 1861, the Virginia Secession Convention had remained at the ready to vote on a three-day notice. The Maryland legislature, only on temporary recess, had a Secession bill out of committee and on the floor with defined districts for each Delegate (matched the Maryland House of Representatives districts) and in many of these districts, voters had selected their Delegates through local election processes. Kentucky, under the guidance of Democrat Governor Beriah Magoffin, was pursuing the same strategy as Maryland, but was further along in selecting Delegates. By August, Governor Magoffin believed he could orchestrate Kentucky Secession through the Convention process in 10 days and through a final vote by the people 10 days later. Except for Louisville, sentiment for secession seemed to have strong support in Kentucky if amplified by a military attack on a seceded State. The Governor of Missouri, Democrat Claiborne Jackson, was eager to advance secession and viewed the only obstacle in his way to be the large German immigrant population that had arrived in St. Louis during the 1850's. The fledgling Missouri Republican Party (although only of significance in St. Louis) had been unusually effective in organizing the Germans of that city into a paramilitary force which had cowed many long-time residents, most of those being of the Southern culture. But agents in the Confederate Secret Service, selected for their skill in speaking German, were making good progress in breaking up the political union between Republican leaders and German leaders, ensuring that Confederate peace propaganda was effectively delivered in the city. In North Carolina, Tennessee and Arkansas, secession conventions had previously met and adjourned. But, the governors of all three States had called special summer sessions of their state legislatures to authorize each of those secession conventions to reconvene in the event the Lincoln Administration called for a military attack on sister States to the South. Democrat North Carolina Governor John Ellis was authorized to convene his state's convention, as were Democrat Tennessee Governor Isham Harris and Democrat Arkansas Governor Henry Rector. So the threat of imminent secession of Virginia, Kentucky, Missouri, North Carolina, Tennessee and Arkansas weighed heavily on the minds of Republican leaders in the Lincoln Administration. Of the eight Democrat-controlled states, only Maryland and little Delaware looked doubtful for secession if provoked. [52]

Confederates Assure Free Use of the Mississippi and Tennessee River

A major aspect of the Confederate peace propaganda was assurance that the Mississippi and Tennessee rivers would be open for steamboat traffic between the Confederacy and the United States. And as every week came and went it was more obvious to people along the Mississippi, Tennessee, Ohio and Missouri rivers that steamboat travel was unimpeded. [53] News in this regard was most influential in St. Louis, Evansville, Louisville, Cincinnati and Wheeling. Furthermore, the Confederate Government had set up steamboat checkpoints near the Mississippi-Tennessee state boundary to quickly inspect cargo and write up cargo manifests to be forwarded to Montgomery and to Washington City. Similar checkpoints were set up where railroads crossed the border. The Lincoln Administration was invited to also man import-export stations at these checkpoints, but throughout the summer, President Lincoln persisted in his fabrication that the Confederate Government did not exist. So the forwarded cargo manifests were only filed away in Washington City. In Montgomery, to support the Confederate peace

---

[52] The history of the threats of secession by Virginia, Kentucky, Missouri, North Carolina, Tennessee and Arkansas rather accurately reflects truthful history, as does the lesser likelihood of secession by Delaware and Maryland.

[53] In truthful history, prior to Lincoln's proclamation of war, free navigation of the Mississippi River was assured by the Davis Administration and ignored by Republicans.

propaganda program, they were totaled up and issued as press releases to newspapers both north and south. The Confederacy did not charge any tax on goods moving south through these river and railroad checkpoints, and the delay for inspection only took about one hour on average.

Confederate Defensive Preparations – James Eads, John Ericsson and Cornelius DeLamater

Considerable progress was made during the summer in strengthening the capability of the Confederate States to defend against military attack. We first examine the efforts to strengthen defense against gunboat attacks from the north.

With the help of Pierre Lafitte, James Buchanan Eads [54] of Missouri was recruited in early May to contribute his remarkable ability toward the best Confederate defenses on the Mississippi and Tennessee rivers and to design and oversee construction of Confederate iron-clad gunboats of the most advanced designs.

Eads, operating under a contract with the Confederate Government, relocated his operations to Commerce, Mississippi and to Baton Rouge, Louisiana. From his St. Louis facility and other smaller facilities in Missouri he brought south his salvage boats and his equipment and tooling. Commerce was a small river town 45 miles south of Memphis, and Baton Rouge was a thriving city with considerable manufacturing capability. Furthermore, his knowledge of older steamboats available for sale and steam engines and other critical equipment was very useful in the direction of a sizable purchase program along the upper Mississippi River and the Ohio River. [55]

But James Eads did not have to work alone in pursuit of the river-defense goals of the Confederacy, for he had the help of John Ericsson. Ericsson was a Swedish-American inventor and noted mechanical and marine engineer. Recruited in 1939 by Captain Robert Stockton of the United States Navy, Ericsson moved to New York City to design a steam-powered warship

---

[54] Born in 1820 in Lawrenceburg, Indiana, on the banks of the Ohio River, just west of Cincinnati, Ohio, Eads had moved west with his parents to St. Louis, Missouri, where he grew up and remained. He was a self-trained engineer who had become wealthy salvaging boats that had sunk along the Mississippi River. He invented a diving bell with which he walked the river bottom, setting up rigging for salvage recoveries. And he knew the river better than even the best steamboat pilots, and river knowledge was a valuable skill indeed, as many wrecks had occurred over the past 40 years, since the beginning of steamboat transport.

[55] In truthful history, the Lincoln Administration successfully won over Eads to design and build iron-clad gunboats for the Federal invasion down the Tennessee and Mississippi rivers, and these Eads gunboats – of superior design and rapidly manufactured by his company – contributed greatly to Federal victories in that theater of war.

for the United States navy that utilized his twin screw propeller technology and other improvements. He was 36 years old. [56]   Three years later, the navy sloop he designed, *USS Princeton*, was launched.   The *Princeton* was a technical success, winning a speed trial in 1843, beating the paddle-wheel steamer, *SS Great Western* – then considered the fastest steamer afloat. However, the celebration was cut short when one of the two big guns on the *USS Princeton* exploded during a test firing demonstration – a most unfortunate event since aboard the ship at the time was President John Tyler, Secretary of State Abel P. Upshur and Secretary of the Navy Thomas Gilmer. Although President Tyler escaped injury, the gun barrel explosion killed Upshur, Gilmer and six navy men.   Captain Stockton blamed the failure of the gun on engineer Ericsson and made every attempt to avoid personal responsibility.   But the facts of the matter pointed the finger at Stockton, for the main gun, still intact, had been designed by Ericsson with iron bands to re-enforce the barrel.   A second gun, the one that exploded, had been designed by Captain Stockton.   It was Stockton's gun that was inadequate.   Although the gun's explosion was unrelated to the ship upon which it was mounted, the United States Navy declined to pursue construction of more warships driven by screw propellers.   And, clever at Navy politics, Stockton's career advanced. [57]   Meanwhile, John Ericsson's career declined. [58]

But John Ericsson remained in New York and continued to work closely with a successful industrialist, Cornelius DeLamater – a relationship that advanced Ericsson's practical knowledge concerning all aspects of foundry operations and metal fabrication.   By 1857, DeLamater Iron Works

---

[56] Born in 1803 in Sweden, John Ericsson had, as a young man, developed impressive skills in surveying and mechanical design.   In 1826, at age 23, he had moved to England where he excelled in naval design – especially the screw propeller, which was to emerge as the replacement for the large paddle wheel.   He had also become expert at steam engine applications and iron-clad battleship design.

[57] You have been reading truthful history.   Captain Stockton's navy career continued upward.   He rose in rank to Commodore and played a leading role in the conquest of the Mexican state, Alta Californio, which became the American state of California, of which he was military governor in 1846-1847.   He was elected to the United States Senate as a Democrat from his home state of New Jersey in 1851, but resigned in 1853 to pursue a private career.

[58] The American navy distanced itself from Ericsson and designs based on the screw propeller – an emotional and illogical decision since the explosion had nothing to do with the warship's propulsion.   Meanwhile, Ericsson looked elsewhere for applications for his advanced naval technology.   In 1854 he presented Napoleon III of France with drawings of an iron-clad armored battle ship with a dome-shaped gun tower.   Although the French government "praised the work," it declined to build Ericsson's battle ship.

was a very large operation, proficient at all aspects of iron fabrication, with hundreds of skilled employees. [59]

At the same time that Pierre Lafitte was recruiting James Eads in St. Louis, two other agents in the Confederate Secret Service were in New York City recruiting naval engineer John Ericsson to work alongside Eads and were seeking to transform Cornelius DeLamater's iron works into a dedicated production facility to work full time secretly filling orders for the Confederacy. Ericsson was easily won over to the cause of the Confederate States, for he was still smarting over how he had been mistreated by Captain John Stockton of the United States Navy, and how it seemed so unfair that Stockton's career had advanced to great heights while his had been "brutally suppressed." Ericsson accepted a generous salary to leave New York and work with James Eads.

It took the Confederate agents a bit longer to win the cooperation of Cornclius DeLamater. He and wife Ruth, married for 17 years, had five daughters and one son. His focus had been on family and advancing metals technology, using his business skills and mechanical engineering skills to advantage. DeLamater was a good man. In hopes of winning his cooperation, the agents explained:

- The seceded States just wanted to be independent, but zealots in the Republican Party were maneuvering to launch a war to prevent it

- The stronger the Confederate defenses, the more likely would be a peaceful separation.

- The Confederate Government would present to both DeLamater and Ericsson opportunities to advance the technologies at which both are so proficient, unleashing their skills for the whole world to see.

Persuaded, DeLamater accepted handsome fees for entering into a secret cost-plus contract with the Confederate Government to supply future orders for a variety of items in sufficient volume to fully occupy his facility and its work force. A deal was struck and DeLamater began expediting the

---

[59] Born in 1821 near the Hudson River, half-way between New York City and Albany, Cornelius DeLamater had moved to New York City with his parents at age 3. He began work at age 16 in a small iron foundry in the city that was named Phoenix Iron Works -- "little more than a blacksmith shop" – learning the business from the ground up. Soon after John Ericsson had arrived in New York City in 1839, he became friends with DeLamater and looked to Phoenix Iron Works to produce most everything he designed. At age 20, DeLamater and his cousin Peter Hogg bought the business, changed the name and continued expanding it. Then, four years later, in 1857, Hogg retired and the business became DeLamater Iron Works. This history of DeLamater and his New York City iron works is truthful.

completion of orders on the books and clearing the slate for anticipated orders from the Confederacy. A secret book of accounts was set up so that men working on Confederate orders were unaware of the true customer. In a sidebar agreement, DeLamater agreed to let the Confederate agents recruit ten percent of his workforce, along with their tools, for jobs within the Confederacy, replacing them with a like number from the Confederacy in need of training in metals technology. A turnover every two months was thought about right. Yes, bringing skilled men into expanding Confederate metal working facilities was just as important as bringing in finished goods. Many of the items manufactured for the Confederacy were components for machining tools, shipped separately, but when assembled in the South, the finished assembly was ready for use in production of firearms, steam engines, etc. Most notable were hand presses designed for resizing brass casings from spent bullets, for it was very important that the brass casings be retained and recycled in the field.

At the same time, Ericsson packed into two bags his clothes and into four crates his engineering resource papers, calculations, designs and notes of all kinds and set out to board a steamer headed to New Orleans. He would be along-side James Eads by early June, and by late-June, the two experts would have a completed design for the Confederate River Defender Gunboat. [60] The revolutionary river craft would be a swift iron-clad gunboat suitable for

---

[60] The Confederate River Defender Gunboat was made of three hulls connected at the top but looking like three large canoes when viewed from below the water. By this method, the design ensured a stable platform for accurate firing and a fast speed. The starboard hull held one forward-facing cannon as did the leeward hull. The propulsion system was an Ericsson design, powered by one steam engine in the center hull, which drove a twin-drive-train gear box with two power takeoffs. The gear box contained two drive trains, each with a manual clutch, a forward gear and a reverse gear and a power takeoff shaft which sloped slightly into the water and drove the attached propeller. Stated another way the craft had one steam engine, one twin-drive-train gear box and two propellers, one between the center hull and the starboard hull, and one between the center hull and the leeward hull. The smokestack presented a very small target for the enemy —it was only 3 feet tall and contained a steam-driven fan to provide a forced draft at the firebox (a manual hand crank got the fire started and, once a head of steam was attained, the fan's steam turbine drove the fan). The deck on top was flat and iron-clad at critical points to deflect incoming artillery projectiles, especially from out in front of the craft, for it would normally be in chase mode. The craft had a draft of 3 feet and a height above the water line of 7 feet. The overall width was 20 feet and the overall length was 60 feet. The guns were aimed by steering the craft directly toward the enemy using a captain's cross-hair sight. With two guns in operation, a round could be fired every 45 seconds. The gunboat was designed to work very well during one-on-one engagements with the enemy, but it could find itself in dire straits if forced to fight off a pack of several enemy gunboats. But that was to be avoided and the fast speed of the gunboat, and its ability to turn around "on a dime" and rapidly flee to safety would prove very effective at the task to which it would be assigned. A favorite attack tactic would be to let the enemy pass by while hiding along the riverbank, then pursue and attack while chasing the enemy downriver, hopefully an enemy in a state of panic.

chasing down and sinking any iron-clad gunboat the Federals might build and bring downriver. The focus would be on compact size, high speed, a low profile, shallow draft, good stability to ensure gunnery accuracy, and two rifled cannon with armor-piercing projectiles and good maneuverability. This revolutionary riverboat would be a shallow-draft, tri-hull design capable of superior pursuit and pin-point firing precision. Eads stayed close at hand directing construction, but Ericsson traveled to Baton Rouge, Montgomery, Savannah and elsewhere as needed to facilitate procurement of parts. When built, the resulting Eads-Ericsson craft would be a sight to behold.

During the summer Eads, taking advantage of his diving bell technology, identified sites on the Mississippi River where snags could be moved into place to concentrate river traffic to narrow passages below which Confederate mines could be laid. A Confederate agent remarked, "Since James Eads is clearly the most skillful man in North America when it comes to removing snags from the river and salvaging wrecks sunk in the river, surely he will be the best at planting snags and mines in the river to sink boats coming down the river." Mines were built at armories in the Confederacy and shipped to Eads to be ready for deployment in the river bed if an invasion force threatened. [61] These mines were designed to be anchored to the river bottom, rest just below the water surface and explode when struck by a steamboat.

The coal torpedo and was also a significant weapon in the hands of Secret Service agents. These weapons were bombs designed to be inadvertently tossed into the fire under steamboat boilers. In one torpedo design, gunpowder and a fuse were built into iron castings made to look like a lump of black coal. The coal torpedo was particularly resistant to deterioration in rainy weather. The torpedoes were taken north to safe houses where Confederate agents could get to them when needed and toss them onto coal piles to be taken by crew onto steamboats. Eventually there would be a huge blast, the boiler would burst and the steamboat would quickly sink.

While Eads and his men pursued advance their work, and while Secret Service agents pursued their goals, the Confederate Army was working to set up artillery to repulse invaders coming downriver. Guns were coming in from purchases made in Europe, and some from islands in the Caribbean were purchased cheaply and brought in for overhaul.

---

[61] The mine was activated when a man in a rowboat pulled the pin connected by a rope to a float. It would then explode when hit. When no longer needed, the mine could be raised to the surface by pulling a second rope and be defused. Sights on the river bank permitted locating every mine by triangulation.

The Summer of 1861, Confederate Strategic Plans Advance while, to the North, Democrats and Secret Service agents Agitate for Peace and Republicans Flounder.

During the summer of 1861 Confederate agents traveled widely in the manufacturing regions of the northern States, recruiting skilled workmen to take good paying jobs in the South and purchasing metal-working equipment to equip southern shops. Target industries were weapons manufacturing and steam engine manufacturing. Further west, agents sought used steamboats suitable for renovation and purchased them when they could. These were loaded with important equipment and supplies and towed downstream to mooring sites near Commerce and Baton Rouge.

Furthermore, by mid-summer, it was apparent to the Republican Leadership in Washington City that they could not be confident of achieving a majority vote in the Federal House or the Federal Senate in favor of a military invasion of the seceded States. The Confederate propaganda campaign had achieved great success within four neighboring States – Virginia, North Carolina, Tennessee and Arkansas – success in each State at building a majority consensus to bring all resources to bear on building a well-armed State militia and in establishing a State Constitutional Convention empowered to proclaim secession at a moment's notice. Further north, in Delaware, Maryland, Kentucky and Missouri, public opinion was firmly against approval in Congress of military action against the seceded states. These eight States, represented in Washington City by 16 Senators and 57 Representatives, were firmly opposed to military action. Maybe Representative Francis Blair, Jr. in Missouri would vote for military action without provocation, but hardly anyone else. Provocation was the issue at hand. Without some sort of military attack upon Federals by at least a few Confederates, public opinion **against** going to war was gaining strength, month by month.

Agitation in most northern States over the summertime arrival of a few families of newly emancipated Negroes added to the problems besetting Republicans – it was harder to demonize southern States people over slavery when northern States were in an uproar over the arrival of a few families of newly emancipated negroes – it was harder to counter Peace Democrats who explained that Negroes would be barred from coming north if they lived in a separate country, a recognized Confederate country. The Abolitionists' higher moral authority was beginning to crumble as passions focused on Exclusionism and Deportationism.

In the Federal Senate, Republicans had started out in March with 29 Republicans versus 24 Democrats and one (1) American Party fellow from Maryland. But, Republican Senator Ed Baker of Oregon had died in an accident and the Oregon Governor, himself a Democrat and opposed to going to war, had appointed a peace Democrat to fill the seat. [62]

That dropped the Republican strength to 28, only 2 more than required to win the "war" vote. But, several Republican Senators – representing states where citizens were becoming more and more opposed to war – were publicly advocating against military invasion. Most notable of this group was Martin Wilkerson of Minnesota and Preston King of New York.

The situation in the Federal House, from the perspective of the Lincoln Administration, was even more troubling. The House was made up of 108 Republicans, 71 Democrats and 27 fence sitters, called "Unionists", "Unconditional Unionists", "Conditional Unionists", or members of the American Party, or whatever. These "27 third party" people were neither officially Democrats nor Republicans, but they were, with few exceptions, opposed to going to war without a provocation – an armed attack of some sort by Confederates against Federals. So Republicans had a caucus of 108 in a House of 206 seats. That meant they needed 103 votes to win a "go to war" vote in the House. But the prospects of losing the support of at least 12 Republicans without provocation was deemed likely and the prospects of gaining the support of even one Democrat was remote at best. Only a few, if any votes from the 27 "third party" Representatives could be counted on. Vote counts by Republican leaders pointed to defections of as many as 7 of their own from New York, as many as 6 from Pennsylvania, as many as 6 from Ohio, and as many as 3 each from Indiana, Illinois, and Wisconsin. [63]

So, by mid-summer, when Republican leaders estimated their strength in a Senate vote to "go to war" and a House vote to "go to war," they continued to postpone any thought of calling for a Special Session of Congress – postpone the call in hopes that somehow, given more time, they could illicit the coveted "first shot" from some undisciplined Confederates.

The Lincoln Paternity Scandal Weakens Support for President Lincoln

Also, by mid-summer, the Confederate Secret Service had constructed a rather complete story about Abraham Lincoln's paternity. His mother was Nancy Hanks of North Carolina – everyone agreed on that. But his father was probably not Nancy's husband, Thomas Lincoln of Kentucky. Secret Service

---

[62] Senator Ed Baker's death is a deviation from true history. He did die, but in battle, and battle had not yet begun.

[63] The vote estimates in the Senate and House are truthful tabulations of Republican strength except for Senator Baker. And in truthful history President Lincoln believed accomplishing his "first shot" political strategy was essential.

agents had considerable testimony from witnesses in western North Carolina and eastern Kentucky supporting the argument that the President's father was Abraham Enloe of the mountains of western North Carolina, who lived in a valley south of the Great Smokey Mountains. Agents obtained evidence that contradicted Lincoln's "Thomas is my father " claim as he had written it in the Bible record he had worked up with his step-mother, Sarah Bush Johnston Lincoln, during a visit to her home a year or two after Thomas Lincoln had died. That would be about 1852 or 1853, about the time Abe sensed new political opportunities may be opening up. Furthermore, Confederate agents aimed to shame Abe for not attending claimed father Tom Lincoln's funeral in 1851. Lincoln's contrived Bible record smelled like a cover-up, and Abe's former law partner, Billy Herndon, was tricked into suggesting the same by a clever agent who approached him during May. Agents had consulted a small group of informed and important people in Kentucky who supported the claim that Abe was two years old at the time of the marriage – stating that Thomas Lincoln was his step-father, not his real father. So in the legal lingo of the time, Abraham Lincoln was a bastard. The true story of the President's father, birth date and place of birth was thus:

> The President's mother, Nancy Hanks, was born in Virginia to Lucy Hanks and an unmarried man, Michael Tanner, Junior. When Nancy was about 2, Michael and his married brother took Nancy to mid-state North Carolina. When Nancy was about 4, Lucy took her to near Charlotte, North Carolina to live with her "Uncle Dicky." Lucy soon moved to Kentucky where she later married. At age 13, Nancy left "Uncle Dicky" to make her own way. She took a job working for Abraham Enloe's young family as an "orphan" house servant. About the time Nancy reached 20, she and Mr. Enloe became sexually involved and she became pregnant.

> Now, Abraham Enloe was a very successful man of notable talents and a community leader. He and his wife were raising a very large family and he had, except for the Nancy affair, been faithful. Nancy gave birth to a baby she name Abraham, after his true father. When Nancy and baby Abe became able to travel, Mr. Enloe took them on horseback to Kentucky, where he arranged for her mother, Lucy, and Lucy's husband to help them get settled there. A year later, Mr. Enloe arranged for a young Kentuckian, Thomas Lincoln, to accept Nancy for a wife, and help raise his son, little Abe in Kentucky. Mr. Enloe gave Thomas a valuable wedding present to seal the deal. When Thomas and Nancy married, there was this little 2-year-old boy "running around"

named Abraham. So the President was illegitimate and about 4 years older than he claimed to be. [64]

The Crisis Accelerates Toward a Showdown in the Federal Congress: September, October and November of 1861

With the Republican Party severely weaken by the propaganda campaign of the Confederate Secret Service and the continuing non-threatening posture of Confederates – including going along with paying a few tariffs at Fort Sumter and unimpeded navigation of the Mississippi River – Republicans were struggling to commandeer the votes needed to win support in the Federal House and Senate for a declaration of war. Once declared, it would be necessary to subjugate Democrat-controlled States that might not have seceded, but be uncooperative, such as would be the likely response in Delaware and Maryland, and maybe Kentucky, and maybe Missouri. After military action in the remaining Democrat States was accomplished, then, and only then, the Federal military could proceed south upon an invasion of the Seceded States and conquer their respective governments and the united Confederate military that would be supporting them.

Space in this work does not permit reporting on the political threats, intrigues and deal-making that surrounded the politics in the Northern States during September, October and November of 1861. Suffice it to say, the efforts were persistent and emotions swung back and forth. And those emotions frequently surged, here and there, as newly emancipated Negro families arrived and sparked Exclusionist anger. And politics worked against the war-hawks in the Republican Party as regularly-scheduled 1861 October-November local and State elections were voted upon and Democrats, more often than not, regained offices previously lost to the Republican advance that had begun in force in 1856 and become so dominant by late 1860.

That said, we now advance to the opening of the Federal House and Senate at the regular scheduled session on December 2, 1861.

---

[64] In truthful history there is a real likelihood that President Lincoln's father was not his mother's husband. It is likely that he was four years older than claimed, and that the real father was Abraham Enloe of western North Carolina. The best overall presentation of this subject is found in *Rebirthing Lincoln, a Biography*, by the author of the book you are presently reading, Howard Ray White (2021). For other documentation several sources are suggested, should you wish to inquire further – The Bostic Lincoln Center Museum (Bostic, NC); *The Genesis of Lincoln*, by James Harrison Cathey (1899); *Lincoln*, by David Herbert Donald (1995); *Lincoln's Herndon*, by David Herbert Donald (1948); *The Eugenics of Lincoln*, by James Caswell Coggins (1940); *Herndon's Informants, and Statements about Abraham Lincoln*, by Douglas Wilson and Rodney Davis (1998); and The Tarheel Lincoln, by Jerry Goodnight and Richard Eller (2003).

Diary note by Carlos Cespedes said, "The five guests are now firm for the overnight sailing trip this weekend. Andrew Houston has good blue water sailing experience and I have named him first mate. Chris Memminger's family has all of those great thoroughbred race horses; so I asked him to join us in hopes he might someday return the favor and invite me to visit his stables and practice tracks. Three girls are joining us three fellows: Emma Lunalilo is so great on the water, I just had to ask her. Marie Saint Martin is such great fun, so I gave her the nod. Conchita Rezanov rounds out the crew. Andrew Houston insisted that I include her and, since he is first mate, I felt I could not refuse. I think Andrew has an eye for Conchita. Why not? She is gorgeous!"

Diary note by Andrew Houston said, "Will be going sailing with Carlos off the coast of Cuba Saturday. Honored to be asked. Will be six of us altogether. I will be the only crew with sailing experience, so Carlos wants me to be his First Mate. His family has a nice sailboat. Very worthy for overnight ocean sailing. He knows the waters and the boat very well and has handled it in stormy seas. Feel good about that. But will have to be on our toes, we will be responsible for three women and one man who have never done this. Conchita is among the girls. To be honest, dear diary, it is the beautiful Conchita on that sailboat that excites me the most."

Diary note by Conchita Rezanov said, "Going to be flying to Cuba with Carlos and four others Saturday morning. Family company has its own jet. Goodness. Is there that much money in sugar cane? Hope to find out. . . . . Concerning this morning's lecture, I am reflecting on a parallel in strategies. The original seven Confederate States refused to ignite a war by firing on Fort Sumter. From that point the strategy was Passive Resistance. My family's Russian America refused to reveal that huge gold deposit in Nome, allowing our region of North America to win independence at a cheap price that we could afford to pay. Deception is often key to success in political maneuvers and often preferable to war."

Book 1, Chapter 6, Day 5 – After Debate the US Congress Chooses War – Virginia, North Carolina, Tennessee and Arkansas Secede and Federal Preparations for War Intensify – Class Lecture, Friday, June 10, 2011

Professor Davis continued with his lectures as soon as the twelve essayists for the Sewanee Project were seated and ready to listen. We will hear Professor Davis' lecture as if we were also sitting in the room.

December 1861: Federal Congress Convenes

The Federal Congress in Washington City did not begin deliberations until the customary first Monday in December, this being December 2, 1861, for President Lincoln and Republican leaders had failed to secure agreement during the Spring, Summer or Fall on calling a Special Session. The Lincoln Administration, the Republican Governors and the Republican leadership in the House and Senate, had been too unsure that, without a provocative "incident," they could get a majority "go to war" vote during a Special Session, so none had been called. Hopes that a few Confederates would be provoked into armed conflict had never materialized, quite to the amazement of Republican leaders.

At the opening of the December secession, the House elected Galusha Grow, Republican of Pennsylvania, as Speaker. The following history about that election of Speaker explains the difficulties Republicans faced in rallying Democrats go to war:

> Although the Republican majority assured a Republican would become Speaker, a "so-called" Republican from St. Louis, Missouri had been given unusual attention. His name was Frank Blair, his brother was Montgomery Blair of Maryland, Postmaster General in the Lincoln Administration, and the father of the two brothers was Francis Blair of Maryland – a newspaperman and historically a king-maker in the politics of Washington City, going all the way back to the days of Andrew Jackson. You see, the senior Blair saw a great political future for his sons if they became prominent Republicans with roots in Southern States, a very rare breed indeed. Some Republicans saw in Blair a propaganda tool with which they could entice Democrats to cooperate with their militant goals.

But Representative Thaddeus Stevens of Pennsylvania had wanted no "pretend Republican" as Speaker – he wanted a "true Republican." He nominated Galusha Grow. Schuyler Colfax of Indiana was also nominated. After a few ballots, Grow was elected. And, as a thank you, Speaker Grow named Thaddeus Stevens as Chairman of the powerful House Ways and

Means Committee, a post from which he would exert almost dictatorial power over the workings of the Federal House. [65]

President Lincoln Asks Congress for Funding and Troops for an Invasion of the Confederacy

The following day Abe Lincoln delivered a written Message to Congress, which was read by the Clerk to a joint assembly of the House and Senate. In his message, Lincoln argued several points of Constitutional law, each designed to twist the truth to support his request for 400,000 men and $4,000,000 for a military invasion of the seceded States.

Regarding the legality of State Secession, Lincoln's Message cast off as "ingenious sophism" the crucial constitutional legal debate over whether the crisis was one of "secession" or "rebellion." He alleged, "The sophism itself is, that any State may, consistently with the United States Constitution, and therefore, lawfully and peacefully, withdraw from the United States Federal Government without the consent of the Federal Government or of any other State. The little disguise that the supposed right is to be exercised only for just cause, themselves to be the sole judge of its justice, is too thin to merit any notice." So it was with this condescending subterfuge that Lincoln brushed aside the most important issue before the State governments and the Federal Government – namely, the constitutional and legal arguments permitting and/or disallowing State secession.

And to underscore his "sophism" argument, Lincoln alleged that "no one of our States, except Texas, ever was sovereign." This was a blatant lie, clearly contrary to the Treaty of Paris where Great Britain had granted independence to each of the former thirteen colonies, each named individually, without mention of any sort of government over any of them. The reality had been that the thirteen Sovereign States, subsequently following their individual independences, had gathered together had and formed a "Continental Congress," later a "Confederation Congress" and afterward a "Federal Government" – in all cases delegating to each sequential new general government only those powers not retained by the States or by the people, which were many, indeed.

And, finally, it must be reported that Lincoln totally ignored the sections of the Federal Constitution that prohibited the Federal Government or a State from taking military action against a State.

---

[65] This history of the Blair's, Colfax, Grow and Stevens is truthful with respect to the men but Grow's election as Speaker of the House and Stevens' appointment as Chairman of the Ways and Means Committee took place in the Special session of Congress called by President Lincoln for July 4, 1861. They remained in those positions for several years.

Had Lincoln sought a ruling or an opinion from the United States Supreme Court regarding State secession? Of course not! From the first day in office, the Administration's policy had been to ignore the Supreme Court as if it did not exist. Lincoln had the United States Army. The Justices only had papers. [66]

Regarding the support for secession among the citizens of a seceded State, Lincoln's Message alleged that, "It may well be questioned whether there is today, a majority of the legally qualified voters of any State, except for perhaps South Carolina, in favor of leaving the United States. There is much reason to believe that voting men who favor remaining in the United States are the majority in many, if not in every other one, of the so-called Seceded States. The contrary has not been demonstrated in any one of them." Of course Lincoln did not intend to suggest that Congress ought to investigate the level of support for secession then existing in the Seceded States. He wanted the question left dangling, for the truth of the issue was that support for secession had not declined from the days of the initial, fully adequate, votes. [67]

Regarding the lack of military conflict between April and the present month of December, Lincoln's Message submitted that, "The leaders over this so-called secession, what is more properly termed rebellion, and so-called Peace Democrats of the North, are clever like the copperhead snake." [68] He went on to explain that the copperhead will hide in the brush, in the wood-pile, even in the grass, seemingly peaceful and of no threat. But anger it too much, come too close to it, and it will strike at you with deadly force. It is still hiding there, for we are not yet too close. But our restraint has persisted far longer than it ought to have. We cannot allow this copperhead snake to give birth to more of its kind, moving ever closer to destroying this government, the government of the United States of America, the greatest government the world has ever known. For far too long we have delayed a decision to deal firmly with the copperhead. That is why, today, I am humbly asking you for the authority and the means of properly dealing with this rebellion crisis.

So President Lincoln asked the Federal House and Senate to approve a bill that called for a military build-up to a 400,000-man army, manned primarily by State militiamen, to be funded by $4,000,000, a huge sum in those

---

[66] Lincoln's insistence on ignoring the Supreme Court is truth history.

[67] These Lincoln quotes of Lincoln's Message to Congress are truthful history, but had occurred in the July 1861 Special Secession.

[68] In truthful history Republicans called Peace Democrats "Copperheads." However Lincoln made no mention of "Copperheads" in his message to Congress in July or December 1861.

days, which would require creative financing. He also asked for $1,000,000 and 1,000 men to fund and operate a stronger navy. He asked the Federal House and Senate to confirm in him the power to, as Commander-in-Chief, use whatever military action deemed necessary to secure the return of the seceded States to their "proper place" under the Federal Government, will all rights restored, subject to Congressional review. He appealed to the Democrat-controlled States to remain loyal to the Federal Government, to avoid being swept up into the secession fallacy, and thereby avoid facing the hard hand of the Federal military. For, he sternly warned, "The power of which I am asking from you, Representatives and Senators, shall be exercised to the fullest extent necessary to ensure loyalty among existing States and to return to the fold those which have already seceded." To Democrat-controlled Delaware, Maryland, Virginia, North Carolina, Kentucky, Tennessee, Missouri and Arkansas, Lincoln warned, with the strongest of words:

> "My friends of these Southern States, let us remain cooperative brethren who have in the past, can today, and will surely in the days of our joint glorious future, settle our differences, as they occasionally arise, with the just rule of law and the fair debate of our respective representatives."

The next day, Thaddeus Stevens of Pennsylvania, Chairman of the House Ways and Means Committee, organized his committeemen and began the process of drafting a bill to give President Lincoln the military force and legal authority he sought for an invasion of the seceded States and to exercise control over non-cooperative States, organizations, newspapers and individuals. Stevens had decided to put all issues under his committee, thereby avoiding going through the three House committees that would normally be responsible for drafting the bills envisioned: the Military Affairs and Militia Committee, the Naval Affairs Committee and the Judiciary Committee. Similar Bills were being drafted in three Senate Committees: the Senate Military Affairs and Militia Committee, under Chairman Henry Wilson of Massachusetts; the Senate Naval Affairs Committee, under Chairman John Hales of New Hampshire, and the Senate Judiciary Committee, under Lyman Trumbull of Illinois.

Confederates Intensify their Propaganda Campaign in the North, Prepare for More Secessions

Meanwhile, telegraph lines to Montgomery, to the State capitals of every Confederate State, and to the State capitals of Virginia, North Carolina, Kentucky, Tennessee, Missouri and Arkansas, were busy relaying messages that were steadily coming down from Washington City in order to keep Democrat leaders across the South fully informed about the situation in the

Federal House and Senate. As it turned out, a Democrat on each of the four committees named above had agreed to feed news of committee activity to a Confederate contact each night. The telegraph messages were nightly converted to code in Washington City and decoded at Montgomery and at each state capital. Coding and decoding was the responsibility of the Confederate Secret Service, which had agents posted at all necessary locations.

Meanwhile, the Governors of the six States most likely to secede — Virginia, North Carolina, Kentucky, Tennessee, Missouri and Arkansas — quietly called each State's respective standing secession convention to assemble within a few days to be on hand at each capital for the purpose of acquiring news and pondering response to anticipated threats. Publicity about the reconvening of these secession conventions was downplayed, but people in the know realized that each of the above-mentioned States had machinery in place to declare state secession within hours of hearing news of a vote in the Federal House and Senate to authorize, man and fund a military invasion of the Seceded states. For the most part, news out of Washington City was interpreted in Montgomery and then relayed by telegraph to the six participating State capitals -- Judah Benjamin and his Secret Service people being primarily responsible for that task. In each State most likely to secede, militiamen were put on alert status and plans were made to seize Federal facilities and arms within moments following secession. Of particular importance were the plans to take over United States military facilities in Virginia, including the Norfolk Navy facility and the armory at Harper's Ferry.

Information was flowing south, as just mentioned, but also flowing north. The Confederacy increased its propaganda messaging to newspapers and influential people in the northern States, especially the metropolitan region in south-east New York State, in certain parts of Pennsylvania where Democrats still had influence, and in southern Ohio, southern Indiana and southern Illinois. Intensified propaganda hammered six key messages. The propaganda:

1. Proved that major allegations in Abe Lincoln's Message to Congress were historically false;

2. Pointed to the peaceful behavior of the people within the Confederacy;

3. Alleged that Republicans planned to round up and deport all Negroes living in the United States (those not seceded), thereby creating an all-white society north of the Confederate States, and declared that a forced deportation plan of that magnitude to be extremely cruel and a violation of the teachings of Jesus Christ;

4. Pointed out that the Confederacy had already begun laying plans for gradual emancipation and in-state jobs for Negroes – a far kinder and more economical plan – to begin after normal diplomatic relations were established between Washington City and Montgomery;

5. Promised to continue tax-free freight passage up the Mississippi and Tennessee rivers and cooperation in collecting Federal import taxes at all Confederate border check-points;

6. Warned that, historically, the people of the Southern States, living in a vast region that was extremely difficult to occupy by military force, had been victorious in all military conflicts encountered in settling the land from the Atlantic out to Texas and would inflict a heavy death toll upon any military or naval attack from the north, accompanied by great weeping by the parents, widows and children of the Federal dead. [69]

In spite of the Confederate propaganda campaign in key areas of the Republican North, militant bills moved forward through the Federal House and Senate. On December 10 Thad Stevens presented his committee's bill to the House floor. It was in three parts – army/militia, navy and judicial. This set the stage for a raging debate between Republicans and Democrats, much of it covered by newspapers in the northern States. Democrats offered amendments, some of which stuck.

On the face of it, there seemed no way for the House to win passage. There were 206 members in the House, meaning 104 votes were needed to pass a bill. Republicans numbered 108, but several were clearly against military invasion. Reluctance to vote with the leadership was particularly strong in south-east New York State, and parts of Pennsylvania, southern Ohio, southern Indiana and southern Illinois.

Over on the Senate side, the bills from the three committees were all introduced on December 12. Immediately afterward, all three were read on the floor, a motion was made and carried that they be combined into one omnibus bill and debated and voted upon as one item. As in the House, debate raged on in the Senate, complete with extensive newspaper coverage in the Northern states.

News continued to flow rapidly by telegraph to Montgomery and the capitals of each Southern State, coded messages no longer being needed.

---

[69] In truthful history the military death toll among Federals, from 1861 to 1865, would exceed that of Confederates.

The Federal Congress Authorizes an Invasion of the Confederacy

As Christmas loomed ahead on the calendar, pressure increased to cut off submission of amendments and further debate. It was late Friday, December 20 when the Senate finally passed its omnibus militant authorization bill. The Senate vote was 28 for and 26 against. The House continued through 3 pm Saturday before it passed its militant authorization bill, which had been spearheaded by Thaddeus Stevens. The House vote was 104 to 102. Clearly, at both sides of the Capitol, several Republican politicians had chosen to avoid being recorded as casting a yea vote if their participation was not essential to passage. Members of a Conference Committee were named immediately after the votes were cast and that group began its deliberations on Monday morning, December 23. A compromise version of the militant authorization bill was agreed upon on at 11:30 on the morning of Tuesday, December 24. By 4 in the afternoon, Representatives and Senators were in their seats and votes were called for in each chamber. The final bill was approved by almost the same small margin as before. But the compromise bill had to be drawn up into an official document for President Lincoln's signature. That was completed on the day after Christmas. In a small ceremony in the White House, with major Republican leaders in the House and Senate at his side, Lincoln signed the bill. It was called the Act to Recover Seceded States by Military Force If Necessary. Final amendments had sharpened the language to avoid the term Rebel or Rebellion. Democrats claimed a small victory in defining the title of the bill and a more significant victory in trimming the size of the military force a little from that requested by Lincoln.

The final bill authorized a military force of 350,000 men, that being a combination of regular army personnel and militiamen operating under the direction of regular army commanders. The final bill authorized an increase of 800 men for the navy. Funds authorized amounted to $3,500,000 for the army and militia and $800,000 for the navy. These funds were to be utilized over fourteen months -- from January 1, 1862 to February 28, 1863. States pondering secession were assured that they and their people would be treated with utmost consideration and respect if participants remained loyal to the Federal Government, even if militia from their region were allowed to not participate in the Federal military action against sister states and, or, seceded states. It was only demanded of states remaining loyal that it was imperative that they allow unobstructed passage and encampment of Federal troops and supportive militia throughout their boundaries, with full access to local supplies, all of which were to be paid for immediately. However, when disloyalty or obstruction was encountered by individuals or groups within states that were officially loyal, Federal forces and Federal courts were authorized to deal with such renegades as harshly as needed to abate such activities. The judicial portion of the final bill directed the Executive to use normal state and Federal courts in all loyal states and to limit martial law. But martial law was appropriate in states that had seceded or where resistance was on such a large scale that its courts were overwhelmed in dealing with the violence. The Executive was directed to permit a free and open dialog in states which remained officially loyal, guaranteeing freedom of speech and publication for all newspapers, pamphleteers, public speakers, etc. Freedom of religious thought was guaranteed. Destruction of private or public property by Federal forces or supportive militia within loyal states was to be avoided wherever possible, and where it did occur, was to be compensated from a $500,000 fund created in the bill to dispense such monies.

Persons of African ancestry were to be excluded from Federal forces and supportive militia, including laborers, and those that were slaves were to remain under their lawful owners, including those who tried to run away to a Northern state where slavery was prohibited.

Seceded states were warned that resistance to occupation by Federal forces and supportive militia would be dealt with harshly according to the rules of nations at war. Even so, the people in seceded states, who offered no resistance to Federal forces or supportive militia were assured that their private property would not be intentionally destroyed, although, in the heat of battle and troop movements, destruction of private property and civilian life was often unavoidable, and there would be no compensation for such destruction. Surrendering troops of seceded states were to be confined in prisoner of war camps until loyalty and peaceful behavior was achieved throughout the seceded states. Most importantly, the bill encouraged seceded states to reconsider their defiant attitudes at the outset, and avoid bloodshed by laying down their arms and returning to their homes. Persons that offered no resistance and gave evidence of returning to peaceful civilian life would not be molested or retained in prisoner of war camps. The bill assured the nation that the object of the military campaign was to secure loyalty in the seceded states and, although the national debate over how to deal with slavery had seriously divided Republicans and Democrats and prompted some to resort to secession, it was not, repeat not, the object of this military campaign to interfere in any way with the laws and practice of slavery in any state where it is presently allowed. [70]

The time for the signing of the bill could not have been worse for the Lincoln Administration. Many men in the Federal army and navy were on

---

[70] In truthful history, the Republican campaign to conquer the Seceded States began with assurances that there was to be no interference in the institution of slavery anywhere.

leave for Christmas and New Years and the militiamen in the northern states were likewise scattered and not easily organized for action.

Across the North, news of the Declaration of War against the Seceded States was met with protests in regions in many locations, especially where the Republican Party was not in control. The Confederate Secret Service and the Department of Confederate Communication had been very effective in sowing the seeds of discontent within the North. The population realized they were under no threat of attack and that Confederates only wanted to be left alone. They saw no purpose in a crusade for emancipation, or in risking life to win a rich man's war to force the South to pay Federal taxes on imported goods. Two days after news of war arrived, the New York *World*, the major Democrat paper in the city and in the North, published a cartoon captioned "Lying Lincoln and Papa," which portrayed two very tall, thin men of similar appearance: on the left Abraham Lincoln in his exceptionally tall hat with a hint of the White House behind him; on the right the older Abraham Enloe with white beard and a hint of tall mountains behind him. [71]

There was a riot in Democrat-dominated New York City against going to war and more than 40 Colored People were chased, harassed, and beaten, three of them suffering death (some protestors blamed Colored People for causing secession and war). The Confederate Secret Service and the Confederate Department of Communication had made important progress in building resistance in the North for a war against the South. Often citizens would protest against State militia as they gathered to drill, parade or get into railroad cars headed south. There was shouting, and spitting, thrown rocks and eggs during such events. [72]

Public support for the war during January and February 1862 was strongest in the Northeast, but even there a religious segment of the population strongly argued against it. Such opposition to the war would be telling when Federal troops were advancing through the Confederate States, first facing little resistance, then, very suddenly finding themselves isolated from the North and in a fight for their lives. Many Federal soldiers, untested in war and feeling no obligation to risk death on the battlefield, looked for the first opportunity to find shelter and then surrender.

---

[71] In truthful history the *New York World* was produced and published in New York City from 1860 to 1876 by Manton Marble. It was the major Democrat newspaper in the North. Thereafter ownership changed twice before the paper was acquired in 1883 by Joseph Pulitzer, the famous founder of the Pulitzer Prize for excellence in journalism.

[72] In truthful history, in July 1863, in response to the widespread Federal draft of immigrants, a horrific riot and race war erupted in Democrat-dominated New York City and lasted four days. The *New York Tribune* would estimate that the violence resulted in 350 deaths (mostly peaceful blacks), 650 injuries, and $1,500,000 in property damage.

Not so in the Southern states.

More Southern States Secede and Execute Plans to Defend Themselves

As soon as the preliminary House and Senate military bills had passed, that being by Saturday, December 21, news of the event and the essential content of the language of those bills arrived in Montgomery and the capitals of all of the Southern states. Democrat Governors in Virginia, North Carolina, Kentucky, Tennessee, Missouri and Arkansas quietly instructed the standing secession conventions to meet and begin deliberations on the proper response for each.

By the day that President Lincoln signed the "Act to Recover Seceded States by Military Force If Necessary", that being Thursday, December 26, the Virginia Secession Convention had declared its state to be seceded. This was all that was needed to authorize the Virginia State militia to overwhelm the thin force at Harper's Ferry and begin the process of loading arms and arms manufacturing machinery on railroad cars and wagons for transport south toward the heart of the state. The Virginians were so swift with their work that over 90 percent of the useful arms, ammunition and equipment was headed south within 48 hours. Likewise at the navy facility at Norfolk, Virginia militiamen and skilled seamen had taken control of the facility to an extent necessary to prevent retreating Federal navy personnel from destroying much of what was left behind. Furthermore, about twenty percent of the Federal navy men then stationed at Norfolk refused to retreat, resigned on the spot, and joined in support of the Virginians. Those resignations were further evidence of the effectiveness of the Confederate propaganda campaign. [73]

The North Carolina Secession Convention declared its State to be seceded on Friday, December 27. The following day, December 28, secession conventions in Tennessee and Arkansas declared their States seceded. In these regions, as well, militiamen were successful in taking control of Federal armories and military facilities within their boundaries.

After stormy debate, the Missouri Secession Convention voted to secede on Thursday, January 2. But unlike elsewhere among the seceded states, Missouri was entering into something approaching a civil war within its boundaries. In St. Louis, the large population of German immigrants was generally opposed to secession, although operatives of the Confederate Secret Service had persuaded about one fourth of that population to forego opposing their State government. Federals successfully defended their armory in St.

---

[73] In truthful history, Federals set fires that destroyed most of the arms and machinery at Harper's Ferry and set fire to much of the naval ships and equipment at Norfolk.

Louis and within a few days moved to Illinois all military supplies within the facility. [74]

Secession in Kentucky would never be fully achieved. The Kentucky Secession Convention remained in session through January 31 without reaching a decision to secede, but it did insist on a neutrality for its state, and demanded that Federal forces moving against Tennessee stay clear of Kentucky land except for three defined in-state corridors: 1) the railroad from Louisville to Nashville, 2) the Cumberland River, and, 3) the Tennessee River. Kentuckians were tied so firmly to the Ohio River and so many Kentucky relatives lived in southern Ohio, southern Indiana and southern Illinois that leaving the United States was too difficult for too many. [75]

At Charleston and Pensacola, Federals possessed staging areas from which they could mount major offensives toward midstate farms, but multiple military advances southward from the north would be chosen by the Lincoln Administration as the preferred line of attack. So militaries at Charleston and Pensacola were ordered to stand firm, collect import taxes, but not advance.

The Confederate Plan to Appear Non-Threatening

The Jefferson Davis Administration had discouraged secession in Maryland and Delaware for two reasons. First, every effort was being made to make the Confederate States appear in the North to be a non-threatening country. Peaceful co-existence and friendly cooperation was the image to be projected, and this was stressed in the propaganda campaign, which was proving more effective by the day. Second, because Delaware was only three counties, a pip-squeak of a state, it was of no use to the Confederacy and, logically speaking, did not merit two Senators anyway. Third, Maryland needed to remain in the United States to give free access from the North to the capital, Washington City. Maryland was a strangely shaped State, too. Baltimore was surely important, but the eastern shore was remote and the narrow strip of western Maryland, squeezed between Virginia and Pennsylvania, was an awkward administration. The population was quite mixed, and only the region around Baltimore and the Eastern Shore held a population that matched well culturally with the people of the Southern States.

---

[74] In truthful history, Missouri struggled but did not secede. All arms in the Federal armory at St. Louis were removed to Illinois. Missourians suffered a civil war within their State.

[75] This account of Kentucky follows truthful history except defined corridors for military advance did not exist. In truth many Kentuckians went south to Tennessee and joined the Confederate military.

In fact, there was already talk in Montgomery about keeping Confederate troops well south of Washington City, providing a buffer zone that would not be defended. This was considered another tactic to appear non-threatening. But there was one more idea behind it. A defensive plan called "Envelopment" was gaining traction in military defense discussions. The Davis Administration was adopting a military tactic focused on capturing large Federal armies in hopes Confederates could negotiate peace and permanent boundaries in exchange for releasing tens of thousands of captured Federals. The "Envelopment" strategy might succeed if Confederates were to be facing multiple Federal armies advancing southward simultaneously, on the same time schedule. Under this joint invasion threat, Confederates could pretend weakness as they retreated southward while working to cut off supplies from the Federal rear and disrupting communications between invading armies and Washington City. And this Confederate retreat and appearance of weakness could be coordinated among the defending armies so as to tighten the "Envelopment" noose around each opposing army at about the same time, forcing surrender of most of the men in each invading army, all within a short span of only a few days, mostly before the Lincoln Administration realized what had happened.

Although classical military strategists viewed the Confederate's "Envelopment" plan very difficult to accomplish, there was little reasonable alternative – prospects for victory in a protracted, several-years-long war looked worse. You see, strategists in Montgomery believed that fighting, retreating, fighting, retreating, again and again would only draw out the conflict, promote escalation, on and on, season after season, until the more populous North overwhelmed the South with its much greater resources in manpower and weaponry. Quick, decisive military movements, aimed at taking captive and imprisoning large groups of Federals – the "Envelopment" plan – was thought the best way to force Republicans to sue for peaceful acceptance of State Secession.

Men of Color Are Recruited into State Militia

You will recall encouragement at the Seven States Emancipation Conference to induct Negro men into the militia of the various Confederate States. By September, 1861 this idea was being rapidly accepted, first this State, then that State, and the idea snowballed. Those inducted were fighting men, armed and trained. The rule requiring that they be evenly dispersed among the militia units, always only as a small minority, seemed to assure the White population that it need not worry about a Nat Turner style rebellion surfacing. Some who volunteered were free Colored men who simply wanted to show their patriotism. Others were free Colored men who planned to stay in their unit through thick and thin with expectation of gaining emancipation for a wife, and/or children who remained bonded. But more than half were owned as slaves and had struck an agreement with their owner to volunteer to serve with the owner's knowledge that success would result in emancipation for the volunteer and in many cases for his wife and children, but additional family emancipations varied depending on the State and on other factors. Often a volunteer Colored man was a close friend of a White volunteer – for example the farmer's son and one of his slaves of about the same age. But it was strictly forbidden that the Colored volunteer behave as a servant to the White man. In fact, in a few instances, where servant-master behavior was discovered, the White man was discharged, but the Colored man was retained under the presumption that he had been a victim of abuse. The presence of Colored men in Confederate State militia units was known to Republicans when Congress voted for a military invasion. And some historians believe the presence of Black Militiamen caused some Congressmen and Senators to worry they were again losing the high moral ground. For example, visions of White militiamen of Massachusetts fighting against and killing Virginia militiamen in a crusade to emancipate Black slaves in Virginia made far less sense when some of the Virginia militiamen were Blacks. Massachusetts Abolitionists were struggling to win there case for a holy crusade against evil Southerners.

January through April 1862: the Federal Military Buildup and Confederate Preparations

From the beginning of January, the Lincoln Administration began a massive military buildup aimed at conquering each of the seceded states. The Administration had vowed to not recognize the existence of the Confederate Government in Montgomery, but, instead, recognize what had been the state government of each seceded state and, by conquering the capital of each seceded state, force each seceded government to repudiate secession, dissolved itself, and demand that its officials pledge allegiance to the government of the United States – that completed, a new "Reconstructed" government for each state would be created under Federal oversight. The capitals were expected to surrender to Federal forces in the following sequence: Richmond, Nashville, Baton Rouge, Raleigh, Jackson, Columbia, Little Rock, Milledgeville (Georgia), Montgomery, Tallahassee and Austin.

A State-by-State conquest strategy had evolved from contentious debate among members of President Lincoln's Cabinet, certain leading Republican governors, and certain Senators and Representatives. Some warned that it would be better to carefully probe Confederate defenses before committing to a massive coordinated invasion by Federal armies that was aimed at all of the state capitals. But others, fearing Confederate defenders would just shift about to concentrate on one invasion force, then another, advocated a simultaneous attack on all fronts to prevent Confederates from shifting about and concentrating forces. Lincoln made the final decision: it would be a coordinated simultaneous attack aimed at all state capitals. Why not just aim to conquer the Confederate capital in Montgomery? Well, Lincoln decided against that, asserting:

> "Since I will not recognize the so called Confederate States of America as a valid government, I will not force it to surrender and hand over control of each seceded state. Therefore, I firmly argue that the object of our simultaneous attack should be the conquest of and submission of the capital of each seceded state. If we simply go after the Confederate Government it will retreat from Montgomery when threatened and transform itself into a ghost on the run. We will not go chasing a ghost pretending to be a government that does not legally exist." Furthermore, Lincoln declared, "each Federal army is to be assigned the mission of progressing along its designated path from capital to capital until every capital on its assigned list has been conquered and has submitted to Federal rule."

Although state capitals could pretend to become mobile to escape subjugation, mobility was much easier for the Confederate capital at Montgomery. The Montgomery capital was newly established and Confederates stressed State Sovereignty over National Sovereignty. Republicans figured they could capture one state capital after another and steamroll toward victory, giving no special priority to far-off Montgomery, Alabama.

The missions, as agreed to and endorsed by Lincoln, were to be achieved by five major military divisions:

1. The mission of the Federal's Virginia and Carolinas Division was to force the surrender of three state capitals and the surrender of the corresponding state governments of Virginia, North Carolina and South Carolina.

2. The mission of the Federal's Tennessee and Georgia Division was to force the surrender of two state capitals and the surrender of the corresponding state governments of Tennessee and Georgia.

3. The mission of the Federal's Alabama and Florida Division was to force the surrender of two state capitals and the surrender of the corresponding state governments of Alabama and Florida.

4. The mission of the Federal's Mississippi River Division was to force the surrender of two state capitals and the surrender of the corresponding state governments of Louisiana and Mississippi.

5. The mission of the Federal's Missouri, Arkansas and Texas Division was to subdue the Missouri secessionists and their pro-secession government by occupying the state capital of Jefferson City,

and then proceed south to force the surrender of two state capitals and the surrender of the corresponding state governments of Arkansas and Texas.

A very small percentage of Federal soldiers and cavalry were from the Democrat States of Delaware, Maryland, Kentucky and Missouri. Furthermore, in Ohio, Indiana and Illinois, the rural southern counties contributed few volunteers, for, in those three States, the northern Ohio River Valley, stretching up to the headwaters of tributary rivers and streams, had been mostly settled by people of the Southern Culture and they wanted no part in a war against kinfolk. When looking at the origin of troops gathering to invade the Confederate States, historians would remark how clearly the battles were between fighting men of the Northern Culture and fighting men of the Southern Culture. [76]

Notwithstanding Lincoln's refusal to recognize or negotiate with the Confederate Government, everyone knew that the great prize would be given to whichever division conquered the Confederate capital at Montgomery, Alabama – the seat of power for the Confederate States of America. And a sense of a competitive race was hard to avoid, for Lincoln's military division to first conquer Montgomery would surely win the greatest glory. Thus, the urge to move rapidly toward objectives, in hopes of winning the big race, so to speak, was to contribute to reckless overreaching by Federal commanders and to facilitate Confederate efforts to lure the Federals into traps where tens of thousands could be forced to surrender. Although, the Tennessee and Florida Division ought to first reach Montgomery, if its progress were to be delayed, the glory of that accomplishment could be grasped by the Tennessee and Georgia Division, following its conquest of Milledgeville; by the Mississippi River Division, following its conquest of Jackson, or by the Virginia and Carolinas Division, following its conquest of Columbia. On the other hand, if the Navy could follow up its success at New Orleans with a successful attack at Mobile, enough troops might be brought to that landing site to mount a successful attack on Montgomery. Most likely, two or more of these Divisions might join forces outside of Montgomery at the same time to create a huge unstoppable force and to share in the glory.

By this Time Confederate Defensive Capability, a Guarded Secret, was Greatly Improved

Fortunately for the Confederacy, the Lincoln Administration was unaware of the Confederate strategy of "Retreat, Envelopment and Capture"

---

[76] In truthful history the battles were primarily between fighting men of the Northern Culture and fighting men of the Southern Culture.

and of improvements gained in gunboat technology, repeating firearm and metallic cartridge technology, and in an expanded cavalry and enhanced troop mobility. There were rumors in the North of Confederate weapons advancements, but Republican leaders refused to believe them, thinking it to be one more example of Confederate propaganda. We only have space to present an overview of the status of these advancements as of April, 1862, the month that Confederates anticipated they would soon be facing the invasion of the Federal divisions.

Confederate Progress Concerning Enhanced Gunboat Technology

Unlike the weakening Northern resolve to support a war of invasion, determination in the South for a patriotic and hard-fighting defense was continuing to gain strength. In parallel with the Department of Confederate Communication's campaign to weaken Northern resolve to fight a war of invasion, was its campaign to strengthen Southern resolve to defend mightily against an invasion should it come. And Southern resolve to mightily defend was encouraged by knowledge of Confederate advances in weaponry.

The program of gunboat design and construction overseen by James Eads and John Ericsson was highly successful. By mid-April 1862, ten Confederate River Defender Gunboats had been produced in construction yards at Commerce, Mississippi and Baton Rouge, Louisiana. Toward that goal Caleb Huse had found ready success in purchasing steam engines in England, Scotland and Europe, many arriving before March 1862, in ample time for installation in nearly-completed boats. He also acquired rifled artillery guns of high muzzle velocity and penetration capability for mounting on Eads' gunboats. The Confederate gunboats (see earlier footnote for design details) would prove very effective in crippling invading Federal gunboats advancing down the Mississippi River. With the help of the stores of hundreds of coal torpedoes and firewood torpedoes positioned along the Mississippi River and dispensed by the Confederate Secret Service, and with the help of James Eads' river snags and river mines, the Federal advance down the Mississippi would hopefully be halted not far downstream from Memphis, and halted not far upstream from New Orleans.

Confederate Progress Concerning Repeating Firearms and Metallic Cartridges

Caleb Huse, acting as a purchasing agent for the Confederate Government had been especially successful in support of Josiah Gorgas' efforts to bring in large quantities of repeating rifles and introduce metallic cartridge technology. Huse and his team had acquired much of this improved technology weaponry from the United States, Great Britain, Belgium, the

German States and France. Cotton was paying for it all, with credit liberally extended. Some of the acquisitions from Caleb Huse's team are presented in the following paragraphs.

Invented by Dr. Jean Alexander LeMat, of New Orleans, repeating short-range LeMat 9-shot pistols were produced in large quantities for use by Confederate cavalrymen. This unusual weapon, utilizing a 9-shot revolving cylinder for bullets, was capable of firing solid bullets out of the rifled pistol barrel or one round of "buckshot" out of an adjacent larger bore "sawed-off-shotgun" barrel. Either paper cartridges or brass cartridges could be used in the LeMat pistol. A cavalryman could fire this weapon at the rate of 9 rounds per minute, adding great firepower to a cavalry charge. About half of the LeMat pistols would be produced in France under a Caleb Huse contract, the remaining being produced in the Confederate States with imported machine tools. [77] By mid-April 1862, Confederates had received and distributed 15,000 LeMat 9-shot pistols, enough for every tenth cavalryman and many army officers.

Another important multi-shot pistol acquired in large numbers was the 1861 Confederate revolver pistol, which was produced under a Caleb Huse contract in Belgium. This revolver-style six-shot pistol was based on the design of Casimir Lefaucheux, a French gunsmith – a designed upgraded to use an improved brass cartridge, pioneered by Benjamin Houllier. [78] By mid-April 1862 Confederates had received and distributed 25,000 Lefaucheux-design six-shot pistols, enough for every seventh cavalryman and most officers.

Confederates also applied revolving cylinder technology in the design of five-shot rifles. History would prove that the Confederate 1861 revolver rifle was, in its day, the most advanced rifle in existence. A large order for parts needed to assemble the rifle had been placed by Caleb Huse and filled by factories in Belgium, France and England. This rifle was capable of firing five rounds at a one and a half minute reload cycle. In five minutes, the time it would take an attacking army, on the run, to cover one-half mile, the Confederate rifle could deliver 15 well-aimed defensive rounds per man. By mid-April 1862, the five Confederate divisions had on hand 60,000 Confederate 1861 revolving rifles, enough to give a 5-shot rifle to every third soldier in a unit, and they would be distributed in that manner.

---

[77] By the way, Dr. LeMat was a cousin to Confederate General P. G. T. Beauregard.

[78] This revolver-style, six-shot pistol was used by Confederate cavalrymen and also by ground troops when a backup sidearm was needed in close-range combat. By April 1862, 25,000 of these state-of-the-art pistols were in use by Confederate troops.

This multi-shot rifle and the two multi-shot pistols mentioned above used cartridges, each made of a brass shell into which was inserted a copper-encapsulated compression cap, black powder and the lead bullet. The Confederate brass cartridge contained a copper-encapsulated compression cap, only slightly smaller in diameter than the shell, followed by black powder, then the lead bullet (cylindrical at the base, tapered in the middle and pointed at the top). By mid-April 1862, Confederates had obtained and distributed 5,000,000 brass-style cartridges designed to fit the revolving weapons, enough for 50 shots from each corresponding weapon. This represented a lot of new-technology firepower, but Confederates were cautioned to use bullets carefully to maximize kills and minimize wasted ammo. But empty brass shells were to be kept where possible and used in field reloading presses to make new bullets. [79]

---

[79] The assembled cartridge was then gently compressed under a calibrated spring and then the top of the shell was crimped around the tapered part of the bullet to complete the job. Assembly was possible at armament factories and in the field – Confederates were required to collect in spent shell bags their spent shells so they could be reloaded at field cartridge reloading wagons which accompanied the divisions.

Most impressive was the 1861 Confederate 5-shot repeating rifle. The footnote below presents details. [80]

Confederate Progress Concerning Field Artillery

Confederates had also made impressive progress in improving field artillery. Confederate artillery batteries had gained key firepower through additions of three innovative acquisitions, all made possible by the months gained during the first 14 months of Lincoln's presidency.

---

[80] The 1861 Confederate 5-shot repeating rifle consisted of 10 parts, made to exacting tolerances at various factories. Ten percent of production was selected randomly and secretly assembled at two locations in Europe to verify tolerances. The remaining parts, labeled as machine parts, etc., were shipped loose to the Confederate States to be assembled and test-fired at the receiving end. The parts were:
1. The rifle barrel, rifled and lapped at the back end.
2. The rear stock, made of wood.
3. The barrel grip, made of wood.
4. The cylinder, bored through to receive five brass cartridges, then lapped at both faces to exacting tolerances.
5. The hammer and spring.
6. The trigger and spring (a very light, predictable pull on this trigger).
7. The cylinder pin, which held the cylinder in position and around which it rotated.
8. The cylinder ratchet lever, at the side used to quickly rotate the cylinder to the next bullet.
9. The cylinder compression screw, push plate and lever assembly, of three parts the screw, push plate and lever, to be cranked down just before firing in order to close the gap between the lapped cylinder face and the lapped barrel back face to a near-zero clearance, thereby producing a near-perfect gas seal. This solved the grave problem of gas blowback into the shooter's face that had prevented the success of the Colt revolving rifle of 1855 design.
10. The component housing, a metal casting to which was attached the barrel, the cylinder, the trigger and spring, the hammer and spring, the ratchet, the cylinder push plate and compression screw with lever, and of course, the wooded grip and stock.

The Confederate 1861 revolving rifle could fire five rounds in the following manner:
1. Take rifle off shoulder and prepare to advance cylinder, 2 seconds
2. Advance cylinder to next bullet, 2 seconds.
3. Compress cylinder, 2 seconds.
4. Pull back hammer, 2 seconds.
5. Raise to shoulder and take aim, 4 seconds.
6. Fire, 1 second.
   - Total time for a firing cycle, 13 seconds.
   - Rounds fired in one minute, between 4 and 5.

The rifle could be reloaded with five new rounds in the following manner:
1. Time to eject spent brass casings into recycle pouch, 6 seconds.
2. Time to insert five new brass cartridges, 10 seconds.
   - Total time for reloading, 16 seconds.

The Confederate horse-drawn 12-pounder Smoothbore Field Gun resembled the "Napoleon," a smoothbore gun-howitzer often cast of bronze, sometimes of iron. By mid-April 1862, Confederate divisions had on hand 500 of these guns, some obtained from Federal arsenals in seceded States, some from State militia companies, but most from France, purchased as used artillery and renovated in Confederate shops. [81]

The Confederate Pack-Transport 12-pounder Smoothbore Light Gun was much like the model 1841 "Mountain Howitzer" used in the war against Mexico. The barrel and carriage could be quickly separated and loaded upon two stout mules, one set up to carry the 220-pound gun, the other set up to carry the 280-pound carriage (consisting of the axle, two wheels, and the tongue). By April 1862, Confederate divisions had on hand 100 of these mule-transportable smoothbore guns. Some had been taken from Federal arsenals in seceded States; others had been produced in Mexico, England and France.[82]

Confederate Progress Concerning Enhanced Troop Mobility

First, Confederate military strategists wanted horses, lots of horses, both for cavalry and for pulling wagons and artillery batteries – the higher the percentage of fighting men who had access to horses, the better. Mules were also sought. The population of mules and asses in the Southern States (below the Maryland-Kentucky-Missouri northern boundary) totaled about 800,000, compared to only 330,000 above that boundary, so there was no way to quickly boost the mule population. On the other hand the corresponding horse population north of the boundary was 4.4 million, compared to only 1.7 million to the South. So Confederates looked to the North for added horsepower and lots of it. To that end, the Confederate Secret Service and patriotic men and organizations had been purchasing horses from beyond the Confederacy. Kentucky is worth mentioning. A horse provisioning network

---

[81] The Confederate horse-drawn 12-pounder Smoothbore Field Gun used a 2.5-pound charge of black powder and a 12-pound spherical solid shot for knocking down defensive breastworks at a distance of up to 1,600 yards (5 degree discharge angle), or an explosive shell of the same size to kill and wound enemy troops at long distances, or a canister of grape shot intended to spread out many iron balls like a shot-gun charge and kill and wound enemy troops at short distances. The gun and carriage weighed 2,500 pounds and, with ammunition limber attached, required a team of six horses for transport along roads or fields.

[82] The Confederate Pack-Transport 12-pounder Smoothbore Light Gun was cast of bronze, used a charge of 0.5 pounds of black powder and could fire explosive shells, spherical case and canister, but not the heavier solid 12-pound solid cannon ball. It was capable of delivering an explosive ordinance against enemy troops at a distance of up to 1,000 yards (5 degree discharge angle), and was very effective at short distances when firing at enemy troops with canister shot. The advantage of this gun was the ability to secretly transport it through woods and over trails and to surprise the enemy by firing upon him from camouflaged, concealed positions.

there, operating for Confederate interests and with Confederate money, had been scouring southern Ohio, southern Indiana and southern Illinois, buying all good animals available and bringing them into Kentucky. From there they were delivered south, some by steamboat, some by the Louisville and Nashville Railroad and some, actually most, by young Confederate men riding and leading groups of twenty or more animals along roads and trails into the Confederacy where they were placed on good pasture where found, ready to incorporate into Confederate military divisions. Horses were also procured from Pennsylvania. There was an axiom in play here – a good horse obtained from the North diminishes the future mobility of the Federal army. By November 1861, on the order of 100,000 good horses had been brought south into the Southern States, below the Maryland-Kentucky-Missouri northern boundary, easily sufficient to double the fraction of Confederates fighting as cavalry to just under one-third of fighting men.

Perhaps the most innovative horse-drawn item was the cavalry travois, and this clever device would prove very effective in carrying out rapid troop movements to and from battlefield positions, these being essential maneuvers to enable the capture of sizable armies. [83]

Many horse-drawn wagons had been procured from tradesmen to meet specific needs. In addition to caissons and wagons for artillery support and general-purpose freight wagons, there were cook wagons, covered ambulances and cartridge wagons, the most advance units being equipped with the tools and hand presses necessary to resize and reload spent brass

---

[83] The cavalry travois employed the concept of using the cavalryman's horse to rapidly relocate four armed foot soldiers in addition to the rider. To facilitate this ability, each cavalry horse was dressed out with straps across the chest and just below the saddle which did not interfere with normal cavalry functions, but to which could be quickly attached, on the left and on the right, the forward ends of the travois tow-poles. The travois tow-poles consisted of two saplings about twelve feet long that ran from the attachment at the horse, which was cushioned for comfort, to the ground behind. Two cross-poles ran from side to side, the lowest about a foot above the ground, the highest about three feet above the ground. In addition, a center pole ran from the forward cross-pole to the aft cross-pole to the ground. Two brace-poles were also incorporated, positioned in an "X" pattern to maintain the necessary travois shape. A three-inch-by-twelve-inch skid plate was carved and strapped to the bottom of each pole where it scooted along the ground. All seven poles were light and slightly flexible saplings of selected wood types allowing for toughness during use. A travois could be constructed in the field using a hatchet and knife to cut down and prepare the poles and strips of leather for binding. When needed, four foot soldiers could gather behind a cavalryman, tie a travois to the horse, sling their rifles across their backs, hop onto the bottom cross pole, hold onto the forward cross pole and be rapidly repositioned. Progress across open ground and roads was good. When encountering rough terrain, fences or small streams, the four riders could hop off in a second and run behind the horse, carrying the travois until the situation improved sufficiently to permit renewed riding. This maneuver was practiced often enough to make it effective and wagons containing fifty travois were part of an army's supply train.

shells. Another essential item was the horse-drawn forge wagon, a blacksmith forge on wheels. These were built in large numbers.

Federals Plan Five Major Coordinated Attacks for Early May, 1862

By the first of May, 1862, the Lincoln Administration had managed to recruit and organize the five major military divisions needed for the coordinated invasion of the Confederate States. Made up of state militia and Federal troops, the five Federal divisions had been strengthened to the following manpower levels, each organized under its division commander:

1. The Federal's Virginia and Carolina Division, gathered near Washington City, consisted of 130,000 men, of which 17,000 were cavalry – Irving McDowell of Ohio, commanding.

2. The Federal's Tennessee and Georgia Division, gathered at Franklin, Kentucky, consisted of 70,000 men, of which 9,000 were cavalry – William Rosecrans of Ohio, commanding.

3. The Federal's Alabama and Florida Division, gathered near Murray, Kentucky, consisted of 70,000 men, of which 9,000 were cavalry – Ulysses Grant of Ohio and Missouri, commanding.

4. The Federal's Mississippi River Division, gathered near Cairo and Mound City, Illinois, along with four armored gunboats, just finished at Rock Island, consisted of 40,000 men, of which 5,000 were cavalry – Don Carlos Buell of Ohio, commanding.

5. The organization of the Federal's Missouri, Arkansas and Texas Division had been slowed by the fighting in Missouri between the State militia and anti-secessionists. But, by the end of April, the State militia had been driven to the southern region of the state and the capital at Jefferson City was firmly in the control of anti-secessionists and their Federal backers. So, the Missouri, Arkansas and Texas Division, consisting of 40,000 men, of which 5,000 were cavalry, was prepared to move south to push resistance out of the state and then proceed into Arkansas, then Texas – John Fremont, with family ties to Missouri, commanding.

Prepared to Meet the Federal Attacks Were Five Confederate Divisions, Trained for Tactical Retreat, Envelopment and Capture

By the time that the five Federal divisions were in place just north of the Confederate boundaries, five Confederate divisions were positioned to entrap them at some strategic region along their path of advancement toward their respective State capitals objectives. The five Confederate divisions are now described, as of mid-April, 1862.

1. Positioned to entrap the Federal's Virginia and Carolinas division was a division of 80,000 Confederates, which included 25,000 cavalry – Division 1, Robert E. Lee of Virginia, commanding. [84] The strategy was to permit Federal advancement southward into Virginia along a route from Washington City toward Richmond, with entrapment and forced surrender of the bulk of the Federal forces planned before reaching the capital. In support would be irregular forces known as the Virginia State Rangers, such as the "Moccasin Rangers" led by Captain George Downs. They would be particularly effective at harassing and confusing the untested advancing Federal soldiers and their commanders. [85]

2. Positioned to entrap the Federal's Tennessee and Georgia division was a division of 60,000 Confederates, which included 20,000 cavalry – Division 2, Braxton Bragg of North Carolina, commanding. The strategy was to permit Federals to occupy the Tennessee capital, Nashville because it was too close to Kentucky to be defended. Afterward, the strategy was to retreat before advancing Federals hoping to entrap them near Tullahoma. As in Virginia, Irregular State Rangers would be involved in enabling the entrapment.

3. Positioned to entrap the Federal's Alabama and Florida division was a division of 55,000 Confederates, which included 18,000 cavalry – Division 3, Sidney Johnston of Kentucky and Texas, commanding. The strategy was to allow Federals to advance along the Tennessee River, through western Tennessee, because in that region surrender could not be forced; then to make a stand at Pittsburg Landing and there inflict significant damage to the troops and their supplies, forcing them eastward of their planned line of advance toward Corinth, Mississippi. Eventual capture was anticipated in northeast Mississippi or northwest Alabama, in the hill country south of the Tennessee River. Here irregular State Rangers would be engaged to ensure success.

4. Positioned to entrap the Federal's Mississippi River division somewhere along its descent down the Mississippi River was a division of 30,000 Confederates, 10,000 of them cavalry, plus a fleet of Confederate River Defender Gunboats designed by Eads and Ericsson and built by Eads' workforce in Mississippi – Division 4, Pierre

---

[84] In truthful history, Robert E. Lee had not, at the beginning of the Federal invasion of the Confederacy, achieved a rank high enough to merit the command described in our alternate history. But history does show he deserved to take high command.

[85] In truthful history, nine 75-man companies of the Virginia State Rangers were authorized by the Virginia General Assembly in March 1862. Captain George Downs led one company, known as the "Moccasin Rangers."

Beauregard of Louisiana, commanding. Success in entrapping Federals descending the Mississippi River was dependent on preventing the capture of New Orleans, a task relegated to the Confederate Navy, Confederate artillery, and teams of Confederate mine-laying experts.

5. Positioned to entrap the Federal's Missouri, Arkansas and Texas division was a division of 35,000 Confederates, 12,000 of them cavalry – Division 5, Sterling Price of Missouri, commanding. Capture was anticipated about half way between the Arkansas border and the capital city of Little Rock. Irregular State Rangers in Missouri and Arkansas would harass and confuse advancing Federals.

Since all but the Federal's Virginia and Carolinas Division were well west of Washington City, the Lincoln Administration had placed Henry Halleck over the four divisions that would be moving south through Kentucky and Missouri. So, Halleck, a seasoned military administrator, coordinated the efforts of Rosecrans, Grant, Buell and Fremont. But he was to remain rather far from the front lines, keep abreast of the situations by messengers and telegraph and take no part in battlefield decisions. Aware of this, Confederate Secret Service agents were active at intercepting messages going to Halleck and substituting misleading messages suggesting that the four advancing armies were proceeding as planned.

The Davis Administration organized its defensive command in a similar way. In Virginia and the Carolinas, Robert E. Lee was given full authority to direct all operations. But west of the mountains, where the greatest fighting was anticipated, overall coordination of the Confederate divisions was needed. That job was handed to Joe Johnston of Virginia, who, from a considerable distance beyond battlefield actions, and with good telegraph and express messenger support, stood ready to coordinate the efforts of Bragg, Sidney Johnston, Beauregard, and Price. The Confederate Secret Service, under Attorney General Judah Benjamin was responsible for maintaining telegraph communications to every state capital and gathering, analyzing and disseminating intelligence concerning troop strength, location and direction of movement. Furthermore, the Confederate Secret Service had developed a network of agents who spied on Federal activities, cut telegraph lines useful to Federals, repaired telegraph lines useful to Confederates, and distributed torpedoes.

Friday Evening Selected Diary Postings

Diary note by Chris Memminger said, "All set for trip to Cuba for overnight sailing adventure. Our airplane landed at the airport late afternoon today, just before sunset. Although a jet, it is capable of landing on short runways, like here at Sewanee. That capability fits our sugar company needs well. Plan to be flying away to Cuba at 8:00 am in the morning. Will have light breakfast in flight.

"The music get together this afternoon was great. I even hit a few licks of Guantanamera to give the group a feel for Cuban music. It was appreciated. Think that Allan Ross and I will play well together. He plays country and western well enough on his guitar. In fact, everyone in the group contributes. Professor Davis? That man can play that banjo."

Diary note by Professor Davis said, "I did not give much consideration to musical ability when choosing the members of the Sewanee Project. But we were lucky to be blessed with musicians: five of the twelve can contribute in pleasing ways. Good time this afternoon finding out how we can mesh as a group."

Diary note by Allen Ross said, "Hope the sailing group has fun and that all goes as planned for them this weekend. I gave Carlos six frozen bison steaks for the on-board meals Saturday night. He says the sailboat has an above deck charcoal grill. Those steaks ought to taste real good. Music get-together this afternoon encourages me to believe we five can really make music together. I cannot match Carlos on Guantanamera, but we can play together in country style. Liked Amanda's play on the piano. She can just about play by ear, but finds sheet music helpful. Marie is compiling a list of songs and will be downloading music for all of us so it will be available the next time we get together."

Book 1, Chapter 7, Days 6 and 7 – The First Weekend and Six
Go Sailing – Saturday and Sunday, June 11 and 12, 2011

Six of the twelve Sewanee Project Participants spent the weekend on a sailing trip out of Mantanzas, Cuba. The story of that trip fills the pages devoted to Saturday and Sunday, June 11 and 12, 2011. The host is Carlos Cespedes, skipper. The guests are participants Andrew Houston of South Texas, first mate, Emma Lunalilo of Hawaii, second mate, and crew Conchita Rezanov of Russian America and South California, Marie Saint Martin of New Orleans and Chris Memminger of South Carolina. We begin the story at the Sewanee Airport.

The Carlos Cespedes sailing party left the airport at 8 am Saturday, June 11, bound for Mantanzas, Cuba. All six were excited in anticipation of the overnight sailing trip that Carlos promised. They would be aboard the family 50-foot sailing yacht, *Independence*, named for the July 4, 1870 independence of Cuba from Spanish rule, led by great-great-great-grandfather Carlos de Céspedes.

Getting to Mantanzas looked to be just as exciting. The Wright Executive Six, a six-passenger jet, was fast, sleek and comfortable, owned by the Cespedes family sugar company.

The jet landed at the Mantanzas airport at 10 am. By one that afternoon the yacht was provisioned and skipper, mates and crew were furnished with a fine lunch at the marina café. By 1:30 they were departing the harbor under partly cloudy skies and moderate winds – good sailing weather. Carlos was skipper (some call it "captain"). Andrew Houston had previous experience crewing on ocean sailing yachts, so Carlos logically named him "first mate." Emma Lunalilo was second mate based on her significant ocean sailing experience and her expert swimming and surf board experience off Hawaii beaches. The other three were new to ocean sailing (otherwise known as "blue water sailing"). So they were "crew." Conchita Rezanov was athletic and a whiz on the tennis court, but not a sailor. Marie Saint Martin was considered the boat entertainer based on her singing experience. Andrew Houston has brought along is guitar to accompany her. Chris Memminger was the typical passenger – no experience at sailing, an average swimmer in pools and lakes, and quite comfortable on dry land with his thoroughbred horses. Good crew and passenger mix. Should be fun.

Under diesel power the beautiful sloop-rigged sailboat left the harbor as crew looked back at the receding landscape. Once fully clear of land, Carlos turned the bow into the wind and crew began raising the sails, which were luffing as they rose. First the 1,200 square foot mainsail unfurled from the roller boom as the head of the sail traveled up to the top of the 70-foot mast.

Then crew unfurled the jib sail that was rolled up on the spool that ran from the bow to a few feet short of the top of the mast. Carlos gave directions on how to set the main sheet (landlubbers call it a rope), which held the boom in position to enable the mainsail to best catch the wind, and the jib sheet, which held the jib sail in position to best catch the wind. That accomplished, Carlos cut off the engine and moved the wheel back to the right, setting the rudder to aim the sailboat toward the desired course.

Carlos set a course out of Mantanzas harbor due north so the crew could not complain that he was just a coast-line sailor. No, Carlos was a fine navigator, had all the charts and navigation aids, including radar and GPS, and was just fine on blue water north of Cuba, anywhere between Florida and South Texas.

The brisk 20 knot wind out of the west filled the sails and the sleek craft eagerly surged forward. "The wind is quite brisk," Carlos said. "Leave about two feet of sail rolled up on both main and jib. Do not extend it all out." Carlos gave first mate Andrew some instructions on trimming the two sails (winching in the main sheet and jib sheet just the right amount) to shape both sails to best advantage. That done, the crew found comfortable positions aboard the craft and settled in to enjoy the beautiful afternoon. It was exhilarating! The sailboat was heeled over quite a bit and crew was encouraged to mostly sit on the upwind side of the boat (the port side) so their weight would slightly serve to hold the boat a little more upright. Chris said he felt a bit seasick, so Emma gave him some ginger cookies and encouraged him to keep his mind off his queasiness and just look at the horizon. That seemed to help. The seas were choppy, but not rough. Four to five foot seas. Some waves breaking at the top. Just exhilarating. The waves were being pushed by the wind out of the west and the boat was sailing north, so, as each wave rested upon the port bow, the craft tilted further toward starboard and crew seated along the port side rose a foot or so, then fell about the same amount, then up again and down again, on and on. But the ginger cookies and Chris's focus on the horizon was allowing him to get by.

Carlos told everybody that time at the helm would be rotated every three hours. He would man it until 4 pm. Andrew would man it then until 7 pm. Emma would take it until 10 pm. Then Carlos would be on again from 10pm until 1am. Then Andrew would go at it again. Ocean traffic was not particularly busy, but all crew was encouraged to call out any vessel it spotted so the helmsman would be sure to know.

Soon after Andrew took the helm, Marie called out, "Get your Spanish guitar, Carlos, and let us have some music." With Marie's strong New Orleans-bred voice and the skipper's fine Cuban-bred guitar strumming, the sailors soon burst into song. Far out in the ocean, with no one else within sight, the six enjoyed being far away from the crowd and lost in themselves. "Michael, row your boat ashore" got the whole group singing along. When Carlos led off with a Cuban standard, Marie got the hang of it and away they went. Helmsman and crew joined in upon the singing of what is undeniably the most famous Confederate church hymn: "Say Brothers." You will find this one to be familiar:

> "Say brothers will you meet us; say brothers will you meet us; say brothers will you meet us; on Canaan's happy shore." Then came the refrain: "Glory, glory, hal-le-lu-jah; glory, glory, hal-le-lu-jah, glory, glory, hal-le-lu-jah, for ever, ever, more." Perhaps the most heartily sung song was "I wish I was in Dixie's Land."

The singing lasted a full hour until someone asked about setting out some drinks. Oops!

Skipper Carlos replied. Folks my voice is giving out a bit and I believe drinks are in order. However, as skipper I must say that, while we are under sail, out in the ocean, no one is allowed to have any beer or alcohol. That is my rule. Mixing drinking alcohol and sailing is too dangerous. Sorry. Groans were recalled as having been heard, but they were brief. Conchita and Emma went down below and prepared drinks for everyone: fresh lemonade, Coca-Cola's, and iced tea, plus some more ginger cookies for Chris, who was barely controlling his sea sickness.

At 7 pm Andrew turned the helm over to Emma. Time to prepare supper while daylight is available. Conchita and Marie descended into the galley area below and got the supper provisions out of the refrigerator. "Wow!," came the exclamation from the galley. "We have bison steaks for tonight. Where did they come from?"

Carlos confessed in little secret. "Well, mates and crew, as you know, Allen Ross's family has a huge herd of bison on the hoof back in Sequoyah. In fact, he is serving bison steaks to the other six of our group in Sewanee tonight. He wanted us to have some, so he packed six on ice and I snuck them on the airplane and into the provisions for us to have for our supper. Nice, don't you think?" All agreed. Along with the bison steaks, the sailors would be having Cuban sweet potatoes; lettuce, cucumber and tomato salad; Cuban melons; and, for desert, peach cobbler with vanilla ice cream. Carlos had already started baking the sweet potatoes, so they would be ready just a soon as the steaks were done. After showing Conchita and Marie how to work the galley appliances, Carlos returned topside, announcing, "My galley work is done, it's topside for me."

Chris volunteered, "I will go down and help the girls." The rather large galley grill could handle three steaks at a time, so everything would be ready in about 30 minutes. The oven would be warming the cobbler as it cooled off.

Conchita launched into cutting up the salad and filling up six salad bowls. Those would be passed topside as they became ready. But trouble was a-brewing even before that. Chris, bounded up the stairs to top-side and exclaimed. "Oh, I am bad sea-sick. No way I can endure down below with these rolling seas."

Carlos agreed. "You had better stay topside all through the night. We will make a place for you on the bench right there on the starboard side."

Supper was eaten while the sun descended, and was about over when it flicked out of sight along the western horizon, the sailors feeling fortunate to be blessed with a break in the clouds at that very important moment. During supper, Carlos gave Emma a short break from the helm to allow her to enjoy the meal. As the sun went out of sight, Robert asked Conchita and Marie how they had learned to be such good cooks.

Marie, replied, "We did not do all that much. The sweet potatoes were so easy, cutting up the salad was not hard at all, just as long as you braced yourself in the galley too avoid cutting yourself. It is a-rolling down there. Do you think, playing tennis has helped my balance?"

Carlos replied, "Doubt it. You are just naturally good at whatever you do." Marie blushed and let it drop.

Conchita added, "We are Confederate girls, you know, and, by and large, Confederate girls learn from their mothers that the way to a man's heart is through his stomach. So, learning to cook good Southern food is part of our family upbringing."

Marie challenged, "Well, I will make one comment about that. "The girls in New Orleans often grow up to become the best cooks of all. None across the Confederacy can please their man better than a girl from southern Louisiana."

Carlos finished off the patter with this observation: "Come on, you all. None of us is married and to my knowledge none are even close to becoming engaged. So this talk seems a bit premature all around." Then Carlos turned on the night lights (lights on the sailboat must be muted so the helmsman and look-outs can preserve their night vision) and he and Andrew descended into the galley to clean up the dishes.

At 9:30 pm Carlos figured it was time to turn the sailboat back toward home, giving instructions to maintain a southerly course at 189 degrees on the compass. He helped Emma turn the boat back toward Mantanzas. The wind was gusting up to 25 knots. So he cranked the roller reefing boom to wind down another three feet of mainsail and rolled up a corresponding amount of jib sail. Sailors call this reefing the sails.

Carlos helped Chris set up a row of cushions on the port topside bench and provided a sheet for him. Chris would be sleeping topside in hopes he would not be seasick. Andrew was topside, too, ready to take the helm from Emma at 10:00 pm. Andrew and Chris would be the only ones top-side from 10:00 pm to 1:00 am. There would be no moon until 3:00 am and clouds would be blocking starlight. Carlos had warned Emma and Andrew about the importance of scanning the horizon every five minutes and maintaining good night vision.

Carlos went below and helped everyone prepare their sleeping bunks and made sure the night ventilation was good. He then retired to his bunk, read for a bit in his bunk and fell asleep about 10:30 pm.

Thirty-nine minutes past midnight Carlos was startled by Andrew screaming at the helm:

"Shit!! Man overboard!! All hands on deck!! Shit!!"

Before he could exclaim the third "Shit" Carlos was bounding up the stairs and Emma was close behind.

Chris had fallen overboard. No time now to explain how it happened. It was quite dark out there. No moon expected for three more hours. It was cloudy and rain had begun to fall. Lightning and thunder was blowing in rapidly from the west.

"Where is he now," Carlos shouted. "What course were you on?" "190 degrees as instructed, sir." "Give me the helm and point and keep pointing. Do not blink. Keep that arm extended toward Chris so I will know." "This boat is coming about to 10 degrees, heading north on the course we have come from." Carlos was turning the boat around to back track toward the man overboard, a practiced maneuver. But this was a sailboat and the boom, mainsheet and jibsheet had to be reset in the squalling wind and rough seas. By this time, Marie and Conchita were at the winches manning that chore, carefully listening to instructions from Carlos.

With Andrew's help, Emma had spotted Chris with help from a lightning strike and was keeping a steady eye on that course. She had already fastened on one life jacket when she asked, "Was he wearing a life jacket?" Andrew, without turning away from this lookout task replied, "No, he had been trying to sleep on the port-side bench there when he jumped up and rushed to the side of the boat to vomit. So sea-sick. A big wave and gust of wind healed the boat suddenly and he fell overboard. I tossed a life ring in his direction as soon as I could grab it." Lighting flashed again. Emma announced, "I just saw him." There was a splash off the port side. Emma was diving into the ocean. She had buckled a second, larger life jacket on top of the first, grabbed a water-proof flashlight and dove into the ocean life-saving style, without losing sight of the cloud pattern that defined the direction she would swim as she progressed toward Chris.

Now Emma was an exceptionally strong swimmer and used to those huge surfing waves along the Hawaiian coast. But, a second man overboard was not recommended procedure in circumstances such as these. But she sensed a terrible crisis at hand. The storm coming in from the west was now churning the ocean and she had learned from conversation that Chris was only an average swimmer. He was in grave danger of losing his life.

It took time to turn around the sailboat. The sails hung up briefly during the coming about maneuver. It was so dark. The lightning flashes were the only means now of glimpsing Chris among the rolling seas, and then only if the flash coincided with Chris being atop the crest of a wave. If he was down in the trough when the flash occurred, he was not seen. Same for Emma, as she swam head erect, eyes staring ahead. "Shout, Chris. Shout as loud as you can so I can hear were you are. I am swimming to you. Chris. Shout to me." Then she heard a shout. "Emma." "Here." "Emma." "Here." Although Chris was doing his best to be heard, he was gasping while trying to stay above water and the wind and rain was making a lot of noise.

Maintaining the desired course was difficult in the high wind and maneuvering toward Chris for pick-up would be difficult. Carlos shouted, "Roll in both sails, I've turned on the engine." Conchita and Marie did as directed, and soon both sails were all rolled up.

Now in normal "man overboard" sailboat maneuvers, it is very unlikely that a swimmer would reach the victim before the sailboat could be brought about and return for a pick-up. Not so this night. Difficulty in seeing the victim in the darkness and among the surging waves greatly complicated this rescue. And ocean swimmers of Emma's caliber were seldom aboard a sailboat. Of course Emma was wrong to dive in without permission from her skipper. But Emma had a mind of her own on this occasion. And away she had gone. She was off swimming back to the north while Carlos was only halfway through maneuvering the sailboat around to a northerly course.

"Emma." "Here." Those shouts were key to Chris' survival and he was doing his best to keep his throat clear for shouting.

Back on the sailboat, a grave mistake was made. At one flash of lightning, Andrew spotted something floating in the water at a distance that matched where Chris ought to be, but twenty degrees toward the east. He had not seen Chris for about 3 minutes, and figured that object was him. Not good. Andrew would be guiding the sailboat toward some floating debris. If that did not match the direction toward Emma's flashlight, the skipper's priority had to go to Chris, who had no life jacket.

Emma's swimming upon the rolling seas topped by white-caps and foam was a thing of beauty and efficiency. Fortunately the two life vests fit snuggly and did not impair progress as much as would be expected. Stroke after stroke, head high, hoping to catch sight of Chris atop a wave crest, Emma progressed toward the sound she faintly heard.

"Emma." "Over here."

Emma knew something was wrong when she observed that Carlos was on a course about 20 degrees divergent from the direction she was swimming. The sailboat, being faster, even passed her well off to the right. But she doggedly continued her powerful strokes, feet kicking and arms stroking down through the water.

"Emma."

She knew she was getting close. Then a lighting strike revealed a struggling swimmer.

"I've got you, Chris." "Do not fight me." "I have two life jackets." "One for you and one for me." "I am getting yours ready now." "Here it is." "Let us put this on." "Good boy." "I will buckle you up." "Snug and comfy."

"There." "Let me hear you cough." "Swallowed a lot of water?" "We deal with that back at the boat."

"I have a flashlight." "Carlos will see it and come to us." "Something must have thrown him off course." "But he will return."

"Emma." "Thanks to God you came." "I was about to drown."

Chris and Emma embraced among the rolling seas as she signaled Carlos with the flashlight. Before long Chris broke down in tears and uncontrollable sobs. He had faced death and survived -- an experience that would alter this young man's outlook on life forevermore.

Five minutes later, Carlos brought the sailboat alongside Emma and Chris. A ladder was lowered and Chris, then Emma climbed aboard. Then Chris just lay down in front of the helm and started to cry again. Emma understood. She went below for blankets and asked Conchita to make hot coffee and hot tea. Chris was to get one or both, along with the remaining ginger cookies. When they were ready she sat down beside Chris and helped him regain his composure. He had chosen the hot coffee. Emma said she preferred the hot tea and would like a sandwich to go with it. You see, that girl had been doing some hearty swimming and it was time to recharge her batteries.

"Conchita, make more hot coffee, but make it real weak. Chris needs to dilute the salt water he swallowed among his struggles. He needs to be doing some serious peeing." "I've have some more hot tea, as well."

By dawn, the storm had passed and the winds had substantially subsided to a comfortable 15 knots, still out of the west. Breakfast was good. Blueberry pancakes with butter and a mixed topping of fresh fig compote and pure maple syrup. Melon to boot.

The sailing party was back in Mantanzas harbor by noon. Carlos had supplemented the sailing with some diesel engine motoring to ensure that the diminishing winds did not make them late.

There was lunch at the marina and swimming in the club pool. Seems like the sailors were a bit salty. They claimed that they were now "blue water sailors." None disputed it. Then showers and dressing for the plane ride back to Sewanee.

The sailors would arrive in the Sewanee airport at 7:00 pm. Whow! Would they have stories to tell.

During the plane ride back to Sewanee, Andrew Houston and Conchita Rezanov sat across the aisle chatting and talking about all sorts of stuff, including tennis, of course. It was obvious to others that Andrew really, really liked Conchita. Without a doubt they would be seeing more of each other.

The next row of seats was taken by Carlos Cespedes and Marie Saint Martin. They were becoming fast friends. He was quite the charmer when strumming along on his guitar and she had a wonderful singing voice and wide range of musical interests. They would be seeing more of each other as well.

The back seating on the airplane stretched from window to window because no aisle was needed behind it. On that sat Chris Memminger and Emma Lunalilo. They chatted for a while, but Chris was still visibly shaken by the night's ordeal at sea. He was emotionally and physical wiped out. They laid back their seat and felt needed sleep coming on. Before long, Chris was asleep with his head on Emma's bosom, as she cradled him with both seats laid back. She was OK and he was OK. Everyone understood.

Now as the writer telling you this true story, I feel the need to explain. Chris was not a sissy. He had been working with horses since he was just a young pup. He had broken young horses. He had raced horses on flat tracks and over steeple chase jumps. On land, Chris was a tough as most any man. But on the ocean, among those waves, gasping for air in pitch black darkness, that experience had brought this tough guy to his knees.

Sunday Evening Selected Diary Postings

Chris Memminger's and Emma Lunalilo's diary notes for Sunday are considered confidential. We do not wish to pry.

All the others on the Cuba trip wrote about the sailing and how thankful each was that Chris and Emma were OK.

Diary note by Carlos Cespedes said, "As skipper, I would never have permitted Emma to go into the water in hopes of rescuing Chris. In all of my sailing training, that was a definite "No, No". But I am so thankful she did it. Considering the gale-force winds; the pitch black darkness; and our error in mistaking debris for Chris when we got a glimpse during that lightning strike, I fear we would have lost Chris to the sea. I do not know how I would have ever forgiven myself. Thank God for Emma.

Diary note by Andrew Houston said, "When the man overboard crisis hit, I was the only person top-side except for Chris. The wind out of the west must have been gusting to 30 knots, so it kept the boat heeled over on the port side. One could practically reach the water when a wind gust struck the sail. Chris was bunked on the port side bench when he sensed he was about to throw up. Damn it! Chris was so damn careful to not vomit on the side of the boat that he leaned too far out over the water. That was just when the worst wind gust struck the sail. Chris simply fell head first into the water. I saw it, but it all happened so fast. All I could do was grab a life ring and toss it into the water while shouting that dreaded cry: "Man Overboard."

Diary note by Conchita Rezanov said, "Like the rest, when I heard Andrew shout, "Man Overboard," I raced up the gangway to topside and helped in every way I could. Following Carlos's directions, working the lines and winches to get the sails down so we could better maneuver by the engine. Straining to see Chris or Emma in the darkness or hear a shout among the roar of the wind and waves. At the same time I was praying for Chris and Emma. It is a miracle that we all got back to the harbor safely. Yet, I do believe I will go sailing again. Up until that horrible crisis, I know that I deeply loved it. Oh, yes. Andrew and I are going to play tennis first chance. I think he is a very good tennis player, but I might have to go easy on him so as not to hurt his feelings. Men are so sensitive about getting beat by a woman. I like him, too. It will be fun. I sense he likes me in a romantic way. That's OK with me."

Diary note by Marie Saint Martin said, "I know Chris was deeply shaken over the Man Overboard crisis. Up until that time, I was having a great time and felt safe even though the wind was howling and the waves were pretty high. Carlos had a way of assuring everyone that we would be fine, that the sailboat was capable of far worst weather and he had sailed it is such conditions. I was enjoying the adventure. I like Carlos. We really had fun yesterday afternoon when he played the guitar and we all sang. We are definitely going to do more of that. Perhaps I should take the lead in getting a music group started. Our group could include Carlos and Allen Ross on guitars and Amanda Washington on piano. We can include Tina Sharp. She plays the French horn very well, I am assured, so I am confident that she can sing as well. Might even lasso Professor Davis to join us with his banjo. I aim to look into it Monday afternoon."

Diary note by Professor Davis said, "Just learned that the overnight sailing trip off of Cuba almost ended in disaster. Chris Memminger was so sea sick that, while trying to throw up over the side of the boat, he fell overboard at the moment that a gust of wind and a big wave hit the opposite side. Was pitch black dark, a gale had come in from the west and he almost drowned. Emma grabbed an extra life vest and flashlight and dove into the ocean and swam . . ."

"Thank God Chris is OK. Emma is some kind of surfer woman. I had no idea she was capable of doing that, or that she would be willing to risk her own life like that. She is our heroine for sure."

Book 1, Chapter 8, Day 8 – Having Finished Subjugating Maryland, Kentucky and Missouri, Federals Launch Coordinated Attacks against Confederate States – Class Lecture, Monday, June 13, 2011

It was hard on Monday morning for the Sewanee Project team to settle down and focus on Confederate history. Professor Davis had prepared a fine lecture about the military contest, clearly to be a highlight of the four weeks together at Sewanee. It took a little over fifteen minutes to settle down and began to listen. Professor Davis began as we listen in.

President Lincoln Issues the Attack Order, Targeted for May 5, 1862

On May 1, 1862, the Lincoln Administration issued orders to all five divisions to launch their respective attack strategies simultaneously, on the morning of Monday, May 5. The Confederate Secret Service intercepted the May 1 telegraph, decoded it, and alerted all five Confederate division commanders. The grand Confederate strategy of "Tactical Retreat, Envelopment and Capture" was about to be attempted on five fronts. But first, the Federal divisions had to be allowed to advance with only token resistance, to build an overly-confident attitude and to lure them away from their lines of supply and into terrain that facilitated envelopment and forced surrender.

May through Early June, 1862 — Tactical Retreat, Envelopment, Capture, and Imprisonment

The success of the 1862 Confederate military campaign, termed "Tactical Retreat, Envelopment and Capture," would become the focus of study by students of military strategy all over the world, even to this day. The history of the successful Defense of State Secession in North America would be as well known in military schools and textbooks in Russia, or France, or Germany or Japan, as it would be at West Point and Confederate military schools. And the essence of our 1861-1862 history is well known – to varying degrees of thoroughness, to be sure – by Confederates living today. So, only a few pages of this book need to be devoted to the story – an overview will do nicely – allowing the reader to devote more time to understanding "Why" the Confederacy is the "Greatest Country on Earth."

Federal Virginia and Carolina Division Advances Southward (May 5 to May 25)

As previously mentioned, the mission of the Federal's Virginia and Carolinas Division was to occupy Richmond and force surrender of the

Virginia State Government; then proceed to Raleigh and force the surrender of the North Carolina State Government; then proceed to Columbia and force surrender of the South Carolina State Government. Made up of militia and volunteers from the northeastern states, this division had gathered near Washington City and departed on May 5 on its march south to first conquer Richmond. This division consisted of 130,000 men, of which 17,000 were cavalry. Irving McDowell of Ohio was commanding.

Positioned to entrap this Federal division was Confederate Division 1, consisting of 80,000 Confederates, which included 25,000 cavalry. Nine companies of irregular Virginia State Rangers were in assigned positions to harass and confuse the Federal advance. Robert E. Lee of Virginia was commanding. The Confederate strategy was "Tactical Retreat, Envelopment and Capture" somewhere west of Richmond.

History shows that, from the start of the Federal advance on May 5, McDowell's Virginia and Carolinas Division appeared to Federals to be relatively unopposed as it advanced southward from Washington City toward its destination of Richmond, encountering – as it appeared to advancing soldiers, cavalry and commanders – only token resistance from Confederates. Federals found it much easier than expected to get through Fredericksburg. Confidence grew at they proceeded further south toward Richmond.

But the resistance anticipated by the Federals to be at their front, materialized instead at their rear as, after eight days of the Federal's southward march, Confederate cavalry and irregular State Rangers began attacking supply lines, capturing horses, wagons and supplies, along with the troops responsible for those functions. Yet, the raids on the supply train were so swift and unnoticed, often during the night, that the general alarm was not fully sounded.

But when the Federal army reached the Pamunkey River, near Cedar Fork, the Confederates appeared in great numbers, causing the Federals to veer westward toward a perceived attacking position west of the capital city. Yet the big fight did not occur, for telegraph messages from Montgomery were advising Robert Lee to delay Envelopment a few days so that Washington City would not become alarmed by a Virginia defeat before defeats west of the mountains could be consummated. Must continue to make the Lincoln Administration believe that the invasion was going well.

By the night of May 17, the Federals were encamped on the east side of the James River. By that point, Confederates had completed their capture of the wagon trains and outlying Federal cavalry. And, over the past several days, Confederate cavalry had swept into the Federal army, at spots when opportunities arose, and seized many of the Federals' artillery pieces. Virginia State Rangers, such as Captain George Downs' company, and North

Carolina Rangers had been particularly helpful in these captures of supply trains and artillery units. Lee's army was now ready to attack the Federal foot soldiers. It was there, with the James to the Federal rear, that Confederates would surround the Federal army and make a fierce attack with the full force of Lee's army and cavalry, employing the enhanced firepower of repeating weapons and many field artillery pieces.

An hour before dawn, the following morning, Confederates mounted a general attack from the east, the south and the north while cavalry and dismounted riflemen prevented retreat across the river to the west. Within three hours, all remaining Federal artillery was disabled. As darkness begin to set in that evening, May 18, 70,000 Federal troops and remaining cavalry, the fit and the wounded, laid down their arms and surrendered. The remainder of the 130,000 invasion force was dead (17,000), had been captured among the wagon trains (12,000) or managed to get away and flee back north (31,000). Most effective in forcing the surrender were the troops under Thomas Jackson. Most effective in directing the operation was the direction provided by the commander, Robert E. Lee. Within three weeks, by June 9, the 70,000 captives would be in 14 prisoner-of-war camps hastily established in the Piedmont region of North Carolina, between Greensboro and Charlotte, carefully dispersed to facilitate food supply, to minimize disease, to maintain a degree of secrecy, and to impede a mass rescue. The Lincoln Administration received news of the defeat on Wednesday, May 27, but the status of the 70,000 missing and their whereabouts was unclear.

Federal Tennessee and Georgia Division Advances Southward (May 5 to May 25)

As previously mentioned, the mission of the Tennessee and Georgia Division was to conquer Nashville, force the surrender of the Tennessee State Government, proceed southeastward, skirting Chattanooga, turn south into Georgia skirt Atlanta and force the surrender of the Georgia State Government at Milledgeville. While honoring Kentucky neutrality, an invasion force had gathered in southern Indiana, not far north of Louisville in preparation for moving down the Louisville and Nashville railroad to Franklin, Kentucky, the last sizable town along the railroad before crossing into Tennessee. By late April this division had fully arrived at Franklin and was making ready to move south into Tennessee to capture and occupy the capital city of Nashville. The Tennessee and Georgia Division consisted of 70,000 men, of which 9,000 were cavalry. William Rosecrans, of Ohio, was commanding.

Positioned to entrap the Federal's Tennessee and Georgia division was a division of 60,000 Confederates, which included 20,000 cavalry – Division 2, Braxton Bragg of North Carolina, commanding. Because Nashville was so close to Kentucky and so easily attacked by Federal gunboats on the Cumberland River, the Confederate strategy was to permit Federals to occupy the Tennessee capital, feign surrender of the Tennessee State Government, then to allow Federals to venture southeastward along the railroad through Murfreesboro, then allow further advancement toward the southeast, but thereafter springing the trap to force surrender in the vicinity of Tullahoma.

History shows that, from the start of its advance on May 5, the Federal Tennessee and Georgia Division was allowed to advance southward toward its destination of Nashville, encountering, as it appeared to the soldiers, cavalry and commanders, only token resistance from Confederates. The march from the Kentucky State line to Nashville was only 40 miles and it was covered in four to six days, the first arriving on May 9. Although most of the city and state government officials and employees had evacuated, a few spokesmen remained to give the Federal commanders confidence that political reconstruction of the Tennessee State Government would not present unusual difficulties. A Federal detachment of 5,000 troops, of which 1,000 was cavalry, remained in the vicinity of Nashville throughout the month of May, while political agents from the Lincoln Administration obtained pledges to rescind State Secession and decreed that all men who resisted Federal occupation of Tennessee were denied the right to vote for the remainder of their lives.

Meanwhile, on May 13, Andrew Johnson – the only senator of a seceded state to have remained in Washington after secession and now an enthusiastic supporter of the Lincoln Administration – departed Washington City for Nashville, expecting to be sworn in as the Provisional Military Governor of the Reconstructed State of Tennessee. [86]

Also on Tuesday, May 13, the bulk of the Federal Tennessee and Georgia Division moved out of Nashville toward the southeast, aiming to occupy Murfreesboro, 30 miles distant, which had been the original capital of the state. Again, only token resistance was presented by Braxton Bragg's Confederate Division 2 on the march to Murfreesboro, because entrapment further down the line of march – against the Cumberland Plateau in the vicinity of The Barrens, west of Tullahoma – would be more certain than among the open farmland surrounding Murfreesboro, or even against the Highland Rim, which surrounded the lowland country of Middle Tennessee.

---

[86] In truthful history, Nashville fell easily to Federal occupation and Tennessee Senator Andrew Johnson accepted President Lincoln's offer to become Provisional Governor. Later Andrew Johnson would be nominated as the Republican's 1864 vice-president candidate. In truthful history, after President Lincoln was killed by Maryland actor John Wilkes Booth, Andrew Johnson took the reigns as President and played a significant role in the political reconstruction of the conquered Confederate States.

Federals arrived in Murfreesboro on Friday morning, May 16, and occupied the town without resistance. Only a token representative of the local government was present, and this small group pledged its loyalty to the reconstructed government in Nashville.

On Sunday, May 18, the Federal Tennessee and Georgia Division moved out, continuing its southeasterly march toward Chattanooga, never veering far from the track of the Nashville and Chattanooga Railroad, which ran in a southeast direction, rising through Bell Buckle Gap onto the Highland Rim and on to Wartrace. From Wartrace it continued southeast, crossed the Duck River and arrived at Tullahoma, where it joined another railroad line that ran northeast to McMinnville. The Federals reached the vicinity of Wartrace by Thursday morning, a distance of 20 miles. After the Federals left Wartrace, Bragg's Confederates and Tennessee Rangers began springing the trap, for the resistance anticipated by the Federals to be at their front, materialized instead from their rear, across the Highland Rim as Confederate cavalry began attacking supply lines, capturing horses, wagons and supplies, along with the troops responsible for those functions. Again, the raids on the supply train were so swift and unnoticed, often during the night, that the general alarm was not fully sounded. By the time the bulk of the invasion force reached a point midway between Wartrace and Tullahoma, on Friday, May 23, Confederate forces began turning the invaders toward their left, due east toward The Barrens and Savage Gulf. Surrenders were gained in stages, first this regiment and then that regiment, the troops on foot being the first to give up. By the time the remnant of Federals were driven into Savage Gulf, surrounded by imposing ridges of the Cumberland Plateau – high ground occupied by Confederate cavalry and artillery -- they were whipped. It was Sunday, May 25th.

After five days of fighting and retreat, of the 65,000 Federals who left out from Nashville, 11,000 had been killed, 30,000 had surrendered, a number of these wounded, and 24,000 had managed to escape the trap, most of them finding their way back to Nashville or to Kentucky. Of the 30,000 that had surrendered, 4,000 were cavalry. There were 3,000 wounded among the captives. The 30,000 captives were taken to 10 prisoner-of-war camps hastily set up at remote locations east of the Cumberland Plateau's eastern ridge and west of the Tennessee River, spread out between Lewis Chapel and Grand View. Within two weeks, by June 9, the captives were in their respective POW camps. The Lincoln Administration learned of the defeat on Tuesday, May 27, but the status and whereabouts of the 30,000 missing Federal troops was in a state of confusion.

Federal Alabama and Florida Division Advances Southward (May 5 to May 26)

As previously mentioned, the mission of the Federal's Alabama and Florida Division was to invade western Tennessee, heading due south along the course of the northward-flowing Tennessee River, proceeding to the Mississippi State line; then turn east into Alabama and then southeast through that State to occupy Burmingham, then move on to Montgomery and force the surrender of the Alabama State Government – and also force the surrender of Confederate Government officials that might have remained. Toward this objective, an invasion force had gathered in the vicinity of Metropolis, Illinois, which was just north-east of where the Tennessee River flows into the Ohio at Paducah, Kentucky, and not far east of where the Cumberland River flows into the Ohio. In groups, this invasion force had moved up the Tennessee River to a staging area west of Murray, in southwest Kentucky, some riding horses, some walking and some coming up-river by steamboats. They were preparing to invade Tennessee along a path paralleling the Tennessee River, where a fleet of gun-boats and steamboats would support the advance into southern Tennessee, as far as the Mississippi border. Since further support by gun-boats and steamboats would be arrested by the rapids at Muscle Shoals, the invasion force planned to proceed overland to Grand Junction, at Corinth Mississippi where existing railroads could be seized to transport the army east into northern Alabama. From there it would advance through northern Alabama and proceed south to force surrender at Montgomery. The final goal was to force surrender at Tallahassee, Florida. The Alabama and Florida Division, commanded by Ulysses Grant, of Ohio and Missouri, consisted of 70,000 men, of which 9,000 were cavalry.

Positioned to entrap the Federal's Alabama and Florida division was a division of 55,000 Confederates, which included 18,000 cavalry and State Rangers from western Tennessee, northern Mississippi and northern Alabama. This was Division 3, which was commanded by the able Albert Sidney Johnston of Kentucky and Texas. The strategy was to allow Federals to advance southward, up the Tennessee River, through western Tennessee, because in that region surrender could not be forced. Then, after Federals left the protection of their gunboats and steamboats at Pittsburg Landing, to make a fierce and rapid attack from the northwest about midway between Pittsburg Landing and Corinth, Mississippi, to incite panic and force retreat toward the southeast, in hopes of effecting surrender and capture in northeast Mississippi or northwest Alabama, in the hill country south of the Tennessee River.

History shows that, from the start of the Federal's advance on May 5, the Alabama and Florida Division suffered extreme losses to its fleet of gunboats and steamboats as they steamed upstream against the heavy spring flow of the Tennessee River. For the most part, Federals did not understand what was happening. Disasters occurred often: suddenly, without warning, a boiler would explode, killing many of those aboard (if a gunboat, few of the crew survived). History reveals that the carnage was the result of torpedoes sneaked into the fuel supply and mines planted in the riverbed, many with associated river snags that encouraged pilots to steer free of a snag, but right over a mine. [87]

Unlike the river vessels, the cavalry, supply wagons and marching troops suffered little resistance as they progressed southward, never very far from the river. When, on May 19, the Federal division arrived at Pittsburg Landing, the jumping off point for Corinth, the different units – those on boats that succeeded in getting upstream, foot soldiers, cavalry and supply trains – were, to their surprise able to join up without harassment. The 66,000 Federals who succeeded in getting through Tennessee, of which 8,500 were cavalry, consumed May 20 and 21 getting organized for the march into Mississippi to attack Corinth and the railroad junction between the Memphis and Charleston Railroad and the Mobile and Ohio Railroad, located 10 miles distant to the south-southwest.

The Federals were confident and eager to be the first to reach Montgomery. The sense of a competition between the five Federal invasion forces was stronger than ever, especially a passion for the top commanders.

The Federals departed Pittsburg Landing during the morning of May 22, a Thursday. By mid-afternoon all units were on the road toward Corinth. It was then that the Confederate attack struck from the northwest. A massive attack in which 18,000 cavalry hit the Federal lines like a hammer, disrupting order and prompting many to retreat toward the southeast. Confederate foot soldiers joined in the push, along with mobile field artillery, such as the 12-pounder smooth bore guns carried by two mules. Both the Confederate travois and conventional wagons were used when helpful in bringing troops rapidly forward by a few miles here and there to maintain pressure on the retreating Federals, not allowing time for them to organize into defensive lines or erect protective breastworks. Some Federals succeeded in escaping back to Pittsburg Landing, but over half were driven across Yellow Creek into a rugged wilderness area south of the Tennessee River town of Hamburg,

---

[87] Successes against Federal boats coming up the Tennessee River were the work of Confederate Secret Service agents, working in the field, placing torpedoes and mines, produced with technical support from James Eads and Confederate munitions experts and fabricated by teams located in various shops. Operating from well concealed hideouts dug into the river banks here and there, were small teams of mine operators who made sure all was in readiness; they often released mines just when a Federal craft arrived, using concealed control wires that ran from the hideout, under the water and to the mine release pin. In truthful history, Confederates used coal torpedoes to trick Federals into mistakenly shoveling one into the firebox of the steam engine.

Tennessee. One would think the retreating Federals would make for Hamburg, in search of Federal gunboat and steamboat protection, although over half of those vessels had been destroyed, but Confederate cavalry and State Rangers prevented many from turning north toward the river. It was at Yellow Creek that the Federals were forced to surrender. During the panic, over 10,000 Confederates had raced around the retreating Federals to the south, along the Memphis and Charleston Railroad, crossed over the headwaters of Yellow Creek and then turned north along the east side of the creek to establish a stout defensive line that prevented the harried Federals from retreating further. Panicked just west of Yellow Creek, Federals were surrendering like dominoes, one unit after the other. This took place during the day of May 26, a Monday.

The final haul of captives totaled 35,000, of which 4,000 were cavalry. Approximately 3,000 captives were wounded. The Federal dead totaled 5,000. Within two weeks, by June 9, the captives would be distributed into 12 prisoner-of-war camps located in the remote northern Alabama hills, between Burleson and Peach Grove. The Lincoln Administration received word of this disaster on Thursday, May 29.

Future historians are often puzzled over why Washington City was unable to understand that its five Invading Armies were not in serious trouble. Well, part of the deception that blinded Washington City and the top Federal military command was the stream of messages passed along surreptitiously by the Confederate Secret Service, which assured that this army and that army was proceeding along its designated invasion path without difficulty.

Federal Mississippi River Division Advances Southward (May 5 until Stalled)

The mission of the Mississippi River Division was to gain control of the navigation of the Mississippi River from the Ohio River to the Gulf of Mexico, and to force surrender of the Louisiana State Government at Baton Rouge and the Mississippi State Government at Jackson. Toward this object, construction of iron-clad gun-boats had begun in haste at Rock Island, Illinois, to be used in descending southward down the Mississippi River. Also Navy warships and transports were upgraded in New York with improved armaments, in some cases with more powerful steam engines, and organized into an invasion force to enter the mouth of the Mississippi River and advance upstream to New Orleans and then force the government surrender at Baton Rouge. From the New Orleans-Baton Rouge staging area, armies would then be dispatched to force surrender of the Mississippi State Government at Jackson. The Federal's Mississippi River Division had gathered near Cairo and Mound City, Illinois. It was led by 4 armored gunboats, just finished at

Rock Island and it consisted of 40,000 men, of which 5,000 were cavalry. Don Carlos Buell of Ohio was commanding.

Positioned to entrap this Federal division somewhere along its descent down the Mississippi River was a division of 30,000 Confederates, 10,000 of them cavalry, plus a fleet of 5 Confederate River Defender Gunboats designed by Eads and Ericsson and built by Eads' workforce in Mississippi. This was Confederate Division 4, commanded by Pierre Beauregard of Louisiana.

Success in preventing Federal navigation of the Mississippi River depended also on preventing the capture of New Orleans and Baton Rouge, a task relegated to powerful Confederate artillery, to three Confederate River Defender Gunboats, to a few Confederate Navy warships, and to teams of Confederate mine-laying experts.

Except for Federal cavalry, which proceeded south on horseback, the foot soldiers and supplies for the Mississippi River Division had been advanced southward from its staging base at Cairo, Illinois in shifts during April, as units and steamboats were available. By early May the division was set up just north of Tennessee and ready to invade further down the Mississippi River. As with the other four Federal divisions, the Mississippi River Division, departed into the Confederate portion of the Mississippi River, as directed from Washington City, on May 5. Federal cavalry did not experience difficulty until it arrived at the Chickasaw Bluffs, located north of Memphis in southwest Tennessee. But from the start at Island Number 10, just south of the Tennessee-Kentucky line, Federal vessels suffered considerable losses from explosions, the cause of which was at the time baffling. Defenses at Island Number 10 were significant, but designed to allow Confederates to escape down-river when needed to avoid capture. And at other points along the river, the emphasis was on getting coal torpedoes onto the invading boats and steering them above mines of the James Eads design. But the most important Confederate weapon was the Confederate River Defender Gunboat. Often, after a group of steamboats and/or gunboats passed by the hiding place of a CRDG, it entered the river and gave chase from behind, quickly catching up to within the range of its two guns, then firing. Within four rounds, the enemy vessel was normally stricken and put out of service or on its way to the bottom. No Federal gunboats ever reached the Mississippi State line. The torpedoes, slipped onboard by Confederate Secret Service agents, most of them African Americans, were very effective in disabling or sinking southbound steamboats.

Federal Navy Advances Northward up Mississippi River (May 5 until Stalled at New Orleans)

Meanwhile, far to the south, a sizable fleet of the Federal Navy entered the mouth of the Mississippi at the Gulf of Mexico, but experienced difficulty in proceeding upstream to New Orleans. The three CRDG vessels and crew were generally effective in fighting off or sinking Federal craft coming upstream, but the most helpful deterrent were the snags and Confederate mines placed in the river. The fleet began its advance up the Mississippi on May 5, as directed by the Lincoln Administration, and it looked like, for several weeks, that it would never reach New Orleans. But, eventually about half of the fleet survived to approach the city. The Confederate Government in Montgomery decided to save the city from a bombardment from what remained of the Federal fleet and ordered the city to surrender. The surrender became official on May 26. But the fleet, weakened by the ordeal of getting upstream from the Gulf, stayed at the City, too weak to challenge the Confederate defenses at the capital city of Baton Rouge without support by Federal troops and cavalry. But Federal troops far to the north were experiencing great difficulties above Memphis, at the Chickasaw Bluffs. Fighting persisted between Federals and Confederates for a full week, but an Envelopment and Capture opportunity never occurred. Confederates had to settle for forcing the Federals to retreat north back into the northwest corner of Tennessee, where they would await reinforcements. By early June, it was apparent to the Lincoln Administration that gaining control of the Mississippi River south of Tennessee and north of New Orleans would take many more months of gunboat construction and a far larger concentration of troops and cavalry.

Federal Missouri, Arkansas and Texas Division Advances Southward (May 5 to May 21)

As already mentioned, the organization of the Federal's Missouri, Arkansas and Texas Division – commanded by John Fremont – had been slowed by the fighting in Missouri between the State militia and anti-secessionists. But, by the end of April, the State militia had been driven to the southern region of the state and the capital at Jefferson City was firmly in the control of anti-secessionists and their Federal backers. So, the Missouri, Arkansas and Texas Division, consisting of 40,000 men, of which 5,000 were cavalry, was now prepared to move south through southern Missouri, pushing resistance out of the state, then proceed into Arkansas, force surrender of the State Government at Little Rock, then proceed into Texas and force surrender of the far-away State Government at Austin. John Fremont, with family ties to Missouri, was commanding.

Positioned to entrap the Federal's Missouri, Arkansas and Texas division was a division of 35,000 Confederates, 12,000 of them cavalry. This was Confederate Division 5, commanded by Sterling Price of Missouri. Envelopment was anticipated about half way between the Arkansas border and the capital city of Little Rock.

As ordered by the Lincoln Administration, on May 5 the Federal force departed Rolla, Missouri, located on the Gascouade River, and headed south toward Cedar Bluff. Resistance from Confederates and/or from Missouri Secessionists was minor, and only a few supplies and horses were lost to raiders, and the units remained intact. Progress on to Gainesville, Missouri was also relatively unimpeded. The raids on outliers intensified a bit when the division crossed over into Arkansas and crossed the White River at North Fork, but progress continued in spite of raids by State Rangers and the confusion they caused. By May 15 the division was at Kinderhook on the Little Red River. Three days later the division was at Lewisburg on the Arkansas River. A day was consumed crossing the Arkansas. And, although the objective, the capital city of Little Rock, was but 40 miles downstream, resistance had thus far been manageable, losses being confined to 500 troops and about one seventh of the supplies. The division departed the Arkansas River on the morning of May 20 toward Perryville, Arkansas, about 10 miles to the south. It was then that all hell broke loose. Confederate troops appeared on the east flank and on the west flank and cavalry closed in behind the back of the Federal division. In response, the division quickened its pace toward Perryville.

But at Perryville, it encountered dug-in Confederate troops, arranged in an arc. The Federals closed ranks, seeking protection from each other, making the damage of the Confederate artillery even more deadly. Confederate cavalry attacked nearly all who attempted escape. By sundown, the Federals sensed that they were surrounded. Mutinous declarations permeated the night. When dawn broke the following day, Wednesday, May 21, white flags began appearing and Federal deserters begin crossing over to the Confederate lines, hands raised in abject surrender. By 2 o'clock in the afternoon John Fremont -- the proud, cocky "Pathfinder" – the husband of the politically influential Jessie Benton Fremont – the largely incompetent commander of the Federal's Missouri, Arkansas and Texas Division – and the former 1856 candidate for President for the Republican Party of the northern States – sought to negotiate. Sterling Price, commander of the Confederate Division 5, and the dejected Fremont met in a tent erected between the lines and struck a deal. If the Federals would lay down their arms, and submit to a lottery, then, Federals could bury their dead at a gravesite within their lines, all of the wounded would be allowed to retreat back to Missouri and all of the healthy would be subject to a 50/50 lottery – heads you are a captive to be escorted to a prisoner-of-war camp somewhere in Texas – tails you may high-tail it back to Illinois or points beyond under Confederate cavalry escort, never to ever again take up arms against the Confederate States of America, Missouri of any State that seeks to secede. Fremont had no choice. His men preferred to take their chances in a coin toss than be certain of imprisonment.

So within an hour, lines for surrender were formed up and Confederate officers began listing each surrendered individual in the "book of life." An entry was made for each Federal – name, age, home town and state, next of kin, where born, citizenship, if an immigrant the year of arrival, healthy-sick- or wounded and where, if healthy, was the toss, Heads or Tails. All was completed and movement north and south began at 9 in the morning of Saturday, May 24. In graves lay 4,000 dead Federals. Headed north under Confederate escort were 4,000 surrendered wounded Federals and 15,750 healthy Federals who had come up "tails." Headed for Texas under Confederate escort were 15,750 healthy Federals who had come up "heads." By June 7, they would be dispersed in 7 prisoner-of-war camps stretching from Jacksboro to Quitman. The Confederates would terminate the escort at Licking, Missouri, giving rise to the ditty composed by a notable captive:

> "On the way down to Perryville, Ol' Fremont led us through Licking.
> But when we got to Perryville, Fremont's fair boys took a Licking.
> For the lucky ones returning, he made us revisit Licking."

The Lincoln Administration received news of the disaster at Perryville, Arkansas on May 28.

Over a Four-Week Span, The Lincoln Administration and the North Receives Repeating and Devastating News

News of the failures of the five coordinated invasions of the Confederacy hit the Lincoln Administration in repeated blasts. The arrival dates of each devastating military report, in chronological sequence, were as follows:

- Virginia and Carolinas Division defeat: May 27. [88]
- Missouri, Arkansas and Texas Division defeat: May 28.
- Alabama and Florida Division defeat: May 29.
- Mississippi River Division and New Orleans stalemate: early June.
- Tennessee and Georgia Division defeat: May 27.

The count of Federals imprisoned in Confederate prisoner-of-war camps totaled 150,000. Federal battlefield deaths totaled a little over 40,000. Confederates had captured huge quantities of modern firearms, ammunition

---

[88] It was with remarkable coordination that Confederates had been able to steer Federals along an extended path to the James River, west of Richmond, and consume valuable time in order to delay the envelopment two extra weeks so as not to alarm the Lincoln Administration prematurely.

and artillery, horses, wagons – so much of what an army needed to wage war. The Federal army was decimated, with no hope of rebuilding a new invasion force prior to the November 1862 elections, which meant that Republican candidates had no way to offer encouragement to their electorate. Confederate propaganda – effectively distributed by the Secret Service – was persuading many in the northern States to advocate, "Let Them Go in Peace." The height of the election season – July, August and September – was on the horizon. Several states actually voted in October and those would surely go Democratic. Recognition of the Confederate States of America as a sovereign among the nations of the world was clearly anticipated, with Great Britain and France likely to lead the way. Abolitionists had, through their campaign against the Southern States, built political support in Bleeding Kansas and empowered the rise of the new Republican Party in the Northern States, but could it at this late hour somehow resurrect renewed enthusiasm for conquering the seceded States? Or would the Abolitionists' plea against slavery be recast as a plea to rid their region of people of African ancestry – a plea for racial cleansing – a plea to drive Colored people out of the northern States and into the Confederate States? The Lincoln Administration had decided to throw all of its military might against an untested Confederate army without first testing the strength of their adversary. If it had worked, all the seceded States would have been forced to rescind secession, State by State, and bow to Federal might. But the untested Federal troops sent south simultaneously on paths of invasion – having no passion derived by a need to defend family and home – having no passion derived from a cause worth fighting for – having no passion derived from desperate battle experience – having not yet seen the elephant – did panic when the elephant was seen, failed to match their foe and soon surrendered in large numbers. [89]

Monday Evening Selected Diary Postings

All diaries commented on the weekend's near-disaster sailing trip, but we need not put those comments here. Those selected below present other thoughts.

Diary note by Amanda Washington said, "Benedict Juárez is such a nice man. At 27 years he is about the oldest of our group. Has already built a small house he calls his "bachelor pad." Seems to be so handy with tools and making most anything. A philosophy major with remarkable hands-on building skills. Only one I have ever known. Don't see that where I am from.

---

[89] The importance of testing an enemy's military strength before committing all of your forces is often found in human history. An example is the First Battle of Bull Run (Manassas) at the outset of the truthful history of the War Between the States, in which Federals turned and fled in panic when Confederate's started to gain the upper hand.

Had supper together. He spoke again of the Monterrey Way – 'If it can be made, we can make it best.' He probably has more to teach our group than any other person, including me. . . . . Loved today's lecture. One important reason that our Defense of Independence was so successful was the cooperation and bravery of brave Colored people, who helped the Secret Service by carrying out tasks, like delivering messages and propaganda and mines and torpedoes. They succeeded because Federals were blind to the idea that a person of African ancestry could be supportive of the Confederate cause. And the vast majority was faithful to their slave-holding families, allowing the men-folk to leave home for military service. That too, the Republican mind did not think possible."

Diary note by Robert Lee said, "Supper with the heroine herself. None other than Emma Lunalilo, surfer and ocean swimmer extraordinaire. She told me about the man overboard rescue . . . . My thoughts about Emma as a person: impressive; self-confident; compassionate, intelligent, perhaps a future governor of her state of Hawaii. I came away most impressed. Would I go out with a surf board on those huge waves? No way. I had much rather write about events and people that to be central in the story. Have a short story already in my mind. Perhaps I should call it. 'Man Overboard: Crisis and Heroic Rescue'."

Diary note by Conchita Rezanov said, "Andrew Houston is a big, tall Texan. Also 23 years old. Says he is an accomplished tennis player – played on the Hughes-Sharp tennis team. I just now checked their record on the internet – not so good. But I need a fast workout and men are normally stronger players. So we will be on the court for an hour before supper tomorrow. A tall handsome dude. I like him – will consider this 'a date'. But can a petroleum engineer lighten up and not be overly serious?"

Diary note by Andrew Houston said, "Finally got my turn for the supper date with the beautiful Conchita Rezanov. I am smitten. Have a date to meet at the tennis court tomorrow at 5:15 pm. People know me as a very good tennis player: big serve, firm and well-placed ground strokes, sharp volleys at net, quick about the court. But, if I lose, it will be the most beautiful loss of my 23 years. . . ."

Book 1, Chapter 9, Day 9 – Confederate Military and Political Strategy Succeeds, Resulting in Montreal Negotiations Over the Boundary and Relocation of Colored People – Class Lecture Tuesday, June 14, 2011

This morning, the twelve members of the Sewanee Project were ready to settle down and listen to Professor Davis present the history of the negotiations, boundary settlement and relocation of Colored people southward into the Confederate States. This is an important aspect of Confederate history and can be confusing to some. So all were eager to hear Professor Davis explain it in his words.

Great Britain and France Recognize the Confederate States of America

Great Britain and France would soon grant recognition to the Confederate Government in Montgomery. William L. Yancey of Alabama, the Confederate Ambassador to London had, over the past 12 months, developed a good working relationship with Lord John Russell, the British Foreign Minister, and it was becoming apparent in London that the States joined together in the Confederate States of America had successfully and jointly defended their respective secessions and their honor, and were deserving of recognition by the world's leading powers. Furthermore, Confederate propaganda concerning future emancipation of bonded African Americans had encouraged the British and the French to view the emerging country more favorably than at first. The critical meeting between Yancey and Russell took place on Monday, June 16. Russell had already received reliable reports from the British embassy in Washington City, so the details of the situation submitted by Yancey's just-arrived documents were readily accepted as factual. And a sense of trust and respect was solidifying. It was clear that secession had been defended successfully and any remaining Republican Party hopes for surviving the October and November 1862 elections, and afterward mobilizing a new, better equipped, and larger Federal invasion force were quite remote at best. Meanwhile, in Paris, Pierre A. Rost, the Confederate Ambassador to the French Government had conferred over the past 12 months with leaders in the government of Emperor Louis Napoleon III and developed a warm relationship – what could be termed a "wait and see" but friendly relationship. Well, by mid-June the waiting was over and the seeing was at hand. From Washington City a message from Henri Mercier, the French Minister to the United States, had been recently received, laying out the case for recognition and strongly recommending immediate action toward that goal. So, between June 17th and June 20th, diplomatic conversations between France and Great Britain concluded with a decision to recommend official approval of joint recognition. In London, Parliament concurred. In Paris, French authorities concurred. And the joint decision to formally recognize the government of the Confederate States of America was announced on June 26. The news reached Washington City and Montgomery on July 4th in time to contribute to the celebration of the Independence of the original thirteen colonies, a victory won on battlefields in the Carolinas and Virginia 81 years earlier.

August through November, 1862 – The Decline of Republican Party Power

In the United States the election season began in earnest in early August. At stake was control of the Federal House and Senate and elections in numerous States, counties, towns and cities. All seats in the Federal House were up for election. One-third of the seats in the Federal Senate were up for election. The Democratic Party was re-energized.

The Stephen Douglas Peace Plan

Senator Stephen Douglas of Illinois, who, four years previously, had won the 1858 Illinois Senate election contest, which featured the famous seven Douglas-Lincoln debates, was considered the leading northern States Democrat when it came to formulating a unified Democratic Party peace plan. [90] And being the leader that he was, Douglas contrived a peace plan, discussed particulars with other leading Democrats, and all agreed to keep the plan secret until it had been discussed with President Lincoln. The Douglas Peace Plan stipulated:

1. Formally recognize the Confederate States of America and its States as a free and independent country.
2. Enforce an immediate cease fire.
3. As temporary measures, withdraw Federal troops to positions north of the Confederate boundary with three exceptions: 1) troops to remain in Nashville to enforce the Reconstructed Tennessee State Government, Andrew Johnson, Military Governor; 2) Troops and navy support to remain at Fort Sumter and Fort Pickens, and 3) a modest navy presence to remain at New Orleans.

---

[90] Senator Stephen A. Douglas of Illinois, the recognized leader of the Democratic Party in the Northern States during the 1850s and up to the start of the Lincoln Administration, in truthful history, died on June 1, 1861 of throat cancer. But in our alternate history of that time, the throat cancer that would debilitate Douglas during the last month of his life, would not take hold of him until five years later. In this alternate history he remains vigorous with impressive leadership ability for five more years, not passing away until June 1, 1866.

4. The 150,000 prisoners-of-war captives held by Confederates are to be cared for humanely and allowed to communicate by mail with family.

5. Great Britain and France are to serve as moderators to facilitate a negotiated settlement of issues that divide the northern and southern States with particular emphasis on: 1) Transfer a strip of land in northern Virginia to Maryland to aid in preserving the capital at Washington City; 2) Transfer Virginia land near the Ohio River to Maryland so that River is all beyond the Confederacy; 3) In general, establish a boundary from the Atlantic to the Pacific that facilitates control of immigration and cross-border tariff collection; 4) Transfer to Confederate control, the land west of Arkansas that has been settled by Cherokee and the other four "Civilized Tribes," 5) Cede a sizable strip of arid western land between Texas and southern California to give the Confederacy a Pacific seaport.

6. Restore open navigation of the Mississippi River with Federal import duties collected at Cairo, Illinois and/or New Orleans.

7. Satisfy the demand of the vast majority of White people of the Republican States that Colored People be excluded from their region. Since the Republican Party was launched in 1854, its primary political demand had been to exclude slaves from all National Territory and future states. Now, with a failed military invasion campaign and 150,000 northern troops imprisoned, the passion for Exclusionism in the Republican states – for an all-White society – had risen into a deafening roar. That vast political majority demanded relocation of all slaves and free Colored people who lived on land that would remain in the United States following the boundary settlement. They demanded that even the 238,315 free Colored people who presently lived among them in the Republican States be relocated elsewhere.

7a. Accordingly, the Douglas Peace Plan called for resettlement somewhere in the Confederacy of all slaves living on land that would remain in the United States following establishing the boundary. New owners in the Confederacy must purchase resettled slaves, but commit to making them the first in line for emancipation after the promised Confederate Emancipation Program is launched. The money paid to purchase the Negro slaves would go half to the owner forced to sell and half to a Federal compensation program to aid families of soldiers killed under fire during the 1862 invasion.

7b. Each State remaining in the United States would decide on the disposition of its free Colored population. As for Illinois, Douglas advocated issuing modest travel grants to all Illinois Colored people and ensuring that they be safely relocated to a sister State in the Confederacy, Liberia, Haiti, Central America or wherever – the receiving country or State being responsible for the welfare of those received.

8. At the time of implementation of the agreement, the Confederacy was to hand over the 150,000 captives at border locations convenient to the home State of each man.

The Amazing Douglas-Lincoln Meeting at Soldier's Home

Considering the arguments presented by both Douglas and Lincoln during the famous 1858 debates, few expressed much surprise that the Douglas plan was heavily weighted toward a program of Exclusion, of racial cleansing. When completed in rather short order, the United States would have no noticeable population of Colored people. Although Whites and Negroes might live in harmony in the Confederate States, the issue of race would never again become a divisive political weapon in the North – in the United States. But Douglas had to persuade fellow Democrats and gain some traction with Lincoln himself.

Most notable of the meetings and discussion among political leaders was the August 4 meeting between Douglas and Lincoln, held at the Soldiers' Home, near Washington City, a favorite get-away for Abe and Mary Lincoln during the hot August weather. [91]

I am able to present the meeting of Judge Douglas and the President as it took place on Monday, August 4, 1862, complete with the conversational dialog. This detail of history would not become known publicly until after the death of Judge Douglas, when son Stephen Douglas, Jr. would discover a report of the discussion his father had written up the day following the meeting with Lincoln, afterward tucking the pages into a hidden drawer in his desk. Here we have a great opportunity to live history as if we were there.

Senator Stephen Douglas, known as Judge Douglas for many years due to a brief stint as a judge in Illinois, walked up to the entrance of the Soldiers' Home, and, after giving evidence regarding his identity to a guard, advanced and knocked on the door. Answering at the door was Captain Derickson, who was of a small detachment of Pennsylvania troops, known at the Bucktail Brigade. Douglas introduced himself: "I am Senator Stephen Douglas of Illinois. Have known the President since before he was married and, although I have no appointment, I anticipate that he will allow me to visit with him a bit to discuss some important political matters. Would you be good enough to

---

[91] Many of the reflections presented in the conversation between Douglas and Lincoln are based on true history, including past quotes by both men. All quotations based on historical fact during this meeting are provided to you in italics so that you are aware of that.

notify him that Judge Douglas has come to the Soldiers' Home in hopes of seeing him today?"

Captain Derickson replied, "Please take a seat in the front room while I inquire about the President's availability."

After about 10 minutes, Derickson returned and said, "The President and the First Lady are presently occupied in a spiritual gathering, but he hopes to be able to break away within the hour, and wishes that, if you have time to wait, that you are made comfortable." [92]

Sure enough, about 45 minutes later, the door opened and the tall, lanky President entered the front room, extended his hand and exclaimed, "Judge Douglas, I am glad you are here today. America is in a pickle of a predicament and, to the extent that you might help us out of this mess, I look forward to learning about your ideas, your advice. Let us go into that room over there where we can talk in private."

The short stocky Douglas replied, "Thank you for seeing me today. I was telling your bodyguard that we have known each other since before you were married. I know the loss of your son Willie must still be hard to bear. It's not yet quite six months since you lost that dear eleven-year-old boy. So hard. When I arrived, Captain Derickson told me that, at the time I arrived, you and Mary were involved in a spiritual gathering. How is she doing; does she receive comfort through the church?"

Lincoln answered, "Well . . ." then pausing a while, continued, "Well, because you have known Mary as long as I have, and can perhaps understand, I will confess that she has been consulting mediums, what some folks call the occult, holding séances in search of a connection to poor Willie's spirit. She is still in one of these sessions as we speak. Most of the séances she has arranged have taken place without me, but I have been dragged into a few, including the one this morning."

"Does Mary believe she has connected with the spirit of son Willie?"

"She tells me that she thinks she has, but the connection has been fleeting and only made her more determined to keep trying. She seems to be happier when she senses a spiritual contact with poor Willie, even a fleeting contact. If it restores some happiness in her outlook, then I figure it may be productive."

---

[92] Fact: true history records that Mary Lincoln engaged many times with mediums in an effort to reach out to Willie's spirit and that Abe was present at these séances on a few occasions. Willie was Abe and Mary's deceased son, who had died six months previously of "bilious fever," probably being typhoid fever, at age 11, in February 1862.

Tell me, Mr. President, when you join in one of Mary's séances, how does it affect you?

"Frankly, Judge Douglas, I feel the whole weight of the world is pressing down on my shoulders. This morning I even asked the medium to help me connect with some source of divine guidance capable of giving me direction in the office to which I have been elected. Believe me when I tell you in confidence, if I may, some days I wish you had been elected President instead of me. If you, as the leading Democrat of the northern States, held this office, the southern States would not have left us and I would have not felt the necessity to go to war to force them back in. Oh, what a mess we have on our hands now, my friend. Why has God dealt us this horrible hand of cards?"

"You are right about secession. With a Democrat in the White House, South Carolina and the other southern States would still be a part of the United States. But, concerning the hand that God has dealt us, I was always of the opinion that you were a religious skeptic and only quoted the Bible in speeches for political effect. I vividly remember your 'House Divided' speech four years ago. Tell me if you will, are you now a Christian, Abe?"

Abe cautiously replied, "Again, my answer is given in confidence: Mary and her preacher say that I am outside the church and I suppose, by the teachings of the Bible, I must be. I am spiritual Judge Douglas, but in a different way. But, enough of this 'spirit talk'. How can you help the United States? Tell me about your thinking."

At that point Judge Douglas leaned forward and began introductory comments that would set the stage for his plan for extricating the United States from the grip of the failed military invasion of the Confederate States.

"Mr. President, the mid-term elections are only weeks away and I am certain that Democrats will win control of the House and be very competitive in the Senate, perhaps in control. The nation is demanding an end to the military invasion of the Confederacy and the return of the 150,000 prisoners of war. We have only enough combat ready troops and weaponry to assemble one invasion force of sufficient strength and commitment to conquer, perchance, even Richmond, the State capital nearest to your greatest political strength and our greatest industrial and financial strength. For over three weeks, recognition of the Confederacy by London and Paris has been widely known. Politics in a democracy being what it is, Mr. President, the people are earnestly speaking and it seems to me you have no alternative but to negotiate a peace settlement with the Davis Administration in Montgomery. They have never sought to conquer us, as you know in your heart, in spite of your political posturing. They only want secession to be recognized so they can proceed in building a separate country, a country which, in time, ought to be our best friend."

Judge Douglas paused, hoping to glean a sense of how Abe was going to react. Then the President said, "Are you about to propose that we two tired old politicians bury the hatchet and work together to bring about the settlement you envision?"

"Yes, Mr. President, I suppose that I am."

"Then tell me where you would draw the boundary, how you would handle navigation of the Mississippi River, how you would secure the border and collect the tariffs and, most importantly, what you would do with the Negroes."

"Well, Mr. President, irrespective of the political struggles in Kentucky and Missouri, first your administration must declare a cease-fire and recognize what is obvious to everyone – that the Confederate States of America exists as a legitimate government of the eleven seceded States. We must drop the political rhetoric, the silly notion, that we are fighting rebels who seek to destroy us. We must accept the truth of the fact that we are fighting secessionists who just want to live separately and peacefully apart. That means you establish diplomatic relations with Montgomery, even if on an informal basis. Abe, we have to begin to talk to one another."

"If your Democrats support recognition, I believe I can agree to it. What then."

"And tell me Judge Douglas, what about our troops in Nashville, who have secured the Reconstructed Tennessee State Government, which is pledged to rescind secession? Do we have to give that up? Kentucky might hang in the balance."

"Not yet, not at first, Mr. President. For the time being, as negotiations play out, we keep troops in Nashville and we sustain the government we set up under Military Governor Andrew Johnson. We also keep our Navy forces at New Orleans, Fort Pickens and Fort Sumter in Charleston harbor. But all of our forces act under a cease fire, ordered not to fire unless fired upon."

"But, Judge Douglas, the Confederates have us on the run, what prevents them from attacking our meager outposts at Nashville, New Orleans or measly Fort Sumter. God, knows, I wish I had never heard of that pile of rocks in the center of Charleston harbor."

"Mr. President, please doubt not my loyalty to our country when I tell you that I have contacts with the Confederate Secret Service, led by Judah Benjamin, and they assure me that the government in Montgomery can sustain a peaceful cease-fire if, but only if, that government is recognized as legitimate and diplomats are exchanged for the purpose of beginning the search for a settlement."

"What about London and Paris, Judge Douglas, if we accept their oversight in the negotiations, will they oversee them in a fair manner?"

"Again, Mr. President, rest assured that my efforts have been honorable when I tell you that, over the past three weeks, I have been in conversations with Henri Mercier, the French minister, and he assures me that, if asked to do so, London and Paris will jointly oversee negotiations and will do so fairly."

"Where?"

"He suggests Montreal."

"So, Judge Douglas, where do you foresee drawing the boundary lines? Confederate Virginia is just across the Potomac River. I can see it from southern windows in the White House. Must we move the United States capital to Philadelphia or . . . , you name it?"

"Mr. President, reliable sources have told me that Montgomery and Virginians are willing to barter a land trade to give Washington City a buffer zone to its south. I am told that even the victorious Confederate General Robert E. Lee would be willing to give up his estate – Arlington, on the south side of the river, also within your view from the White House – if a good overall land trade was agreed to on both sides. In exchange for a comfortable swath of northern Virginia and the return of our imprisoned troops, the Confederacy seeks western land that connects it to southern California and the Pacific Ocean. That is mostly dessert, they will argue, not worth much to us, but considerable to them. So they give us what is dear to us, and we give them what is dear to them."

Lincoln asked, "What about Kentucky and Missouri, do your sources give a clue to what would happen there?"

Douglas replied, "I have heard it proposed that elections by county might be held in Kentucky and Missouri, for the purpose of guiding negotiators in splitting those two States. We might, in the long run, lose southern Kentucky and southern Missouri to more secession demands, but retain the south side of the Ohio River and St. Louis and all of the Missouri River. We have a shot of gaining western Virginia along the Ohio. By recognizing the right of State secession, the consequence of recognizing the Confederacy, we keep alive secession political struggles in Kentucky and Missouri. It might be best to divide those States for the sake of unity within our country. Nip the southern Kentucky and southern Missouri secession blight in the bud. Our people want peace, Mr. President – an end to the struggle between the Southern culture and the Northern culture. A boundary line that gives southern Kentucky and southern Missouri to the Confederate States will go a long way toward defusing future demands for State Secession,"

"My goodness! You present the struggle as one between the 'Southern culture and the Northern culture.' What about the 'slave power?' I thought we were fighting the 'slave power.' Now you say we are fighting the 'Southern culture.' Explain that for me, Judge."

"Mr. President, we have both been exposed to the Southern culture through our marriages. Your wife Mary was born and raised in Kentucky. Well, I was 34 years old and in Congress when I married Martha Martin of North Carolina. You may recall that I met Martha through her cousin, Congressman David Reid of North Carolina, who occupied the seat next to mine in the House chamber. Romance blossomed and we married. We had two boys, Stephen, Jr. and Robert. The following year Martha's father died and she inherited a 2,500-acre cotton farm in Mississippi, along with more than 100 slaves. That was 14 years ago, in 1848. I managed the farm mostly from afar, but made periodic visits. I also traveled the Southern States on campaign trips. As a Democrat, I have enjoyed close relationships with many political leaders from the Southern States. So, taken all together, Mr. President, I have acquired a rather detailed understanding of the Southern culture. Being born and raised in Vermont and upstate New York, I have also acquired a rather detailed understanding of the Northern culture. There are differences, and the reasons for them go way back to the first settlers to arrive here from Europe – differences between settlers at Jamestown, Virginia, and settlers at Massachusetts Bay and New England. [93] As you know, Martha has been dead a long time; died of complications during the birth of our daughter, who also died a month later. That was a sad, sad time in my life. Six years of happy marriage, then she was gone. Yet it helps me understand the hurt you and Mary feel over the loss of Willie. By the way, for some time the Mississippi farm has been in a trust for the boys, and I have no control over it at all. It's best that way. Senator Douglas owning slaves is bad for politics in Illinois. Yes, for a man living in Chicago and Washington City, I understand both cultures rather well. [94] But, Mr. President, with all due respect, sir, I fear that your understanding is a bit wanting."

"A bit wanting, you say?"

"Frankly, Mr. President, you have never traveled in the Southern States to a meaningful degree. And I don't want to sound harsh or threatening, but I owe it to you to give you the full story so you will know what you are up against, in total, not just in part. Although you were born in the South, your youth was spent in Kentucky and Indiana. Now, I perhaps should not mention

---

[93] Students and writers of truthful history have long recognized the existence of two cultures, one prominent in the North and the other prominent in the South.

[94] Stephen Douglas' biographical sketch of himself is truthful history.

this, but some knowledgeable Kentuckians question your paternity as you wrote in the Bible record you worked up with your step-mother, Sarah Bush Johnston Lincoln, during that visit to her home a year or two after Thomas Lincoln died. You are aware of how agitators against this war have called you "Lying Lincoln" and claimed that your true father was a North Carolinian named Abraham Enloe. I know that hurts, but let me assure you I have had no part in such bastardy name-calling. I want to trust your word – that Thomas Lincoln was your true father. But trust in this regard is hard. Your Bible entry was made in 1852 or 1853, about the time you sensed new political opportunities may be opening up for you. Although you decided to forgo attending your claimed father Tom Lincoln's funeral in 1851, you made a special trip to visit your step-mother for the apparent purpose of establishing your birth date in that newly purchased Bible. That smells like a cover-up, my friend. And your former law partner, Billy Herndon, suspects it as well. A small group of informed and important people in Kentucky attest to that being the truth of it. Thomas Lincoln was your step-father, not your real father. So in the present legal lingo, you are a bastard, if you will pardon my language. Does the true story of your parentage go like this, as I understand it from reliable sources?

"Nancy Hanks was born in Virginia and living in North Carolina when she became pregnant with you, my friend. Since a young teenager, your mother, Nancy, had been a servant in the home of Abraham Enloe and his wife and children for many years. She became pregnant by Abraham Enloe, a well-to-do married man with wife and family. As soon as mother and child were able to travel a long distance, Mr. Enloe took them north over the Smoky Mountains, across Tennessee and into Kentucky. Later he arranged for a young Kentuckian, Thomas Lincoln, to accept Nancy Hanks as his wife, and to help raise little you. Mr. Enloe gave Lincoln a very generous going-away present, as well, as I hear it. Therefore, when Tom and Nancy married in eastern Kentucky, there was this little 2-year-old boy in attendance, who was you, my friend. So you are about 4 years older than you say you are and your father is not Thomas Lincoln as you claimed in your campaign biographies.

"Mr. President, I would not use this information to tarnish your image because that is not the way I conduct my political affairs. But there are people who would use it if they saw no other way to gain your political cooperation. Enough said about this, Mr. President.

"Allow me to say we both should take this issue off the table and commit to saying nothing more about it. I just wanted you to know what I have been hearing and that it is coming from reliable and capable sources." [95]

"Judge Douglas, I know not of these so-called reliable sources, but let me assure you that my father was Thomas Lincoln and the birth date I wrote in the Bible of which you refer is the truth. My mother always said I was large for my age, even when I was little, and that is the sum total of it. If you have nothing more constructive to say, let me suggest that this interview is over."

"Regarding your father, Mr. President, I have nothing more to say, and rather regret that I mentioned the subject. It just slipped out as I was beginning to discuss your perception of the Southern culture. Pardon me for that impropriety. I will speak of it no further. But I do have more to say concerning the grave issues before our country, and assure you my further comments will not be unpleasant or threatening."

"Very well, Judge Douglas, you clever fox, tell me what I do not understand about the Southern culture."

"Mr. President, the short of it is that you have had little exposure to the Southern culture. You've made a few visits to Mary's relatives in Kentucky. As a very young adult, you made two flatboat trips down the Mississippi River. Those experiences do not afford a fellow an understanding of a people and their culture. Your political friends in the Republican Party, frankly sir, share your relative ignorance on the subject. When it comes to understanding the people that your Massachusetts Abolitionist friends so passionately despise, I must tell you those know-it-alls are the most ignorant of them all. For that reason, it is advisable that you seek out and strongly consider the advice of folks who do understand the Southern culture. Such understanding is necessary to make sense of what ought to be done with our divided nation and our Negroes during this time of unprecedented crisis."

"So, Douglas, I suppose you want to teach me about the Southern culture and the Negroes. Fire away. Your elaborate preamble now completed, please deliver the meat of your message. Are you now going to tell me about the Negroes?"

---

[95] In truthful history there is compelling, though inconclusive, evidence that Abe Lincoln's father was not his mother's husband, Thomas Lincoln. Abe Lincoln was likely four years older than he reported and born out of wedlock. The belated family Bible entry is truthful history. If not Thomas Lincoln, the most likely father was Abraham Enloe of western North Carolina. See my recent 2021 book, *Rebirthing Lincoln, a Biography*, available as a paperback book, hardback book, e-book and audiobook. See Amazon and book stores.

"Mr. President, the Southern culture is a by-racial culture, made up of White people and Colored people. The races are accustomed to living together in communities and often on the same farms and plantations. It is a successful culture that began in Virginia, was mostly responsible for winning independence from Great Britain, and has subsequently expanded across the Ohio River Valley, to Missouri and to the Republic of Texas, now the State of Texas. In the South one sees a broad spectrum of personal relationships. On occasion a Negro slave is abused, to be sure. But so often, one finds friendships between Whites and Negroes who live in the same communities and even on the same farms and plantations. They often grow up together, play together, work together, hunt together, and go to church together. In a nutshell, that is the Southern culture. So different from Massachusetts or land along the Great Lakes."

"To further explore our relative understandings of the Southern culture, Mr. President, let us review your speech before the Illinois Republican Convention at Springfield on June 17, 1858, 4 years ago, when you were launching your campaign to take my Senate seat. There you proclaimed:

> *"A house divided against itself cannot stand. I believe this government cannot endure, permanently half slave and half free. I do not expect the Union to be dissolved – I do not expect the house to fall – but I do expect it will cease to be divided. It will become all one thing, or all the other. Either the opponents of slavery will arrest the further spread of it, and place it where the public mind shall rest in the belief that it is in the course of ultimate extinction; or its advocates will put it forward, till it shall become alike lawful in all the States, old as well as new – in the North as well as the South."* [96]

"You see, Mr. President, that speech was essentially non-sense. Why? Because it was not based on an understanding of the Southern culture. The people of the Southern States have never intended to enslave people living in the Northern States, such as Illinois – have never intended to move with slaves into Illinois and take up residence. There was no threat of enslaving people in the North. End of story! You proclaimed that a house divided against itself cannot stand, but that you did not expected it to fall. Mr. President, if it cannot stand, it must fall. In fact, just weeks before you became President, it fell."

Lincoln replied, "That's what I said in Springfield and soon afterward I maneuvered you into allowing me to join you in seven debates, scattered

---

[96] This is the exact wording, as presented in italics, of Lincoln's speech in Springfield, Illinois on June 17, 1858.

across the State. The Douglas-Lincoln debates. I suppose you want to quote something I said there as well. Do you?"

"Might as well, Mr. President, quote you, and quote me as well. By recalling quotations from the two of us during those seven debates, I believe we can gain a measure of understanding regarding what we ought to do with the Negro today."

"At the debate in Ottawa, Mr. President, you submitted:

> *"I have no purpose, directly or indirectly, to interfere with slavery in the States where it exists. . . . I have no purpose to introduce political and social equality between the White and Negro races. There is a physical difference between the two, which, in my judgment, will probably forever forbid their living together upon the footing of perfect equality; and inasmuch as it becomes a necessity that there must be a difference, I, as well as, Douglas, am in favor of the race to which I belong having the superior position."* [97]

"Mr. President, in those remarks you confirmed the attitudes of voters all across the North. The people of the Northern States do not want Negroes living in their communities. For God's sake, the Illinois State Constitution forbids a person with only the slightest drop of Negro blood from taking up residence within our borders. [98] We can divide into three categories the attitudes of Northern people toward people of full or partial Negro blood. The vast majority belong in a category I call "Exclusionists." These people want to exclude Negroes and Colored people from their State. Others belong to a category I call "Deportationists." They want to round up Negroes and "colonize" them in Africa, Central America, South America, or somewhere else. Many influential people like this idea. But there is a third category, to which very, very few people belong. That is the category I call the true "Abolitionists." A true Abolitionist wants to help slaves become free, even purchasing them and training them to be self-sufficient, one would presume. But to this category very, very few belong. Mr. President, I am sure that, in your heart, you recognize that almost everybody who calls himself an Abolitionist merely wants to meddle in someone else's business, not help the Negro."

At this point President Lincoln countered: "You have been quoting me, Judge Douglas. At our 1858 Illinois debates you were the Senator from

---

[97] This quotation in italics is the exact wording of Mr. Lincoln's remarks at the debate in Ottawa, August 21, 1858.

[98] The prohibition against any person appearing to have even a small fraction of African ancestry taking residence in Illinois was in the State constitution, was enforced, and is truthful history.

Illinois, a leader in the Democratic Party in the Senate and standing for re-election by our state legislature. As a Republican, I was opposing you. Quote for me something you said at some point during those seven debates that might help us sort through the mess we find ourselves in today. Quote from that debate again, if you can."

"Mr. President I do believe I can do that. It was at Alton, the last debate on October 14, that I warned you before a crowd of 5,000 the following truth:

"I said, our founders had agreed to form a government over thirteen States, uniting them *"together, as they stood divided into free and slaves States, and to guarantee forever to each State the right to do as it pleased on the slavery question. Having thus made the government, and conferred this right upon each State forever, I assert that this government can exist as they made it, divided into free and slave States, if any one State chooses to retain slavery. Mr. Lincoln says that he looks forward to a time when slavery shall be abolished everywhere. I look forward to a time when each State shall be allowed to do as it pleases. If it chooses to keep slavery forever, it is not my business, but its own; if it chooses to abolish slavery, it is its own business, not mine. I care more for the great principle of self-government, the right of the people to rule, than I do for all the Negroes in Christendom. I would not endanger the perpetuity of the Union. I would not blot out the great inalienable rights of the White man for all the Negroes that ever existed. Hence, I say let us maintain this Government on the Principles that our fathers made it, recognizing the right of each State to keep slavery as long as its people determine, or to abolish it when they please"."* [99]

"You make a valid point, Judge Douglas. But that water is over the dam. All but four Southern States seceded. The Union is broken. We cannot remake the history of it. But we must do all we can to prevent further secessions. So, Judge Douglas, what should we do now?"

"Mr. President. You are right. We must avoid further secessions. We must not let future fusses over Negroes ever again divide our citizens. We agree that the people of the Northern States do not want Negroes for neighbors. That is the fact we face. They want them to remain in a Southern State where they are accustomed to living, or be "colonized" elsewhere. That's what the so-called Underground Railroad was all about – keeping runaway slaves moving north until they left the United States and self-colonized in Canada. And that should be our goal in a negotiated settlement

---

[99] The portion in italics is the exact wording of Douglas' remarks at Alton on October 14, 1858.

with Montgomery. We should tell Confederate ministers that, 'Together we will draw a boundary between our governments, but it must be agreed that all Negroes north of that boundary must be resettled to somewhere south of it, and that no Negroes can ever cross northward-bound over the boundary to live among our people, in our country.' You said it yourself in Springfield in 1858. 'A house divided against itself cannot stand.' Our house is the Northern States and it will stand for hundreds of years if we remove the divisive issue of Negroes and Whites living in the same communities."

"If we act as statesmen instead of politicians and negotiate a reasonable settlement, we can cast off the Confederate States and reconstruct the remaining United States into the greatest nation of peace and prosperity and opportunity that ever existed for White people."

"So, Judge Douglas, in your judgment, a plan as you have described, will return the 150,000 soldiers presently held captive in Confederate prisons. When do the people in Illinois regain access to commercial river transportation to the port at New Orleans?"

"As you know, Mr. President, after the secession of Mississippi and Louisiana, the river was open to free trade and Federal tariffs were being collected at the Mississippi-Tennessee border, but that capability was terminated by Montgomery in December, on the same day you signed the bill authorizing military force against the South. I anticipate the river being opened to commercial traffic very soon after signing a cease fire agreement."

"In your judgment Douglas, will our Federal Government have the legal authority to free slaves living on land that remains in the United States, or will authority to free them and define emancipation details and procedures reside in the individual States?"

"That issue will only concern Delaware, Maryland, Kentucky and Missouri. We can count on little Delaware to cooperate. The southern boundary of Maryland will substantially expand, if my thinking prevails, when it receives some of northern and western Virginia and that prize will encourage the cooperation of that government. Kentucky and Missouri may well divide, smaller southern portions going to the Confederacy, expanding Tennessee and Arkansas. Those people have a big job in sorting all of that out. We ought to leave the emancipation details to the people of the Southern culture who best understand the issues involved. So, in short, our Southern States – Delaware, Maryland, Kentucky and Missouri – must define emancipation details and deportation procedures pertaining to the Negroes residing within their borders."

"What about the free Negroes, Douglas, will the Federal Government have authority to exclude them from our nation, to forcibly colonize those who do not leave willingly?"

"Mr. President, let me assure you that free Colored people will depart swiftly as White people will make it known that such people are not welcome to remain in their communities. Most will resettle in the Confederacy, with some going to Canada and some by sea to wherever. I can only hope that Canadians do not try to block migration into their country, but we cannot be sure. I do believe the Confederacy will accept all free Colored people who migrate south, and I assure you they will remain free, they will find the Southern culture an attractive destination."

"Douglas, I have devoted much time and political capital toward colonization of Negroes. I rather firmly believe that Confederates will refuse to accept any more Negroes. They have more now than they need, for Heaven's sake."

"Mr. President, do not be so sure of that. I know the people of the South much better than you know them. If we negotiate in good faith, Confederates will accept our Negroes, slave and free, and give them good homes. Those who are now free will remain free and those who are still slaves will have opportunities to learn to be self-sufficient and to gain freedom in a reasonable length of time. We just have to negotiate this plan, which gets rid of our Negroes, and, at the same time, gives Abolitionists in our Republican States the rights to boast that they freed the slaves."

"I remain doubtful of Confederate acceptance, Douglas. The Federal Government may yet have to arrange for and pay for deportation to Africa, Central America or South America. Congress recently appropriated one million dollars to pay for a colonization program and that is already available. Thad Stevens pushed a $500,000 colonization bill through the House, and you managed to expand the funding to $1,000,000 in the Senate. [100] That will give us a good start."

"Don't be too hasty, Abe. Give Confederates a chance to accept our Colored people."

"You are probably dreaming, Judge Douglas. My government ought to begin immediately with the resettlement program, starting with the Negroes living in Washington City who are being emancipated now – that is, those not taken to Maryland at the last minute and sold. Immediately after the cease fire

---

[100] In truthful history, on July 16, 1862, the Federal House and Senate approved a bill, subsequently signed by President Lincoln, which appropriated $500,000 to finance deportation (colonization) of African Americans – money that would be spent for that purpose. This truthful history preceded the fictional Soldier's Home meeting by over two weeks. In truthful history Senator Douglas was dead of throat cancer. Here, in our story, Douglas is alive and remains as the leading Democrat in the Senate. He is reminding Lincoln that he had succeeded in doubling deportation funding to $1,000,000.

agreement, we ought to be able to free up ocean transport to begin the movement of these people."

Lincoln then said, "I have already supported colonization in Haiti and some want to establish a Negro colony in Central America at a place they call Chiriqui. In addition to our standing colonization destination of Liberia, my administration has, during the past few months, collected invitations to receive colonists at St. Croix, Surinam, Guiana, British Honduras, New Granada and Ecuador, and more invitations are expected. How many, in your opinion, Douglas, would we need to send off?" [101]

Douglas replied, "That depends of Confederate acceptance or rejection. There at about 240,000 free Colored people living in our Northern States. Half may migrate willingly, but we may need to apply pressure to see the remainder off. There are about 550,000 Negroes living in Delaware, Maryland, Kentucky, Missouri and here in the District of Columbia. [102] Many will probably be living in regions that will be taken by the Confederacy and their status would not change. Many will be relocated within their respective States to land that is taken into the Confederacy and their status would not change either. Overall, we may need to resettle by law one quarter of that population. That presents a resettlement burden of about 250,000 individuals. But let us hope Confederates will accept these people."

"Douglas, I am still anticipating colonization. That may require more than $1,000,000, but our military will probably shoulder much of the cost, providing soldiers to help gather individuals to seaports and get them boarded, plus Navy transports to take them to their respective destinations. We can do what we need to do."

"Well, Douglas, you've presented and argued for an impressive a list of suggestions, quite a plan, I must say. Are you through, or is there more?"

"Mr. President, this seems like a good place to conclude my remarks. How can I be of further help?"

"Douglas, I believe the issue now sits in my lap, and, unlike you, I remain doubtful of Confederate willingness to accept more Negroes. But, I have called a Cabinet meeting for day after tomorrow, on Wednesday, August 6. I will place your plan before them for discussion. If they see merit in it and if Democrats and Republicans in our country can bury the hatchet and agree

---

[101] In truthful history the Lincoln Administration actively deported Negroes to land set aside in Haiti and engaged in negotiations to allow deportations to foreign lands elsewhere. Relocating Negroes to Africa (Liberia) was a long-standing American program supported by so called Abolitionists.

[102] Truthful population figures from the 1860 Federal census.

on a plan that saves us from further unnecessary divisive political agitation, while, at the same time, resettling the Negroes living in the North and bringing back our captured troops, then it seems to be in our best interest to draw an intelligent boundary between the secessionists and ourselves, a boundary that preserves our capital where it is and gives us the best land on both sides of the Ohio River Valley."

"Thank you, Mr. President. Then I will take my leave."

With that, Senator Stephen Douglas departed the room, walked to the front door of the Soldiers' Home, said goodbye to Captain Derickson, and departed. Moments later, Abe Lincoln walked over to the room where he and Mary had been in séance with the medium, wondering if contact had been made with dear Willie's spirit — the results of which are lost to history.

But what is not lost to history is the determination in the Republican States to forcefully implement ethnic cleansing within their respective regions and in portions of Democratic States that would remain under the Federal Government. And history would prove that Colored people, free and slave alike, who migrated south into the Confederate States would be so, so glad to have been welcomed there and given the opportunity for success in their lives, the lives of their children, the lives of their grandchildren, and their descendants yet unborn.

Selected Tuesday Evening Diary Postings

Diary note by Tina Sharp said, "Robert E. Lee IV and I shared a table at supper tonight. One would think that, being descended from the great Confederate General, this man would be too proud to care about me and what I am doing. But he really seemed to care and I found the time together enjoyable. He wanted to know about my career as a nuclear engineer and about the Comanche Peak Nuclear Station renovations. Perhaps it is the aspiring writer's mind set: always wanting to know about other people and their cares. Always gathering information for the next story, the next book. Very handsome and easy to like. Knows far more history than I do. If he resembles his ancestor, General Lee, then I can understand why the first Robert was so effective at building a team and leading his men. . . . . After supper we musicians gathered in the faculty lounge to play and sing together for almost two hours. This group is fun and capable of putting on a show. Amazing! Look forward to the next get together."

Diary note by Robert Lee said, "Giving up much of Virginia's territory in its north and west was hard for my beloved State, the mother State of our former country, the United States. My ancestor Robert E. Lee, after such brilliant leadership in the Defense of Virginia and Richmond, lost his beloved home along the Potomac River across from Washington City. As you know,

Virginia had given the Federal Government control over what became Kentucky and far more than that, for the Mother of States had held title to that vast expanse of territory extending far to the northwest, out to Chicago and beyond. What became Ohio, Indiana and Illinois was territory that belonged to Virginia during colonial days and at the conclusion of the American Revolution. [103] But, it seems that Virginians were continuing the tradition of Nation Building, agreeing to give up valuable settled and developed land in exchange for a far greater western expanse of arid land awaiting settlement and development. All Confederates should be appreciative of Virginia."

Diary note by Marie Saint Martin said, "Just got back from playing together with our musicians. After supper we played in the faculty lounge for a couple of hours. Was great fun. I had gathered up some music off the internet, and this was especially helpful to Amanda on the piano. This group seems capable of putting on a respectable performance by the weekend of the Confederate Celebration. Tina Sharp, although a French horn player, improvises harmony and sings it well. I have always sung lead, and relied on others to harmonize. Great fit, us two girls."

---

[103] It is truthful history that Great Britain acknowledged that Virginia held title to vast land stretching out to the northwest. It is also truthful history that Virginia gave the right to manage the settlement of that land to the American government soon afterward. This, among other facts of American history justifies recognition of Virginia as the "Mother State" that gave birth to much of the United States.

Book 1, Chapter 10, Day 10 – Negotiations at Montreal Result in a Boundary Line from the Atlantic (in Northern Virginia) to the Pacific (in Southern California) and Resettlement of all Colored People North of that Boundary– Class Lecture, Wednesday, June 15, 2011

We now settle in to our seat alongside the twelve and listen to Professor Davis' next lecture as Book 1 of our trilogy nears a close.

President Lincoln and His Cabinet Debate Alternatives

Two days later, as planned, on August 6, President Lincoln sat down with his Cabinet, all of them Republicans, in search for a way out of the military crisis. Present was Secretary of State William Seward of New York, Secretary of War Simon Cameron of Pennsylvania, Secretary of the Navy, Gideon Welles of Connecticut, Secretary of the Treasury Salmon Chase of Ohio, Attorney General Edward Bates of Missouri, Postmaster General Montgomery Blair of Maryland, and Secretary of the Interior Caleb Smith of Indiana.

The meeting began at 1:00 in the afternoon. By 2:00, the thoughts of various Cabinet members had been offered and briefly discussed. It was about that time that Lincoln presented, in some detail, the plan he had received from Senator Stephen Douglas, widely recognized as the leader of the Democratic Party, alleging that the plan was mostly his own thinking, but that Judge Douglas had suggested an item or two. From that point forward, the discussion centered on what we know to have been the Douglas plan. Blair of Maryland was enthusiastic about a boundary that gave his State a swath of northern Virginia, including land belonging to Robert E. Lee. And others saw merit in a boundary that avoided the embarrassment of relocating the capital. Bates of Missouri quickly endorsed moving all Negroes out of States north of the boundary line, emphasizing:

"Clearly, going back to the War against Mexico, our history proves that the major divisive factor in our country is the issue of Negroes living among us, whether slave or free. If Negroes are moved south of the boundary, this agitation will be gone and happiness will return. I personally know several families on large farms, with fifty or more slaves each, who would love to reduce their work force, but see no way to do it. This gives them an out. The future of the southern States is a growing Negro population destined to become a burden on Southern society. We do not want that to happen to us. Have it happen to them! Let us relocate ours now, while we can. That, gentlemen, will be our victory and the secessionist's loss."

Caleb Smith of Indiana, offering his viewpoint as the Secretary of the Interior, agreed that, with slight exceptions, the desert region west of Texas was of little value to the United States:

> "Concerning New Mexico Territory, we might keep the territory capital at Santa Fe, but to the west there is nothing but desert and canyon country. Concerning the State of California, if we retain Monterey and everything north of there, we are only giving the secessionists the southern California desert. It seems to me that the Gadsden Purchase of that strip of Mexican land, now in southern New Mexico Territory, was money wasted in 1853 by the Franklin Pierce Administration, wasted for a railroad never built. Good riddance, I say. Desert land from Texas to the Pacific in exchange for good land east of the Rocky Mountains and removal of our Negroes would be a good trade, if carefully negotiated."

Secretary of State William Seward submitted that, given a chance, he was confident he could strike a hard bargain in negotiations, and viewed the relocation of the Negroes to be essential to any acceptable plan. Secretary of War Simon Cameron expressed his great concern for Federal troops held in Confederate prisons and argued that the sooner they are brought home, the more lives would be saved.

Secretary of the Navy Gideon Wells promised that navy warships and transports could be fitted to move thousands of Negroes to Central America, South America and/or Africa, and that the colonization program could be carried out economically if it was begun very soon, while seamen remained enlisted and ships remained in a seaworthy condition.

Salmon Chase also stressed a rapid resolution to the crisis, submitting that every week of delay would cost the Treasury several million dollars.

The Cabinet resumed their discussions the following day, August 7. At the point in time when Abe Lincoln thought he had the votes, he proposed the following question:

> "Resolved:
>
> 1. "That the United States Government, for the purposes of securing a negotiated settlement, does recognize that eleven States have seceded and fought with some success to militarily defend said secession; and does recognize that the Confederate States Government is the proper agency to negotiate on behalf of said seceded States; and does recommend a cease fire on both sides; and does recommend that the United States Government appeal to diplomats in Great Britain and France to jointly manage negotiations toward goals of:

2.   Drawing a logical boundary between the two parties;

3.   Arranging for Negroes living north of the boundary to be resettled into regions south of the boundary or elsewhere;

4.   Arranging for all prisoners of war to be freed and returned to their home States;

5.   Ensuring free navigation of the Mississippi River;

6.   Ensuring collection of standing tariffs on all listed goods moving across said border;

7.   Arranging that said border be secured, to the extent possible, from illicit cross-border movement of persons, animals and goods, including Negroes."

The Cabinet voted. The resolution passed. At a press conference that afternoon, President Lincoln presented the approved resolution to newspapermen and political leaders. Announcing that Senator Stephen Douglas had given his support moments earlier, the President encouraged speedy review of the Resolution in the House and Senate – both just now returning from a two-week temporary recess, which had allowed members to visit their home States and districts for consultations with constituencies.

The Montreal Treaty Negotiations

Events were moving rapidly, to say the least. Within a few days, the Confederate Government in Montgomery voted to approve the resolution as a suitable framework for immediate negotiations. Likewise, under the leadership of Senator Stephen Douglas, the House and Senate approved resolutions of endorsement. Both Great Britain and France agreed to jointly facilitate the negotiations at Montreal. And that they did. All parties understood the urgency of the issue.

On Monday, September 1, 1862, the parties gathered and negotiations began. History knows the full story. But space has only been set aside in Book 1 of our trilogy only for a presentation of the results, so the reader must look elsewhere for stories of the gives and takes and the individuals involved.

By the way, Confederate negotiators arranged for the Federal Government to purchase Arlington plantation, the ancestral home of General Robert E. Lee's wife, Mary Custis Lee. The Lee's were obviously sad over the loss of Arlington House and Arlington plantation, especially Mary and the children, but emotions gave way to reason. The family realized it no longer wanted to live directly across the Potomac River from Washington City, with that magnificent view of the capital, now controlled by the Republican Party, which had waged war against the South. The family owned plantations further south in Virginia, such as the 4,000 acre White House plantation and the 3,500 acre Romancoke plantation. There and elsewhere the family's future surely lay. Mary had a good cry, but reason returned. The price paid for Arlington House and the surrounding 1,100 acres was just. Soon afterward, the Federals would transform Arlington plantation into a huge military cemetery, and, over the next few years, many Federal soldiers who died in the invasion of the Confederacy would be exhumed, transported to Arlington and reburied there. The Lee family's acceptance of the transfer of valuable northern Virginia land in exchange for vastly more far-western arid land was trumpeted as an example of Confederate patriotism, and many other land owners in the transferred portion of Virginia accepted the boundary settlement as a reasonable division of the two countries. [104]

We now advance to presenting the settlement itself.

The Negotiated Boundary

The agreed boundary was defined thusly: "Beginning on the Atlantic shore at the northern boundary of Virginia (near 38 degrees 0 minutes latitude) follow the existing boundary to the Chesapeake Bay, then across the Bay to the mouth of the Rappahannock River, then follow the stream in a northwest direction until reaching 78 degrees 0 minutes longitude, then proceed north on that line until reaching 39 degrees 0 minutes latitude, then west on that line until reaching 81 degrees 0 minutes longitude, then south on that line until reaching 38 degrees 0 minutes latitude, then west on that line until reaching 84 degrees 0 minutes longitude, then south on that line until reaching 37 degrees 30 minutes latitude, then west on that line until reaching 85 degrees 0 minutes longitude, then south on that line until reaching 37 degrees 0 minutes latitude, then west on that line until reaching the Mississippi River, then upstream until reaching 38 degrees 0 minutes latitude, then west on that line until reaching the existing boundary separating Missouri and Kansas, then south on that boundary until reaching 37 degrees 0 minutes latitude (the southern Kansas boundary), then west on that line until reaching the eastern California State boundary, then southeast along that boundary until reaching 36 degrees 0 minutes latitude, then west on that line until reaching the Pacific Ocean.

The negotiated boundary was to be a guide, not a rigid routing of the boundary. Refinement of the boundary, during surveying, allowed a deviation of up to one-quarter mile to avoid unnecessarily dividing a group of related buildings or a small town. And the line could be moved up to 5 miles from the negotiated route to get around major obstructions in the terrain that prohibited practical road building. This flexibility was permitted for a period

---

[104] In truthful history Arlington, the ancestral home of Mary Custis Lee, is the national military cemetery on the south side of the Potomac River. Mary (Mary Anna Randolph Custis) was the daughter of George Washington Parke Custis, the grandson of Martha Washington and the adopted son of President George Washington.

of five years following the settlement, after which the boundary was fixed. A boundary road and secure fence was a firm demand of United States negotiators who insisted that every effort be made to prevent Negroes from entering their country and to prevent smugglers from bringing goods north without paying the Federal tariff. [105]

The location of the following landmarks helps in visualizing the routing of the boundary:

- In Virginia, that portion of Fredericksburg on the south side of the Rappahannock River remained in the CSA, but a large amount of northern Virginia was transferred to Maryland and the USA, including Alexandria, Manassas, Reston, Winchester, Morgantown, Clarksburg, Wheeling, Parkersburg, Charleston and Huntington.

- Southeastern Kentucky below Mount Sterling was transferred to Virginia and all of extreme southern Kentucky west of London was transferred to Tennessee, including Mount Sterling, Hazard, London, Somerset, Middlesboro, Corbin, Monticello, Glasgow, Bowling Green, Hopkinsville, Murray and Mayfield.

- The southern third of Missouri was transferred to Arkansas and the CSA, including Rolla, Carbondale, Malden, Poplar Bluff, Springfield, Nevada and Joplin.

- Native American lands west of Missouri and Arkansas, south of Kansas and Colorado, north of Texas and east of New Mexico Territory was designated as being within the CSA and to be reserved as a Territory for Native Americans and their descendants. This large area would become the Confederate State of Sequoyah, but the treaty did not address that issue. The so-called "panhandle" in the west of that Native American territory was immediately transferred to Texas.

- Most of New Mexico Territory was transferred to the CSA. From it, two new Confederate States would be created, but the treaty did not address that issue. The eastern half, including Santa Fe, Albuquerque and Las Cruces, would become the Confederate State of New Mexico and the western half, including Flagstaff, Phoenix, Tucson, Las Vegas and the Grand Canyon would become the Confederate State of Arizona, but the treaty did not address that issue.

---

[105] The boundary road and fence was to be completed in five years' time, which was comprised of a graded roadbed, 45 feet wide, sloped from the center toward the outside for drainage of water. Along the center-line of this road, which matched the exact boundary, was to be constructed a strong ten-foot high fence. Both sides of this graded roadbed were to be cleared for easy visibility to a distance of fifty feet from the fence. Locked gates were to be provided every 10 to 20 miles. A gate would be unlocked by Federal revenue and border control agents when permitting and monitoring import/export trade and passage of individuals.

• A major portion of California, essentially the arid far-south, was transferred to the Confederate States, including Bakersfield, Santa Maria, Santa Barbara, Los Angeles, Palm Springs and San Diego. This Confederate State would be known as South California, but the treaty did not address that issue. Federal negotiators did not realized that, in the future, with expanded technology and electric power, Colorado River water could be impounded and distributed to enable development of this arid desert land. So they greatly underestimated the value of the land they were relinquishing in the trade.

On Friday, September 19, 1862, the Montreal Treaty was signed by negotiators for the United States and the Confederate States as well as the ministers representing Great Britain and France. It was sent immediately to Washington City and Montgomery with expectations of quick ratification by both governments. The United States Senate and the Confederate State Senate were both already in session, awaiting receipt of the treaty. One week later, on Friday, September 26, the treaty was ratified by the Confederacy, and three days later, likewise by the United States.

The British and French Joint Boundary Monitoring Commission

Neither the South nor the North fully trusted the other side to honor the treaty just signed. Confederates had witnessed too many broken treaties with Native American nations to fully trust the Great White Father in Washington to honor a treaty. Republicans in the North did not fully trust Confederates to collect import taxes on goods moving north across the negotiated boundary. Some even feared escaped slaves and colored people might migrate north across the boundary. Monitoring the flow of goods coming up the Mississippi River looked to be enforceable, but, the land boundary was thousands of miles long, and smuggling was a real danger to the collection of Federal import taxes. So both sides agreed to the proposal that a joint British-French team of boundary monitoring officials would help ensure honest law enforcement along the boundary. It was to be clearly marked with a fence line, and both sides of it were to be cleared for horse-drawn wagons to ride alongside, except for rough terrain, where a path for a man riding a horse would be provided. Furthermore, a telegraph line was to be run along the fence line from the Atlantic to the Pacific, with many stations along the way to ensure speedy and reliable communications involving Confederate Boundary officials, United States Boundary officials and British-French Monitoring officials. The cost of the services of the British-French Monitoring officials was to be shared equally by the Confederate States and the United States. Since the boundary matched the northern edge of eight Southern states, the British-French Monitoring team was to consist of fifty officials: five for each state boundary section, five for Davis and five for Washington City. Of course, these fifty officials were not capable of riding the boundary and manning the designated boundary crossings and import duty stations. That was not their role. Their role was to judge the behavior of the two treaty signees and cry foul when dishonesty was discovered. This program would work well as the decades would roll by. In the year 1912 the Confederate States and the United States would agree to discontinue the British-French Monitoring program. It had worked well for 50 years, but no longer was thought to be necessary.

The War Between the States Was Over

In accordance with the treaty provisions, all captured Federal soldiers were soon moving north under Confederate guard in convoys, to be turned over, at various points along the boundary, with documentation and one man at a time, to receiving United States Army officials. Within five weeks' time, all men had been thusly processed and the resulting documentation of the process seemed acceptable to both sides.

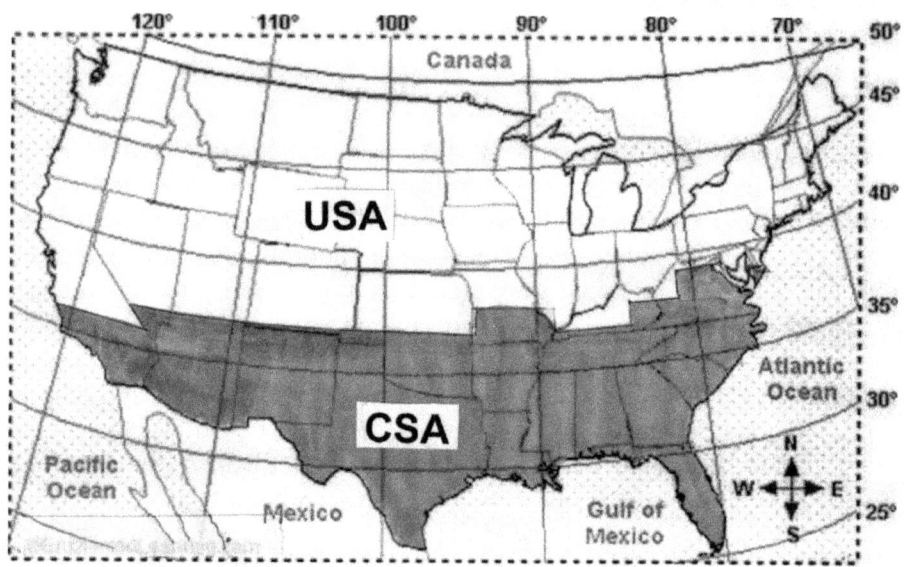

A map of our country as negotiated in Montreal, Canada in September, 1862. Remember, in our story the Lincoln Administration did not carve West Virginia from Virginia. So Virginia continued west to the Ohio River and gave to the North considerable land near Washington, D. C. and the Ohio River. These boundaries are the extent of our country prior to inviting Cuba, six states from northern Mexico, Russian America and Hawaii to join us. Read Part 2 to enjoy those exciting historical stories.

Also, in accordance with the treaty provisions, Federal soldiers, working north of the boundary, gathered up all Colored people, even including those with barely noticeable African ancestry, and began the processing of each. However, history of events in Maryland, northern Virginia, northern Kentucky and northern Missouri shows that about one-third of the bonded Negroes living north of the boundary at the time of the cease-fire, had, over the previous few weeks, been sold by their owners to other persons living south of the boundary as private transactions. Those sales obviously reduced the number of bonded Negroes that Federals had to process and relocate in accordance with the terms of the treaty.

Federal soldiers brought Negroes to processing stations where officials first attempted to group together all members of the same family and extended family. Even friends were grouped together for processing, for such groupings were very important to the future welfare of all, especially the children and the elderly.

For each person perceived to be independent (not a slave to someone else) detailed paperwork was prepared to document each individual's status, past work experience, family relations and friends, and all were assigned to cohesive groupings. Groups were escorted under Federal guard in convoys, to be turned over, at various points along the boundary, to receiving Confederate immigration officials, who reviewed the documentation of each person, further inquired about family ties, work skills and religious affiliation, confirmed acceptability of each grouping or modified it, and then coordinated each group's further migration to a State and county where they were to initially reside, with a letter of introduction for the county court house where their settlement was to be coordinated to ensure, although free, these people would be successful in their new environment.

Federal officials interviewed each bonded Negro and, if available, his or her owner, and prepared documentation regarding former owner (name and address), past work experience and family relations and friends. Speedy freedom was promised to all, but indenture for three years was thought a wise move for many to ensure they were successful as independent persons. All were assigned to cohesive groupings and also moved to the border to be delivered over to Confederate immigration officials. Because these individuals had no experience living independent lives, Confederate officials paid particular attention to each person's apparent ability to succeed without going through a transition period. Inquiry was made regarding religious affiliation, if any. Most did need to experience a transition period because of immaturity, dependent children or dependent parents, or lack of competitive skills. For those needing to experience a transition period, border officials sought to place groups in States and counties where coordinating officials were standing by to place them in transitional three-year indenture contracts. Accordingly, with interviews and documentation completed, groups were escorted by Confederate guides, selected from among former soldiers, to their selected destination and there turned over to the local indenture coordinators. This program of transitional indenturing would prove a great success, with almost ninety percent of adult individuals deemed suitable for independent living at the end of their three-year's service. The remainder entered into a second three-year contract. At the end of that period, everyone was, by law, declared independent. Success of the program is proven by the very small number of immigrant Colored people requiring subsequent State welfare support after six years of indenture. Colored children without support from family or friends were turned over to a welfare organization which arranged for foster care. The sick or lame were also treated with appropriate care through church-affiliated groups. [106]

Although during the meeting at the Soldier's Home Senator Stephen Douglas recommended to President Lincoln that a sizable portion of the Negro population in the North ought to be "colonized" overseas, that need never developed. The Confederacy was clearly the choice destination of Negroes living north of the new boundary. It was never necessary for the United States Government to "colonize" Negroes in Haiti, Africa, South America or anywhere. A few went to Canada, and a smattering went overseas, but the vast, vast majority accepted the Confederate proposal for resettlement in the South. By far the most common destination was to Texas, New Mexico Territory and South California.

We are now arriving at the final events that need to be reported concerning the Confederate's defense of independence.

Final Events Concerning the Defense of Independence

The final events suitable for reporting here can be presented in a punch list of statements:

---

[106] It will be hard for many readers to understand how successfully Colored people transitioned from slavery to independent living under the training and guidance of former slave owners, and oversight by Confederate officials. But, our alternate history is far different from truthful history. In truthful history, the South was devastated; the economy was destroyed, jobs were few, food was scarce for several years and sickness was so prevalent among Colored people that an estimated 200,000 died as a result of diseases spurred by the War and the Political Reconstruction that followed. Furthermore, the enormous disruption of Negro family groupings fed immoral and criminal behavior. In our alternate history, a far more moral and successful Colored population is sustained going forward through future generations.

- The counties along the northern boundary of the Confederacy were reorganized by respective State legislatures to stand alone or merge with neighbors.

- Elections of the fall of 1862 were held as scheduled, and a new census was taken in 1863, to be effective in organizing districts for elections scheduled for the fall of 1864.

- The Confederate Constitution remained unaltered over the subsequent few years, and was judged to apply to the western regions of New Mexico Territory and South California.

Having concluded his presentation on the successful defense of State Secession and the negotiated boundary treaty and the resettlement of Colored people, Professor Davis invited all twelve essayists to a celebration party he had arranged immediately following supper:

"Everyone, you are invited to join me for a celebration party beginning an hour before supper. I have arranged for supper to be delayed one hour, we will all have the normal free time allotment this afternoon. We have much to celebrate! So, with that said, please join me and my wife near where we normally have supper. This treat is on me. You all are going to be magnificent when presenting your essays before the television cameras on our sesquicentennial celebration on July 4. So let us celebrate the first phase of our country's success this evening."

Marie Saint Martin replied: "I have an idea – let's bring our instruments and play a couple of relevant songs during the celebration party. We have worked up two that would be fitting. There is a piano there for Amanda. Allen, will you bring your guitar? With Professor Davis's banjo in hand, we can do it."

Professor Davis agreed: "I will bring my banjo. It is a done deal. Fifteen minute limit. Judith suggests we dress up in the Southern tradition. Coats and ties for men, dresses for ladies."

Independence Celebration Party

Professor Davis's celebration party was splendid. Joe and Judith Davis were a handsome couple to be sure. Andrew Houston and Robert Lee seemed to be competing for time with the beautiful Conchita Rezanov. Chris Memminger seemed to be forever thanking Emma Lunalilo for saving his life, while Skipper Carlos Cespedes seemed to have accepted Emma's decision to dive into the stormy and dark ocean with flashlight and life jacket in a desperate swim toward the shouts for help. Isaiah Montgomery and Amanda Washington, both looking fine, seemed to be enjoying sharing conversation.

Allen Ross, dressed in fine western gear, was questioning Robert Lee about the trip to Big Bone cave planned for the coming weekend. Marie Saint Martin, dressed in fine New Orleans style, and Tina Sharp, dressed like – how do I say: like a nuclear engineer? – were discussing the upcoming singing while Judith looked on. Then Judith turned to Tina and said, "Why don't we get together tomorrow night and play some French horn duets. Will be fun." Tina replied, "Sure. I know I will learn something from you. My endurance will be suffering from lack of play. You know, the lip loses its stamina and flexibility through inaction." Benedict Juárez and Professor Davis were discussing agricultural management and how to maintain harmony among the shareholders, when Marie interrupted and announced, "Time for music, you all."

With that, the musicians among those attending gathered around the piano and made ready to perform. Seated at the piano, Amanda keyed notes to help Professor Davis tune his banjo and to help Allen and Carlos tune their guitars. Tina and Marie took a sip of water to clear their voices. The six were ready. To the others, Amanda said, "You all will know these two songs, so please join in."

"As you all know, we Confederates love to sing 'Dixie,' but with revised words that change the perspective to a Southern viewpoint: change it from a person up north looking at us "away down south" to we "here at home" looking at ourselves. As you know, the 'Dixie" we love goes this way:

> "We're . . .
> Proud to be in the land of cotton.
> Old times here are not forgotten.
> Gon'a Pray. Come what may.
> Gon'a stay, in Dixie Land.

> "In Dixie Land where I was born.
> Early on one frosty morn.
> Gon'a pray. Come what may.
> Gon'a stay, in Dixie Land.

> "I'm so glad that I'm in Dixie.
> Hooray! Hooray!
> In Dixie Land I'll take my stand
> To live and die in Dixie.
> Hooray! Hooray!
> We Love, Love, Love . . . our Dixie!"

Thanks for joining in. Now let us close with our Confederate States Anthem, our beloved, 'Diversity' song [107].

"We are one.
We are free.
We are the Great
Diversity

"From Carolina's sandy beach,
Westward to our Pacific shore,
From Artic ice beyond our reach,
To warm Gulf waters we adore.

"We are one.
We are free.
We are the Great
Diversity."

The brief party hosted by Joe and Judith Davis was good fun. And it represented another step toward bringing the twelve essayists together as a united group focused on doing their very best to understand "Why the Confederate States are the Greatest Country on Earth" and to prepare to explain the "Why" of it before a vast television audience as the sesquicentennial celebration would be drawing to a close in 19 days.

Wednesday Evening Selected Diary Postings

Diary note by Isaiah Montgomery said, "Benedict Juárez and I shared supper tonight. Most interesting fellow. He is of almost pure Native American ancestry. Real proud of the manufacturing powerhouse in his State of Costa Este. Monterrey is the main city and he lives there. Has a Ph.D. in philosophy and a bachelor's degree in history and came across as a great

---

[107] You will read much about "diversity" in *The CSA Trilogy*. Although in truthful history, in the year 2011, the word "diversity" means many different things to many different people – in our alternate history of the Confederate States of America its meaning is more narrow and is understood as a feature of Confederate society to be celebrated. In the CSA, "diversity" speaks of the range of racial and ethnic ancestries of the Confederate people. Confederates do not all look alike and their talents and abilities vary broadly. But they are Confederates, true and true. They speak the common English language. Immigrants who have arrived since 1865, most of them from Europe, had learned and continue to learn English and blend into Confederate society. So "diversity" to a Confederate does not mean diverse cultural behaviors, does not mean that Muslims can disrupt the Christian social norm, does not mean that racial and/or ethnic gangs can get away with bad behavior, does not mean that political agitators can desecrate the monuments erected to honor long-ago Confederates. Stated in a positive way, the diverse peoples within our States have subordinated their former cultures to become compatible with the Southern culture and the governments within the various States and the Confederate Government at Davis.

conversationalist. So interested in my Mississippi farming background and how my African American ancestors carved out a farming cooperative for ourselves. Was interesting to compare our backgrounds, experiences and interests. I like him a lot and expect we will become pals over the next three weeks – not because we are alike, but because, although we are so unalike, we both are so interested in other people. . . . . Today's lecture was on the Boundary Treaty and Resettlement of Negroes. I was reminded that quite a few of the people who today live in and work in Mound Bayou Corporate Plantation are descended from Negroes who resettled in that part of Mississippi from north of the Boundary Line. And they hold stock in our corporation like I do. Although a minority of the population when they arrived in our area from up North, their contributions were greatly appreciated. Many had arrived with more education than their new neighbors and took pride in teaching others.

"There is a relevant story passed down by my Montgomery ancestors, two slaves owned by President Jefferson Davis and his older brother Joseph. They say that President Davis, upon accepting the position of Provisional President, anticipated leading the Confederate States as an honorable and truthful political leader, and as an experienced and successful military leader. That was his background and that was consistent with his character. But that attitude experienced helpful change when, on the day of his inauguration, President Davis met Jean Lafitte, the old, but reformed, former pirate made famous by Andrew Jackson at the Battle of New Orleans. With Judah Benjamin's help, Jean opened Mr. Davis's eyes to the value of a strong Confederate Secret Service and the artful, widespread and persistent application of clever propaganda aimed at the Northern States and the political attitudes of the people within each. And many Southern Negroes, accepting assignments as Secret Service Agents, went North, carrying messages, dispensing propaganda and warning people that a Federal conquest of the Confederate States would result in hordes of Blacks migrating North to become their neighbors. The message: let the South live in peace, nationalize your practice of prohibiting immigration by Blacks, and keep your States even more pure in the skin color of its dominant people. At Mound Bayou we honor these Negro Secret Service Agents every July fourth. Have a monument to them at Mound Bayou, too. It is a lovely monument."

Diary note by Allan Ross said, "I am so proud of my Cherokee ancestors and how they supported the Confederate States and won for themselves and our other four neighboring civilized tribes the independence available to us through the Confederate Nation/State of Sequoyah. I firmly believe that, if Confederates would have failed to win their independence, we Native Americans would have suffered great abuse and would forevermore be treated as a sub-class in North America. [108] We can certainly look to our north, to the United States, and clearly see Native Americans suffering in so-called Reservations: poor, forced to live on the worst possible land, with restricted opportunities, and dependent on Federal subsidies.

"At the party, Robert Lee and I talked about a caving trip he wants to make this coming weekend. Calls it Big Bone cave. Says lots of salt peter vats constructed during the War of 1812 and the War Between the States are still present in the cave because the cave has remained exceptionally dry over the past 150 years. I have never been caving. Will give it a try."

Diary note by Marie Saint Martin said, "We played pretty well at the party this evening. Will do better as we practice more. I will add more songs to our play list. Judith complemented us. That goes a long way. As I prepare for bed, I am thinking of the heroic men of Louisiana that were so effective in defending our independence. A special thank you bedtime prayer goes to my ancestor Jules Saint Martin, who was so effective at helping the Confederate Secret Service under the overall direction of Judah Benjamin, Confederate Attorney General. Without our very effective Secret Service during 1861 and 1862, it remains doubtful that our Confederate ancestors would have successfully defended our independence against the large and well-armed, but untested, army gathered up by the Lincoln Administration and the cooperative Republican governors of the Northern states."

Diary note by Chris Memminger said, "My great, great, great grandfather, Christopher Gustavus Memminger of South Carolina, President Davis's Secretary of the Treasury, has passed down through descendants this important message: A major reason that the Confederate States succeeded in acquiring the best in military weaponry during 1861 and the first months of 1862 was because Confederates enjoyed a strong positive balance of trade and a strong Confederate dollar. And I believe that Secretary Memminger had a lot to do with that success. I toasted him tonight at the party to a rousing response from others, especially Professor Davis, who shouted. 'Bravos to Secretary Memminger'!"

Diary note by Robert Lee said: "You heard a lot in Confederate military history about my great-great-great-grandfather General Robert Edward Lee. He did a fine job leading the Confederate Division charged with defending the advancing Federal army as it progressed southward through Virginia, aimed at capturing Virginia's capital, Richmond, and then proceeding further south toward State capitals in North Carolina and South Carolina. He embraced the Confederate strategy of Retreat, Envelope and Capture, and, to an extent, his was the most difficult to accomplish. His great challenge was to deceive the

---

[108] Truthful history supports the prediction presented in Allan Ross's diary entry.

advancing Federal army into a sense of confidence, contentment and patience, and delay springing the trap for many days. If General Lee had too soon Enveloped and Captured the opposing Federal army, the Lincoln Administration would have signaled the other Federal divisions to close ranks, maintain a path of retreat and respect the fighting spirit of the Confederates. Lincoln would have warned that Confederate retreats were not from weakness, but designed to draw Federals into a trap in which they could capture most of the weaponry and most of the Federal soldiers, still green untested troops, in one bold stroke. I am proud of General Lee and proud to carry his name. I like to think Conchita would be proud of the Lee name, too.

"Oh well, going caving this coming weekend. To Big Bone cave. Have permission from the land owner to enter the cave, which is normally locked up to protect the bats. Allen Ross will join me. I have received word from a Nashville caving friend of a crawlway recently discovered. We will go equipped with knee pads and dust masks, and prepared to do one hell of a lot of crawling. Will return Saturday night, probably totally exhausted. But there is hope that we will enter into a cave passage never before seen by humans or at least never seen since those long-ago salt peter mining days. "

Diary note by Andrew Houston said, "Played doubles with Marie against Conchita and Professor Davis. We lost. I was easy on my serves to Professor Davis in the early going, but picked up the pace in the last set, hitting volleys at him and in efforts to pass him. Conchita covered three fourths of the court, allowing Professor Davis to just stand his ground and use his quick hands to return volleys at Marie. It got vicious. Did not seem fair. Of course we lost. Oh, well. Great party tonight. My ancestor Sam Houston did not favor Texas secession, but was outvoted on the matter. He lived to see its successful defense. I just wish he could see the Confederate States today and observe our great diversity and our great success – to hear people say that the Confederate States are the greatest country on Earth. Time for night night."

Diary note by Amanda Lynn Washington said, "My ancestor, Booker T. Washington, of Virginia would be proud of the success today of the Confederate States of America. He played no role in the Defense of Secession, but he sure was a leader in the education of Colored people in the following decade. Makes me laugh – just thinking about how those holier-than-thou Northern Puritans thought they had won a great benefit for the United States by forcing the Confederates to accept their deportations of people of African descent to south of the negotiated boundary. Ha! Serves them right! We taught them a thing or two! But will their descendants ever come to realize the value to society of a diverse population?"

Diary note by Professor Davis said, "I played doubles tennis this afternoon with Conchita, Andrew and Marie. We were a bit rushed, because we had to quit in time to shower and dress before the celebration party. Was fun in spite of the fact that Conchita's ability on the court is far beyond any of us. Her closest competitor is Andrew Houston. Has a very good game, has the genetic male advantage, and has played singles with Conchita since arriving in Sewanee. Hear she let him win one of the matches they have played so as to not overly bruise his ego. They seem to be great friends. I had an easy time of it, for my partner was Conchita. Andrew and Marie were partners across the net from us. Had some trouble with Andrew's powerful serve, but played well enough for a seniors player. Was fun and needed the exercise. We won. Will do this again." As we prepare for bed, Judith tells me that the party was very successful. She believes it was a great way to bring the twelve essayists closer together and will pay great dividends over the coming two and a half weeks.

The Close of Book One, of Our Trilogy

Dear reader:

Congratulations! You have completed Book 1 of our trilogy. Book 2 and Book 3 continue the story. The Sewanee project continues. Professor Davis will next be telling the twelve essayists the history of the French Intervention in Mexico, the consequential secession of the provinces of northern Mexico, their successful fight for independence, and the region's transformation into six States within the Confederacy. There will be more: the story of Cuba, Russian America and Hawaii.

Beyond that, in Book 2 and then Book 3, you will experience the amazing continuing CSA history, including our amazing technological achievements and our success in the War against Imperialist Japan, going forward to the 2011 sesquicentennial celebration at the All Saints' Chapel at the University of the South at Sewanee. Professor Davis hopes to see you auditing his remaining classes. More weekend adventures await you as well.

Now, just proceed to Book 2, *How We Confederates Invited Cuba, Northern Mexico, Russian America and Hawaii to Join Our Federation of States, 1862 to 1977.*

About the Author, Howard Ray White

I was born in Nashville, Tennessee on August 4, 1938 to parents Howard Ray White, Sr. and Martha Bell White. Dad went by Ray and I went by Howard. Ray was a school teacher as a young man, but his main career of 25 years was to lead the Nashville Boys' Club, and oversee the building of Nashville's fine Boys' Club facility on Thompson Lane, which was dedicated by Richard Nixon in 1965. Martha was a high school teacher for 26 years, primarily teaching home economics and English at Hillsboro high school. I attended Hillsboro high school and then Vanderbilt University, also in Nashville, where I earned a degree in chemical engineering.

After completing my junior year at Vanderbilt, I married Judith Hunt Willis, also a Vandy student. Judith and I celebrated our 60th wedding anniversary in 2019. Judith and I have three sons, two living. We have lived in Charlotte, North Carolina since 1972.

I became interested in history in my early fifties and eventually focused on a study of the politics before, during, and after the War Between the States, a horrific period in American history of which none other compares. I generally set aside the study of military aspects of the conflict to more clearly focus on the political and cultural aspects. My first published books were a vast record of our history before, during and after the War. It was published as four volumes, under the overall title of ***Bloodstains, an Epic History of the Politics that Produced and Sustained the American Civil War and the Political Reconstruction that Followed.*** [109]

During this time, I hosted eighty-one 30-minute television shows on our local cable TV station. A show was presented every Tuesday evening at 8 pm and they have continued to be presented every week for almost 20 years, reruns being presented now since I no longer produce new episodes. The television series is titled "True American History." You can view some of my shows on vimeo.com.

---

[109] In addition to *Bloodstains*, other published books by Howard Ray White include his mother's autobiography, *Springfield Girl, a Memoir*; his grandfather's poetry, *Understanding Granddad through his Poetry*; his father-in-law's Ph. D. thesis, *Advancing American Reading Achievement During the Great Depression*; Howard's assessment of Biblical teaching, *Understanding Creation and Evolution*; Howard's study of the Fort Sumter incident, *Understanding Abe Lincoln's First Shot Strategy*; Howard's study of abolitionists propaganda, *Understanding 'Uncle Tom's Cabin' and 'The Battle Hymn of the Republic'*; two quick reads by Howard, *How to Study History when Seeking Truthfulness and Understanding* and *Why and How the North Conquered the South*; Howard's Southern history, *How Southern Families Made America*; a wartime Virginia novel, *R. E. Lee, Edmund Ruffin and Slavery* about a slave family struggling to keep safe and stay together; and Howard's unique, must read biography, *Rebirthing Lincoln, a Biography*.

Soon after the completion of **Bloodstains**, Dr. Clyde N. Wilson of Columbia, South Carolina and I jointly founded the **Society of Independent Southern Historians**, a web-site based, nation-wide organization of folks interested in reading and writing truthful American, Southern and Confederate history. A bit later, Dr. Wilson and I co-edited a publication by the Society that included fourteen other writers, all Society members. Published by the Society in 2015, and titled, **Understanding the War Between the States**. This book of only 80 pages, is considered by many to be the most effective resource available today for teaching truthful history concerning the War Between the States, especially regarding political and social aspects. The book's targeted audience is "middle school, high school, college and beyond." A variation of this book was published in 2018, especially for home schooled students and parents. It is titled, **American History for Home Schools, with a Focus on Our Civil War.**

I have presented my background above to help you, the reader of the three books comprising our *CSA Trilogy,* better appreciate my in-depth and comprehensive understanding of **truthful and relevant** American history, which is essential to a writer who is conceiving of an **alternate history** where the South wins a negotiated settlement of the War Between the States.

The emphasis in the first book of our *CSA Trilogy* concerns Confederate political deception and delaying tactics. That derives from my understanding of the 1861 and 1862 political and cultural situations. Believing that, after the 1862 elections, defeating Federals by conventional warfare would have been impossible, I constructed a concept of "retreat, envelope, capture and imprison." It further logically flows that the negotiated CSA-USA boundary wins approval by east-dominated Republican leaders. With book 1 completed, I was then free to construct my subsequent Confederate world history.

You are encouraged to proceed toward reading the second book in this Trilogy. You will find it a fun story about inviting others to merge into our Confederacy. The French Intervention in Mexico is easily transformed into a story of the secession of northern Mexican states, their independence from Mexico City and their inclusion into the Confederate States. With CSA help available, the Cuban Revolution is easily transformed from a Spanish victory to a victory for Cuban Independence fighters, and inclusion into the CSA as the State of Cuba. Far to the north, the purchase of Russian America by the United States Federal Government, at the time protested as "Seward's Folly," is transformed into independence for Russian America settlers and inclusion into the CSA. And, to complete the story of the Great Confederate Expansion, adding the mid-Pacific Hawaiian Islands as a CSA state so nicely blends with the Russian American story that the reader feels naturally happy over the outcome.

After reading the second book, please proceed to reading the third book. You will find it a satisfying story of the growth of our country as it strives to become the greatest county on earth. In my alternate history, talented and inventive men come to the Confederate States far more often than to the United States. And free enterprise flourishes. CSA technology rapidly advances. The story of the war against Fascist Japan – and how the Confederates and Chinese Nationalists supported each other so effectively to drive the Japanese out of mainline China and Korea and force unconditional Japanese surrender – is very different from truthful history, yet plausible and far more satisfying.

I enjoy telling happy stories, and the three books comprising our *CSA Trilogy* is one that readers admire. I was inspired by the great histories written by the late, great Texan, James Michener (*Hawaii, Texas, Centennial,* and so many more). I remain ever grateful to Michener for teaching me and the world how to tell truthful history as a story of many generations, of families, and of heroic men, in a style that resembles a compelling novel, but teaches supremely. Proceed to live the history in books 2 and 3, enjoy my story telling talent and give special thanks to James Michener.

Closing Commentary and a Few of the Historical Resources Utilized in Preparation of Book 1 of this Alternate History/Historical Novel

The following is a sampling of resources that helped the author understand the truthful history from which he departed in creating his fictional alternate history/historical fiction novel. For twenty years the author studied, wrote and sequentially published his four-volume history series, *Bloodstains.* These twenty years of study enabled him to formulate a logical alternate history of 1860 through 1862 that was consistent with many of the sectional North-South cultural, political and racial passions – passions that were, at the time, driving the truthful history along the course it, in fact, did take.

There is historical precedence for a Confederate victory over invading United States troops. In truthful history, the first major battle of the war was the Battle of Bull Run, in Northern Virginia. There, truthful history shows defeated and panic-stricken Northern troops abandoning their weapons and running back to Washington City. Our alternate history draws on this nature of a first battle between untested invading troops and untested defending troops.

The author realizes that much of the story involving attitudes toward slaves, slavery and race, as presented herein during the 1860's, is hard for people today to understand. He realizes how difficult it must be for people today to believe that, in 1862, the people of the North did not want Negroes living in their communities, and that people of the South were accustomed to it and were agreeable to accept immigration of Negroes from the North into the Confederate States, both those that were free and those soon to become free. The idea that the Party of Abraham Lincoln would give up what would become Oklahoma (Indian Territory), and arid New Mexico, Arizona and Southern California for far less, but bountiful, land in northern and western Virginia is also hard to believe for most. But the author reminds these people that, the North was eager to get rid of Indians, and the far away southwestern land was mostly occupied by people of Mexican ancestry, plus a few Southerners, and was extremely dry. Republican leaders wanted to ensure they retained Northern California and the States of Oregon and Washington, and believed that shedding the arid southwest would prevent any future agitation for a Western State Secession movement. Although this eventually gave Confederates four additional States, it greatly reduced the likelihood of a future State Secession movement. And, preventing another State Secession movement was very important to political, financial and economic leaders of the Northeastern States, who dominated the Republican Party at the time.

After creating the fictional story of the successful military defense of the Confederate States and the subsequent boundary separating the two countries, the author recognized that this major alteration in the history of North America readily facilitated a much happier history for Northern Mexico, Russian America, Cuba and the Hawaiian Islands. So, happily, he then proceeded to create these four alternate historical outcomes, all in the flash of only a few years. By this rapid inclusion of nine additional States, the Confederate States created a truly multi-racial society, including a large population of persons with significant native ancestry, and/or Spanish ancestry, and/or African ancestry, plus a few with Asian/Polynesian ancestry. These people added to the original Confederate people of European ancestry, yielding a multiracial society of divergent and complementary skills and talents.

The author apologizes that more of the story in Book 1 of our trilogy is not devoted to heroic and accomplished People of Color. They were very important to the success of the Confederate States, providing vitally needed talents and energy. Their cooperative attitude during and after the war enabled successful emancipation and living as independent persons afterward. The reader should realize that, in truthful history, Political Reconstruction, which was implemented by the Republican Party for ten years following the conquest of the Confederate States, drove a lasting wedge between the races in the South that forced Southern Whites to contrive methods to rescue their towns, counties and States from ruin under Carpetbagger rule.

Much of the historical information gathered in support of creating our trilogy was obtained through internet searches and small books and essays, too numerous to mention. But it does seem appropriate to list several of the major resources utilized in the writing of this work. That list follows:

The author drew heavily from his early American History studies, beginning with the South's earliest colonial days in Virginia to the creation of the Republic of Texas in 1885. That history is revealed in his published four-volume history, *Bloodstains, An Epic History of the Politics the Produced and Sustained the American Civil War and the Political Reconstruction that Followed.* This is a large work in four volumes. Volume 1: *The Nation Builders* (2002), Volume 2: *The Demagogues* (2003), Volume 3: *The Bleeding* (2007), and Volume 4: *Political Reconstruction and the Struggle for Healing* (2012).

The author co-founded the Society of Independent Southern Historians in 2013 and helped the membership cooperate in writing a teaching aid for schools, colleges and parents. This concise but comprehensive book of 80 pages is titled *Understanding the War Between the States*, 2015. A recent variation is titled: *American History for Home Schools.*

Concerning Fort Sumter, see: *Understanding Abe Lincoln's First Shot Strategy (Inciting Confederates to Fire First at Fort Sumter)*, by Howard Ray White, 2011.

Concerning Abraham Lincoln and the Republican Party of the North, see: *Lincoln*, by David Herbert Donald, 1995. By the way, Howard Ray White, in 2021, published a very revealing book, *Rebirthing Lincoln, a Biography.* You are encouraged to put that one on top of your reading list.

Concerning Stephen A. Douglas and the Democratic Party of the North, see: *Stephen A. Douglas*, by Robert W. Johannsen (1973).

Concerning Jefferson Davis and the Democratic Party of the South, see: *Jefferson Davis*, by Hudson Strode, three volumes: *American Patriot*, 1808-1861 (1955), *Confederate President*, 1861-1864 (1959), and *Tragic Hero*, 1864-1889 (1964).

Concerning Native Americans of Southeastern North America, see: *The Southeastern Indians*, by Charles Hudson (1976), *History of the Choctaw, Chickasaw and Natchez Indians*, by H. B. Cushman (1899) and *After the Trail of Tears, the Cherokees' Struggle for Sovereignty, 1839-1880*, by William G. McLoughlin (1993).

Concerning Sam Houston, the Cherokee Nation and Texas, see: *The Raven*, by Marquis James, 1929.

Concerning Judah Benjamin and the Confederate Government, see: *Judah P. Benjamin, Confederate Statesman*, by Robert Douthat Meade, 1943.

Concerning the races of Mankind, see: *Understanding Creation and Evolution*, by Howard Ray White (2018).

Concerning people of African ancestry after the end of slavery, see *Up from Slavery*, by Booker T. Washington (1901), *The Negro Problem*, a collection of seven essays, edited by Booker T. Washington (1903). The author is happy that People of Color are perceived as being far happier and successful in our Confederate States today as compared to the corresponding truthful history.

www.ingramcontent.com/pod-product-compliance
Lightning Source LLC
Chambersburg PA
CBHW072054170626
46813CB00004B/1353